Praise for the acclaimed novels of Robert Holdstock . . .

"Holdstock has done an impressive job blending reality, history, and the supernatural into powerful fiction."
—*Locus*

"Masterful. Holdstock brilliantly evokes the vertiginous spirals of history." —*The Washington Post Book World*

"Tightly crafted, crammed with lyrical language and evocative scenes." —*The San Diego Union-Tribune*

"An excellent fantasy." —*Science Fiction Chronicle*

"Beautifully written and conceived . . . hard to shake off."
—*The New York Times*

"The scope of Holdstock's imagination expands the further one delves into it." —*San Francisco Chronicle*

"Dramatic. Powerful. Enjoyable." —*New York Newsday*

"Exquisite characterization and prose."
—*Chicago Sun-Times*

"Brilliant." —*Magazine of Fantasy & Science Fiction*

By the same author

Eye Among the Blind
Earthwind
Necromancer
Where Time Winds Blow
In the Valley of the Statues (collection)
Mythago Wood
The Emerald Forest
Lavondyss
The Bone Forest
The Fetch
The Hollowing
Ancient Echoes
Unknown Regions
Merlin's Wood
Celtika: Book 1 of The Merlin Codex

ROBERT HOLDSTOCK

GATE OF IVORY, GATE OF HORN

A NOVEL IN THE MYTHAGO CYCLE

A ROC BOOK

ROC
Published by New American Library, a division of
Penguin Putnam Inc., 375 Hudson Street,
New York, New York 10014, U.S.A.
Penguin Books Ltd, 80 Strand,
London WC2R ORL, England
Penguin Books Australia Ltd, Ringwood,
Victoria, Australia
Penguin Books Canada Ltd, 10 Alcorn Avenue,
Toronto, Ontario, Canada M4V 3B2
Penguin Books (N.Z.) Ltd, 182–190 Wairau Road,
Auckland 10, New Zealand

Penguin Books Ltd, Registered Offices:
Harmondsworth, Middlesex, England

Published by Roc, an imprint of New American Library,
a division of Penguin Putnam Inc.

First Roc Hardcover Printing, November 1997
First Roc Paperback Printing, November 2001
10 9 8 7 6 5 4 3 2 1

Cover art: Ron Walotsky
Designer: Ray Lundgren

REGISTERED TRADEMARK—MARCA REGISTRADA

Printed in the United States of America

PUBLISHER'S NOTE
This is a work of fiction. Names, characters, places, and incidents either are the products of the author's imagination or are used fictitiously, and any resemblance to actual
persons, living or dead, business establishments, events, or locales is entirely coinci-
dental.

BOOKS ARE AVAILABLE AT QUANTITY DISCOUNTS WHEN USED TO PROMOTE PRODUCTS OR
SERVICES. FOR INFORMATION PLEASE WRITE TO PREMIUM MARKETING DIVISION, PENGUIN
PUTNAM INC., 375 HUDSON STREET, NEW YORK, NEW YORK 10014.

For Annie, our "glimmering" girl.

Take, if you must, this little bag of dreams;
Unloose the cord, and they will wrap you round.

—W. B. Yeats, from *Fergus and the Druid*

False dreams come through the Gate of Ivory,
True dreams through the Gate of Horn.

—Virgil

PART ONE

THE VALLEY
OF THE CROW

PROLOGUE

This morning, when I opened my eyes and saw the spring sky above me as I lay in the shallow boat, I realized that my long journey from the heart of the forest was over, and that I had come home again.

Oak Lodge was there, across the meadow, empty and silent. And yet I could not step through the trees and go to the house, as if the wood, so difficult to enter from the outside except along the brook, was now reluctant to let me go. So for a while I walked *back* into that consuming gloom, following an old track, one I knew to be there, and coming after an hour or so to the clearing my father had called the "Horse Shrine," for the crumbling, ivy-covered statue of the animal that stood in that place, a wooden shield propped between its forelegs.

Here, I decided that I must write down what had happened to me, to give an account of it, something that I might refer to later when the details might have faded, since I cannot believe that I will not be returning to the heartwoods again and again. Though I am tired and confused now, I shall keep going back. I have left someone behind and I intend to find her.

And I will start this account with a truly haunting memory, the memory of a boy watching his mother dance furiously on the lowest branch of an oak. A day that ended a week of wonders. A day that shaped the boy for the rest of his life, although he couldn't know it at the time.

And because that day is no longer mine, though it once belonged to me, I shall tell of it briefly, and in a different voice.

George Huxley was on his knees by Christian's bed, his hand resting lightly on the boy's shoulder. Chris woke quickly, aware of a pale, predawn light on the man's unshaven face. He could smell the waterproofing on his father's cape, the leather of the bulky backpack, the polish on the heavy blackthorn staff.

"I'm going into the wood again," the man said. "Just for a few days."

"Hunting shadows?" the boy asked quietly.

His father smiled. "Yes. Hunting shadows. Shadows of the past, strange and wonderful shadows of the past."

"Shadows in the wood."

"I'll be gone for a few days only. Take care of things. I trust you to take care of things. Of your mother . . ."

All night Chris had listened to his mother's shouting, her sobbing, the crash of crockery and pottery, the bass grumble of his father's voice.

"Mummy's upset," he whispered, and Huxley frowned. The man's breath was cheesy, the black stubble along his lip flecked with crumbs. There was sadness in his pale eyes, the lids hooded, lines of discomfort on his brow, on his temples. A watery gaze, a tired look, but a glance or two of affection, something that Chris's brother, Steven—away, staying with an aunt—never received.

"Don't go away again," Chris whispered, but Huxley merely kissed the boy's cheek.

"I've left a note for you in the journal. The latest one. Read it, don't get it sticky, don't tear the pages. Do you understand? When you've read it, put it back on the shelf and lock the cabinet. Put the key in the drawer of the desk. Do you promise me?"

"Yes."

"I'll be gone a few days. Just a few days. The torches you saw by the wood last night are important. Someone of very great interest to me is very close to us. You'll find his name in the journal, too."

"And the horse?" Chris said. "I saw a gray horse. There was a girl on it, a girl with white hair. She was watching the house."

"Be careful of her," his father said. "If my ideas are right—she's no girl. I shan't be gone long, Chris. You *must* promise me to comfort your mother. She's a bit . . . upset."

Chris remembered the desperate voice: *Don't go, George! You've only just come back. How do you think it is for your sons? For me? To see you wounded with arrows, covered in . . . covered in mud, and dung. And blood! Stinking like a farmyard, like an old tramp! You keep leaving me here! I'm going out of my mind, George! Don't go to that bloody wood again. . . . What do I tell the boys?*

"I'll make her some breakfast," Chris said to reassure his father. "I'll tell her everything's all right."

"Good boy. I know I can depend on you."

"Daddy . . . ?"

"I have to go, Chris."

"How *far* . . . do you go? Into the wood . . . ?"

George Huxley's hand swept gently across his son's unkempt hair. "Very far indeed. There's a river in Ryhope, a river that flows from the beginning of the world. It's a river at the heart of the wood, the very heart of the wood. Strange ships sail there, and strange sailors watch me watching them. I'm learning so much, but I've only just begun. One day you'll know. One day, your brother Steven will understand, as well . . ."

He leaned forward and kissed his son, then rose and

stepped away. At the door he murmured, "Don't play with
the white-haired girl, if she comes again. She isn't a girl.
She's older by centuries than she seems. She's dangerous.
Promise me."

"I promise."

By sunrise his father had gone. Chris put on his clothes and
made a pot of tea. His mother, dressed for some reason in
her Sunday suit, was huddled by the dead fire, staring at the
ashes. She didn't respond when her son put the cup and
saucer on the table and touched her shoulder. The boy
walked quickly to the study and opened the bookcase, taking out a thick leather volume, his father's latest journal.
Opening it to the last written page, sitting by the window
that opened onto the brooding edge of Ryhope Wood, he
tried to understand a little more about what he had seen during the few days before.

Huxley had written:

> I am as sure of this as I am sure of anything—
> which is to say, not sure at all. But my guess, on the
> evidence, is that the group which has ventured beyond
> the Horse Shrine and is gathering at the edge of the
> wood is of the *Iron Age*. I suspect aspects of classic
> Celtic *questing,* the searching for cauldrons, or grails,
> or swords, or great pigs, emblems of magic and mys-
> tical attribute.
>
> I am tempted to think this may be a form of Kylhuk
> and his entourage of knights from King Arthur's court,
> occupied and obsessed with the many strange and
> wonderful tasks he must accomplish to win the fair
> Olwen, or die at her father's hands. To these questing
> men (and their ladies!) the edge of Ryhope is the edge
> of the world.

I must leave poor Jennifer again, to go in search of them, but Christian is a sensible boy. He will "guard the fort." Young Steven is still confused from my failed and foolish experiments upon his perception and sense of time, and he will stay away from the house for the rest of the summer. I know my eldest boy will exercise caution in all things, and make Oak Lodge safe for my return in a matter of days. He is not a curious boy; I trust him not to interfere in things he doesn't understand.

When Chris went back to the sitting room, his mother was no longer by the fire. He saw she had drunk the tea. He found her in the kitchen, bottling tomatoes. The front of her green tweed suit was splashed with juice. The red liquid squirted over the table as she pressed a lid into place and snapped down the iron lock of the preserving jar.

Chris wanted to ask her if she was all right, but the words wouldn't come. His mother hummed to herself, increasingly drenched in the red juices. She should have been wearing an apron. She was bottling unscalded tomatoes; they would go rotten in a matter of days. She was doing nothing right and Chris felt like crying. His mother's mouth and eyes looked bloody where she had wiped her hands across her lips and brow.

"Go outside and play," she said suddenly, looking at her son. "You know how your father hates to have you under his feet when he's working."

"Daddy's in the wood. . . . He's gone into the wood."

"Nonsense! Daddy's *working*. And you should be playing. Go on, now. Go and do something constructive with your time. Make a model ship. You make good models. You'll be an engineer one of these days. Off you go."

"Why are you in your Sunday clothes?"

"Why do you think? It's a special day. Now, off you go."

What special day? he wanted to ask, but the feeling of "absence" from his mother dried the words in his mouth. He wanted to cry, his eyes moistened. He reached out to her, hoping for a quick kiss, a warm pat on the cheek, that little smile that always reassured him, but she went on squashing fruit, her head shaking as thoughts tumbled inside her head. Chris quickly left the house, drying his eyes on his sleeve, then kicking angrily at everything he could see before running to the stream which he and Steven called the stickle-brook.

Here, last year, the two of them had launched HMS *Voyager*, a two-foot, single-sailed model that had swept into the wood so fast they had hardly had the strength to follow it and see it vanish. Lost for six months, the vessel had turned up again, almost as good as new, caught in the mud on the Shadoxhurst side of Ryhope. The return of the ship had sent his father into a fever of work and writing. Even now, Chris wasn't sure whether the hours of questioning that early spring had meant approval or anger from the man whose moods and obsessions dominated the atmosphere in his home.

By the millpond, later that day, Chris sat for an hour or more, hoping to see the same furtive movement across the water that usually denoted the "Twigling," an odd creature disguised in the dull greens and browns of an outlaw, and with sticks and twigs tied about his head to make a crude and hideous wooden face. Today, all was still.

He wanted Steve. His brother was full of dreams and full of stories. His imagination had fueled the brothers' games. Without Steve, Chris felt isolated. He longed for night, when the wood might again become alive with fire and voices, horses and garish human figures.

By the evening, he had walked as far as Shadoxhurst, playing on the village green for a while with friends from school,

spending his meager allowance on chocolate before heading
back along the hedges toward the sprawling estate on which
his parents had their lodge. The fields were waist high with
barley, the seeds about to burst. It had been a fine summer
and the harvest would begin two weeks earlier than usual.

When he came to the sticklebrook, he followed it to the
thistle field and the dense border of scrub wood and nettle
that made Ryhope Wood so hard to enter. He was close to
home, but surrounded by a bosky silence that thrilled him.

Suddenly, out of that silence, out of the wood, a white-
haired girl rode toward him, cantering along the bank of the
stream, leaning low in the saddle as she passed the boy and
reaching out to strike him on the head with a thin stick,
strips of red rag and white feathers streaming from its shaft.

She laughed as she achieved this deed. Then the horse
reared up, leaped the stream and she trotted back on the
other side, the coup-stick held loosely in her left hand while
the right tugged at the crude bridle, slowing down the impa-
tient gray.

Chris stared at her in awe and astonishment. The ride had
been so sudden, her appearance startling. Her face was so
pale that she might have been a ghost, but there were thin
dashes of color at the edges of her cheek and he realized that
she was painted. Her hair, too, was whitened with some
paint or other; it was long and quite stiff, not flowing freely
as she moved. Several braids had been wrung through these
sculpted locks and tied with string or cord. One braid alone
was decorated with leaves and feathers, and this she ab-
sently tugged with the hand that held the crop as she gazed
at her prey.

She was wearing a short tunic of red-and-green check
and cloth shoes. Her legs were otherwise bare; there was a
glistening sheen of sweat on her throat and arms.

This girl was *centuries older than she looked,* according
to his father. But she seemed to Chris to be no older than

some of the girls in the village. He said to her, "Why did you hit me?"

Instead of answering him, she shouted at the wood behind him, and when Chris glanced round, he saw a tall man in a white cloak, standing with a black horse and gently stroking its muzzle. The man frowned, growled fierce, warning words at the girl, then pulled back into cover.

The next thing Christian knew, the sweating gray was splashing through the brook, snorting loudly, and the girl was reaching down to grab him by the shirt. She hauled him onto the horse with astonishing strength, verbally abusing him in a way that suggested he might help himself a little, and he grabbed at the rough saddle and the coarse mane, somehow righting himself astride the beast's back. Suddenly they were off, at a heavy, painful canter through the fields of barley, ploughing a trail that wound and weaved toward the glowing sky where the sun was setting. The girl laughed and called out, kicking the young gray until it was galloping dangerously fast. Chris felt bruised by the saddle, but was more aware of the firm touch of the girl's fingers around his waist, and of her breath, sweet like fresh fruit, as she shouted and urged the horse along, her cries of delight clearly indicating her pleasure at the ride.

Her gaiety ended quite abruptly. She screamed suddenly, tugged so hard on the reins that the horse reared and the young riders fell heavily into the soft crop of corn. The girl was shaking, clearly in pain and very frightened. She tugged at her tunic to cover her legs, then twisted round to a kneeling position, breathing hard and shaking her head.

Chris tried to touch her, but she pulled away. He could feel a bruise on his knee and blood in his mouth, but the girl was in much greater distress, though the reason defied his eyes and his understanding.

Riders were coming across the cornfield, five of them, their faces painted a violent scarlet, white hair in spikey crests across their crowns, colorful cloaks streaming behind them. They rode in silence, spreading out to form a wide arc around the boy, long spears held loosely, points grazing the ears of the corn. The girl stood up and whistled for her pony. One of the oncoming men pulled up, shouted, the others swung round and dismounted quickly. The field of corn stooped to a sudden breeze that chilled Chris as he stood nervously, watching the events.

With a sharp word, then a laugh at him, the girl swung onto her gray's back and kicked toward the wood. One of the red-faced men slapped at the horse as it passed and his companions began to follow her. This one, though, beckoned to Chris, and the boy walked slowly toward him.

Close up, the apparition was frightening. The red paint was cracked across cheek, brow, and chin, and was like dripping blood where it had been rubbed into the full, curling mustaches. The horse was edgy, held by its reins but wanting to return to the trees. Below the full-flowing cloak the man wore a chain-link coat of dull gray metal and patched rust-colored cloth trousers tied below the knee. A broad, intricately patterned scabbard was strapped to his left thigh, and the jutting pommel of the sword it enclosed was shaped like a dead man's face, blind-eyed, long mustaches drooping around a gaping mouth.

This protecting warrior talked angrily at the boy, his free hand waving, punctuating his points, emphasizing the sibilant, fluid words that flowed through Christian's head like a smooth, welcoming dream. He recognized something about this man, but couldn't place it. The lesson was stern, but somehow forgiving. Whatever had angered the red face, it had more to do with the foolishness of youth.

Eventually the man slapped his heart and said, "Manandoun."

Christian said his own name. Manandoun nodded, puffed out his cheeks, and exhaled in exasperation, then pulled the horse round, mounted up, and rode quickly back to the wood, while Chris ran in pursuit, through the deep path left by the wild rider.

There was silence at the edge of Ryhope, where the sticklebrook flowed into the gloom.

But a moment later he heard the girl's whistle. Ducking below branches, she came quickly out of the trees on the gray pony, shrugging off the angry cries from behind her, and flung something toward the watching boy before vanishing again. He ran to fetch her gift, and held the feathered stick, her skull-cracker, her pony-whipper, and felt a sudden sense of wonder and joy.

He wanted to show the crop to his father. He wanted to stand in the light from the desk, watching as his father turned the piece of decorated wood in his hands and nodded with satisfaction.

"This is much more than just a riding crop, Chris; it's a talisman capable of calling for power, a magic stick, something I've never seen before. . . . Priceless, wonderful . . . I'll analyze it and display it in the cabinet, among the spears and arrows, and the masks, and the carved pieces of ivory and horn. . . . A real treasure . . ."

But his father was in the wood, called by his own needs, his own obsessions.

In the evening, while his mother stared silently at the fire she had laid, sweat beading on her skin as the unnecessary heat in this scorching summer made the room like a furnace, Chris prowled his father's study, circling round the desk that occupied the middle of the room and staring at the glass-fronted cabinets, where the labeled, numbered exhibits were displayed in quantity. George Huxley was a man of application and orderliness, but his museum was cluttered.

Chris had always been fascinated by the weapons and crossed the room to his favorite display. Five longbows were

arranged side by side; the first, with crude carvings of ante-
lope and bison, was labeled CRO-MAGNON, ca. 50,000 B.C.;
next to it was a smaller, simpler piece of wood, with gut
string, marked HITTITE. The tallest of the bows, blackened
with charcoal and decorated with simple bands of red paint
on either side of the arrow-nock, was labeled intriguingly:
AN AGINCOURT BOWMAN CALLED ALAN LEANBACK (NOTE PUN
IN NAME): CANNOT FIND STORY ATTACHED TO HIM.

In another cabinet, figurines in clay and bone, bronze and
wood were arranged by subject, rather than period: Snake-
Goddesses, Lords of Animals, Power Figures (made of
wood, their bodies wounded with shards of bone or metal to
release their anger), Keepers of the Hearth, grotesquely
obese icons for Fertility and Fecundity, Battlefield
Guardians with hawk or owl attributes, Animal Totems,
Spirit Houses, and others. Chris stared at the range of
horned faces, fat-bellied women, crouching ghouls, terracotta statues with their arms raised and snakes, or ropes,
draped around them, and distorted animal faces that peered
malignly at him from dulled ivory, or greened bronze, or the
battered, ragged gray of flint; suddenly something reached
out to tug his heart, drawing him closer to the cabinet until
he found his nose against the cold glass and his breath misting to obscure these grim and gruesome tokens of so many
lost and forgotten peoples.

It took a moment for him to realize what it was that had
attracted his attention. Then his mind focused where his
eyes were staring: at the dead face, blind eyes, gaping
mouth, the same, or a similar visage, to that which had
adorned the grip of Manandoun's sword. The effigy was
clearly part of a similar weapon, Chris now realized; it was
not the same face; it was *akin* to the Manandoun face—
brothers in death, perhaps.

For reasons he couldn't understand, he felt unwell, disturbed. He started to leave the study, but became weary and

sat down behind the heavy oak door, staring across the room, across the wide mahogany desk at the garden windows, at the gathering dusk.

He fell asleep and woke when the desk lamp was switched on. His mother was sitting there, hair awry, head shaking, her hands moving over one of his father's journals like scurrying, frightened animals. She was flicking through the pages, whispering words, hissing sounds, scanning the tight and tidy writing. She hadn't seen her son, although she was facing him. He remained curled up, half hidden by the open door, listening to the stream of words.

After a while he drifted into sleep again, huddling into his body, feeling chilled, aware of a flickering but persistent light beyond the glass door opening onto the garden.

He awoke again, this time to the sound of breaking glass. The study was alive with shadows, cast by the torches held by figures which emerged slowly into the room from the garden. He could see his mother, but only in silhouette. She was standing by the desk, facing the intruders, her arms limp, her body quite still. A tall man walked about the room; a sharp, unpleasant odor followed him. He leaned down to Christian, bringing an acrid flame close to the boy's face. Chris saw gray eyes, black beard, scars across a high brow, glittering rings in the man's ears, the sharply stylized face of a horse on the bulbous pommel of a sword that was slung across his belly.

"*Slathan!*" the man breathed, and then repeated the word, as if questioning, "*Slathan?*"

A woman's voice answered from behind him, the words like a low growl.

"*Slathan . . .*" the man said again, menacingly, then reached out and used a tiny knife, a green metal blade, to nick the edge of Christian's brow, at the same time touching the healed scar by his own right eye. The boy sucked in a breath and touched a finger to the gash, but he remained quiet, watching as the shadowy figures smashed the cabinets, rifled the exhibits, laughed and shouted at the things they were finding, and all the while his mother stood in silence, in frozen silence, staring through the open garden doors at the flame-lit wood.

A cry of triumph, and the scarred man turned away from where the boy crouched. There was a moment's laughter and the invaders left the study, all save a strangely long man, a figure so tall that he had to stoop below the high ceiling of the room. He smashed the cabinet containing the bows and drew out the one which had been labeled AN AGINCOURT BOWMAN CALLED ALAN LEANBACK. He flexed the yew and listened to it, then nodded with satisfaction and followed the others to the wood, cracking his skull on the lintel and complaining loudly to the amusement of his comrades.

A cowled woman came back into Huxley's den, facing Jennifer's motionless figure. Chris thought it might have been his friend from the horse ride, but he suddenly glimpsed a face below the cowl that was gaunt and moon-silvered, and old. While outside, horses were led away from the house, men shouted, and torchlight flickered and streamed into the night sky, this matron whispered something in Jennifer's ear, then went quickly around the room, marking each wall with ash symbols, shapes that Chris couldn't fathom. Finally, she used a knife to spend several minutes hacking a criss-cross of lines along the vertical edge of the door frame, before backing away from the study.

Outside, she stuck a carved pole into the lawn a yard from the house, then turned and ran after her fellows.

By the desk, his mother had started to wail, and when Chris went to her, touching her gently on the arm, she turned, shrieked, and ran. She fled to her bedroom, closing and locking the door behind her and refusing to respond to her son's urgent and frightened questions from the landing outside.

What had the old woman whispered? What could she have said that could have so terrified his mother?

It was the longest night he had ever spent, though in years to come he would know greater fear and a greater need to see the light of a new day, to banish shadows. He kicked through the glass of the smashed cabinets, picked up the artifacts that had been scattered, and tried to place them back where they once had been displayed, studied the smeared symbols and the cuts on the door. He shuddered as his finger felt the vertical line of tiny scars, a premonition of the meaning that would come some days later, when his father interpreted them:

Kylhuk turned away from the Ivory Gate and broke this place. He took what he had been seeking. He marked the boy as slathan. *The burden of quest is now lighter for the ever-searching, fearless man, Kylhuk.*

The journals, six volumes of his father's obsession, were still on their shelf, and he reached to take one down, but got no further than this before the sound of running upstairs made him push the volume back again and call to his mother. In fact, she came into the study, furious and frightening, chasing him out.

"Look at this mess!" she said loudly, kicking at the broken glass. Her son watched her apprehensively. She had washed her face, combed her hair, changed the juice-stained blouse for a new one.

"Are you all right?" he asked her.

"Get out of here, Chris. I'm going to lock the room. Heaven knows what your father will say when he comes home. Go upstairs, now. Go to bed!"

She was speaking as if the lines were learned and familiar, mouthing the words without any real feeling; she was acting, Chris thought; her mind elsewhere as she paced around the study, murmuring her annoyance.

He reluctantly left the room. His mother closed and locked the broken windows to the garden, then locked the study door, pocketing the key as she moved away into the darkness of the house. Chris had watched her from the landing; now he crept into his room, crawled below the covers on his bed, and cried with loneliness.

He woke sharply at first light, alert and clear headed, as if someone had shouted at him. He was still dressed in his holiday clothes. He rubbed at his eyes, then went to the window, aware that it rattled, that a stiff late summer wind was blowing from the east. There were rain clouds looming over Ryhope Wood. The gate to the garden was swinging and several chickens were pecking in the hedgerow, their feathers bristling. Somewhere in the house, a door banged.

Then he saw the figure in the distance, and recognized his mother, moving like a shade through the rippling field of barley, her direction toward Shadoxhurst. Something about the way she walked, leaving a dark, snaking line behind her in the field, whispered to Chris that something was terribly wrong.

He followed her, running into the barley, picking up her path across the rise and fall of the land. Was she running, too? The faster she went, the more she seemed to be ahead of him. And he noticed, too, as he brushed at the windswept corn, that she was bleeding; she had cut herself, perhaps; there were regular spots of blood on the flattened stalks.

Then the trail divided and he stood in astonishment, aware that someone had walked at right angles to his mother's route, heading directly for the wood. Indeed, as he stretched on his toes to see who had made this second trail, he thought he glimpsed a dark shape entering the underbrush. A familiar head, a determined way of walking, his mother certainly. And yet he could see her ahead of him, emerging from the barley onto the low rise of ground that led toward Shadoxhurst, the path running close to the tall, broad oak known locally as "Strong Against the Storm."

The blood trail led toward the tree and confused though he was, he moved past this second path, noticing that the ghostly figure had vanished now, and soon was walking over the fallow field toward the somber spread of the summer oak, where his mother stood facing him, dark against the brightening dawn sky.

She watched him approach. She was still in the stained Sunday suit, and had combed out her long hair, pinning it back only above her ears to reveal pearl earrings, bright like drops of dew. Her mouth was a slash of garish red. A rope was round her neck, slung over the lowest branch and waiting to be tied.

"What are you doing? Mummy!"

"Go away!" she shouted, but Chris began to run toward her. As he moved, so she jumped, reaching up to grab the branch, tugging at the rope to shorten its drop, dangling one-armed as she threaded a securing knot, a wild, mad dance on the lowest bough, then taking her weight with both hands, hanging there, watching him, her fingers digging into the grooves and knots of the umber bark.

He stood a foot away from her, staring up as she stared down, aware of the tears in her eyes and the blood on her shoes.

"What are you doing? What are you doing?" he wailed.

"Ending the pain. Starting a new life . . ." As she spoke her gaze flickered briefly to Ryhope Wood. The wind gusted strongly and the tree swayed, his mother's body swinging left to right. Christian went up to her to put his arms round her legs, but she kicked out savagely, her right foot connecting with his tearful face and sending him sprawling.

"What are you *doing?*" he screamed again, adding "What have I done?"

She laughed as she dangled.

"Nothing. Yet. But it will turn out very badly for you."

Her strength was giving out, her face strained, her fingers slipping on the branch.

"What did that old woman say to you?" the boy wailed.

"Nothing I hadn't dreamed of already. Nothing that wasn't already pain."

"Tell me what I've done," Chris said again, fighting tears and struggling to his feet. "Please don't die. . . ."

He couldn't bear the thought of it. His mother gone; no smile, no laughter, no knowing hug and gentle words after his father had raged and ranted about some madness or other. She couldn't die. She couldn't leave him.

His mother shook her head, blood suffusing her cheeks, her eyes watering with effort. "My son is gone," she whispered. "I have seen what you will do! My poor boy. My poor little boy . . ."

"No! I'm here! I love you!"

"He's gone; they're both gone. Now it's my turn. . . ."

She dropped and the rope stopped her fall, making her gasp, making her instinctively scrabble at the hemp around her neck, her face bloating almost at once. Chris sprang to her again, screaming in his panic, throwing himself at the dangling legs to take their weight, his voice an animal howl as he held her, aware that she was limp, now, limp and warmly liquid, her eyes unfocused, everything about her at peace as she swung in his arms.

He let go. Climbed the tree. Crawled up the branches to the heart of the oak, where he and Steven had often made a camp. Here he curled into a warm and huddled ball, listening to the wind and the creak of branch and rope below him.

After a while he heard voices. Several men were coming from Shadoxhurst. They didn't see Chris in the tree as they lifted down the corpse and carried it on a stretcher back to the village. Two of the men, one a policeman, set off round the cornfield toward Ryhope and Oak Lodge. Chris watched them go, watched them cross the two trails in the barley, the one that had brought the woman to the tree, the other that had taken the image of his mother into the wood.

He wondered if she was watching from the underbrush; or had she followed her husband inward, to the cauldron of strangeness that Huxley claimed to have found at the heart of the forest?

And he was aware, though distantly as he huddled in the tree, that the seed of a great and terrifying knowledge had been sown—but like a butterfly that flits beyond the net, the precise form of that thought eluded him as he tried to grasp it through his grief.

CHAPTER 1

I had stayed in the tree, Strong Against the Storm, for a day or more. The manor cooperated in the search for me, and had called out the hounds and the local hunt, scattering widely to search the fields and woods around the heart that was Ryhope. None, of course, entered Ryhope Wood itself, where the paths were known in local lore to turn back on themselves and confuse the senses.

It was my own father who found me, and then only because I think he intuited I would be there. He had come from the wood and discovered the tragedy. He had walked across the barleyfield at dusk, to stand below the tree and stare at the branch where the body had recently kicked.

Whether or not he saw me, I shall never know. But after an hour, with the light now gloomy, he suddenly called out to me, "All right Chris. Down you come. Your brother Steve's home. We have to go home, now. We have to face this together."

He started to walk away and after a minute or so I swung down from my hiding place and followed him back to Oak Lodge.

A silence more oppressive than that in the gloomy study pervaded the house for more than a year.

Steven mourned for our mother. I anguished at the loss of

a woman who had been a friend. My mother had always stood between me and my father, protecting me from his occasional anger and frustration with me. Her words, her caresses, had reassured me that all was not as bleak and terrible as it seemed. And in this way, and after picnics in the fields, and games and laughter with a woman who seemed to have so much time for me, so the sounds of fury, the sounds of anguish at night, the gasping cries of pain and indignity as Huxley used her (yes, Huxley! that is how I often think of my father, now), blindly, callously, and without love, all became as no more than bad dreams.

A hand gently stroking my hair, an ice-cream cone, a walk, hand-in-hand through the meadows as the sun dipped below the trees and the distant spire of the church in Shadoxhurst, these from my mother were enough to banish the shadow of my father.

Her violent and angry words to me, as she died, had been shocking and incomprehensible to me.

When at last Steve began to accept that she had gone, so Jennifer Huxley crept back into my own dreams, crouching by me at night, whispering to me, almost urging me to remember her, to find her. Suddenly, these were frightening encounters with my mother, though I longed for her to come home again and would have welcomed a ghost in *any* form.

Over the years, I often woke to find myself standing at the very edge of Ryhope Wood, damp with sweat, convinced that the shade of my mother had beckoned to me, urging me to enter, to follow, to find her, to bring her home! And she seemed to call out: *A girl, centuries older than you think, took you on a wild ride. Chris! She, too, was ghost-born. Open your eyes! If you listen to me, it may not be too late!*

Her words, her warning I now realize, came in my dreams, insubstantial, yet affecting.

And yet, how quickly I dismissed these sensations as no

more than guilt and grief at the loss of a woman who had mattered to me so much.

Despite my childish longings, I was not yet ready to believe in ghosts.

There was something else which struck me as strange, in those last years of the 1930s, before the war in Europe would change our lives forever: Whenever the field by Strong Against the Storm was ripe, with corn or beets, or grass if fallow, two trails would appear on the anniversary of my mother's death, one leading toward the tree, the other leading to the wood.

To stand where the track divided was to hear an unearthly song, the sound of wind from a cavern; it was to smell the deep earth, to hear lost voices. Perhaps I was catching a glimpse, by odor and touch, of the twin gates that would one day confront me; those of Horn and Ivory, of Truth and the Lie!

I have often wondered if my father at this time entered into an odd form of dialogue with me, he writing in the pages of his journal, me responding with naive, awkward questions which he dismissed to my face, but seemed to answer later in his ungainly scrawl.

Frequently, I prowled the closely written pages of his journal and fought the wildness of his mind, finding in my reading a certain satisfaction, since my awareness of the wood and of events was slowly broadened. In this way I discovered the meaning of the *ogham* inscription that Kylhuk's "marker" had left that time before . . .

He has marked the slathan. . . . *The burden is lighter for the ever-searching, fearless man, Kylhuk.*

And I read that, Kylhuk, according to legend, as a young man had arrogantly enlisted the help of Arthur of the Britons and his knights—Kei and Bedevere and the rest—to help in his marriage to Olwen, a "giant's" daughter. Olwen's father had set Kylhuk a series of wild and wonderful tasks, from the ploughing up of whole forests in just a day, and the finding of magic cauldrons, to the rescue of an entombed God and a confrontation with animals older than time.

But there was nothing in Huxley's journal to suggest a meaning for the word *slathan,* which settled upon my youthful shoulders like some silent, watching bird of prey.

Only the reference to "the Ivory Gate" openly puzzled my father. All he wrote was:

> According to the Roman writer Virgil, false dreams, dreams that delude the sleeper, enter the world through the Gate of Ivory; and true dreams, truth, if you will, through the Gate of Horn.
>
> This legend does not link with the other, that of Kylhuk, and the reference is perplexing.

I noted this entry with interest, but was too young at the time to understand the significance of these mythological "dreamgates."

All of the entries in Huxley's journals, convoluted and confused as they were at times, related to manifestations of mythological creatures and heroes that my father called myth-imagoes or "mythagos" (I shall keep the man's eccentric spelling of the coined word).

The "forms" of these mythagos, he believed, arose in Ryhope Wood as a result of being *seeded* by the human minds close by. They would first appear at the edge of vision, in the peripheral area of awareness where imagination and reality co-exist in shadowy tension. But the very fact that they could be glimpsed here, haunting ghosts, vague, startling movements seen from the corner of the eye, meant that in the deeper forest they were being given *form,* and *life,* and certainly a *past* . . . a history and a role in myth, born with the solid flesh, and a life that functioned as it had functioned in prehistoric times, perhaps. They could arise time and time again, conforming to memory and legend in many ways, but utterly unpredictable. And dangerous!

Indeed, there was a short entry referring to my mother that saddened me deeply, though again I couldn't grasp its full significance at the time:

> Jennifer sees her. Jennifer! Poor J. She has declined. She is close to death. What can I do? She is haunted. The girl from the greenwood haunts her. Jennifer more often hysterical, though when the boys are around she remains coldly silent, functioning as a mother, but no longer as a wife. She is fading. Giving up all hope.
>
> Nothing in me hurts at the thought of this.

The girl from the greenwood? Not the "whispering woman," I imagined. And surely not the impish girl on the gray horse! So to whom had he been referring? And what role had this "greenwood girl" played in my mother's suicide?

There were no answers to be found at the time, and life at Oak Lodge settled into an uneasy and grim routine.

CHAPTER 2

Years passed. A devastating war swept across Europe, and when Steven and I came of age we were both called up and saw action on the Front. When the war ended, I returned as soon as possible to Oak Lodge, and the brooding and obsessed presence of my father. I'd hoped Steven would be there, but he sent an enigmatic, oddly sad letter: He was staying on in France, with the family of a nurse he had met in the field hospital.

He was well, recovering from a shrapnel wound, basking in the warmth of the South of France and quite at peace with himself.

This announcement made me feel very melancholy, very alone.

And I was still wallowing in a feeling of loneliness and pointlessness on the day, in December, when my father finally turned on me like a wild creature. I had not anticipated the sudden shift of mood.

A heavy snow had fallen during the night. I'd stayed in the village, sleeping on a couch at the local hotel, but woke at six, made tea, then gratefully accepted a lift on a passing truck as far as Ryhope Manor. The main pathways on the estate had already been swept clear of snow, right down to the farm, and from there I followed the tracks of the tractors that had been out at dawn with hay for the animals.

By following the hedges and the stream, where the snow was thinner, I came quite soon to the garden of Oak Lodge. As I jumped the gate, I noticed what I can only describe as a *panic* of footprints in the snow of the garden, as if there had been a chase, or a wild dance, circles of impressions leading from the kitchen door, through the spiral formations and then to the gate. The single trail then crossed the field to the wood. The impressions were small. Deeper marks in the snow showed where the person had fallen or stumbled.

These were not my father's footprints, I was certain of that. Whose, then? A woman's, I felt.

The house was in chaos; someone had ransacked the kitchen, opening and emptying cupboards, battering at cans of food, smashing jars of preserved fruits and vegetables. There was blood on the surfaces, and in the sink, and a towel was bloodstained where it had been used to mop at a gash. Nervously I walked through the rest of the house. My bedroom too had been ransacked, though nothing was missing that I could see at that time. In his own room, Huxley lay naked and in a deep slumber, facedown on the bed, his skin scratched and grazed, his eyes half opened. His right hand was clenched as if holding something, or frustrated by the loss of something onto which he had been gripping firmly.

"What *have* you been up to?" I whispered at him. "And what have you been eating?" I added, because I had suddenly become aware of the odor in the room; not a human odor, not animal at all; no smell I could associate with winter. Indeed, there was the scent of summer grass and autumn berry in the atmosphere of this disrupted room.

"Where have you *been*?"

I left him where he was, went downstairs and laid a fire. The house was freezing. And it was as I struggled to light the kindling in the grate that my father suddenly lurched into the room, still naked, his flesh pitted with the cold.

"Where is she? What have you done with her?"

His appearance was frightening. The growth of graying beard on his face and the strands of disheveled hair made him look wild. The watery gaze was hypnotic; the wet slackness of his mouth after he screamed the words at me stunned me into silence. He looked quickly round the room, then lurched for one of the two shotguns stacked in the corner. He grabbed the weapon and swung it round.

"Don't be mad!" I shouted at him, throwing up my hands as he pulled the triggers. The two dull clicks brought me back to furious reality. In the past, those guns had been kept loaded, the breeches broken.

He advanced on me with the empty weapon, his thigh bruising against the edge of the table, his eyes still shining.

"Where is she? The girl! What have you *done* with her?"

"There's no one here. Dad, put the gun down. Get some clothes on. There's no one here—just you and me."

His answer was to swing the stock round to crack against my head, but I was too quick for him, avoiding the desperate blow and grabbing the barrel. We struggled for a few seconds and I was astonished at his strength, but I had learned a trick or two in the last few years and disabled him with the briefest of kicks. He howled, hunched over his battered flesh, clutching himself in agony. Then, like some berserk creature of old, he was on me again, hands at my throat, musty breath in my face.

"Where is she? Where is she? I've waited too long for this encounter. . . . I won't let you interfere with it!"

"There's no one here. You. Me. An unlit fire. Footsteps in the snow. That's it. Dad, stop fighting me."

He seemed shocked, staring hard into my eyes, his own eyes wide with alarm. "*Fighting* you? I'm not fighting you, Chris."

"What, then?" I whispered.

And he answered quietly, "I'm frightened of you." Then he almost collapsed against me.

His words astonished me. I was too stunned to speak for a moment as I stared at the gray, apprehensive figure of my father in all his filthy glory. Then I simply asked, "Why? You have nothing to be frightened of. . . ."

"Because you saw me . . ." he said, though he said it as if the statement should have been obvious. "Because you know . . ."

"I don't understand."

"You know what I *did*. You saw me!" He was suddenly exasperated. "Don't pretend!"

"You're making no sense."

"Aren't I?"

He was shaking, now, tears spilling from his eyes. I held him close to me. His body slackened, his gaze dropped, fatigue catching at his strength. I didn't understand his words, but they had distressed me. There was an emptiness in this cold house again, a hollow sense, that I had last known when my mother had danced for me on that terrible day and I had felt that—because of a whisper—I was the cause of her anger, her hatred, and her suicide.

I tried to speak, but the words caught in my throat. I wanted to cry. I wanted to be anywhere but here. For some reason the fire, which had refused to light at my urging, suddenly caught, and the dry kindling crackled in the flame. I helped my father down onto a sofa, suddenly more than conscious of his nakedness and of the bruising on his groin. His hand stroked and soothed the wounded limb and he slumped to one side, tears rolling on his cheeks, glowing with the sudden fire. I pulled the cloth from the table and covered him, and like an old man he clutched at the edges, drew the warming blanket up to his throat.

"She was here," he said quietly, and for a moment I thought he meant Jennifer Huxley, but he had never referred to my mother with such tenderness in his voice.

"Who was here?"

"*She* was here," he said. "I went with her. She was everything I had expected. She was *everything*. Everything I'd imagined. Everything . . ."

"The girl from the woods?"

"The girl . . ." he whispered, touching a shaking hand to his eyes to wipe the tears.

"Guiwenneth, you called her. . . ."

"Guiwenneth," he repeated, clutching at the blanket. "Exactly as her story had said. But she is mine. Created from my own mind. I had known that. But I hadn't known what it would mean. . . . Poor Jennifer. Poor Jennifer. *I couldn't help it*. Forgive me . . ."

"What *does* that mean? The girl was yours, you said. What does that mean?"

"They reflect our needs," he said, then turned his head to look at me, and suddenly all weakness had gone, only the canny look, the hard look of the thinking man that I had known for all my life. It was as if his face tightened from the flaccid mask of despair to a stone-hard look that concealed all emotion. "They *take* from us. I should have known that. They reflect us, and they *take* from us. We are them. They are us. Mythagos! Two shadows from the same mind. I was curious; therefore, so was she. I was angry. Therefore, so was she . . . I longed for her in certain ways. Why should I have expected anything different from her?"

Suddenly he threw the tablecloth aside and leaned toward me, hands at first seeming to go for my throat so that I pulled back defensively, but I think he had merely wanted to embrace me. He said, simply, "Did you see her? Any sign of her?"

"She danced in the snow."

"Snow? Is it snowing?"

"Last night. It's quite deep out there. She went back to the wood, but she'd danced first."

"Back to the wood . . . If that's so, then I can follow.

There'll be a way in for a moment. Into the wood. The way is open more clearly for a moment. . . . Chris, make me some tea. Please! And a sandwich or two."

"Yes. Of course."

And the man, so recently mad, so recently feral, walked from the room, a tablecloth for modesty, reappearing minutes later dressed for a winter's walk, indifferent to me once again.

CHAPTER 3

I watched him go. He inspected the disturbed snow in the back garden, then quickly followed the strange trail into the scrub that led up to the wall of oak and elm that marked the near-impenetrable wood. He didn't look back; he was swallowed by the winter darkness of the trees in an instant.

My curiosity got the better of me and I dressed warmly, intending to follow. But first I entered the study, found his journal, and read the last few entries.

They were very matter-of-fact, and I was struck by how repetitive many of his observations were. There were also several macabre references to my mother, written as if she was still alive.

I put these out of my mind. It was the recent visitor to the house who now fascinated me, and I had a name to go on! I leafed back through the volumes and found entry after entry referring to Guiwenneth. The two that excited me the most were these:

> The girl again! From the woodland, close to the brook, she ran the short distance to the chicken huts and crouched there for a full ten minutes. I watched her from the kitchen, then moved through to the study as she prowled the grounds. . . . The girl affects me totally. Jennifer has seen this, but what can I do? It is the

nature of the mythago itself. . . . She is truly the ideal-
ized vision of the Celtic Princess, lustrous red hair,
pale skin, a body at once childlike yet strong. She is a
warrior, but she carries her weapons awkwardly, as if
unfamiliar with them. She is Guiwenneth-of-the-
Green!

Jennifer is unaware of these details, only the girl
and my helpless attraction. The boys have not seen
her, though they have certainly seen strange activity at
the edge of the wood.

And from a later entry I learned this:

She is a warrior-princess from the time of the
Roman invasion of northern Europe, but her charac-
teristics, the essence of her story, are older of course.
She is beguiling, intelligent, fast, and vulnerable. Is
she a benign and seductive form of the enchantress we
know as Viviane? Or Morgan le Fey? This is an interesting heroine indeed, and she is as curious about me
as am I of her. It is not surprising that my heart leaps
to see her.

This time I cannot fail. She will be my guide to a
greater understanding of all that rises from the past
and is sustained inside Ryhope Wood itself.

I was intrigued. I too dressed warmly and went into the
woodland following precisely along the line of the girl's
tracks, ducking below the branches and following the winding route between the trunks, aware that the snow was thinner here and that the light from above was rapidly fading—
not because the day was advancing into dusk, but because
the whole nature of Ryhope was changing with every pace!

Suddenly, the winter had vanished.

Bemused, I stood and smelled spring. A brighter sunlight

beckoned me forward and I entered a wide glade, a leaf-strewn clearing, criss-crossed with winter bramble, a fallen tree, now very rotten, cutting across its heart. All was stillness. All was silence. But this was not winter and my body was pricked with apprehension, my head whirling with the sudden sense of being watched.

By closing my eyes, the fear subsided. But to stare steadily ahead was to experience movement, an intriguing movement, right at the edge of vision. To search for that movement with more direct gaze was to see nothing but shadow and woodland. To hold steady was to experience a whole world of life and attention, so far into the corner of my eye that it might have been heat or light playing tricks on the budding leaves that had no business on the branches in this deep, December day.

I remembered something else that Huxley had once written: that the wood somehow *turned you around,* confusing the senses and sending you back to the edge. Small though Ryhope was, it guarded itself against intruders, and I was now an intruder. A sudden panic gripped my senses. I turned, and ran, bruising and grazing myself against the trees, finally bursting from the edge, falling in the snow, scrabbling and swimming in the cold, refreshing mush.

"Damn!"

Sitting up, I stared back along the way I had come.

For the first time in my life I had experienced the sensation that I was sure had first intrigued my father. Encounters with strange figures had featured large in my childhood years, but never this sense of being drawn in, turned inside out, scanned, approached, scrutinized, and finally kicked *back* to the reality of snow.

"Wonderful!" I shouted to my father in the wood. "You're on to something wonderful! I've always known it.

It's always been here! I've never *felt* it so strongly, until now."

Not even as a child, I thought grimly.

I flopped back in the snow, laughing loudly, giving in totally to this moment of release and exhilaration.

"What *have* you found?" I asked the image of my father. "What *is* going on?"

And I sat up abruptly, remembering Kylhuk, *slathan,* cuts to my face ... and my mother's urine soaking from her shoes onto my shirt as I held her and tried to keep her back from that terrible valley.

"And what have you done to me ... ?"

Later, seated miserably in the cold enamel tub, lukewarm water to a depth of eight inches as I washed, I heard the tentative movement of someone in the house. The bathroom looked out over the garden and I shivered and peered from the window, noticing a new set of tracks from the wood. Wrapped in a towel, I crept out onto the landing, peered over the banister, and was at once struck on the back of the head by a stone. As I slumped in confusion, I glimpsed and smelled the woman who darted from my father's room. She crouched briefly on the turn of the stairs, staring at me as she breathed in that shallow way that denotes fear and flight, then was gone, leaving me to slow recuperation of my senses.

Dried and dressed again, I searched for her, found only traces of her presence. I added wood to the fading fire and crouched in its welcome warmth. Then I sat in the chair where years ago my mother had stared into her future through similar flames.

The girl was still in the house. When I walked through the rooms I knew she was watching me, but she stayed out of sight, darting and slipping through the shadows, adding to my sensory confusion.

I could smell her. I called to her. I tried everything. I tried to make myself nonthreatening. I even sang a jaunty song and cooked a pot of broth, hoping that the smell of food would entice her from her shifting lair.

She was biding her time, no doubt watching me, trying to work me out.

She confronted me in the late afternoon, as the light was going and I had switched on the lamps in the sitting room. Movement in the kitchen caught my attention and I went to investigate. The kitchen was empty, the pot of barley and chicken broth gone, the back door open into the snow-shadowed dusk. My breath frosted as I called for her again, then closed the door. But when I returned to the blazing fire, there she was, sitting in my own chair, the pot held to her lips as she drank the cold soup. Her eyes watched me over the iron rim. A vicious-looking weapon, a leather sling tied around a stone, lay in her lap. She was clad in loose woolen trousers, vaguely patterned, and with a heavy cloak still tied around her shoulders. Her feet were bare, small, pale toes warming at the fire. When I smiled, she nodded, then lowered the pot; a yellow froth of soup lined her upper lip and she briefly frowned into the vessel before placing it to one side and letting the fingers of her left hand twine with the leather of the skull-cracker. She made no effort to move, simply stretched out her feet a little more, wriggling with clearly implied satisfaction.

In all this time her gaze never left me, green-eyed, slightly frightened, very wary, her face a pale oval between long locks of fire-reflecting auburn hair.

"I can make you a better supper," I said. "The soup was very thin."

"Huxley," she said, and I fancy there was a question in the word.

"Yes. Huxley. Christian." I patted my chest. "Christian Huxley. My father is George. George Huxley . . ."

"George," she echoed, her eyes narrowing, her grip tightening on the stone skull-cracker.

I raised my hands in a gesture of pacification, but she had risen to her feet, every muscle tense, her gaze on mine, but her awareness wider, now: listening, sniffing, alert for betrayal.

"He's not here," I said to her. "I promise you. He followed you into Ryhope Wood." I was making dancing and walking motions with my fingers, simple gestures to emphasize and direct my words. "You're quite safe with me."

What arrogance! What assumption!

She smiled at me, bowed slightly, and started to walk past me, the soup pot in her hand, for all the world as if she were going to wash up her dirty pan. As I stepped to one side I saw the blur of her fist, heard the exhalation of her breath, and then for the second time in my life felt my head cracked and my world go black.

This time when I roused myself, I found the fire burned low, the carpet charred where embers had spilled from the blaze and not been extinguished, my head sore from the blow, Oak Lodge filled with the sound of breaking glass. Weak and shaking, I hauled myself to my feet, and cautiously walked through the house to the sound of mayhem. Guiwenneth had found framed photographs of my mother and was systematically smashing them, screaming abuse at them as she did so, flinging the buckled, splintered remains across the study floor.

"What are you doing?"

At my feet was the crushed portrait of Jennifer Huxley that for all my life had adorned the mantelpiece of my parents' bedroom. She was young here, smiling brightly, half turned to the camera, her cheeks highlighted from the studio lights. This was a woman perhaps no older than myself, her life ahead of her, her dreams filled with beauty, her hopes so legion that she had no hopes at all, simply expectations, anticipation, the exhilaration of looking forward.

Now smashed, now ruined by this creature from my father's furious, feral mind!

"Stop this!" I shouted. "These are precious!"

The stone sling blurred toward me and I snatched it from the air, flung it to the floor where the handsome, youthful woman watched me from the creases in the photographic paper, through the jagged edges of the glass, the twisted metal frame.

"Enough!" I hissed.

She crouched. She launched herself at me, her feet striking me, her nails raking me, her teeth gnawing me. And then she was gone, out into the evening snow, floundering in the deep drifts, cold and lost and frightened, calling for something or someone, desperate in her loneliness, desperate in her fear, oblivious of my calls to her to *come back, come back,* that I really wouldn't hurt her.

She was a frail shadow against the crisp and moon illuminated field of snow, falling below it and flailing within it, like a fish leaping and splashing in an icy river. She stumbled and vanished and at once was quiet. It was too cold to follow, and I was too disturbed by the thought of the reception I might receive if I made to pursue her.

I found enough kindling to make a crude torch, tied it together, lit it, placed it in the open kitchen door to the house. As the evening passed, I kept feeding the simple beacon, but soon the meager supplies from the woodshed were exhausted; and I was exhausted too; and night was black and bleak, and the snow came heavier.

My father came home at dawn, and he was not a happy man.

By the beard on his face, he had been away a week, I thought; he quickly checked the calendar, then—as if not

quite believing me when I assured him of the day—he
turned on the wireless and sat hunched beside it, listening to
the voices, waiting for the first chimes of the new hour and
reference to the day itself.

"I was here only this morning."

"Yes. She's been and gone. . . ."

"Guiwenneth?" he shouted, startled and angry.

I shifted the loaded shotgun into the crook of my arm,
facing him across the room. "Guiwenneth," I said. "She's
bruised me, battered me, confused me, and fled."

The animal in his eyes was back and I snapped shut the
breech of the shotgun, keeping it pointed away from him,
but my fingers close to the trigger.

"She was here looking for *you*, not me. She's gone. She's
angry. Whatever is happening to you, please either sit down
and talk about it with me, or go away and leave me alone.
Do you see the bruise on my face?"

His watery, wild gaze flickered to accommodate the yellowing and painful mark that was still aching and distracting
me.

"She did that?"

"She's a bit of a fresh one, Dad. More than a touch lively.
You taught me not to walk behind a lathering mare after the
hunt, in case she kicked; you forgot to mention trying to
pacify one of your . . ."

I hesitated, then used the word: "Mythagos."

"Myth*aa*goes," he corrected. "From 'Myth Imagoes.' "

"I've read what you've written," I said patiently. "I know
the source. I don't understand what they are, these *mythagos,* but I know the coinage. And I know that you think they
come from the wildwood, beyond the house, and from our
own unconscious minds."

"Primal woodland, Chris. Unchanged for twelve thousand years. The home of *living history*. . . ."

"I don't know much about that. But I *can* tell a woman

who's jealous of another. . . . She's smashed my mother's photographs."

"Smashed them?"

"Went berserk. In your study."

He seemed startled. "She's smashed them all? All the photographs?"

"Not beyond repair."

"Not beyond repair," he echoed, a curious smile on the unkempt face, in the sad, tired eyes. "No. Of course not. Not beyond repair. Pictures and statues, the earth itself . . . all can be damaged. But not beyond repair. Not like us . . ." He sat down behind the desk, slumped forward, head in hands. "I'm weary, Chris. And hungry. And cold. Is there anything to eat?"

"Not much. I'll fix you something. A hot drink."

"Wine," he said. "Bring me anything red. Don't bother about letting it breathe. Just pour it."

"Barbarian," I said as I left the room to follow his instructions.

The wine was a mistake. He got drunk and aggressive and at two in the morning was raging at me in the darkness of my room where I lay in bed. "What did she say to you? Tell me everything she said! What are the two of you doing behind my back? I told you, Chris . . . leave us alone! I've waited too long for her. She doesn't belong to you."

Frightened that he might have the shotgun with him, I stayed quite calm, watching him carefully. He was holding a blackthorn walking stick, a deadly enough weapon if used deliberately, and I gently prompted him to put it down. He did so but came toward me, leaning down and hissing like a cat through near-clenched teeth, his lips drawn back. "Don't touch her. I won't let you touch her. I know your game! I've always seen it in your eyes. You know what I did. You saw me—"

"I don't know what you mean, Dad. All I know is, you're drunk." His breath reeked of wine. I suspected he'd opened a second bottle.

"You saw me," he repeated nervously, his words of yesterday. "That frightens me."

"I don't know what you mean. Go back to bed—"

But before I could say another word, he had leaped at me again. His hands closed on my throat briefly and I threw him back, flinging off the counterpane to defend myself more effectively. But again, like a cat he had slipped from the room, an angry shadow, taking the stairs two at a time, banging below me through the house and finally trudging out into the snow. I watched him go from my bedroom window, a sad, lonely man, a hunched shape, head bowed, using the staff he always carried to help him through the deep snow of the field, back to the wood, back to his dream.

The snow kept falling and I decamped to Shadoxhurst again, to a room above the Red Lion Inn. Whether or not Huxley returned to Oak Lodge in that time I do not know, and at the time couldn't have cared. When I went back myself, on the last day of January, the snow was on the melt. I laid a new fire. The photographs of my mother were still where they had been smashed. The wine cellar had not been further raided and I removed several bottles and locked it up again.

In the evening I heard the sound of carrion birds and went out into the garden. A small flock of crows was circling a part of the field, where a dark shape was half exposed as the snow melted around it. Shocked and apprehensive, I ran across to it, waving my arms to scatter the noisy birds. I had expected to see my father's grim, disheveled features staring from the ice, but it was the girl who lay there, her pale face white as the snow around her, the skin drawn in to expose the skull, the eyes dull below half-opened lids. The crows had not yet started to feed, and though they mobbed me, screeching, I kept them off and covered the corpse while I returned to the house for a blanket.

I hauled the fragile body into the woolen shroud and was surprised that it was as light as a doll. Indeed, she might have been made of hollow wood, her skin as brittle as an autumn leaf. I stored the sad remains in the empty coop, wondering what to do about reporting it. If my father was right, this woman did not exist in our own world. If he came back and found her dead, he would assume the deed to have been of my own doing. Better to bury her, leave her in peace, and forget that she had ever existed.

And this I did, where the chickens once had run, where the earth was deep, where she would rot down well away from the house itself, forgotten bones in a forgotten corner of the garden.

CHAPTER 4

It should have been easy to forget her. Who had she been, after all, other than some strange woman from a strange place, hostile, uncommunicative, beautiful, yes, but an entity nonetheless that had in no way impinged upon my senses?

So why, then, did she haunt my waking hours, and whisper to me in my dreams? Sometimes I woke crying; my mother seemed to drift away, a shadow in the room, her words fading into obscurity but my muscles and stomach still clenched with the pain of the loss. Other times, it was Guiwenneth who called to me, and there was something in the look, something in the smile, something that I should have recognized but for the moment could not.

These edge-of-the-mind intrusions became increasingly distracting. I realized quite suddenly, sometime in the spring, that I had become as obsessed with Guiwenneth as my father had been, and this prompted me to read his journals through again, to commit to memory great tracts of what he had written, to think more deeply about the things he'd seen, the lands he'd visited, beyond the gate and the brook, in this tiny patch of English woodland.

I tried to find the entrance to the wood, but nothing "opened" in the way that Huxley had described. Nevertheless, if my father had been right, there ought to be some gap, some opening in the wood's defenses. Huxley himself had used various devices, all of them handheld, all of them strange, which he had called "residual aura detectors" or "vortex focusing sensors" or other such nonsense. I found two of these in his desk drawer and tried to use them, but though they responded, I had no idea what they were signaling to me.

I decided to sleep on it, and explore the edge first thing in the morning, with or without the strange detectors.

I'm glad I waited.

A sound like the bellowing of a metal bull woke me from a spirit-haunted sleep, disoriented and cold. When the sound came again, a short, rising call, I went to the window to peer out through the crisp dawn at the dew-covered trees of Ryhope Wood. And at that moment I had my first glimpse of visitors from the deep for more than two months.

Pale light reflected off gleaming metal, a strange and hideous animal's head, open-mouthed, swaying in the tree line at the end of a long, curved neck. This metal grotesque pulled back into the underbrush almost instantly. A man's face, pale and beardless, replaced it for a moment, peering at me hard, then that too was gone.

I had never seen an instrument like this vertical horn before, though I had heard them several times in my childhood. I imagined they had been used in war to frighten the enemy; they certainly made the pulse race.

The two blasts had been a summons to someone in the house, but not for me. I sensed rather than heard the doors to the garden open and a few seconds later a woman ran lightly from my father's study toward the gate. Her long, red hair had been tied into a single braid; she wore a leather tunic of the Roman kind, and sandals. When she glanced back at the house I could see she was in her "war paint," purple spirals on her cheeks, a band of black across her eyes. Even so, she was both beautiful and recognizable.

I had buried the bones of a "form" of this woman last winter. Here she was again, the same and different, and altogether less feral.

The girl again, from the wood . . .

And this time she was *mine*!

As she caught my eye, she hesitated at the gate; the smile that touched her lips was both enigmatic and impish. She seemed to have taken something from the study, but what she raised to me in acknowledgment was a riding crop, feathered and brightly painted, similar to that which she had used to "count coup" on me as a boy.

For the first time I realized that the white-haired girl rider of my childhood and "Guiwenneth-of-the-Green" were the same, separated only by the span of years of adolescence.

I felt both stunned and elated. There had been something in the look of this Guiwenneth that was more than familiar—it had been *knowing*. The girl rider had come back! And she was signaling to me to follow.

She had gone then, running fast over the field and into the wood, and though I waited a few seconds, hoping for a further glimpse, I knew there was not a moment to lose. If my father was right, mythagos left trails through the dense and convoluted defenses of Ryhope Wood, openings into the deep that would grant me an access so often denied. Even now, this new doorway, like a wound in flesh, would be slowly closing up.

There was grass and leaf matter on the floor of my bedroom. The heady scent in the room was alarming and arousing—more than just flowers, then. Dust danced and swirled through a thin shaft of light from between the curtains.

The woman had been in here, I realized, and had charmed me in some way, sending me deeply to sleep. Waking me *just* at the moment of her departure. Had she *wanted* me to see her as she made her escape from the dawn raid upon Oak Lodge? Of course she had! Why else wave at me? She had spent time exploring while I slept. Now I was being called inward.

An hour later, Huxley's strange detectors in my pack, I reached the glade where previously I had been turned about. This time there was no such attack upon my perception and I pressed on, deeper into what was now a forest of great and ancient growth. If I was following a track, I was not conscious of it, but my path seemed clear, and my journey, if claustrophobic, seemed directed.

And in due course—by now time had ceased to register—I came to the greater, darker clearing among the massive oaks, the shrine, well known to my father, that was the place of the Horse Goddess. I had heard the rattle of the skulls tied to the lower boughs and that morbid sound drew me from the darkness into the circle of light that illuminated the massive statue at the center of the sanctuary. Made of bones and branches, the Horse faced me, eerily watching me from the eyes that had been shaped in the bridled head. There was a strong breeze and the leather trappings that adorned the hundred skulls around the edge of the clearing whipped like tendrils, clattering where their metal decorations clashed.

I hated this place; I believe Huxley had hated it. But it was the entrance to the inner forest, and all things passed this way, and therefore Guiwenneth—*my* Guiwenneth, the wild girl grown older—had passed this way, too.

A sudden shaft of daylight, released as the canopy rolled and shifted in the wind, illuminated the brilliant shield that stood between the statue's legs. And I remembered something that my father had written about just such a shield, which changed according to who or what passed by:

If there is significance in the restless decor and patterning of the shield, I have yet to find it. But that it *does* change is of great interest. The designs seem to reflect the latest visitor from the heart of the wood: Wessex warrior priests of the Bronze Age fading into the figures of Aegean dancers, and then to Viking dragon ships or lost Roman legions—each mark, each picture, each symbol telling a tale, or suggesting a route if the puzzle can be pieced together.

The shield was oval and as tall as a man. Rimmed and with a central boss of iron, patterned in bronze on the outer leather, it was made of oak so thick that I could not lift it. It was certainly not meant to be used in war or combat, at least not by men of my own physical stature.

I examined the detail of the latest design to cover its face. Five ravens circled the top of the shield; a white horse, curiously elongated and catlike, graced its center; and a white-faced mask, framed in luxuriant auburn hair, stared at me from the lower quarter. This mask appeared to be the object of desire of two crudely drawn wrestling warriors, whose interlocked arms and grimacing faces formed a circle above it.

I stared at that image for a long time. I couldn't help feeling that it signaled, yes, that Guiwenneth had passed by this way, but also that my father was still alive and in the deep, still searching for the woman who obsessed him.

To the naked eye there was no way of telling which direction among the great oaks the party had taken some hours previously. But Huxley's inventiveness, his "residual aura detector," should at least be able to indicate the general direction of the departure. This small gadget, like a flashlight, but with neither bulb nor glass at its end, only a series of copper needles fanning out like a pin cushion, functioned (he had claimed) by responding to the residual "life energy" of those who had passed by. Huxley had been infatuated by the notion of *ley lines* and patterns of energy and memory in both earth and in the confined spaces of glades and clearings, even in the root network of the heartwood itself. A small dial indicated the highest source of this "residual aura" by the simple device of a needle flicking to maximum and then dropping again, as a magnet might respond to a lodestone.

To my surprise—and to my admiring delight—the needle duly flicked and I began my journey to the heart of the wood, passing to the right of the statue of the horse, following the route suggested by this unlikely piece of electronics. There was a heavy scent of mold in the air, and a claustrophobic darkness for a while, but in a minute or so the oppressive sense of enclosure dissipated, as I had known it would, and I was on a wide track, a summer sun overhead, the land opening before me and dropping away, perhaps to a river. In the distance that land rose again into the great swathe of primal forest that would soon be my home for as long as I remained in Ryhope Wood.

The ridge ahead of me was like the hunched back of an animal, topped with a spine of conifers that reminded me of quills. This was the "Hogback Ridge," a place which Huxley had often visited and referred to in his journal. Indeed, as I tentatively explored the rocks and wind-curled thorns that fringed the rise of land, I found the rusting remnants of more of his strange detectors, fragments of metal, broken dials attached to trunk and branch, their function long since dead with time.

How often had my father paced to the summit of this ridge, I wondered? And what had his machines told him about the ebb and flow of myth and legend in this place? It was a strange sensation, for a while, to know that the man had made his camp here, surveying the inner wood perhaps from this very spot.

But Huxley was now deeper, engaged on his own journey. He was beyond this ridge, and beyond the river that I knew curved around the bottom of the hill, taking the traveler through deep gorges and toward the setting sun. To dwell on the flux of time and space in this realm was to go mad with confusion. At any moment, the man might come striding through the spine of trees, aged by tens of years, perhaps by days only. And the possibility was strong that he lay in cold indifference somewhere, consumed by the earth itself.

These thoughts occupied me for a while. I was reluctant to leave this place of open hill and rusting intellect; it was my father's shrine, in every sense and in every way as significant as the gruesome Horse that marked the multitude of cross-roads into the past.

But after an hour I had made a sort of peace with this place and ascended to the spine of the ridge. Rarefied, clean air, a crisp breeze, a wonderful silence, these were the sensations as I stood between two tall conifers, my arms outstretched like a man on the cross, or a man embracing the far horizon. I was heady with triumph and with anticipation. I had already seen a coil of smoke curling from the forest below me. Light shimmered on movement for as far as the eye could see across this ocean of wildwood. Something, or someone, was out there waiting for me, and the thought of this was both frightening and exhilarating. And I assumed, also, that Guiwenneth herself would be there, at the edge of the inner forest. And it was with confidence, if caution, that I began the walk down to the hidden river, and that enigmatic curl of smoke.

I had begun the journey, and I had made my first mistake.

PART TWO

THE FORLORN
HOPE

There is no limit to my foreignness; every word means something to someone somewhere. I will find one you know.

—Alanna Bondar, from *Agawa host*

CHAPTER 5

I had expected to find a camp at the riverside below me, smouldering embers signaling its position. In fact I found a funeral pyre, crudely and hurriedly erected, only half consumed by flame, sufficient to char but not cremate the long body that lay upon it, its hands on its chest. The pyre was still glowing and in time the journey of the particular dead soul would be achieved, but for the moment it stood in a clearing among smoke-blackened crack-willows, both a tribute to the loyalty of friends and a consequence of the need of those friends to travel quickly.

Everything about the arching corpse, its grim mouth gaping, suggested that it was a man. Four crudely shaped wooden poles had been erected at the points of the pyre, and ogham symbols had been hacked upon them, but without a knowledge of that code, the meaning was elusive. I noticed, though, a fragment of bronze, a segment of tube that had been placed upon the dead man's chest, perhaps, before rolling off as the cadaver had writhed in the first, fierce heat. And at once I was reminded of the vertical bronze trumpet I had glimpsed from Oak Lodge. This might have been the mouthpiece.

How this man had died I couldn't tell. I approached, but a gust of wind enflamed the smouldering embers and the fire licked high for a few seconds before dying down. I stepped back to a respectful distance.

In a second clearing however, some way from the river, I gained a fair idea as to how the trumpet blower had met his end. There had been a hard fight here, and the sour-sweet smell of it was strong on the humid air. A severed hand lay in the protecting curl of an elm's root; long locks of black hair, scalp attached, were caught in cracks in the bark of the same tree; slices of bloodstained leather and linen clothing lay everywhere. The trees showed the marks of slashing blades, powerfully deployed. And huddled together, as if asleep, two dead men had been placed in the overhang of a thorn bush, side by side, heads tucked down, knees drawn up, arms folded, They might have been Buddhist monks in deep contemplation. They were naked, no doubt since clothing and weapons were always of value to someone somewhere, and I guessed that these had been the enemy of those who had built the pyre.

There had been an encounter then, but with whom it was hard to tell. That the two dead men were tattooed was not surprising. Huxley had written several times that: *It seems all life in prehistoric ages boasts body decoration of this type; like a coded script, the designs contain more information than is first apparent.*

I could not read them!

Their hair was long, formed into braided locks interwoven with strips of leather and colorful beads, all bloody now. They were fly ridden and beginning to stink and I didn't linger long. But I was sure that Guiwenneth had been taken by surprise by these men, and she and her group had fought hard for their lives, losing the trumpet blower before continuing their inward journey, whose direction I soon discovered as I prowled the edge of the river.

An exposed bank of sand stretched out from below the low-hanging foliage and I saw where people had passed, walking toward the setting sun. A hundred yards from the spit of sand, the bank was furrowed where canoes had been stored and launched.

One small boat remained, without paddle or seat, like a floating coffin, perhaps, but a hulk of oiled wood and patched hide that at least was river worthy. Had it been left for me? Who could tell? But surely, if there had been a fear of being followed, my party would have taken the boat to frustrate my pursuit.

I was to drift with the current, it seemed to me, and await further contact.

What Fates, what forces were guiding the flow of my own journey? It hardly seemed to matter. To enter Ryhope was to enter a confusion at the *edge* of things, a sensory cacophony of sound and vision—glimpses and echoes that could not be grasped—that was both frightening and seductive. I had experienced these feelings on a previous occasion, and had become determined to fight through the fear, to fight the dizzying defenses of this semi-sentient wildwood, to find that certain moment when a definable and welcome peace replaced the screams of the anxious intellect and the tricks that the forest was playing. It was a moment when a hand seemed to reach out and soothe everything, from mind to brow. There was a certainty attached to this moment, a feeling that the direction was right, that the events which were being witnessed and the loss of control were all being carefully monitored. I was like a child, secure in the assertion and confidence of a parent, unaware, of course, that the parent was trained to respond to my fears in just this way.

Previously, I had turned about when this catharsis had occurred. Now, however, with the rediscovery of Guiwenneth as my goal, I fought against the feeling to return and let events take their course.

I thought of Longfellow as I launched the short canoe; I

lay back, my pack at my head, my arms over the sides of the
simple, smooth-hewn craft; I let the river take me and
watched the sky through the over-reaching branches of the
trees. I let the motion of hull and water become the movement of time itself, taking me backward, ever backward,
into a distance of which I had only dreamed.

This was the edge of the Wilderness. It was the true entrance to the past and to the Otherworld and I became afraid
to watch it, aware of its beauty and its confusion. To try to
see it, to document it, would perhaps have been to find that
it ceased to exist; and it would spit me out, hurl me back into
the bright air near the cornfield by Oak Lodge, drifting again
on a stream in England rather than on a river that flowed into
the realm of ghosts.

I thought of Longfellow, and his Hiawatha.

I thought of Arthur on his way to Avalon, stretched out in
his barge, three Queens tending to his mortal wounds. And I
rued the lack of women, black cowled or otherwise. How
nice, how pleasant it would have been, to have had their
strange company on this sluggish journey to the past.

And so this simple boat of fate brought me, by the hour,
toward my first encounter with the bloodied, angry group
that had been to the edge of their world to find me, and
which had suffered a terrible loss as they returned to the garrison that protected them.

I drifted for a long time, though precisely how long is hard
to know. For a while I stared at the watch on my wrist, noting the second hand mark the passage of minutes, but this
objective observation soon ceased to relate to the subjective
experience, and within a few hours the mechanism had
wound down and I left it so.

Like a leaf on a stream, the canoe turned slowly in the
deeper water. It grounded in the shallows and I lazily
reached over the side to push the craft back into the flow.

Night descended then departed, and at dawn I was dew covered and shivering, but still at peace. That same dawn, as I stared through the broken canopy over the water at the brightening sky, a massive human shape stepped across the river and across my boat, startling me. Untrousered and massive, I saw no more than the legs and the bulbous droop of the swinging genitals as the stride was taken, and heard a sound like rolling thunder that might have been its voice. Sitting up, shaking languor from my eyes and my mind, I began to take more interest in the direction of my travel.

A while later a second figure appeared in mid-river, walking toward me, waist deep in the water. The current carried me rapidly toward this bearded human male; he was large, a giant, though not like the river-striding man I had seen before, and he grinned as I came toward him. He carried ropes over one shoulder, each attached to a boat, ten in all, some small and sleek, some simple, one ornate and masted like a royal barque. From what I could see of him I reckoned him to be ten feet tall at least. His hand, as it reached ahead of him to stop my own canoe, was the size of a dinner plate. Strong fingers gripped the prow and he struggled to keep my craft from turning and twisting away from him. He had kindly eyes, lank black hair, a water-saturated beard, and gleaming teeth. He wore a green and patterned shirt that gaped open to his huge meat-fattened belly.

"Elidyr," he said loudly, and repeated the word.

I realized it was his name and slapped my chest, calling, "Christian."

"Elidyr," he repeated again, then pressed the boat's prow against his belly, releasing his hand for a moment to make an odd little walking movement in the air, then touching the tips of his fingers to his chest and cocking his head. "Elidyr," he said softly.

"Christian," I said in the same soft tone of voice. He looked puzzled.

I could learn little of the man at this stage of our encounter, of course, but because he would stay with me for a
while I would learn that Elidyr meant "guide," though the
nature of his guidance was far more complex than I realized.
He certainly seemed confused, however, standing there with
the river flowing and soaking him, and the ten small boats
shifting restlessly in his wake. Bodies lay in them, I could
see, and smoke rose from two.

Elidyr kept looking back downriver, back to the east.
(The sun had risen in that direction, so I considered it to be
the east.) Then he would look ahead of him, to where I had
come from, and frown and sigh. It was decision time, that
much was clear, and he was having a terrible time with it.
His sighs made the leaves tremble. The anxious beating of
his free hand against the water made waves break against
the rocks. Had he been looking for me? Did he recognize
me? Had I arrived unexpectedly? Whatever was inspiring
this indecision, it was clear that Elidyr was confronting a situation he had not anticipated.

After a while he let go of five ropes and let the boats slip
away from him. The river turned them, the low branches
snagged them, but they were swept away downstream and
had soon vanished. When they had gone, Elidyr waded to
the bank and tied the other boats to the bough of a fallen
tree. He unfurled a coil of rope from his waist and secured
my own canoe, then walked up into an outcrop of rocks,
stripping off shirt and trousers and slapping them against the
stone, beating out the water. He was certainly about ten feet
tall and I was in awe of the man.

As he attended to his rough ablutions, I inspected his
charges, and was shocked by what I saw.

In a round coracle decorated with the eyes of animals on
its oil-skinned sides, a gray-haired brute, clad in tooth-
decorated buckskin, lay as if softly sleeping, a fistful of
thin-shafted, flint-tipped fishing spears by his side. A

mangy-looking hound, more wolf than dog, was draped across his belly, eyelids fluttering to expose the dark eyes that struggled to see from its hunt dream. It was the breathing of this hound that gave the illusion of life to its owner.

By contrast, in an ornate riverboat painted in sumptuous blues and reds, with an eagle prow and roaring-lion stern, a man lay on rain-saturated and now moldy cushions, a scimitar across his bloody body, one hand on the gash that had opened his belly and stained the green and purple silk of his shirt and billowing pantaloons. His beard was neat, in ringlets, his hair tied into a tail and draped over his shoulder. Gold and rich blue lapis lazuli adorned his wrists, ankles, and ears. I thought immediately of Saracens.

A third boat, shrouded in white satin and filled with red flowers, was occupied by a sleeping beauty, pale skinned, her closed eyes shimmering with purple dye, her lips glistening with rouge, her hair jet black and shoulder length, her clothes similar to the Saracen's, loose and light. A strange, symbol-covered staff was all she had with her in the way of a weapon; and a small, red-beaked carrion bird was tethered to her wrist. Very much alive, its eyes flicked and flashed as it watched first my movements, then those of Elidyr, away in the trees. Small though it was, I felt it was protecting her, even though her life was lost.

The other two canoes were similar to my own. In one of them, his face still twisted with the pain of the mortal wound to his breast, lay a man in an iron-studded leather jacket and a pair of cloth trousers that were striped in the dull green of moss and the fading purple of dying heather. A thin, bronze torque was wound around his neck, the heads of wolves on the overlapping ends. His mustache—saffron-colored, like his hair—was elaborately fashioned, curling down over his chin above the grim set of his mouth. His hair was odd, drawn up on each side of the crown of his head, the parting in the middle shaved in an inch-wide line, the bare scalp pricked out with purple chevrons.

He lay, in death, noble and magnificent, and with all the despair of his lost life etched into the frown and gape of his face.

And in the last, small boat, his companion perhaps during the journey to the edge of the wood when I had seen her, Guiwenneth lay asleep, her left hand still holding a bronze dagger, a small oval shield on her breast, its pale wood painted with the image of a leaping stag. Her face was intricately decorated with circles, spirals, and other symbols. As I looked at her, I began to cry. I couldn't help it. There was a truth I had to face and I couldn't face it.

I had glimpsed this woman for only a moment from my bedroom window. But the look she had given me, and the way I now felt for her—whether by guile or magic, or simple love at first sight, I could not imagine, I did not care—I knew only that I was in pain, and that I longed for that gentle face to *open* again, to look at me with a wink and a knowing smile, a look of longing that would echo my own.

It was not possible that she was dead. There could be no point in her being dead!

Tearfully, I leaned over her. I could see no wound on her, but neither could I detect any breath from her mouth, and for a few moments I was confused, and perhaps this helped to keep despair at bay.

I was still staring at her when a hand like a giant claw wrenched me by the shoulder, pulling me back from the tethered boats. The naked Elidyr scowled at me, pushed me aside, then bent over each body in turn, patting the cheeks, tugging the ears, touching the gashes on the "dead." As he probed the belly wound in the Saracen, the man stirred and growled. Ironjacket's mouth opened as his ribs were parted by the probing fingers of the guide, an expression of pain half felt through rising consciousness.

I laughed out loud, but it was with relief and delight, since Guiwenneth, too, was stirring. They were still alive, then. All of them. They had burned their dead, the trumpeter, back below the Hogback Ridge. These were the wounded survivors of the skirmish.

But who or what was Elidyr, and why was he dragging them back along the river?

I had no answer to this at the time, and to my disappointment, the five sleeping figures continued to do just that: sleep soundly, though the hound, like the red-feathered bird, was now alert and very noisy. I crouched by her boat and stared at Guiwenneth. And for the first time a shadow passed across my vision. I remembered the woman whom my father had summoned, as beautiful as this sleeping figure, but warped and made sinister by the man who had brought her into life.

It was not possible—was it?—that Huxley had left others like her in the wood? It was a cold thought in the mind of a drowsy man.

I was being called by name and came out of my reverie.

Elidyr was watching me closely, leaning down toward me, his big hands making gestures that I thought were pacifying.

"Chris! Chan! Chris! Chan!"

He was waving me toward my boat, indicating that I should enter it and—by his elaborate gestures—that I should fall asleep. I declined vigorously, pointing to Guiwenneth and referring to *her* by name. This surprised the river walker and sent him again into an agony of indecision. He stalked back among the trees, scratching at the fungal rings that wreathed his waist and buttocks, slapped at the branches, swore at the air, then grabbed his damp clothes and dragged them over his limbs, returning to the water's edge.

"Guiwenneth!" he agreed loudly, nodding. Then he moved his pointing finger to Ironjacket, the proud Celt, and raised his hands in that universal gesture that says, "I just don't know."

I think he meant that he didn't know his name.

The dark-haired woman was "Issabeau," and he added a word that sounded sinister, waving a hand toward the sky, then simulating the cutting of his throat three times, his eyes popping with meaning.

"Thanks. I'll be careful of her."

The Saracen was "Abandagora." The buckskinned primitive was apparently called "Jarag."

"Thank you for the introductions. But why are they all asleep?"

Elidyr stared at me. "Huh?"

I tried to ask my question with gesture. The big man grumbled and said with emphasis, "Gureer! Gureer! Gwithon. Angat. Ankaratha! *Gureer!*"

I repeated, "Gureer?"

Elidyr waved a hand in front of his mouth and repeated, "Gureer," then tapped a finger from his lips to my ears.

An interpreter! He was ruing the absence of an interpreter, a *gureer,* or a human of that name.

I made walking motions with my fingers and said, "Let's go and find this *gureer*. You lead the way."

He seemed delighted at my decisiveness and busied himself at the tethers on the fallen tree, waving me to my canoe as he did so. I stepped in gingerly and sat quite still as he untied his sleeping charges and slung the mooring ropes across his shoulder. I had expected him to continue up the river, but with a loud sigh and a grumble that seemed to go on forever, he let the six boats float out ahead of him and drift downstream, tugging them back against the drag of the current, leaning back and taking their weight before slowly returning the way he had come, waist deep in the water.

* * *

For a while, facing Elidyr, I was fascinated to watch the big man at his work, reminded of stories of the Irish hero Bran, who had dragged great ships across the Irish sea to effect an invasion of Wales; reminded of the boatman of the Styx, and all the boatmen of all the rivers of the underworld; and I wondered what role in legend this worried giant filled, and why, indeed, every action he took seemed to fill him with an anguish of indecision?

As he walked through the deep river, tugging at the ropes, struggling to prevent one small vessel from drifting to the bank, or snagging on a broken branch, so he watched me, the furrows in his brow as restless as a sea of snakes as his mood and thoughts changed.

After a while he reached a hand toward me: "Go to sleep," he seemed to say.

I remembered *Treasure Island.* "Neither oxen nor wain-ropes could make me sleep in this terrible place," I asserted, and tightened my grip around my knees.

"Huh?"

"Never mind."

He sighed wearily, hauled at the Saracen's barge, brushed aside the heavy bough of an overleaning willow, then grunted with effort as the river suddenly deepened and became more turbulent, running through glistening granite rocks formed from gigantic, broken statues.

But I could not stay awake. One moment the sweating, bearded face was staring down at me from above the burden of coils of rope. . . .

. . . the next, the sun was dappling my vision through a breeze-blown lacework of high foliage. I was on the ground, my pack below my head, the sound of voices and laughter touching my awareness as I surfaced from swirling dreams of my mother's death and my father's anger.

The chatter stopped. A man's voice spoke in tones of alarm; a woman's sounded calming. A moment later, Guiwenneth crouched over me, her hand a gentle touch on my chest, her hair a tickling presence on my face. She smelled fresh. Her cheeks were pale, the painted spirals washed away, and from the way she looked at me, and smiled at me, she certainly knew me.

"Guiwenneth," I whispered and she cocked her head, raised her eyebrows, repeated her name with a hiss and a glottal stop that I knew I would never reproduce. And then she said, "Christian," and I agreed quickly, adding, "I'm glad to find you."

And now I was certain: This was not the angry woman I had met before, my father's diabolical creation. At least, she was not the same manifestation. Something, certainly, connected the one with the other, but the look in her eye, the sense of familiarity and belonging, was comforting and warming. She helped me to my feet, brushing at my clothes, talking in her fluid language to the unnamed man, the Ironjacket, who leaned on his sword and regarded me coolly, answering his companion in monosyllables.

The others paid me brief acquaintance—the Saracen touching his hand to his head and heart, the sorceress Issabeau repeating her name to me without much interest, the elk-skinned hunter slapping his hands together as if crushing shells, which it turned out he was doing, and he tossed me the river food that he had been processing, a gritty, slimy mollusk that he indicated I should eat.

I ate.

It was an unpleasant snack, but it seemed a courteous thing to do.

These introductions over, the band went about their business, allowing me to observe what I soon realized was a coming-to-terms with a new situation. In truth, they were amazed to be here. Their laughter came from astonishment. Watching their body language, it was clear that Abandagora and Ironjacket did not expect to be alive, and were discussing the reason for this sudden return to the mortal world. Jarag had formed a ring of stones and sat inside it, whittling heavily on a piece of bone with a flint blade. Beside him, apparently ignoring him, Issabeau crouched and whittled at her staff. The staff, I could see, was damaged, mostly by burning. She was reshaping the symbols using a thin, iron blade, cutting down to the wood again, refreshing the magic.

But what magic!

As she touched here, then there, so her face became a shadow of a beast, now a wolf, now a lion, now a snake, hints only, glimpses only of the power of the animal world that was condensed into this patterned shaft. Jarag watched her suspiciously, and when her face briefly transformed into a dark-furred dog, she growled; when a cat she spat; when a deer, she blinked; when the features of a monkey shimmered on her eyes and lips, she chattered; and as Issabeau herself, she smiled darkly, keeping to her task, bringing back a craft and a talent that had perhaps died with her on the occasion that had brought her to the river, in her funeral boat drawn by her otherworldly guide.

CHAPTER 6

In the late afternoon, the lassitude in the group as they recovered from their river journey changed to fierce activity, hunting for food, the building of a basic camp, mostly a foraging for dry wood to construct a fire at the river's edge. By dusk, Ironjacket and the Saracen had constructed a clumsy pyre as high as the tall men themselves. Jarag stripped off his skins and swam twice across the river, dragging his clothing and four lengths of newly hewn birch behind him. Dry and clothed again, he erected these posts in a row on the far bank, then chipped at them, making symbols, before crouching down in front of them, staring up the stream.

As dusk became twilight, Issabeau lit the fire, and when it was blazing, she, too, went to the river's edge and sat down, singing softly as she cast small stones into the water.

It was a cool, breezy evening. I sat on the ground, close to the warming flames, and drifted into the sounds of fire and river. After a while, Guiwenneth sat down beside me, flicking mischievously at my legs with her feathered riding crop, firelight shining in her eyes and on her lips as she watched me.

"Christian, Christian," she whispered, and I responded, "Guiwenneth, Guiwenneth."

Then, to my surprise, she leaned her head on my shoul-

der and took my hand in hers. My world closed down to encompass her body and her fragrance and nothing else. Her
touch was gentle and curious, her fingers squeezing each of
mine in turn, then running lightly over my wrists and arms.
And she talked to me in that soft and sibilant tongue that I
supposed to be the language of pre-Roman Britain. It was a
mellow and comforting sound. Sometimes she seemed to be
emphasizing a point; once she slapped my hand as if in rep-
rimand. Twice she said something and turned her face to
mine, and when our eyes met, and when she looked down at
my mouth, I wanted to kiss her. I think she saw my longing.

"I've been with you but not with you," I said quietly.
"How do I explain it? I was with the *wrong* you. But truthfully, you *are* that wild rider; you *are* the white-faced, chalk-
haired girl who galloped me through the barley, all those
years ago. God knows, it's good to find you again, even in
these strange circumstances. And you have cast a spell on
me, and I certainly won't complain about it. . . ."

"*Agus acrath scathan,*" she said by way of agreement,
then pointed to the river. "*Gwyr. Ambath criath. GWYR.
Hoossh!*"

"How can I be *hoossh* when I want to kiss you?"

She relaxed into my arms again. Ironjacket walked past
in the firelight, glancing darkly at me, then at Guiwenneth.
He muttered something and she told him off. He laughed
and made a quick movement of his right hand and Guiwenneth growled at him again.

"He's big, looks very strong," I said with a smile. "But
useless with a sword, I expect. . . ."

"*Hoosshh*" was the reply to my nervous observation.

I had already made connections between the Saracen and
Issabeau, a pair, I thought, despite their different origins;
perhaps part of the same story? But their intimacy, what little had been demonstrated, might have equally been that be-

tween brother and sister—or people in the same business?—
as between lovers in dire circumstances.

Ironjacket was intrigued by Issabeau, I noticed. And she
seemed perturbed by his presence, and they kept apart. But
the proud man kept a protective eye on Guiwenneth, especially where I was concerned, and again I was unsure of his
relationship with her. They spoke the same language, I had
easily noticed that. And though they spoke different words
from the Mesolithic hunter, the Saracen, and the medieval
sorceress, all five understood each other, and very little in
the way of signs and gesture needed to be used.

As Guiwenneth relaxed in my tentative embrace, awaiting the results of river fire and totem poles, I watched the
tall, saffron-bearded Celt. He was very fussy about his appearance, continually stroking his mustache and those weird
and wonderful wings of hair above his head. I had noticed
earlier that rings of tightly interwoven snakes were tattooed
or painted on his arms. Though his clothes stank, and were
ragged and battle torn, something in his demeanor suggested
that he was less a tramp, more a warrior.

It may seem strange to observe this, but all of this motley
group suggested more than they displayed. I might have
been in the presence of royalty (as much as a Mesolithic
hunter might be described as royal), or in the presence of
knights of their age.

I had to remind myself constantly that I was in the presence of *legend*; and if Huxley was right, then these people,
each in his or her way, had been a hero of their time, even if
forgotten by later generations. But a hero once, and now
alive again.

That thought indulged me in a moment of inappropriate
paternal protectiveness; for they might all have been of my
own creation. These wildwood warriors might have come
from my own unseen dreams.

Certainly Guiwenneth had. I was in no doubt about it.

The woman had touched my heart from the moment I had seen her at Oak Lodge, and then again, wounded, perhaps dying in her boat of fate.

And if she was my creation now, then she had been mine then, those years ago, when she had disobeyed her guardian—Manandoun, was it?—and galloped headlong from the forest. And if she had been part of the raiding party that night, then they, too, were from my deep unconscious, my most secret dream, and I had called them to mark me.

Slathan! Whatever it was, whatever it meant.

I had not thought of *slathan* for years. The two nicks in my brow were all but invisible, though now, as I remembered how they had been inflicted, they began to itch again.

"Slathan," I breathed softly and Guiwenneth looked up sharply, frowning; then touched a finger to my lips and nestled down again. I remained hypnotized by the flame, aware of Issabeau's crouching figure and the murkier shape of Jarag on the other bank.

I fell into a light sleep, roused by a sudden cry. Guiwenneth stood up quickly, then tugged at my hand. I followed her to the water's edge and stood with the others, watching the approach of a boat whose hull was illuminated by flaring torches.

It sailed toward us slowly, turning in the flow. A tall, familiar shape stood in the stern, tugging and twisting at the rudder; a leaner, harder-looking man, trim bearded, occupied the prow, regarding us coolly. I noticed that Issabeau had put her hands to her mouth and was staring in shock. The Saracen and Ironjacket were dismayed as well. Guiwenneth was shaking her head, smiling at some secret realization. She raised a hand and acknowledged the man in the prow, and he raised a hand to her, a grim smile touching his lean features. She glanced at me and whispered, "Gwyr."

I got the distinct impression that whatever this group had

been calling to, with their fires, they had summoned more than they had bargained for.

Jarag and Ironjacket waded into the shallows and Elidyr cast a rope to the Celt, who caught it and pulled it taut, helping to slow the drifting vessel. Jarag swam back to the fire and all of us helped to draw the boat onto the bank. Elidyr unloaded several small, clay amphorae and four sacks of foodstuff. The newcomer tugged at the reins of two gray ponies which had been lying on sacking in the deeper part of the vessel's hull. They were small animals, shaggy maned and ungroomed. They struggled and stumbled to dry land, protesting loudly, but became calm when Guiwenneth embraced them like old friends, whispered to them, and gave them a thorough once-over by the light of the fire.

The Saracen had opened one of the sacks and laid out food of varying types on his shield, inspecting the morsels critically and without much enthusiasm. Ironjacket cut the beeswax seal on one of the flagons and took a long draught of its contents. I smelled sweet wine on his breath and he spoke to me in a much warmer tone of voice than before. Guiwenneth was crouched by the shield, picking at fruit and chunks of gray meat. Jarag and Issabeau joined her, but Issabeau selected only an apple and walked back to the river to join the sulking Saracen.

Elidyr watched all this from the gloom of the woodland behind us. His arms were crossed, his body hunched as he stood, his face drawn into a worried frown. The man seemed plagued by uncertainties and concerns. When Ironjacket carried the wine to him he nodded his thanks without a smile and took a drink. He bent his knees to tower over the Celt by a mere two feet. They talked for a minute or so and from the giant's quick glances toward me I knew that I was the subject of that conversation.

Agreement on something was reached between them, and

Ironjacket went to Guiwenneth and quietly talked to her as well.

I was too tired to be further wearied by all this mystery. I assumed that if something was happening that involved me, I would be told about it in due course.

Ironjacket called to me. He was crouched by the shield, beckoning to me, grinning broadly, though I had to guess at that fact since his drooping mustaches were so enormous. I sat by him and he pointed to the various meats and fruits, naming them and indicating that I should eat. Everything smelled of decay! From the rancid stink of fatty meat to the heady, suspicious odor of failing fruit, this feast was stomach churning. But I picked at it, and welcomed the wine, which was savory, pine scented, and slightly sharp; perhaps one of the resinous wines from the Aegean that I had read about but never tasted.

And it must have been strong in alcohol, too; soon, all of my companions were curled up next to each other, like spoons in a drawer, close to the fire, beneath the cover of a hastily erected tarpaulin.

The embers flared and glowed, and the river beyond glittered with reflected fire. Drowsy, aware that Elidyr still watched from his place among the trees, I lay down behind Guiwenneth and tentatively let my head rest on the spill of hair that covered the roll of clothing she was using as a pillow.

A voice called to me and I woke in the silent night to see Elidyr standing over me, his eyes bright with the moon. There was a strange atmosphere in the clearing, an ethereal presence in the trees, which reflected a pale, ghostly light. The others still slept, their bodies covered with dew, a sleep so still and quiet that for a moment I felt a touch of panic, and reached to Guiwenneth. But Elidyr stopped me, taking my hand in his and helping me to my feet.

He beckoned me to follow him. When I walked, it was an odd sensation, as if the ground were cushioned. Something was not right about this midnight rising. The big man walked ahead of me, passing into the gloom beyond the trees, and as I followed him, and glanced back, my heart skipped as I saw that the fire and my companions had disappeared.

Elidyr said nothing. I experienced the sensation of being touched and stroked by tiny hands; it might have been insect wings. It alarmed me at first, then I grew used to it. From the corners of my eyes I seemed to see faces, eyes, movement, watching creatures, never there when I turned to look at them.

The pre-mythago forms first appear at the edge of vision . . . words remembered from Huxley's journal. Was I being taken to see the place where mythagos were born?

Suddenly the woodland brightened. Elidyr glanced back at me, his face friendly. The brightness grew stronger, and with it the verdancy of leaf and fern. We had passed into a summer wood, which burgeoned and ripened around me as I stepped deeper through its spaces.

And then, remarkably, flowers started to erupt in increasing swathes of color and bloom. They grew up from the ground, and out from the massive trunks of oak and elm. Reds and yellows, trailing greens, and vibrant whites, the forest bloomed until it was so rich with color I was dazzled.

A step further and a pricking on the skin of my face and hands made me realize that from these surfaces too, flowers were sprouting. Elidyr was swathed in briar rose, with lines of white petals down his back. Luxuriant, spongy tree fungus grew out from his legs; white-capped mushrooms from his shoulders—and from mine, too! A step further and he was so swathed in red rose and green fern that I had to struggle to see his eyes when he turned to me. Archimboldo had

never painted so strange a sight! I brushed at my hair and
leaves shed their dew across my face.

Elidyr spoke to me and the words flowed around me
meaninglessly.

Holding up hands covered with red orchids, I said, "I
know people who would kill for a gardener like you!"

And Elidyr sighed. He hesitated, looked in the direction
of travel, then back the way we had come. He shook his
briar-cloaked head and came to a decision, indicating that
we should return. He had wanted to show me something but
had changed his mind.

"Where are we, Elidyr? What place *is* this?"

He raised the mossy stumps of hands and shrugged. I
turned again to follow him, shedding nature, returning to
moonlight, to the fire, and to a sleep that took me faster than
I could realize, Elidyr fading from my eyes even as I lay
down by Guiwenneth, entering at once into the same dream
of my mother that I had recently deserted. . . .

I was awakened in rude and painful fashion, Gwyr kicking
me in the buttocks and grinning as he barked instructions
that were incomprehensible to me. My face was wet with
dew. The experience with Elidyr had taken on the strangeness and the insubstantiality of a dream, and I truly wondered whether that indeed is what the whole adventure had
been.

I had no time for reflection though. Gwyr was holding
the two ponies by their rope bridles and was certainly urging me to my feet.

Already Issabeau was bathing in the river, and the Saracen was crouched at the water's edge, his head stretched
back as he looked at the sky. Guiwenneth and Ironjacket
slept in each other's arms, the tall warrior snoring loudly
through open mouth, the long hair of his mustache fluttering
like a leaf in the wind. I felt a long moment's shock and ir-

ritation at this display of intimacy and Gwyr saw my look; he slapped me on the shoulder, still smiling, and shook his head.

Was he saying, Just the way they ended up in sleep?

More important to this man was that I got into the saddle and rode with him, and this I did, uncomfortable on the broad but drooping back of the smaller pony, my feet practically touching the ground. Gwyr showed me how to grip the rope rein with one hand and the creature's mane with the other; a kick at the flanks made the ponies canter, but the blanket tied over the coarse hair was not thick enough to stop my bones from being jarred, and my flesh from being bruised.

After a while he slowed the canter to a gentle walk through sun-dappled glades, following a narrow track away from the river. And at this point we began to exchange names for things, with Gwyr indicating or slapping those parts of nature or his own body that he wished me to describe. His own words, similar in sound and intonation to Guiwenneth's, were forgotten by me as soon as I heard them, but Gwyr echoed what I said, sometimes frowning, sometimes laughing as if he had just realized a fact that should always have been obvious to him.

For an hour or more our conversation was a listing of words: "Arm, hand, chest, breast, or bosom . . . leaf, ivy, bark, twig . . . oh, Lord, *gallop,* trot, snort—whinny? Sneeze!—sigh, weep, laugh . . . sap, sweat, blood!"

He explored more difficult concepts by inviting the expression with gesture and playacting.

"That looks like lovemaking, making love; that's cuddling or hugging . . . throat cutting, beheading, disemboweling—you certainly change the subject fast!—um, dueling, swordplay, stabbing or cutting, admonishment, anger . . . affection, heart-throb, longing or needing . . ."

The thesaurus came in a shifting, startling way, each phe-

nomenon of nature that we passed causing a change in the
direction of his questioning.

"Sunlight, sheen or shimmer, rustling leaves, gloom . . .
That might be a shady grove—that's *sudden movement,*
edge of vision . . . stink or stench, a fart, flatulence . . . I
think you mean *long ago,* the past, history, time . . . the future . . . wildwood! Legendary figure? Understanding . . .
language . . . communication, chatter . . . interpretation or
interpreter? Interpreter of languages?"

And suddenly, my companion astonished me by talking
to me:

"Interpreter of *Tongues!*" Gwyr said in English. "That is
what I am. That is what I was born for. To take the knots out
of gabble and see it for what it is. And I am here at last, and
you and I are together at last. *I have you,* as the saying goes.
I have you now. I have touched the magic in your tongue. "

At which point of triumph he fell from his pony, thudding
into the fresh fern. I jumped down to help him up; the man
was shaking, his body drenched with sweat, his pulse racing.
He was exhausted and I dragged him into the shade, prop-
ping him between the massive roots of a tree. I carefully
pursued the ponies, which had run astray, and persuaded
them back, leading them and tethering them close to where
the Interpreter of Tongues lay recovering from the effort of
the past few hours.

When at last he woke, he stretched and scratched, urinated with a great sigh of satisfaction, then drank from his
leather gourd before turning to me, his face still showing the
effort of his work.

"Well, that was difficult, and I will not pretend otherwise," he said, dark eyes glittering as he watched me, dark
beard still wet with sweat. "I am tired to my bones. But I
was born with the ability to disentangle the tongues of
strangers, and I have disentangled yours, and know you,
now, for your thoughts and your words. I will instruct the

others in your language and then they will be able to tell you their own stories, which have nothing to do with me, though of course I am aware of them."

"How do you do?" I said, extending my hand, which he ignored.

"For the moment," he went on, "you should know this: That you have been accepted by us, and are now a part of our group. We are known as the Forlorn Hope, because of what we do. We are at the head of Kylhuk's Legion. We have had two terrible encounters, on each occasion with the Sons of Kyrdu, who are a malign and evil presence in this time. It is only by your arrival that we have survived, and for that we thank you."

"How do you do?" I said again, dizzy with the spill of words, my hand waving toward him in a vain attempt to be courteous. He glanced at my fingers curiously, then again ignored me.

"I in particular wish to thank you. Elidyr fetched me back from the pyre, where I was already charred bone and ash according to his own words, and this was a great deed and a great concession."

"Your arrival was a bit of a shock, I think."

"Indeed. They had been signaling to Legion. Because of you, though, Elidyr has looked kindly upon me. I have a reprieve from the pyre!"

"You were the trumpet blower, I think. I saw you at the edge of the woods, near to Oak Lodge. A terrible sound. Like the dying of bulls."

"Somebody has to do it," Gwyr said, pain etching his face as he stared at me. "Blowing the war horn, that is. The 'trumpet' as you call it. And I have the strongest lungs. It is said that I can make the call of the bull's mouth speak to everyone who hears it."

"You certainly can."

He looked away from me. "I had thought the effect more musical than you seem to have heard."

I realized he had been stung by my comment. "I'm sorry. I have no true appreciation of music."

"Clearly. It's of no consequence, however," he said with a smile. "My only objection is that the *horn* is so heavy! I'm glad it's gone, lost in the river."

"You called Guiwenneth back from her raid on my house."

"The sanctuary?"

"Call it what you like. I followed you into the wood, through a place that is a shrine to horses."

Gwyr shuddered noticeably, shaking his head. "That is a strange and evil place. At the edge of the world—I had heard of it and came to it without realizing it!"

I didn't know how to pursue that observation, so I completed my question. "You were together, then, the two of you. And all the others?"

"Indeed, we were together then, the two of us. And all the others. And now I am here because of your arrival, and for as long as I am here I am in your debt. Truthfully! Despite your insults, your coarse appreciation, your lack of tact, your lack of—"

"I'm *sorry*. I'm sorry for my lack of tact."

"Well said. Your words are accepted. And make no mistake," he went on airily, "you have friends with you even if they scowl and grumble and put you to the test."

"I hope I shall prove worthy of any and all tests to which I am put."

"I share that hope," he said with a serious look at me, and for a few moments I felt warmed by his companionship. But he quickly treated me to the comfort of Job, saying, "And be assured, a terrible time awaits you, and a terrible discovery if you fail to keep your wits about you. A strong arm would help." He glanced without much enthusiasm at my physique. "And we have time to improve on that, but you must be prepared to be strong in all aspects of heart and mind. That is the purpose of the Forlorn Hope, and it is why we scout ahead of the Legion."

"Am I part of the Forlorn Hope, then?"

"I have told you that already." He peered round at my right ear. "The hole in your head appears to be open, but perhaps there's a sparrow's nest inside! Pull your horse round, now, and get on its back. It's time to return to the others."

I stood my ground for a moment. "If you can talk to me in strange tongues, tell me what *slathan* means. The word is meaningless, but it gnaws at my neck like a bird of prey."

Gwyr scratched at the back of his own neck, perhaps in response to my metaphor, and thought hard before saying, "It's a word that Kylhuk uses, but not a word from his own language. It's older." Irritably, he added, "He's always doing things like that. He thinks it gives him stature with enchanters."

"And does it?"

Gwyr tugged at his thin beard. "Now you mention it . . . yes. I suppose it does."

"And *slathan*?"

"Slathan. Yes. I'll try and find out, if it's important to you."

"Truthfully, it is important."

"Put it from your mind, Christian. It is a question that will be a long time being answered. And now we have a long journey ahead of us and it will be bad for us if Kylhuk abandons all hope and changes his direction as a consequence. Without his Legion, we are all lost."

CHAPTER 7

Gwyr's anxiety that we would be abandoned by Kylhuk and his Legion was unfounded, as I would shortly discover, for even as we rode back to the camp, the great beast that Kylhuk had formed around him, the entity of flesh, stone, and legend that would soon become my home, was moving in its ponderous way toward us, tacking away from its steady progress through time and the forest, drawn, I am quite sure, by a scent from Elidyr, some otherworldly call from the Guide that attracted Legion (as I would come to know it) as powerfully as flame attracts a moth.

It took us several hours to find Guiwenneth and the others, the paths Gwyr and I had ridden having subtly changed and causing us to become lost on three occasions; but the river was there, and each time we reached it, Interpreter of Tongues seemed to find his bearings. I was exhausted with the ride and the humidity of the moist wildwood, and fell gladly into the embracing arms of the woman.

There was a buzz of excitement among the Forlorn Hope. Issabeau was almost in a trance, darting here and there around the boundaries of the glade, peering into the forest, snapping her fingers in quick, sharp rhythms, cooing and calling to her red bird, even as she shouted crisp observations and instructions to the Saracen, who responded in kind. Whatever difference in their magic, they were combining their talents expertly! Though the results, if any, eluded me.

An air of anticipation, then, and indeed there was an "electric" atmosphere around the small fire, as if the whole glade flowed with unseen energy.

Guiwenneth left me and went to talk to Gwyr. Their conversation was animated for a while. Guiwenneth was listening hard, repeating words that I gradually realized were my own words, English words. Ironjacket was listening, too, frowning at me as he concentrated. Jarag and his mangy hound were not around, and when Gwyr came over to me, dropping to his haunches and picking at the undercooked wildfowl that had been grilled on the wood, I asked him of the Mesolithic hunter's fate.

"No fate," Gwyr said, "just hunting. Without him our diet would be poor indeed."

I looked at the string and sinew on the charred bone of the moorhen and thought of times past when Steven and I had been instructed on how to distinguish between the birds of the riverways, the coots and moorhens, the ducks and the waders. I also thought of what I knew about the prehistoric past, and guessed that Jarag's idea of a hunting trophy would be a pile of bivalves and a clutch of gull's eggs.

Ironjacket joined us and sat down, cross-legged, his arms folded across his belly. He stared at me solemnly, his voluminous orange mustache moving side to side as he chewed thoughtfully on the remains of his meal. Gwyr said, "Christian, I must make this man known to you, he has requested it. He is Someone son of Somebody, unnamed at birth because of a tragedy that you will soon hear about, though his true name runs before him, waiting only for the speed of the man to catch it and claim it."

"Pleased to meet you . . . Someone," I said, and extended my hand, which the man shook. He nodded with satisfaction, still staring at me, and scratched at his shaven chin before muttering a question which Gwyr translated.

"He wants to know where you come from. Guiwenneth has said that you come from the same islands in the west as she does. Is that right?"

"Yes."

Someone son of Somebody would not recognize the name England, I guessed, so I said, "Albion. South of Hibernia? No, that's Ireland. East of Hibernia! South of Caledonia? Britain. *Prytain?* Logres . . . ? West of Gaul . . . ?"

Someone, listening to these words, suddenly indicated that he had understood. He spoke to me through Gwyr and I learned that, "Someone comes from the east of you, where two great rivers join near high mountains. The strongholds of his land are many, and the kings are rich beyond measure. Great war chariots often raid across the rivers into Gaul, but his people take ships along the coast to your own country, where they celebrate at the great circles among the forests. His forefathers sailed farther west, to the Island of the Great Boast, where five Queens ruled and may still rule and every head taken in battle can sing for five seasons after being severed."

This sounded like Ireland, where everything in those days, and even now, was larger than life, from its generosity to the battle antics of its warriors. This Someone himself, I gathered, was an unnamed and banished Lordly One from early Celtic lands east of the Rhone, in modern-day Germany, his homeland perhaps below one of the great cities that had so recently been devastated by war.

There was indeed something regal about the man's appearance. Even the hacked and scruffy leather of his jerkin, I now realized, was studded not simply, but with the bright iron heads of mythical animals. The short knife he carried was wide bladed and leaf shaped, more ceremonial than offensive. (His sword was very offensive indeed; I had watched him clean and hone it.) And the way he wore his beard and hair, those elaborate coils above his scalp, shaped and made secure with grease, certainly suggested an attention to appearance that went beyond the traditional Celtic warrior's vanity.

I had not suspected it, but there was a slight ulterior motive to Someone's first, friendly contact, the warmth he gave me. Gwyr said, "He wonders if you know him; if anything about him is familiar? It may help him."

"I'll try," I said, but nothing about the man's look inspired me with any sense of recognition.

Someone spoke briefly about his birth, using Gwyr as translator.

"As far as I am aware, my father was summoned to combat before he could name me. The combat was by chariot, and along the eastern edge of the river that divided our land. The dispute was about the stealing of a bull and five cows that were being taken to honor Taranis. It was the beginning of the winter and when the snow came in that place, one in every three of us would die of cold and hunger. This was an important sacrifice, and my father had intercepted it—the white-and-black bull was a very famous creature, well regarded and envied among our clans—and made the offering himself. He had no time for the other king, who was his brother-in-law, but that didn't matter. A challenge was issued and had to be acknowledged.

"So—as I was told later—the two kings arrived at the river to fight first with spear and then with sword. They rode up and down the sides of the bank, shouting insults at each other until the horses were tired. Then they threw off their cloaks and prepared to hurl spears at each other across the water as a preliminary to the main combat.

"Unfortunately, my father was killed outright by Grumloch's first throw.

"All that saved my life, when Grumloch came to take

possession of the fort, was the fact that I hadn't been named, otherwise I would have been killed along with the selected five knights who were used in place of the animal offering. We were taken to a lake in the forest and out onto the water in small boats. The five knights were stripped, tied, bled from the throat, skull cracked, then tipped into the lake. I was left in a coracle with a wet nurse, forbidden ever to return to the fort.

"When I was weaned, the woman left me in one of the glades dedicated to Sucellus. She never told me my father's name, only that he had known which name to give me, though the secret had died with him. She placed me in a hollow between the feet of the great wooden idol, where it was warm and protected from rain and wind. At night, the great gods roared at each other across the forest, and Sucellus strode around the glade, beating at branches. But he, like all of them, was tied to this place.

"Every so often, masked people came and sacrificed or left offerings at the feet of the idol. I ate whatever was left and Sucellus never complained. Only later did it occur to me that because I had no name, the god could not see me."

I realized he had stopped speaking and was looking at me expectantly, almost hopefully. I think I grimaced and shrugged. Grumloch? Not a name to ring the bells of romance and chivalry.

"No. I'm sorry," I had to say. "Truthfully, if I could help with a name I would, but I know only of Perceval, Kay, Bedevere and Bors, Gawain and Galahad, the knights of Arthur and Guinevere, of Camelot, of Merlin, Morgan and Vivien, all of them introduced to me in stories by my mother when I was a child."

As I recounted my limited listing of Malory's heroes I watched Someone for any sign of recognition, but he simply shrugged, sighed, bade me good-bye and went back to where Issabeau was still engaging with the woodland in her strange way.

Whatever was then said, within a few minutes Issabeau had cried out in what may have been despair, but which was certainly a voice of fear, and run into the gloaming. Someone took off his leather jacket and flung it to the ground angrily, then stomped away in the opposite direction to the distraught woman, swearing volubly, and slapping his left hand against his left buttock. Gwyr seemed to be as bemused as I was by what we were watching. Then he called for Guiwenneth, but without success. The Saracen was agitating to move on, and had been held back only by the antics of Issabeau, but now Gwyr came over to me and said, "We shall have to start walking toward Legion. It's quite close now, but it's well protected and we must be ready for encounters with its defenders."

"We can't go without Guiwenneth or Jarag," I said. And indeed, where was Elidyr, the mournful guide?

"The jarag," Gwyr said, using that form of the name for the first time, "is beyond my knowing. His magic is too strange, his life seems inviolable, and he has become the rock on which this unit of Forlorn Hope has stood; so I doubt if he is lost; he sprouts from the earth like a new shrub, full and green just when you think the earth is barren. Guiwenneth is more vulnerable. We should look for her at the river."

We started to retrace our path to the water, but Gwyr turned back. "You should stay here, I think. I can always follow later if she returns and you then feel the need to move on."

And so *he* had gone.

I stood in this firelit place, utterly confused by the random and seemingly pointless movement of this small band of travelers. My heart longed to see Guiwenneth again, but my head was full of apprehension now, with Gwyr's departure, since he was my voice in this wilderness of incomprehensible sign and song.

A light touch on my shoulder from behind startled me. I turned quickly where I sat and saw Issabeau's doleful face staring down at me from its frame of luxuriant night-black hair. She was holding a small branch of white thorn, stripped and trimmed so that only a single thorn remained, like an elongated nail at the end of a withered arm. She kept this pointed at me as she walked round and sat down demurely, arranging her skirts around her, pulling her cloak across her breast. With the wooden arm of thorn between us on the ground, her liquid eyes almost unblinking as she gazed at mine, she began to murmur words. I heard "Merlayne" and "Vivyane" and asked her to repeat what she had said. There was something indefinably familiar about her words; I was on the edge of understanding, it seemed, and these noticeable names had helped me focus on the tongue, and I heard that it was a dialect of French; and Issabeau was a name that came from the time of Chivalry, eleventh-century French, perhaps, or some variant local to the peninsula of Brittany, a land where so many legends were held in common with the legends of my own country.

In a voice that was as deeply husky as it was sad, she whispered slowly, *"Merlayne eztay mon mayder. Vivyane eztay mon* courz mord!*"*

This last was said angrily, with her right hand extended toward me, gripped into a fist.

"Merlin and Vivian," I said. "Are you part of their story?"

She shook her head, not understanding, then went on. *"Merlayne ez mord. Enabre, enterre, envie ettonmord pondon tomp ayteme! Moie, onfond treez d'onzhontrayz, de courz noy, de fay ett onzhondmond moivayze!*

"Zharm ett onzhondmond!" she muttered furiously, star-

ing at the branch she held. *"Layze yeuze voie surlmon lay monzonge."*

These sounds were run together, sharp and fluid, teasing my awareness, communicating nothing but her passing despair, a sadness that suddenly surfaced in her. I would ask Gwyr about her as soon as I could.

When Someone reappeared, he was wet from the river, stripped to the waist, wringing water from his mustaches. He crouched by the fire, looked around, glanced quizzically at Issabeau, then grunted, "Is Guiwenneth . . . here?"

"Gwyr is looking for her. Gwyr . . . looking! Guiwenneth!"

He understood.

"Kylhuk." He stabbed a finger at the forest. "Men! Chariot! Warrior!"

"I understand! Men and chariots and other warriors . . ."

"Legion! This way is."

"I know. They're coming to find us. I'm glad to be able to talk to you, Someone son of Somebody."

"Uh?"

"What language is Issabeau speaking? It's later than your own, I think. Is it early French?"

"Uh?"

"Never mind."

We weren't quite as far along the path of understanding as I had hoped.

But a while later, Gwyr returned, Guiwenneth and the jarag with him, the two absentees carrying fish and birds across their shoulders. Jarag grinned through his unkempt beard, twirling his snares around his finger, rattling his small, bone-tipped spears in the loose grip of his other hand. His horrible hound was panting with exhaustion, its head shaking from side to side as it recovered from what I intuited had been a triumphant hunt.

I told Gwyr that Issabeau had been trying to speak to me,

that she was mournful. He nodded wisely, spoke briefly with the woman, then told me, "Merlayne was her master; he taught her many ways of charm and enchantment; but Merlayne has been tricked by the black-hearted Vivyane, and is entombed in a tree in the earth. Issabeau has many talents in the way of magic, but there are times when her eyes see only lies, and this is because Vivyane's dark magic is still attached to her. She was upset for a while when you mentioned Merlayne. She thought you were Vivyane's spy. But now she knows better."

"What does she know?"

"That you, like the rest of us, have heard of the two enchanters. They are widely talked about. The terrible things they did when they were together were more devastating to the countries they passed through than war and pillage."

I thought of Merlin, the old, white-bearded wizard, and his haunting presence in the corridors of white-walled Camelot, a benign figure, voice of advice to King Arthur. We were clearly not talking about the same old man from the stories *I* had heard.

And I had no sooner processed this thought than the whole glade seemed to shift.

The fire guttered, then flared high again. The trees had bent in a strange way, as if pressed upon by an unseen hand. The sensation in the earth was that of a mild tremor and I felt shifted sideways, though I had not moved in space, at least as far as I could see; but now, as stillness returned, there was a new electricity in the canopy and on the ground, a tension, as if creatures ran among us, hands touching, fingers pinching, tiny teeth nipping, not unlike the sensation with Elidyr the night before. If a flock of curious carrion birds had invaded this glade, I could have understood the feeling; but there was no sign of the disturbance, simply the *touch* of it.

It was enough for Gwyr.

"Elementals," he said quickly. "They are damned and a

nuisance, though in truth, they always precede Legion and are useful. We've been spotted."

"Is that good?" I asked.

"Of course. Eventually. But for the moment, we are unknown because it is assumed we are dead. So we must make ourselves known again, or be attacked." And he shouted to all around us: "Get your things! Issabeau, take a brand from the fire, then flatten the embers. Guiwenneth, start calling to Kylhuk. Saracen, sing to your sword. Jarag, go ahead of us and enter the shadow of the wood, tell us when that shadow changes. . . ."

Everyone in the glade except for Guiwenneth was staring at Gwyr blankly. He realized with some embarrassment that he had been barking orders in English, perhaps because his head was still full of his latest Interpretation. He repeated the instructions—he was in charge then? I hadn't known this—this time in the tongue they spoke in common, which was his own. Even as he issued orders, I realized I could sense some small meaning in the words.

Gwyr, then, had not just learned from me, but had implanted the seed of new language in my own under-educated language centers.

As activity commenced, Guiwenneth came quickly over to me, brushing at my cheeks with quick fingers and smiling. "There were things I had to do," she said in careful English. "I have been with Gwyr. To know how to talk to you. To know you better. I'm glad to have you now—*Christian*," she said, then repeated my name as if savoring it. "Do you remember me?"

"Oh, yes . . ."

"It was—a long time ago. I was a girl. Very small. Manandoun was still my . . . *guardian*. I was so frightened. Remember? The horse reared and we fell into the corn. I felt . . . so strange . . . as if a cliff had struck me where there was no cliff, and hooks dragged at my limbs where there were no hooks . . . dragging me back to the wood."

"I remember you well," I said, and though I remembered also that Huxley had written how mythagos could never journey far beyond the edge of Ryhope, they simply died and decayed, I chose to keep this knowledge to myself. "I think I must have been waiting for you from that moment on. I was entranced by you, despite your chalked hair and white face. Remember?"

She laughed as she agreed.

"But I hadn't realized how much I was thinking of you until you came back and called to me from the wood, with Gwyr blowing that strange bronze trumpet, the bull horn or whatever it was. There had been a war. I had been fighting in a foreign land. I'm glad you came when you came. And I'm glad to have followed you here, even if it's cold and wet. And the food is grim."

She sighed, partly content with what I'd said, but partly through anguish, I thought. Indeed, there was a quick, strange look in her eyes that I couldn't fathom. But she said, "This is not the best time to meet again. Though truthfully— I'm glad you followed me. If I had remained in the sanctuary . . . where you were sleeping that night . . ." She sighed wistfully, then shook her head. "But I was afraid the Creature was there, and the Creature frightens me. I am glad I saw you. I am truly glad you followed me."

The sanctuary? She must have meant Oak Lodge, my home. Gwyr had used the same word. The Creature? Did she mean Huxley? My father? He hadn't been there that night, but perhaps some scent, some shadow had remained.

I said nothing. Indeed, I could have found no moment to say a word, for Guiwenneth had gone on brightly in her growing confidence with the English she had learned from Gwyr. "Once we are in Legion again, everything will be as it was. Kylhuk is intimidating." She shrugged. "But if you leave him alone, he will leave you alone. There will be a job for you . . . and we can be together. When this great task is finished, Legion will rest. Kylhuk has assured me."

"What task?"

"No one knows. Kylhuk keeps it secret—except from Manandoun! He has sworn secrecy on his life. But Legion is first searching for the Long Person, and when we find *her* we will know. The great task will begin . . . Kylhuk has gathered Legion for this very purpose." She looked at me quickly. "And it is a very great task indeed, the hardest of all that Kylhuk has been set." She put a delicate finger to my lips. "Enough of that. Time to talk about it later. First, follow me, do exactly as I do. And don't at any cost leave the Forlorn Hope. If you do, it will be worse for you than you can imagine."

"So I was told by Gwyr. I hear you. And I understand!"

"Good. I'm glad you hear me. And *understand*. Follow me . . . Christian."

I was amused and delighted at the thrill my name seemed to give her, and by the mischievous look in her green eyes and on her mouth as she teased me.

Another day passed, and another glade found and flattened, protected with a few sharpened branches, a fire started and grim food eaten. The hunt had been poor, and Jarag's hound old and failing.

We ate the dog.

Elidyr settled at the edge of the camp, knees drawn up to his massive jaw, fingers fiddling with the coils of rope he still carried round his shoulders.

I was uncomfortably aware that he was watching me.

As if touched by magic, the Forlorn Hope suddenly lay down on their blankets and drifted into sleep. The fire guttered and I stoked it, putting on a log to make it burn a little brighter, fighting against the drowsy influence of drink, silence, and peace.

The next thing I knew I was being called from a dream. I sat up, blinking through my tears, and again found Elidyr reaching for me, the same otherworldly glow all around us.

"This way," he said. "Something for you to see. To understand."

Perhaps that was why he had turned back previously. He had felt too alienated from me without Gwyr's mediating interpretation.

And so we walked again through a ghostwood that suddenly began to bloom. Since we had traveled several miles from the river during the day, and since this wood was identical to that of the previous night, I realized we had stepped out of the space and time of the Forlorn Hope.

I couldn't help laughing as again we underwent our floral transformation. The air was scented and sublime; the light was gorgeous, and we walked between its pools and shafts like manifestations out of Eden.

Elidyr was not indecisive now. He led the way with a sureness of foot and a firmness of purpose. Once we had become flowered and fungused, the transformation was complete. When Elidyr stopped and crouched, he became like a rotting trunk, vibrant with parasitic growth in full color. I nearly tripped over him.

"Sssh!" he said, and pulled me down by the fern on my arms.

I listened carefully, and heard the sound of a woman singing, and the sound of water.

Knee-deep in iridescent bluebells, we stepped closer to the pool. On one side of it rose a cliff, and a thin waterfall tumbled through the trees that crowded its edge. The woman was dressed in black and was rinsing pots and pans at the water's edge. Her hair was red and was combed but undecorated. Her feet were bare.

Elidyr pointed to the right. A stone tomb, made from roughly hewn rocks, rose among the trees, whose roots were entangled with the stones, as if drawing it closer to their gloom. A small red pennant hung above the low entrance, and simple dolls had been fixed to the lintel, though from here it was difficult to see what sort of dolls they were.

This was a magic place, a luxurious garden in the vibrant forest, and everything but that crumbling mausoleum was alive with brightness.

Elidyr sighed and the breeze he caused flowed through the ferns and passed away. The woman looked up, looked toward us, then returned to her pots, beginning her song again.

"Can she see us?" I asked.

"No. Not looking for us," Elidyr muttered. "I must show you."

He walked into the clearing by the pool and I followed. We crossed the rocks to the tomb and Elidyr ducked down and crawled inside. I glanced at the woman again, but she was quite unaware of me.

Inside the tomb, a man lay on a marble plinth. He was garbed with chain mail over heavy shirt and trousers, and clutched a bunch of flowers to his chest. His sword, which was broken in half, was by his side. A doll lay below his feet, which were crossed at the ankles.

I touched the white face. It was as cold as the stone on which he lay. His hair had been combed. He smelled of flowers and not decay.

After a while, the woman came into the tomb. She walked straight past us, carrying fresh flowers for his hands and a pot of water, with which she washed the dead man's face. When this was done, she kissed his lips, knelt down and prayed to an icon of a woman in white, then left the mausoleum.

Elidyr, in his green disguise, rustled over to the corpse and blew on its mouth.

The knight stirred and opened his eyes. The flowers dropped from his hands and he started to breathe, a ghastly sound as he returned from the dead. One hand reached for the handle of his sword, found it and gripped it as a child grips a finger. But he lay there, on his back, his unfocused gaze upon the corbeled ceiling of his resting place.

A sudden stench made me look down at my body. Everything was rotting where it grew. Elidyr's luxuriant growth of fern and briar had browned and shriveled; insects burst from the fungal swellings. The flowers the knight had dropped wilted, then putrified.

I ran outside, ducking to avoid the lintel, brushing the small cloth dolls, which I swear made sounds like children waking. Elidyr followed me. The woman was on her feet, looking up at the waterfall, where the trees had begun to die, the leaves shedding in a rain of russet, autumn fall. Winter curled through the forest and pool with a malevolence and a speed that shocked me. Ice grew on the pond and spread along the branches of the wood. The cold was so intense I thought the woman had frozen where she stood, but she slowly looked down, then at the tomb, a crease of confusion forming on her brow.

At once, Elidyr was furious with himself. He went back into the chamber. The winter faded, life returned to the pool, flowers bloomed, and the dolls swung in the breeze that came from the big man's breathing. The woman ran to the tomb—I followed—and knelt by her dead lover, but he had gone again, as cold as the marble on which he lay. She cried silently, her hands clasped in prayer across his chest.

Elidyr walked quickly from the place and into the woods, and when he was a long way back toward the region where the forest changed, he howled with anger and with sadness. I had chased after him, shedding my summer's growth, and found him huddled against a mossy rock, tears streaming from his eyes, his great brow furrowed, his fists clenched in his lap.

"Had to show you. Bad to do." He muttered fiercely to himself. "Poor woman. Sad enough."

"You brought life back to him."

"Yes. Not again. Poor woman. Sad enough!" He looked up at me, gray eyes misting, his mouth grim below the straggling hair of his mustache. "You must think about it. *Christian*. I live with it. Waking to sleeping. You must think about it."

"Who are you, Elidyr? Who *are* you?"

"Elidyr," he said unnecessarily, frowning and touching his lips. "I take boats down rivers. Remember?"

"Yes, I know. The wounded and the dead. You carry the wounded and the dead. You guide them to where they must go in the next phase of their life. I understand. And you brought Gwyr back. Back from his pyre. You gave him life."

Elidyr stared at me for a moment, then said softly, "You will *need* the gureer. He will need you. Care for him."

"I will. I surely will. . . ."

He had said, *I had to show you.* Why? Why had he been under such an obligation?

And what significance had there been in that strange fluctuation from summer to winter? The answers eluded me, and perhaps this was because another thought was on my mind, and this I mentioned to the anguished man, trying to be as tactful as I could.

"Elidyr . . . did you once take a boat with a woman who had hanged herself . . . killed herself after Kylhuk had assaulted her? A woman called Jennifer . . . ?"

"Guinevere?"

"Jennifer!"

He stared at me, the tears drying in his eyes, the furrow in his brow deepening. He put a big hand on my face and I flinched, wondering if he was going to do me harm, but his fingers brushed my eyes, his thumb my mouth—

And suddenly I was walking in the river, waist deep and hauling back on long ropes attached to the boats that floated ahead of me!

The vision was startling. The bright sun glinted through the canopy. The narrow river was icy. My feet were slipping as I walked with the flow. The rope cut into my shoulders, rubbing and bruising me. I ached with the effort of this walk, tugging back against a current that was trying to drag me faster. I was hungry. I longed for rest. But there was so far to go, such a huge river to sail, so many small boats to tether carefully, in hidden places, ready for that final pull, that massive guiding of all these floating coffins toward their final destination, beyond the twin gates. . . . And I could rest. . . .

But I leaned forward now, and through Elidyr's eyes looked at the sleepers in their boats.

Fair faces and old faces, and strange faces and masked faces . . .

And suddenly I saw my mother! Her hands were crossed on her chest! Her suit was still stained with the juice of tomatoes. Her hair was still combed and pinned for the Sunday service. She was resting on cushions, and though her face was white, and her chest didn't rise or fall, I could see no sign of the strangling rope with which she had taken her own life. I was twelve years old again. At any moment my mother would sit up, yawn, rub her eyes and see me; and she would smile and tease me. And she and I and Steven would walk around the edge of Ryhope Wood as far as Shadoxhurst or Grimley, and sit on the village green. . . .

"Elidyr," I begged, breaking the trance. "That's my mother! Bring her back. Take her back to Oak Lodge! Don't let the twin gates take her! She still had so much life to live."

"I can't," said Elidyr.

"Why not?" I cried.

"She has already passed the two gates. Besides . . . her death was not as you think."

"Not as I think? What do you mean by that?"

I had seen her death. I had been there! And I had experienced Elidyr's memory of taking her along the river.

And I had seen Gwyr brought back from the pyre, and a dead knight briefly raised, though what message I was supposed to take from that I couldn't quite imagine.

"If you know so much," I yelled at him, "answer my question! What do you mean: Her death was not as I think?"

"I cannot bring her back," the big man said, staring at me stonily. "Only you can. After all. That is partly why you're here!"

I could bring her back?

He rose and stalked away, leaving me crying and staring after him, shouting, "And what does *that* mean? *Partly* why I'm here! *How* do I bring her back?"

"Ask your father."

Huxley?

"Where is my father in all of this?" I screamed at him.

"Waiting for you."

"Waiting where?"

"Go to sleep," Elidyr called back gruffly. "I'm bored with you. Until Kylhuk finds the Long Person—nothing you can do!"

I followed him for a while, but I became lost and confused, blinded by the silver-bright reflection from the trees, a lost soul in a winter's nightmare. I seemed to see my mother's face in every patch of shadow, every shimmering, moonlit fern. She called to me and I cried for her, cried for the life with her that had been taken from me by Strong Against the Storm. How much I longed for her quiet counsel, her gentle reassurance. I had been too young when she died, too young to know what Steve and I were losing. Now, having glimpsed her through the boatman's eyes, a sense both of acute loss and hope snatched at my breath. For some reason the awful words of a hymn came to mind: *She is not dead, but sleeping. . . .*

And I laughed, because the words were associated with a memory of my father singing them during the funeral of his sister, his mind elsewhere, his eyes focused elsewhere.

And then I panicked, not seeing Elidyr ahead of me anymore. I ran after him in this moon-gleaming wood, shouting for him, but I could no longer even hear his long, steady stride.

I finally accepted the truth—that Elidyr had gone—and curled into the hollow of a rock to sleep, only to discover that the rock was Guiwenneth's back, and I had returned to the dead fire, the crude camp, and the slumbering forms of the Forlorn Hope. Elidyr had gone.

CHAPTER 8

Kylhuk, thinking my companions dead, had formed a new "point" to his Legion, a new Forlorn Hope which had been probing steadily toward us, attracted by the signals that Issabeau and the jarag in particular had been emitting, the calls and summonings of the enchanted parts of their lives.

We were running in single file along a thistle-strewn stone road that had been laid between the edges of the wood. It ran in a winding fashion. Overgrown monuments, probably tombs, lined it on both sides. Gwyr ran behind the rest of us, leading the two horses. He had muffled their hooves, and muzzled their jaws, but they still made a loud noise as they trotted, though the rest of us padded through the wood in silence.

Abruptly, Issabeau raised her arm, waved us back. I could see nothing ahead of us save the bend in the road and the dense wall of greenery, but I didn't doubt for a moment the truth of Issabeau's urgent shout that: *"Eelzond ici! On-tond! Payrill ezbroje."*

They are here. Listen. Danger is close.

Almost at once, a part of the forest shimmered and changed, becoming silver and white, resolving into the form of a mounted knight, a grim-faced man in gleaming mail. He was riding with thundering speed toward us, lance arm raised. A javelin sped toward Someone son of Somebody, who stepped aside and almost disdainfully plucked the weapon from the air. The white charger reared, the knight turned, fair hair flowing as he reached for a second spear. Then he rode at us again, this time stabbing low, going for Issabeau, who turned her back and bowed her head. Her red bird flew at the knight, who raised his weapon and stabbed at the screeching creature, sending it to the ground in a storm of feathers. Then he wheeled around and flung the spear at the Saracen, who stooped to avoid the blow.

After that, the knight returned to the edge of the wood and sat there motionless, side-on, stretching up in the stirrups to peer at us more curiously.

"Peril!" Issabeau urged again, her dead protector held to her chest, her eyes glazed with tears. But this time she was looking behind us.

Out of nowhere, it seemed, two sleek male figures came running toward us, hawk faced, green skin gleaming. Someone intercepted them, fighting furiously. His sword struck a face and I realized that the men were wearing tarnished masks of bronze. Even as one reeled back, so the other ducked and the air about him shimmered. Someone became wreathed in fire, his face grimacing as he held his hands outside the consuming flame. I ran toward him, but Issabeau growled, "Stay back!"

A second later, the fire gathered around the warrior's shoulders, formed into something like an animal and jumped into the trees, where it flowed amorphously, hovering in the lower branches. Quite suddenly, it resolved into a white-robed woman, silk clad and with white, silken hair.

There was much shouting. The hawks drew back. The knight kicked cautiously toward us, then sheathed his sword.

Our friend Someone was standing with his arms raised, a gesture of welcome and peaceful intention; indeed, of surrender. Issabeau adopted the same posture. Jarag growled, but grinned, mocking us for a weakness that only he could understand.

Gwyr said to me, "It could have been worse than that. It was an easier encounter than many. They recognized us for what we are despite you, and now Kylhuk will hear of it and soon you will meet him."

"Again," I added.

"Again?"

"I met him when I was a child. He marked me. As *slathan*. I told you before."

"Indeed," said the Interpreter. "The strange word. *Slathan*. Indeed, you have met Kylhuk before, so he will be expecting you. I'll stay close to you when you meet him for the first time, if you wish. If he marked you, he may be intending to kill you. He often does this."

"He *often* does this?"

"He's an unpredictable man. But I am in your debt, so you have only to ask if you wish me to stay close to you."

"Stay close," I said, my whole impression of Kylhuk shifting into a new and darker form. "Your absence made me uneasy, that time before, when you went back to the river to look for Guiwenneth. Now, even the thought of it, the absence of your understanding tongue and wise counsel, makes my head spin."

He seemed pleased with my comments, patting his breast above the heart, and tugging at the horses with greater enthusiasm.

We followed the knight and the woman along the road. The woman walked in an ethereal way, as if floating, her robes drifting in the light breeze. The knight slouched in his high-backed saddle, his attention on the woodland around him, his hand resting on the pommel of his sword. The horse dropped dung at regular intervals and the small file that followed this imperious chevalier wove one way or the other to avoid it. But during the early part of the march, both Issabeau and Jarag stooped to inspect the remains, Jarag flicking pieces of the spoor into the bushes that crowded the boundaries of this ancient road. They showed no sign of alarm or concern at whatever they might have detected.

Someone watched the performance with appalled dismay, however, but when he stared at Issabeau, she simply taunted him by shape-changing into a grimacing animal. The two walked next to each other after a while, but in disdainful silence. When the proud Celt offered to take the dead bird from Issabeau and carry it in a small cloth bag, she reluctantly agreed. It was an odd moment.

Though the two of them were still not talking, they kept glancing at each other curiously.

The two hawks ran beside us, out of sight in the woodland, but not out of hearing. They called to each other, a regular series of screeches and shrill whistles, imitating the birds of prey whose features they had adopted in paint and mask. Listening to them, still remembering their lithe figures running and somersaulting toward us, metal hammers raised for the attack, I wondered from which culture they had arisen as heroes. They seemed unlikely for any role in legend that I could imagine.

But then, by the sound of it, Kylhuk himself—who as *Culhwch,* in love with the fair Olwen, was recorded with great affection in the medieval Welsh romances—was not quite the youthful and proud arrival at King Arthur's court, the determined suitor needing only Arthur's assistance to achieve his conquest, with which my own generation was familiar.

And as I walked in the file, alert to every sound and every sight, I began to appreciate one of the earliest comments in Huxley's journal (it wasn't dated, but must have been written sometime in the middle 1920s; he could scarcely have been older than I am now. I certainly hadn't been born at the time):

> *Curiouser and curiouser. I must repress my expectations and beliefs. I must forget everything I knew and thought I knew. I am in an unknown region, walking unknown paths.*
>
> *In the words of the poet, all is a blank before me. There are no maps, no paths to follow. This is the wilderness.*
>
> *And yet no society of primitives inhabits this wonderful WILDNESS of unshorn hill and rough-banked river I penetrate day by day, adventure by adventure. But rather, a mixture of forms and figures, and strangely familiar images from my studies, that seems to suggest ALL of myth, something timeless yet ever-changing, fragmented, and at any time, in whatever place I occupy, somehow ever-present. I am so curious. . . . I must not too quickly interpret what I see. . . .*

"Then why did they attack me?" I wanted to ask my father from this distance in time, and yet—perhaps—from no distance in space that might be counted as significant on any map. After all, Ryhope Wood was not the broadest or deepest stand of ancient wildwood in this country.

But these thoughts were rattling drums, no more than that, a reflection of confusion, fear, and curiosity—how often I thought of that jibe in Huxley's journal! (*Neither boy seems curious.*) How often I wonder whether he was tempting me, Satan to my Eve, taunting my intellect with an encouragement to question what I could see around me. And I wondered why did he not take me into his confidence? Why taunt me when I would have been such a willing student?

"Why did they attack me? If these people are the memory of heroism, why are they so brutal?"

All is blank before me. There are no maps, no paths to follow. . . .

"Yes, yes. The easy answer—"

"Who are you talking to?" Gwyr asked, startling me from my reverie.

"A ghost," I answered, adding in Gwyr's way of speaking, "truthfully! If I was talking out loud it is because a man walks beside me whom I never understood, and who wishes me harm when I wish only that he would talk to me without secrets. And I don't mean you!"

"Your father?"

"My father."

Gwyr rolled his eyes and sighed. "I know. I know. They get old before they're ready. Women get wiser because of this, men no less so, but fussier. But I don't think I can help you on this occasion. I'm getting too old myself!"

Before I could comment—he didn't look *that* old, though he was certainly older than me—the horses tugged at him, or he made them seem to, and he turned away from me, calming the restless animals as he led them in a soothing circle.

At the first opportunity, I talked to Guiwenneth about Elidyr. She took my hand as I recounted the strange trip into the forest, the far stranger transmogrification of Elidyr and myself, and the lush, luxurious garden around the stone tomb of the knight.

"I remember a story like that," Guiwenneth said. "It was told to us when we were children. It's an old story:

"A man lies dead in a fairy hill, his body guarded by his wife who will not let him go into the valley beyond. The hill is in the bend of a river, surrounded by a deep forest filled with rich fruit, strange herbs, and wonderful flowers. The wife will not let her husband go until she has had a child by him, but the man is dead. There is nowhere for her love to go except into the land, and the land has flourished on this love for years, and is abundant and beautiful, mysterious and welcoming.

"Then, one day, the wife finds a herb growing over the body of a fledgling bird that has fallen from its nest. The bird comes back to life and starts to sing. She takes the herb and plants it in earth in the mouth of her dead husband. He comes back to life and they fall in love all over again. She declares love for nothing and no one but this man and their children.

"But without her love, now given back to her husband, the land becomes wasted and blighted. An eternal winter covers everything. And that is the lesson . . .

"Each of us has only so much love to give, so we must share it carefully between everything that matters to us, no matter how small. That's what my mother told me when she told me the story."

She squeezed my hand, but didn't look at me when I glanced at her. She went on. "Elidyr has shown you this terrible scene for a reason. And by the look of you"—she looked at me, now—"there is certainly something distressing you."

"Yes. He showed me a vision of my own mother. He said—he said I might be able to bring her home." *Back to life . . .* "And then he left. But *how*? How do I bring her home?"

Guiwenneth said nothing for a while, and we walked in awkward silence. She was thinking hard, still occasionally squeezing my hand, gestures of affection that I reciprocated.

At last, she sighed.

"Elidyr the Guide has shown you his dilemma. He is always torn between guiding the dead or giving them further life. He is showing you that there is a consequence to everything. The woman's happiness would blight the forest. Her sadness sustains nature. Elidyr always agonizes over the choice he must make. . . ."

I thought of his crisis of indecision in the hours before he had brought Gwyr back from the pyre. And I watched Gwyr, walking with the horses, and wondered if he knew.

"Gwyr was dead," I said. "Elidyr brought him back. So is he now living on borrowed time?"

"It depends on the consequences," Guiwenneth said. "He might live to be old. Elidyr might take him back tomorrow. It all depends."

She looked up at me with a smile. "I like your words, Christian."

"What words?"

"Living on borrowed time! It's a good way to talk about the gift Elidyr has given to Gwyr."

"Thank you."

"You use so many wonderful images in your talk. . . ."

"I do?"

"They make my head spin. So soothing and charming, so . . . unusual."

Clichés, I thought, but said, "I'm glad."

"I loved the way you talked about our first night together, by the river, by the fire."

"Remind me."

"You said that it was like . . . like a *mid-summer night's dream.*"

"Ah . . ."

"And that's just how it seemed!"

"It did," I said. "I can't deny it."

"You have such a way of using words to make visions. Sometimes when you speak, it's like listening to a poet."

"It is," I agreed. "I certainly can't deny that either."

*   *   *

Between one step and the next we had entered the twilight of the day, and the wood seemed to crowd suddenly upon us. Flocks of birds circled above the canopy, angrily noisy, perhaps because they were being disturbed by activity somewhere ahead of us. Guiwenneth rested a hand on my arm to draw my attention, then whispered, "It's here. Just ahead of us. It's watching us, making sure it recognizes the armored man."

We waited for a long time, standing in a line across the road on the chevalier's instruction, silent but for Gwyr's muttered words of calm to the animals. Then, astonishingly, the wall of forest *split apart,* the edges stretching toward us like a sucking mouth, widening as if to eat us, fires and human figures revealed within its maw; and two men on black horses cantered toward us. These riders came through the mouth, turned back suddenly, and beckoned us to follow, and the chevalier led his own steed forward, the rest of us close behind.

The smells of cooking and animal ordure, and the noise of a military camp greeted us as the hidden gate closed behind us. We were in night and in the forest, and dazzled by the brightness of twenty fires.

Almost at once, a group of runners, two women, seven men, ran toward the forest wall and appeared to merge with it, or pass through it, vanishing from view in any event, a new Forlorn Hope sent to their uncertain fate.

There was so much movement of men and animals, so much barking, shouting, laughing, and clashing of metal on metal, that it was hard to detect who or what was paying attention to us; but the knight was in earnest conversation with a group of men, and the ethereal woman was standing, palm to palm, with a second woman, who scowled as she listened to what was being said, one eye watching me, the other closed, and I guessed I was being discussed as part of the cacophony. Gwyr and Guiwenneth were in deep conversation, too, peering deeper into the camp that was spread through the wood. I sensed they were expecting an arrival. Jarag sat alone on one side of a fire, his skin clothes stripped from his muscular body, whittling happily at a piece of bone with an elegant flint blade. On the other side of the flames, three grim-looking warriors were leaning forward, idly talking as they ran whetstones lazily along their iron knives, taking a scant interest in the prehistoric man who was using their firelight. All members of the same team, I thought, even though there would be no playful banter in this particular stadium.

Of Someone and Issabeau there was no sign, and I hadn't even seen them slip away. I was puzzled by what was happening between the two of them, this odd flux of hostility and affection, with a common tongue continuing to elude them both, although the Saracen seemed able to talk to each of them in turn without difficulty.

I liked Someone. I liked his swagger, and the sudden doubt that seemed to plague him.

Guiwenneth had told me a little more about the proud Celt, who had been recruited to Legion at much the same time as she, though she had been a child at the time and placed in the care of Kylhuk's friend Manandoun, and Someone had been a youth, wandering and making his living as a mercenary as he searched for his identity:

At the moment of his birth, with horns sounding and silver hawks circling above the house where his mother labored, his father was being struck by the spear that had been flung across the river by his challenger. The name his father had been about to announce flew from his lips and was caught on the wind. A woman hovered there, disguised as a great bird of prey, and she caught the name.

"I know someone who will pay well for this," she screeched from the clouds.

Men ran and dogs ran, following the bird, and after a day

the hawk faltered and fell to the river. But before they could find the name it had stolen, the name had been swallowed by a salmon. The salmon was pursued, but was caught and eaten by an owl; the owl then fell prey to a dog-wolf. The wolf was hunted, but gored by an old boar. The boar was hunted, but eaten by a creature that no man or woman had ever before encountered.

And in this way, the name was lost. And because his father had died before naming the child, the father's name was forgotten, too.

It all seemed very unfair to the mother, but that was that—that was the way it worked.

The men gave up the hunt, returned, only to find themselves servants of his father's killer. The boy was exiled. But when Someone came of age, he set out to find the single word that would make him whole.

The way Guiwenneth told it left me in no doubt as to why the man was ill at ease. A great deal indeed was placed on a name.

And as I stood listening to the sounds of the night camp, I realized that I was surrounded by people who seemed ill at ease, continually unsure, always looking around them, always questioning. I wondered whether this was to do with the fact that they were part of what appeared to be an unnatural union in this land of fairy, fey, and fiction. Times fused together, stories welded one upon another, an uneasy alliance of destiny and determination that could only exist because . . .

Because what? Because one man had deemed it so? This Kylhuk?

Legion was not itself a memory of myth and history, like the people and creatures that occupied it. As Huxley scoured the wood for mythagos, to gain brief glimpses of the forgotten past, one such mythago—Kylhuk—had found a way to raise these entities *unnaturally*, to gather them like flowers, subverting their *own* stories to his own, transmuting their legend to his own quest, whatever that quest might have been.

How was he doing it? What "source" of magic or myth was he using to so shape this already supernatural wildwood?

I became dizzy with noise and movement and strange smells, and the sensation of being alone in a huge place, with a crowd which was somehow walking *through* me, as if it were I who was the ghost, and not these ghostly recapitulations of the hopes and wishes and stories of long-gone generations.

I seemed to draw the wood around me, to become the narrowing focus of some creature, invisible to the eye, bending the trees and the forest with its presence as it closed down upon me, sniffing, licking, quizzically eyeing its captive, then pulling back, letting through as if from nowhere a tall man in bright clothes, a man with hair as white as snow, and with a face as hard as ice. He strode toward me, rooting me to the spot with his fierce gaze.

And I knew him. It was Manandoun, Guiwenneth's guardian, and the last time I had seen him I had been twelve years old.

Without a flicker of emotion, Manandoun reached up to grip my face in his rough hands, his thumbs running along the two small scars at the sides of my eyes. Then the icy expression on his face broke and he grinned broadly. He jabbered excited words at me, then fell silent as he realized I was failing to understand him. But when he spoke more slowly, I began to get meaning from his words, though my frown finally encouraged him to shout for Gwyr, who came running over to us, wiping his hand across the back of his mouth. His beard was greasy and he was chewing and swallowing hard, ready to act as interpreter again.

Manandoun said, "I didn't think you would come. You

were so far at the edge of the world that we didn't expect to
see you again. But I'm glad you're here, and Kylhuk is delighted, too. It has been a good day for Kylhuk. The return
of friends we thought were dead"—he glanced at Gwyr with
a slight frown as he said this, and Gwyr stumbled in his
translation for a moment—"and the discovery of a boy who
is now a man and come to help him in the most difficult part
of his quest."

"For the Long Person," I said and Manandoun slapped
me on each shoulder, delighted.

"That's just the beginning of it. But if you know that,
then you know it's dangerous. That's good. You know what
you're up against."

"Truthfully, I don't," I said, still trying to imitate the way
of speaking of Manandoun and Gwyr (which at that time
was an effort for me, though it is an effort no longer). "I
know very little, though I am eager to learn."

"Then don't worry for the moment. Kylhuk will tell you
everything, everything about himself, from his childhood to
wise warrior, of his deeds and his disappointments. Kylhuk
has lived for a long time and not one breath of wind has
passed that hasn't seen a great deed or a great fight or a great
song from that man. Nothing is wasted, not time nor wit nor
the strength of his arm. He is a living legend, every moment
of his life packed with interest."

"When will I meet this man Kylhuk?"

"Tomorrow," said Manandoun, glancing away from me,
almost as if embarrassed. "When he has finished shaping the
great delights of today into a story."

And in English, Gwyr added, "He's drunk."

Manandoun, clearly understanding what had been said,
scowled at the interpreter and reprimanded him. "He is in
the Delightful Realm!"

"I'm sure he is."

"The Delightful Realm!" Manandoun repeated. "From where he can see events from all sides at once!"

"Especially from on his back, looking upward," Gwyr retorted.

Manandoun stared at the other man. "Truthfully, I should take you to task for that insult. But Kylhuk would want me to be forgiving, now that his friends have returned from the far frontier."

"No fight, then," Gwyr said, disappointed.

"No fight," said Manandoun.

Then a thought struck him. He reached out again to embrace me with his fists, feeling my arms and shoulders. "*Can* you fight? Can you throw a spear? Can you drink and run at the same time? Can you use a sling? Does the pain of a wound slow you down?" He peered more intently at me, whispering, "Can you summon the frenzy? Are you willing to shoot an arrow at the Scald Crow? It would be good for us all if you could!"

Before I could attempt any answer to this tumble of questions, Gwyr said, "I can give him some basic training. The man is fast, I've seen him run, but he's younger than he looks, and drinking will be his greatest training."

Both men looked at me and laughed, though I couldn't see the joke. I said, "I have a few tricks of my own, which I'd be glad to demonstrate."

I was thinking of the training in unarmed combat I'd been given in '42. I was certain that I could throw even the burly Manandoun, but had decided to wait for the right moment to demonstrate my skills. I might make a fool of myself using their own crude weapons. It would be useful to have a comeback which might earn me more respect.

"Show those tricks to Kylhuk," Manandoun said. "He is very fond of tricks."

And again both men laughed.

Then with the words, "Legion is an animal that moves on

ten thousand legs. But two extra are more than welcome, Christian . . . *Huxley*," Manandoun bid me good-bye and went in search of Guiwenneth.

He had given me a strange look when he'd used my name, but I thought no more of it.

Gwyr watched him go, then turned to me, tugging at his thin, trimmed beard. "Until recently, he was Guiwenneth's guardian, but now there are others who will begin to care for her. Despite Kylhuk's rage, pomposity, and inclination to visit the Delightful Realm, he truly does see the future, and with Ear, son of Hearer and Hergest Longsight, he can often tell who or what is to come into our lives."

"Did he know that I would come into his life? And into Guiwenneth's?"

"I don't believe so. And this is why Kylhuk must be watched, and his mood determined with great skill. He will be afraid of you, and fascinated by you. He marked you, after all; he needs you for something, that is clear. I very much doubt if it's for your head as a trophy, but I hardly see how it can be for your throwing arm. There is something that disturbs me about all of this, so I shall stay close. Guiwenneth, though, will be parting from Manandoun, so there may be a mood of sadness. Manandoun was in despair when he thought she was lost. Now he must face a different loss. According to Kylhuk, a band of hunters—the Jaguth—are rising from the earth, twelve in all, and Guiwenneth will spend time with them before the next adventure in her life."

"The Jaguth," I repeated.

Gwyr shrugged, saying, "I have heard of them. But Legion has never encountered them, or captured them, so they are not within its gates. They may not even arrive until this adventure is over." I think he was trying to reassure me. He went on: "But you are here, and Manandoun has told me to show you the garrison. Tomorrow you will meet Kylhuk himself, but tonight—are you tired?"

"Not at all."

We had only been traveling half a day before Legion had swallowed us and shifted us away from daylight to night. It was remarkable that Gwyr and the others seemed so accepting of this phenomenon.

"Then we can begin now," said the interpreter. "Legion is a garrison that moves during the day and settles into the forest by night. You must come to know it intimately. You will have to work for your stay here, and you must know of your position inside the beast at any time, otherwise you will be snatched away by the forests of the Long Gone. Stop looking so forlornly at Guiwenneth. She is leaving Manandoun, not you! She has plans for *you*!"

There was a twinkle in his eye and an impertinent edge to the grin on his face as he added, "All things in their time."

"Yes. All things in their time. Unlike this place, Gwyr. Unlike Legion. This is not a *thing in its time*."

But he pretended not to understand my point, though I'm certain he did, and simply led me to the horses.

PART THREE

LEGION OF
THE LOST

CHAPTER 9

I had once read a description of a Roman legion on the march, mile upon mile of cavalry, armored infantry, surly auxiliaries, archers, trumpeters, pack animals and their handlers, siege machines, smiths and cooks and carpenters, baggage wagons and camp followers, an orderly, organized, relentlessly advancing and thoroughly dusty column of battle-weary men that would take a day to pass, and would continue to shake the earth for hours after it had disappeared into the distance.

Kylhuk's Legion was not like this, though it was ordered in its own way and was huge, seeming to stretch forever through the forest, a sprawling beast (now mostly sleeping) laid out according to Kylhuk's needs.

In a Roman legion there were traditionally six thousand men of war. Manandoun had referred to this one as "an animal marching on ten thousand legs," but Gwyr thought that four thousand was more like it, two thousand men, women, and children, although if Manandoun was including the dogs and horses, each of which had four legs, he may have been closer to the truth. Kylhuk's Legion had whole packs of dogs scattered through its line, hounds of all types and mastiffs the size of bulls; also, four herds of wild ponies, which would be broken in and used as the need developed.

Indeed, as we rode down the line later, there was an outburst of angry shouting from some of the fires as a spike-haired boy astride a black, narrow-muzzled wolfhound came bounding past us, leading five angry, kicking horses by rope tethers. He was whooping and laughing, holding the dog by its mane, kicking the beast's sweating flanks with bare feet.

We watched them go and Gwyr said, "One of Kylhuk's first tasks was the capture of the hound Cunhaval from its master, Greidos son of Eiros. That hound has mated with every bitch in Legion and the place now swarms with its bastards. Like the one you've just seen. The children in Legion organize hunting parties—for its fleas!"

And then, as if the moment had not happened, he continued his thought on the number of legs in Legion, saying that as well as horses and dogs, there were also weasels, foxes, sacred hares, and bulls, not to mention owls, eagles, and hawks, none of them tethered but flying free, attached to the column by magic and by instinct.

"And there is a woman who keeps cats," he added as an afterthought, but said no more, looking distinctly uncomfortable even at mentioning the fact.

That first night, as Gwyr and I rode slowly down the line, I was more overwhelmed by the size of the column, the dazzling fires with their chattering, laughing or sleeping groups of fighters and their mates, the confusion of armor and weaponry, the chaos of tents, some of them ornate with pennants flying, some made from bent willow and animal hides, some nothing more than a few skins wrapped around the yellowing long bones of mammals.

We rode through a forest that was alive with light, that droned with voices, and which also flexed and flashed with distorted perception. On many occasions during that first tour of the defenses of the Legion, I saw people emerge from nowhere, trunks giving up the shapes, or the earth opening to disgorge a human form, a fire sucked down, then flaring up again as a man or woman stepped through the flames as if nothing had occurred at all.

If I asked Gwyr a question along the lines of "Who is that?" or "How on earth or in this forest can someone step out of the fire?" he would most often shrug and say, "Truthfully, if I knew the answer to that I'd be a wiser man than I am," which became such an incantation that I began to laugh when he said it, or even voice the words along with him. On an occasion or two he explained that these apparitions were part of the perimeter force that used the secret ways, or the charmed ways, or the ghost-born ways, legendary and mostly forgotten forms of magic, to hold the flank of Legion against those malevolent forces that surrounded the garrison like so many predatory animals.

The flanks were also defended by groups of armed men. These, as in any legion, were formed from groups of warriors of the same culture, and so Viking patroled with Viking, and the mail-clad Norman stood arrogantly debating his fate with a shorn-haired compatriot. I saw soldiers with muskets who might have been from the seventeenth century, Saracens and crest-helmeted men from the Near East, Greeks and Goths, Scots and Sumerians, all of them recognizable because history and the carvings on rock tomb, pottery, and chalice have preserved the form and shape of their beards, hair, and armor. And I saw dozens of other groups whose dress and attitude confounded me, all of them spread down the line, band upon band of them, becoming hundreds, all of them resting now that Legion had dropped to its haunches for the night.

When Legion advanced, the Forlorn Hope spread out before it, and the Setting Sun, as they were called, behind it, for reasons that I would learn later. Behind those scouts at front and rear was a formidable defense, divided between armed warriors and specialists in the ways of magic. Gwyr listed them for me, and I became dizzy with these specialist functions, but I remember that he talked of earth-walkers, spirit-travelers, shadow-fighters, shamans who could become hounds, eagles, salmon, or stags, running or swimming through the forest with an animal's sense. There were "Oolerers," who opened and closed hidden gates, called Hollowings, so that the Legion could slip briefly into another time before slowly flowing back again, avoiding danger.

And the woman who kept cats, he added, shuddering.

There were Arthurian knights, their heavy armor gleaming as they rode, their horses huge compared to the smaller ponies that Kylhuk owned in multitude; and these, those knights, were either ghost-born or holy (Gwyr used the expression hallowed, which I took to mean the same thing).

Ghost-born were not to be interfered with. They were reluctant additions to Legion, parasites on the back of the noble column, seeking a totem that was as dark in its meaning as it was in its appearance. A Dark Grail? I asked.

"Truthfully, if I knew the answer to that—"

"You'd be a wiser man."

He looked at me irritably and I smiled, then laughed as he walked his horse below a low-slung bough and cracked his head.

"Perhaps we have seen enough for the night," he said, composing himself after he had rubbed the area of the blow. "The heart of Legion is around Kylhuk himself." He pointed into the forest. We had ridden ten miles or so in one direction, and returned halfway along the other flank. Circling the heart had taken several hours and my impression was that Kylhuk and his train lay a mile or so from this rim, behind more circles of defenses.

And I was certainly tired now, my backside sore, my thighs aching from the stretch across the horse.

Legion slept. Gwyr and I rode slowly between the fires, returning to where Guiwenneth lay below a woolen blanket, her back to Someone son of Somebody, who lay with his hand on Issabeau's outstretched arm (a pale limb in the night, everything about her so delicate). Guiwenneth stirred as I lay down beside her, Gwyr again having taken the horses to their own station.

She looked at me sleepily, then touched fingers to my cheeks and smiled. "I wanted to come with you," she said. "But you went before I knew it."

"Gwyr has shown me the defenses of the Legion," I said. "I've learned a lot."

"I've missed you," she murmured, then stretched to kiss me, putting a hand round my head and holding my face to hers, her lips on my cheek. Then, after a moment's hesitation, her lips were on mine. "Come under my blanket. Keep me warm."

I went under her blanket. She was a slender shape in my arms, wriggling and snuggling closer to me, reaching a cold hand inside my shirt for my warm flesh. But if I'd hoped for passion I was disappointed. She mumbled and murmured, drifted into sleep again, her hair covering my face. I had to move it away with my chin and nose, since my arms were entwined with hers.

And I slept. And I slept well.

And at dawn, when I woke, I woke to the sight of Guiwenneth beside me, her eyes open, her breath in rhythm with my own, our faces still very close.

"Good morning," I murmured.

"You sleep very peacefully," she said. "I've been watching you."

And then she kissed me again. But before I could kiss her in return, she had thrown off the blanket, risen lithely to her feet and scampered into the cover of the bushes.

A horn sounded a long, low note, then came the frantic beating of a drum. Distantly, I heard the whinnying of horses, the angry barking of dogs, and the shouts of men.

Legion came alive. Its fires were extinguished, its tents dismantled, its human occupants put to their stations after snatching breakfast from wherever they could. Manandoun, white cloaked, white haired, his face painted scarlet, rode up with an entourage of two, one a striking-looking woman, yellow haired and solemn, and with a plethora of weaponry slung across her shoulders, from her waist, even strapped to the high, leather boots with which she gripped the heaving flanks of her sleek and feisty mare. I was not introduced, but in any case, she had eyes only for the distance, as if dreaming of the fighting for which she was clearly well equipped. The other, a man in a silver helmet with stylized face plate and leather armor, was "the Fenlander," according to Gwyr later.

"Good morning to you from Kylhuk, and indeed from me," announced the scarlet-faced Manandoun, as he tried to control his restless steed. "He hopes you slept well on your first night here, and indeed, I have that same hope."

"I slept very well. Thank you."

"Kylhuk feels that you must learn to walk with Legion, which will take some time, and may surprise you. I share this view and would add only this: That when you cease to believe your eyes, your legs will find their true rooting in the earth."

"Thank you for the advice. I don't understand it, not a word of it. But I'm sure I will."

"I am certain that you will. We have all, in our turn, had to find the truth in our eyes and the steadiness of our legs. When you feel confident with the motion of this great Legion, ride back with Guiwenneth to Kylhuk's tent and Kylhuk will embrace you and answer all your questions. There is trouble following us and later you will test your arm, or at any rate, learn the smell of Kylhuk's vengeance!"

"What sort of trouble?" Guiwenneth asked from behind me.

"Kyrdu's sons. What else?"

Nothing more was said. Nothing more seemed needed to be said. Guiwenneth was biting her lip. Gwyr, standing also, had heaved a deep breath.

"Legion will move at the next sound of Kylhuk's horn. Be ready!"

And Manandoun and his companions swung round from us and galloped away, merging with the forest, swallowed by the trees ahead of them.

"She came to get a look at you," Guiwenneth said with a sly smile. "I thought she would."

"Who was she?"

"Kylhuk calls her Raven. They're not lovers, though Kylhuk would like them to be."

"What raven has yellow feathers?" I asked, thinking of that tumble of golden hair.

Guiwenneth shook her head. "He named her for her black heart and the darkness of her humor."

"Magnificent, though."

"Yes."

"And she came to get a look at me," I said, standing a little taller.

"Yes. And it seems she was not impressed."

I had not understood Manandoun's advice to me about the truth of eyes and the sureness of legs, and Guiwenneth shrugged my question off when I asked her to elaborate.

A few minutes later, Kylhuk's horn sounded, distantly but sonorously, and everyone around me turned to face the front of the column, horses held tightly, dogs restrained, wagons ready, armed men in groups of twenty-seven, a number which seemed important but which Gwyr could not explain. A silence such as that at dusk fell briefly on this gathering; it lasted a second or two only, a caught breath in time, and then the second blast of the horn sounded through the camp and everyone stepped forward—

And the whole world lurched with them, like a ship casting off into a turbulent sea!

How can I describe the sensation? The earth began to shudder as Legion, spread for miles through the wildwood, began to advance with a steady step. But the forest *itself* seemed to be dragged forward, each tree and bush, each rock, each gully shedding a ghost of itself, which progressed with us, then faded. I stumbled to avoid hazards that were only images. I struck wood and rock that had seemed no more than illusion.

Two worlds, then, occupied the space of Kylhuk's Legion, one drawn from an underworld that flowed up to surround and accompany us; the other the dissolving reality of a world I knew well, but which was made insubstantial by the power of the advancing beast.

It was disorientating and frightening.

A cliff face suddenly materialized ahead of us and the whole column shifted away from it, not just those who walked and those who rode, not just the wagons and carts and animals, but the ground itself, the *whole of the space around us*. In doing so, we walked through broad-trunked oaks as if through images projected on the air; and a shimmering afterimage of the cliff would come with us for a while, detached from the reality, then fading into nothing.

It must have been like this to walk along the deck of a galleon, swinging in the wind and with the waves. And it was a kind of "sea legs" that I strove to find for balance, and a "focused sight" to tell which of the forests we passed through was real and which was not.

Though even that is wrong, because it was not the case that *any* of these wildwoods was illusion (I learned this later from Kylhuk), simply that Legion moved forward outside what you or I might think of as ordinary space and ordinary time. These were woodlands and rivers and massive stones that in various forms had occupied the space through thousands of years, new and vibrant, eroded and rotted, and the cleverness of Legion, supernatural entity that it was, was that as it marched it used these times to *hide* itself from all who pursued it.

Only when it rested was it vulnerable!

And what strange effect, I wondered, might it have had on any passing prehistoric group, hunting or traveling up the rivers in the past, when Legion flowed for a few seconds through their space and time, pursued by those forces of Nemesis herself that Kylhuk could not shake off?

By such encounters—and Huxley would have agreed with me, I'm sure—were stories begun and myths evolved!

(How quickly I was coming to accept "magic" in my life. But then, like dreams, in Ryhope anything could happen, though unlike in dreams, in Ryhope Wood the presence of the peculiar was defined and *ruled* by its existence in fiction!)

I walked in my group of twenty-seven, aware of the joking, the arguments, the groans as bodily functions needed to be addressed "on the hoof," as it were, the mocking jollity, the lies and exaggerations of the claims and stories told to conquer fear and boredom as Legion advanced into the unknown region, nosing for the first trace of the Long Person, who would guide us to Kylhuk's final task.

The wildwood flowed about us and our ship rocked through time and half-glimpsed worlds, swaying as it moved, settling steadily into its forward rhythm.

How long it took to "find my legs and eyes of truth" I cannot say. I was suddenly hungry, breaking from my column to seek the crude wagon where the cold carcasses of roasted birds and mammals were stacked, ready for distribution. The bread was as hard as rock, baked on hot stones during the nights when Legion rested. But it melted eventually when held in the mouth long enough with wine or water, and we were not short of these commodities, and I was glad to get half drunk like everyone around me.

Riders came through our ranks, and running men, stooped low, heading to the forward tip of Legion, to where the Forlorn Hope was spread out in the unknown world, scenting for danger and for the right path. Behind them came Manandoun, without an entourage. He spoke to Guiwenneth, glancing at me. A horse was brought for each of us and Guiwenneth asked me, "Do you want Gwyr with us?"

"Yes!"

She signaled to the Interpreter, then said, "He'll follow us when he can. Come on now. Come and meet your *marker*."

CHAPTER 10

Some colorful, some grim-faced, some wild, some silent, the raiding bands, the solitary adventurers, all the warriors of Legion marched steadily past us as we rode furiously down the line. Baggage wagons trundled and swayed through the shifting, ghostly forest, burdened beneath screeching children, who clung to each spar and beam. Naked, painted men in wicker chariots charged at us, taunted us, tried to race us as we passed. Spectral figures flickered in and out of vision. Somber, armored knights, some helmeted, some wild haired and youthfully bold, save for the dark look in their gaze, kept their great horses on a tight rein, matching the steady pace of Legion's lumbering walk.

Soon we saw tall pennants rising from narrow, ornately tented wagons, the flags mostly black, but one above all displaying the symbol of a boar's tusk crossed by a rose. There was a confusion of activity now—horse riders, dog riders, masked runners all taking messages and orders between all parts of the garrison.

And there were frightening moments of disorientation: The feeling of plunging into a ravine where no ravine existed, or of being suddenly caught in a burst of fire; birds clawing at our heads, arrows being fired at us. . . .

Guiwenneth had forewarned me of this, the unseen defenses that Kylhuk's enchanters and enchantresses had erected around the heart of Legion, like glowing embers ready to be "ignited" if the pursuing forces broke through the outer walls and came close to the Keep.

So many defenses! So much magic, which Kylhuk had painstakingly recruited at every opportunity during the years in which he had strengthened his army.

"He has spell-casters," Guiwenneth had told me. "Controllers of Time and of Fire, Controllers of Seasons, so we can shift within a year; there are summoners of spirits, speakers to animals, fire-starters, swimmers with fish, runners with hounds, fliers with birds, and cave-walkers—they tread carefully, and only ever walk at the edges of the worlds of the dead, since most of the dead seem to be on our tail!"

Manandoun reined in suddenly, interrupting my efforts to identify this magic, a worried frown on his face. "Kylhuk is not with his train," he whispered nervously. "Something has happened."

He raised a short hunting horn and blew three blasts. After a while, two riders galloped out of the wall of the forest, emerging like black-cloaked phantoms from the greenwood. Both had their faces painted scarlet, and one was suffering from a wound to his right arm, which he had tied across his chest.

"He is at the Silent Towers. Eletherion and his brothers have breached them."

"How many killed?"

"Less at that time, when we left, than now as we sit talking." A glance was cast at me. "He will be in the way."

"He should see this," said Manandoun harshly. "He should see Eletherion, since the bronze man has sworn to kill the *slathan*."

Guiwenneth hissed with anger, distracting me from the shock of that revelation, that I was the target of a death squad. I imagine I was ashen as I looked at her, and she looked hurt and sorry, her hand on her left breast.

"Modron's Heart, Christian, I was keen to tell you that Eletherion also has you marked, but there was a right time to do it, to give you a chance to decide for yourself—"

"Decide what for myself?" I asked.

"To return or to stay. To confront Kyrdu's sons. I'm sorry."

"There is nothing to be sorry for. Later, you can tell me about him in greater detail. Now, I think I should accompany you to the Silent Towers."

The riders were unhappy about this, but clearly there was no time to sit on restless, tiring horses and argue the point.

Some time later, we began to smell death. I have no words to describe how awful is that aroma. There is something about it that is familiar, and yet which instantly tells you that the dead await you. After that, the sky darkened, another shift in space and time, and we were suddenly in a brightly moonlit night, the moon itself low and gibbous behind an earthen mound where a single tree grew, its branches winter dressed, bare and stark. Steel clashed and men were screaming. There was an odd hollowness to the sound. The skirmish was ferocious, but involved few warriors, I realized. Torches streamed, illuminating frantic shapes engaged in combat. Ahead of us, framing the hill, was a wall that rose sheer to a turreted summit. It was shaking with the movement of Legion, of which it was a part, and crumbling before our eyes.

Manandoun at once flung himself into the fray, disappearing into darkness. Gwyr uttered a bloodcurdling cry and also vanished into the gloom, toward the moonlit gleam of a river, where fighting was happening in the water. Suddenly deserted, I turned anxiously to Guiwenneth, but a wildcat leaped at me, silver flanked, black maned, coming right into the saddle, crouching there before me, a carved staff in its

mouth. At once it transformed into Issabeau, who slapped
my face hard and hissed: *"Attonzion!"*

Pay attention!

Then she had dropped to the ground, crouching low,
sniffing the air and shaking her black mane like the cat
whose features she was adopting. She was looking for something and suddenly cried out, following in Gwyr's tracks toward the gleam of the river, where metal rang and eerie light
played.

I looked again at Guiwenneth, in time to see her reel from
the saddle, the sound of a stone from a slingshot cracking
against the bone of her skull, echoing loudly in my heightened consciousness. Stunned in my own way, I was easy
prey for the silent figure that rode at me, face hidden behind
the mask of an owl, chest bared, legs protected by strips of
hide wound round to create a crude armor. I saw the spear
stabbing at me and recoiled quickly. The blade glanced off
my face, but didn't cut. Nevertheless, I tumbled from the uncomfortable saddle and hit the thistles on the ground hard
and my frightened horse cantered away and vanished.

The rider had turned and was coming back through the
darkness, silhouetted by the moon, screaming a challenge,
or an insult, something in any case that chilled my blood. I
rose unsteadily to my feet to face him, watching the gleam
at the spear's tip, anticipating how I would snatch it, but before he reached me, another rider thundered past, flinging a
javelin that pierced the attacker through the shoulder, turning him and sending him screaming from the field. My sav-
ior swung round and reached down for me, gripping me
painfully by the arm and suggesting by every motion of his
large, smelly body that I should jump up behind him. I did
this, cracking my undercarriage against the wooden bar that
marked the rear of the saddle, gripping on to the rolls of fat
that warmed the waistline of this seminaked rider.

He slapped at my hands with a yelp of pain. "Hold my

hair if you must!" he roared, and I did just that, gripping the
long locks, silver and black in the moonlight, jerking his
head back as I got a better grip, then leaning against the tickling jungle of hair on his sweat-saturated shoulders as he
cantered again toward the hill. He had a torque around his
neck, and he rattled with earrings and bits of metal tied to
his hair.

"Manandoun!" he shouted. "Manandoun!"

He rode this way and that, snarling angrily, then drew out
a leaf-shaped sword and struck and hacked at an oak branch
in pure frustration. He seemed to be talking to me sometimes, but I couldn't understand him, and when I leaned forward and asked, "Say that again?" he just pushed me back
with the muscular ridges of his shoulders. When he suddenly kicked the charger into a gallop and I reached again
for safety to the ample flesh of his flanks, he again slapped
my hand away with an irritable shout. I rode behind this
man, using his hair as reins, noticing that as *he* rode, he used
the mane of the horse. The earrings jangled. The gold torque
round his neck struck me time and again in the teeth and I
was lucky not to lose enamel. I hardly had time to think of
poor Guiwenneth struck down by the slingshot, but my anxiety would have been grief had I not noticed her slowly
standing even as my fat friend was rescuing me.

Hopefully, then, she had escaped back to the inner lines.

"Manandoun, you dog! Manandoun! Great Hound!
Come to my side! Old friend . . . call to me!"

My guardian's voice deafened me.

We had reached that turbulent river, the water thrashed
by running men, dogs, and horses, the far bank stalked by
shadow creatures, wolves, and stags, upright, monstrous,
and shifting in and out of vision.

One such apparition was locked in a strange embrace
with Issabeau. She was ankle deep in water, her face and
breast fused with a man whose face and form writhed

through the shapes of animals, as did Issabeau herself. Only her right arm was human. She held tightly on to the left hand of Someone son of Somebody, who was backed up against her, stark naked save for the golden torque around his neck.

The two of them seemed to be protecting each other.

He was fighting against three men in the curious, skull-like helmets of the ancient Greeks, all of them naked, too, but pushing from the river at the proud Celt with shields and long, bronze blades which he was parrying with difficulty, though he screamed abuse at them. When his iron sword was struck from his grasp, I thought it must be over for the shouting man, my companion from the Forlorn Hope, but my guardian flung his own sword into the fray, a spinning weapon that Someone grabbed from the air and, without hesitating in the movement, used to cut down his nearest opponent. The sword was flung back to my paunchy companion, who caught it with equal dexterity. Someone grabbed the dead Greek's sword and shield and rampaged against the others on their own terms. As he forced them back into the river, Issabeau followed him, breaking the spell from her own opponent and sending him flying like a dark bird, screeching into the night, where shapes reached for him and seemed to shred him, like a cloud ripped on the wind.

I saw this over my shoulder. We had cantered uncomfortably along the river, the horse unhappy with our double weight. I saw the Fenlander, and Raven, fighting furiously from horseback, their shouts and challenges bloodcurdling and ferocious.

And again came the anguished cry from my host: "Manandoun! Fall back! Come back! I can't ride to you!"

Then a terrible scream pierced the confusion of night and skirmish. My blood went cold. I know now how that feels. The scream was short lived, but my guardian had broken from hot sweat to cold fear, and his mare became agitated almost beyond control, eventually becoming still under the gentle persuasion of her master. I realized the horse was now limping.

It was as if the whole skirmish had come to a sudden pause, an awful silence. Somewhere in the distance I could hear a rider coming, but my gaze was fixed upon the hill, with the moon full behind it. A man was slowly climbing to the summit, coming into view, dragging the body of another man behind him. When he stood there, to one side of the winter tree, he was taller than the lower branches, a giant of a man then. I struggled to see in this silver light. It seemed to me that the man on the hill wore a helmet with a high, vertical crest and a face plate fashioned with the grimacing features of a church gargoyle. White skin gleamed from the clean-shaven face that showed through the frame of the mask. Hair flowed on one side only from below the helmet. He seemed to be kilted to the knee, but bare chested like my guardian, though moonlight picked out the shine of bronze in a lacework across that body.

He had raised his sword to the heavens.

"No!" said my guardian softly, "not now . . . old friend, don't leave me. . . ."

The sword moved down savagely, then cut again, and then again. The body in the bronze man's grip slumped away from the head, which the bronze man swung round and round by its gray hair, then released, so that the spouting ball came toward us and struck the tree a few feet away.

"*That* is Eletherion," whispered Gwyr grimly from behind me, and I turned to look at the Interpreter, glad not to be looking at that black hill. Gwyr had ridden up to us with a second horse, the great chestnut charger that Manandoun had loved, and my heart sank as I realized who had been slaughtered by moonlight and by this Son of Kyrdu.

"I saw Guiwenneth struck," I muttered, "but she was still alive—"

"She is alive. She is safe," Gwyr said. His eyes were narrowed with pain.

"Where is Kylhuk in all of this?" I asked, suddenly angry, and the man whose lame horse I straddled reached round and grabbed me by the shoulder.

He half swung me from the saddle, but held me, his face inches from my own so that I could see clearly how his lower lip had been ritually cut to make it broader and angrier. Circles of blue dye covered one side of his face; the other was white with chalk. The teeth of small animals and glittering links of bronze were tied to the fringe of his hair. His eyes were dark in this light, but his cheeks glistened with a stream of tears, which dripped from the trimmed beard around his jaw and fell upon my hands . . . hands which still gripped him around the belt line for balance.

"Kylhuk is *here* in all of this," he said in a whisper. "I am Kylhuk. And truthfully, I have looked forward to our meeting, and indeed called you to it earlier today. But this is not the right time, now. I have just lost the closest friend a man could wish. His head is in that tree, caught among the branches. His life is in that man on the hill there, that bronze man, and I must find a way to get it back. Now . . . *let go of my skin.*"

I obeyed and he dropped me like a stone, then turned away, dismounted, and disappeared into the night, leading his unsteady horse.

Gwyr handed me down the reins of Manandoun's steed. "Kylhuk will want you to have her. But she will be grieving for Manandoun, as indeed will we all. So ride her gently, and if she springs for the canter, let her have her head and wait until she finishes the Grieving Ride. I know little about you, but I have seen you gallop, and I have seen your concern for those around you. I know in my heart that you are a man who can understand this creature, and her needs, and her instincts. Her name is Cryfcad, which means 'Strong in battle.' She is brighter than any of Uther's sons, which is not saying much, but she will respond to affection, and to a resolute instruction. Is that clear?"

"Who are Uther's sons?"

"The three Arthurs," Gwyr said, and shook his head despairingly. "All born together when Uther had prepared only one name. I would have thought you would have known of them."

"Truthfully, I know of only one Arthur, a great king."

Gwyr looked at me for a moment as if I were mad, then said, "Never mind that now. Go and fetch Manandoun's head—"

"What?"

"Pick up the head," Gwyr said angrily. "Kiss its lips and eyes and tie it to the mane of his horse. Bring it back to the heart of Legion."

"Why?"

"Why? So that you can learn how to honor a great friend. Or even a great enemy, though Manandoun was no enemy of anyone save a coward. Kylhuk will expect this of his *slathan.*"

"What *is* this *slathan*?" I asked again irritably.

"You are this *slathan*," Gwyr said coldly. "Clearly, you are this thing that you keep questioning me about. But I have no knowledge of it beyond what I have told you. Pick up the head. Do what I have told you. Then follow me."

I had found my legs and found the truth in my eyes, and though Legion made its ponderous way forward toward the Long Person through overlapping worlds of time and the forest, I was now accustomed to the dual movement, and approached the heart of Legion with Gwyr and without difficulty.

As it moved, the heart was no more than a train of wagons, each pennanted with the identity of its owner or the task it fulfilled. The forest was opened before each cart or wagon by either a roadmaker, or a pathfinder, some of these functionaries forming into gangs of laborers laying logs and stones at the front of the column, then picking them up behind; others using the wiles, tricks and magic of their own ages, from prehistoric to medieval to make passages through the tightest thickets and the densest groves of ancient oak and elm.

In this part of Legion, the true specialists that Kylhuk had gathered around himself lived, worked, and journeyed as the garrison forged forward in its final quest, not just the cooks and brewers, weavers, leather workers, saddlers, and all the rest, but stone shapers and metal smiths, who used every bit as much sorcery in their craft as those sorcerers Kylhuk had cunningly stationed behind the Forlorn Hope and at the Silent Towers, at the rear of the column.

But here as well were Kylhuk's accountants, who traded spoils for assistance and exchanged quests with passing knights, or passed on the acquisitions of successful tasks to those who had asked for them. For Kylhuk was now a mercenary and took on challenges on behalf of the faint hearted, or the overburdened, or the just plain frightened.

Since there was often a "hand in marriage" at the end of a task, he had a team of shapechangers who could appear as the triumphant knight, claim the marriage bed, and then be found "dead" in a few weeks' time. These were called the Marrying Men, and their position was keenly sought by all heroes who were blessed with the ability to alter their looks. There were Marrying Women, too, but since they were often required to sleep with giants, there was less demand for this particular station.

Perhaps most important of all were the Cleverthreads, Kylhuk's name for them, a group of women who could hold and weave the complex strands of fate that these many quests and tasks unraveled. Since any one action seemed to involve a host of other actions—as I was soon to find out from Kylhuk himself—these clever, silent women filtered and fashioned the consequences of each deed by each hero or heroine in the column. Without them, there would have been Chaos, and a grim ending to Legion.

Far more powerful than sheer walls of stone, water-filled moats, or armored men, the Cleverthreads were the true fortifications that kept at bay the great enemies of Time, Confusion, and Nemesis. And among them I thought I recognized the woman who had whispered to my mother.

"Who *is* she?" I asked, and Gwyr answered, with an ill-concealed shudder:

"The dolorous voice. If she has a name, I don't wish to know it. She whispers bad news or good news. Usually a simple word that gives a vision either of hope or despair. It is a double-edged gift since its whole purpose is manipulation. We can all act to change the vision—or not! Why do you ask?"

"My mother died because of a word that woman said to her."

Gwyr thought hard for a moment. "Then take back the word."

"Can that be done?" I asked, my heart pounding.

Gwyr glanced at me. "Tell me how she died."

"Hanged by her own rope. From a tree."

"Who *saw* this act?"

"I did. I tried to stop her. I saw it happen."

Gwyr laughed. "I doubt that you did. Not if the dolorous voice had been there first. But take back the word! That's what you have to do. If you can do that, you might find things aren't as you believe."

Elidyr had said that to me!

"How do I take back the word?"

"I don't know. Others have done it," Gwyr said simply. "But don't expect help from the Cleverthreads!"

*   *   *

I was anxious to see Guiwenneth and she had asked to see me.
Gwyr led me to the wagon where she was being cared for.
Someone son of Somebody rode behind the cart, facing backward on his horse, his sword drawn and held across his lap.
He was glad to see me and let me pass. I noticed that he had
trimmed his beard, combed out his hair, and changed his
clothes. On the dimples of his shaven cheeks he had painted
two small images of long-necked birds, one in red and one in
white, their beaks toward his eyes. Gwyr whispered to me,
"That's interesting. He has done something without knowing
what he is doing. That is the prerogative of only certain men."

"The birds?"

"It is a powerful charm to protect Guiwenneth. Interest-
ingly, he has learned it from Issabeau, the sorceress. And the
backward riding! And the hair hanging to his shoulders!
Very significant. But our handsome friend is using magic
without the knowledge of its power. As long as I live, I'll
pay more attention to his quest for his true name. He is certainly noble and what you're seeing is a *geisa*. . . ."

"A *geisa*?"

"Yes! A courtesy he is bound to show, or a taboo he is
bound to honor. He will have several of them, perhaps as
many as ten, so if he ever behaves peculiarly, that is probably the reason. A man's *geisan* are born with him, like a
birthmark, but usually he hears of them from his family as
he grows older. Someone, of course, was abandoned at his
birth, so the *geisan* return to him like bad dreams."

"Which *geisa* are we seeing now?"

Gwyr shrugged, leaning forward in his shallow saddle,
legs dangling by the heaving flanks of his pony. "My guess
would be that he is bound to ride backward and ward off enemies—using any means he can—for seven days after the
death of an honorable man. Manandoun was certainly honorable. It will be something like that. I may be wrong. But
enough of this. Go and kiss the woman in your heart."

Guiwenneth was awake, her head resting on a fat, feather pillow, a wet pouch of herbs pressed against the bruise from the slingshot; her breath was sickly with some medication that she had willingly consumed. Issabeau sat beside her, dark eyes watching me, one slender hand on the pale forehead below the tumble of luxuriant red hair of the wounded woman. She smiled at me as I closed the flaps of the covered wagon behind me. I wondered if it was for her that Someone now rode backward behind the wagon.

"Ellez trizda," she said in that deep, slow voice. *"Ellez trayze trizda, mayze ellez* sauve; *le sonje ez* forta."

She is sad, very sad, but she is safe. The blood is strong.

Issabeau left the wagon. I came closer to Guiwenneth, who reached out for my face with both hands, smiled, and mouthed a kiss to me. There were tears on her cheeks and after a moment she looked at the sack I carried and asked to hold the head of Manandoun for a while, though she kept it inside its leather bag. She talked to him as if he were there in front of her and answering back.

"Trim his beard," she said suddenly and gave me back the bag.

"Every whisker," I avowed, and kissed her on the lips. "Guiwenneth . . ."

"Trim his beard!" she said again, gently dismissing my moment of longing, and I left her, following Gwyr to the oilcart.

Here, under a cover made from the skins of wildcats, a solitary man supervised all such ritual as the oiling of heads and the preparing of corpses. That he was a so-called "druid" did not impress me, since he was neither exaggeratedly dressed for some festival of poetry and singing, nor a wild man, hair disheveled, eyes glowing with the effects of hallucinogenic mushrooms. He was scruffy, his hair long and uncombed, his face covered with a gray stubble and heavily wrinkled, but his hands were very smooth, like the hands of a youth. His whole body was running with sweat (though this was deliberate, I suspected, since every so often he scraped the sweat from his skin with a curved iron knife and let it run into a small pottery receptacle). His manner was very matter-of-fact.

Gwyr explained that it was Kylhuk's wish that I prepare the head for Manandoun's funeral. Although it was customary for a man like Manandoun to be interred with his horse and chariot, it was in Manandoun's fate that he would be burned after death so that he could ride to the Islands of Fire, where a quest was awaiting him, so a pyre had been erected. The druid spread a wolfskin blanket on the floor of the wagon, fur side down, then told me to place the head upon it. Manandoun looked ghastly and bloody, his face still in its final grimace, hair plastered to the skin with gore. Next to it, the druid placed a crudely hewn block of elm wood, approximating the size and shape of Manandoun's head.

The first task, then, was to wash the head and comb through the hair and beard. I did all of these things, the druid patiently showing me how.

Whatever I did to the true head, I mimicked on the block of elm.

When the cleaning was complete, a long iron knife was used to trim the end of the neck; then the neck was covered with a woolen cloth, dyed blue, and tied tightly with a leather thong, to stop any further seepage.

A sharp flint blade was used to shave the stubble from the cheeks, and with a pair of iron shears I trimmed the beard, mustache, and hair into a neat and precise style. On the wood, I scoured simple lines.

With the eyelids closed, and a small stone carved with Manandoun's totem wedged below the tongue, the head was ready for oiling. The druid guided my hands as I massaged the cheeks and the scalp. The cedar oil was pungent and enlivening. An iron awl was used to pierce the septum of the right nostril, Egyptian fashion, and oil was poured into the brain cavity before the entrance was sealed with beeswax.

The wood was oiled, its crude nose pierced with a knife.

Finally, a chalk-and-water mixture was combed through the washed hair with fingers, making a fan, a peacock's display of stiff, white hair, a crest around the head. The same mixture was caked on the block.

When this had dried and the hair was rigid—it didn't take long—Manandoun was ready. I picked up the head and presented it carefully to Gwyr, who took it away and returned it to the dead man's wife.

"Well done," he said as he departed. "Since the way you have made him look is the way he will live for the rest of his life, he will be more than pleased with you. Don't forget the trimmings of his hair. His wife will need them. And the block, that tree-head, is to be buried with the widow when she goes, so treat it kindly."

The druid had already gathered up the trimmings and put them into a cloth pouch. Like a Victorian pharmacist, he was now busy stoppering pottery jars of unguents and potions and sorting out the wagon, where no doubt soon he would receive another corpse to dress.

And that was that for the better part of two more days, during which Legion lumbered forward toward the Long Person and the secret she held, and Issabeau and Someone son of Somebody became increasingly intrigued by each other, and of that, more later. But then Kylhuk sent for us all, all of the Forlorn Hope that had become my friends, to be his guests at the funeral of Manandoun. Jarag had vanished into another season, helping to guide the garrison, but the rest of us went back to where Manandoun was laid out on his pyre, his proud, chalk-whitened head on a stone beside it, ready to be replaced with the wood when the fires were lit.

I rode there with Gwyr.

CHAPTER 11

As we approached the tent with its four pennants, each of a boar's tusk crossed by a rose, Gwyr said to me, "I forgot to mention something. Kylhuk is very angry with you."

I slowed the pace of my approach and looked at the man, who was behaving in a slightly shifty way. "Angry about what?"

"About your comments that he is a fat man, and would be a better warrior and a keener fighter if he was not so heavy around the waist, the flesh hanging on him like great folds of tree fungus, and all because he eats too much and drinks too much and prefers to ride horses, or travel in chariots, rather than running like the younger men you have cruelly compared him to."

I stopped the horse completely and turned it round.

"Is there some problem?" Gwyr asked.

"Yes. I made no such comments, and I have suddenly lost my appetite. Again."

"You made no such comments?"

"Would I dare make such comments?"

"Comments must have been made, why else is the great man Kylhuk so furious with you?"

"I made no comments! Tell the great man that I'm ill. I'm returning to the Forlorn Hope. I feel safer there!"

"You cannot do that. You must face Kylhuk and explain

your insulting behavior, and your cruel slaps and pinches to the fat that you have complained about."

Ah! That was it, then. When he had buried Manandoun in his heart, the funeral had not yet happened; but when the tears had become private and not public, he had begun to remember my inadvertent attempts to hold on safely as he rode around the silent towers, looking for his friend. He had been made painfully aware of his burden of flesh by my painful grip, and in his fury, being the man he was and from the type of warrior caste that he was, he had invented stories and insults to displace and reflect away his own embarrassment with himself. As a Celtic warrior, from whatever period of time or from wherever in Europe, he would have been ostracized for his lazy weight. Because he was a leader, and greatly feared, he was tolerated and respected, but the degree of sarcasm that I had already detected in conversations about Kylhuk, the great man, clearly suggested that this respect was being tested, and indeed, that his own self-respect was being challenged.

The Celts simply did not tolerate a paunch on a man, especially not a young man, and certainly not a king. (Kylhuk was not young, but he *was* a king in his own domain.) And on such dissatisfactions as being overweight, regarded as a discourtesy, were changes in kingship made.

I wasn't sure that I was the young blood to take on such a challenge, but from what Gwyr had said, Kylhuk had fashioned a grand account of my insults with which to test me.

"I didn't say a word," I said to Gwyr, adding, "I grabbed his belly for balance. He slapped me down."

"I know," Gwyr said. "Everyone knows. And it would certainly have been better for us all if you had found something more *heroic* to hold on to. But there it is, it is done, you have failed us. He is now so aware that he must stop eating and drinking if he is to run with the hound like CuCullain, the fleet-footed CuCullain, the iron-bodied CuCullain, and not run behind the hound like Dubno, the thorn-snagging Dubno, the breath-gasping Dubno. He is so aware of this that he is sarcastic at all eating and drinking, no matter who the eater or the drinker might be, man, woman, child, or dog, sarcastic at all feasting unless it is with plums and water."

Plums and water?

Events became even clearer to me! The great man had gone on a diet.

And for "sarcastic" read "critical."

And the great man's companions were not happy about this. Any of this.

It wasn't Kylhuk, I suspected, who would be angry with me, but the warrior guests at his nightly, knightly feast.

"And you, Gwyr," I ventured, turning back to finish the ride to Kylhuk's hold at the center of Legion, "are you angry with me too?"

"Let's see what he offers in the way of hospitality," the Interpreter said with ill-disguised disgruntlement.

I believe I laughed, thinking at the time that the man was referring only to meat and mead. To Gwyr, though, and to all who were of a high caste in the society which had made them heroes, hospitality was as complex a concept as any I could ever wish to know, and single, mortal combat could and would be initiated on so sublimely senseless a notion that a man wearing a red flower, who had not shaved for three days, had been denied the first cup of mead at the moment the king sat down to drink after the death of his champion in combat in a river.

Gwyr hinted this to me as we rode through the thorn-and-wicker fence and the lines of flaring torches that defined the oval funeral and feasting area. The strange notion he had described to me was another *geisa,* that taboo or demand on a noble which might need to be addressed once or many times in life, not one of Kylhuk's in this instance, Gwyr had simply been giving me an example.

For the moment, though, Gwyr led me through the wicker fences, through the shielding torches, through the grim-faced guards, to the cluster of crude tables piled with bread, fruit, and clay flagons of sharp-smelling liquor, where we found ourselves to be not just guests but *honored* guests at the funeral feast for Manandoun, seated with Kylhuk himself, and so at last I met the man face-to-face and not cheek to spine, or fingers to fat!

"Most of this celebration is for my friend, the Wise Council, Manandoun. I miss him, I will miss him all my life in this world—"

He looked into the night sky and roared: "Taranis, hear me, strike me with thunder if I lie! Modron, bring us together to hunt the great-tusked, ever-bleeding black boar, wounded after I put my spear in its side, and Manandoun put his spear in likewise, though less effectively, that deadly boar, the hunter of our world, the silent peril of our woods!"

He looked back at me, softer, sadder. "Yes! that is how much I miss him, and this feast is for him, and on that pyre there, if you look closely, you will see my friend about to burn, to go into a place that I will soon know well, as will you, as will we all. But Christian . . . *Huxley* . . ."

He scratched his chest and stared at me, looking me up and down as he sat there. "Huxley*oros*? Huxley*aunii*?"

Clan names!

"Where do you come from? Huxley*antrix*? Huxley*uranos*? What are you, I wonder? What clan? Why did I mark you? Why did I go so far into the netherworld to find you? Was I mad? I can't remember for the moment. Can you help?"

Before I could respond, he went on, "Anyway, though Manandoun will soon open the gate to a fairer land than this—and a fond good-bye to him, I weep to see him go— this feast is partly for you, Christian, to welcome you, even though you seem to have nothing to say, since you have not said a word since I started speaking, but you are welcome nonetheless. And here is the food; you must eat what you want; you must not hesitate to demand what you want; whatever Legion can offer is yours. Have you tried these?"

He held a plum toward me, watching me keenly.

"It looks like a plum."

"Very well noticed," he said, holding it closer. "It is better for you than that foul stuff over there, that roasting pig meat and the racks of hot-peppered chops for those men in iron." He scowled at the Courteous Men, the chivalrous knights in their colorful tunics and chain-mail protection,

I took the plum, ate it, spat the stone into my hand and tossed it over my shoulder. Kylhuk watched me through furrowed brows. The aroma of roasting pig was making my stomach sing. There was a honeyish, alcoholic smell from flagons being surreptitiously passed around, but between Kylhuk and myself there was only a wide dish of crystal water, with rose-petals floating in it. He pushed the dish toward me.

"Drink your fill. I am told this tastes very good."

I drank from the dish. Kylhuk studied me carefully, leaning forward. "Well?"

"It's water."

"I know it's water. Are you content?"

"No."

The whole feasting place was suddenly silent, all faces turned toward us.

Kylhuk's voice was a controlled whisper as he stared at me. "Why are you not content?"

"Because water satisfies a thirst. But as drink goes, it does not satisfy the need to show a great man like Manandoun the respect he deserves. It is not the right drink to hold up to the flames that will soon accompany a great friend into the Otherworld."

"I agree!" Kylhuk exclaimed emphatically. He rose to his feet, staring down at me darkly. "You speak with the same Wise Counsel as Manandoun himself! Yes . . . the same Wise Counsel . . . And I agree!"

He flung the rosewater onto the ground and stamped on the clay dish, breaking it, kicking the shards all around the feasting area. He seemed very satisfied with the act.

In the middle of the tables, over an open fire, the pig was a poor sight now, being no more than bone from skull and spine to upper haunch, and at the lower part of each leg. Like two obscene growths, the rumps, the prime cuts, were intact, untouched, since it was these portions that were Kylhuk's to enjoy first. With a single stroke of his wide-bladed sword he cut the gruesome carcass across the backside, sending shards of bone and flaming charcoal among the cheering host.

I had expected Kylhuk to cut from the haunch and eat, but instead he flung his sword onto the unlit pyre, calling out:

"That another man has come to take your place does not mean that your place can ever be taken. Not here, old friend. You and I will always hunt for the heart of the beast, and if Twrch's tusks take us, if the beast is too strong, then we'll ride on its snout and tell stories for a year and a day! Manandoun! Wise, gracious Manandoun! Truthfully, I would not have seen you go, and certainly not on the end of Eletherion's sword!"

Then he turned to the pyre makers, snapping, "But he's gone and that's that. So burn him, and burn him well," before beckoning me through the gate in the wicker fence.

As I went to follow, Gwyr flicked his fingers, drawing my attention, and pointed toward the hacked but still unused hindquarters of the fat pig, crisping slowly in the charcoal where they had fallen.

I went over and cut two thick slices of the tender meat, laying them out on a wooden platter. I carried this offering out to the silent man, who stood, staring up at the waning moon.

"Have a little piece of one of Twrch's bastard offspring," I said, holding up the slices. He looked at the wooden platter for a moment, scooped up the meat in his hand, squeezed the flesh until the juices ran, then slapped it down again, wiping his palm on his clothes.

"No. You eat it. I have no taste for it now."

"Kylhuk! If you offer me this meat, this best cut, then I will eat it to the memory of Manandoun. I met him when I was a boy, when he was Guiwenneth's guardian. And again recently, when he impressed me as a man of wisdom."

"Yes," Kylhuk said, turning to face me, his big hands on my shoulders, his dark eyes gleaming, but not, now, with tears. "Yes. He was a man of wisdom! And the best friend a man could wish for. And you are not yet a man of wisdom, though from what you say, I believe you will soon become one. You are a man of impulse and recklessness, of shallow delights and shallow appetite, but you give me hope and heart, because once I was the same. And though you have insulted me, I forgive you. You were right to say about me what you said, though I am certainly not as bloated as the corpse of a dead bullock swelling up on a hot summer's day, as you so coarsely described me. . . ."

On Modron's Heart, I did not! I wanted to cry, but there was a great warmth in this man for me at this moment, or so I thought. And the crackle of the pyre, the passing away of Manandoun, was casting a gentle and doleful sound across us, and I said nothing.

And Kylhuk concluded, slapping his portly places, "You were right. This great man needs to run with CuCullain's hounds, and I will do it, though Manandoun would have thought otherwise! We have time to run as we move toward the open legs of the Long Person. Time to talk, to get to know each other. Time to run with the hounds. Time to *fast*, you and I, to fast as no two men have ever fasted before, and ignore the greedy brutes who have gathered around me, those who feed only on succulent pig meat, tender roasted venison, roasted fowl birds, all of it!"

Still on a diet then, I thought grimly. But I said, "Is it this Twrch Trwyth, then, this giant boar that is your great quest?"

"No. Though I long to hunt it down and take its head. And *will* do so before I ride to the Islands. But no. It's something else."

He grinned at me, then embraced me, a full bear hug. Then he slapped the platter of meat I still held into the air and announced, "I have so much to tell you! And while my dear friend is still alive with the movement of flames, he can listen to me and clip my ear if I tell one word of a lie." He stared at me hard, for a moment, then said softly, "Gwyr tells me that you are confused by what *slathan* means."

"Yes."

"Shall I tell you or shall I not?"

"Tell me."

"But shall I?"

"Please do."

"Once I tell you, you are bound to it, so if I tell you, you must stop me quickly if your courage fails you and you become frightened, because I expect my greatest friends to be true to me until the moment of the pyre."

I ignored the taunt, the insult. "I'll be sure to do that. Truthfully. On Modron's Heart!"

"On Modron's Heart," Kylhuk repeated softly, amused and thoughtful, his gaze meeting mine for a long, too-long moment.

And then, without a further word, we went back into the stronghold, where everyone at the funeral party, for reasons no doubt to do with Kylhuk's cutting of the prime of the pig and the consequent opening of more flagons of a drink stronger than rosewater, was in a rowdy and vibrant mood.

CHAPTER 12

The pyre blazed. Manandoun was lost inside its fire. I watched the wind-whipped smoke rise to the stars. I scented the cedar oil as it burned that trimmed beard and hair. I tried to imagine what Manandoun was seeing as he passed through the hinterland, that place of shadows and tricking gates, and approached his chosen realm.

Manandoun's wife, Ellys, sat on a stool with her back to the flames, a safe distance away, her arms crossed over her breasts, her husband's battle torque over her wrist, his small knife on her lap, a pouch containing the trimmings of his hair around her neck. The wooden head was mounted on a stone beside her. Her two sons, both youths, knelt beside her, scowling at the ground, no doubt thinking of Eletherion and his brothers.

Each woman in the host went over to the widow and stood before her for a while. Then each man in the host went over and gave her a token, kneeling as they did so. Kylhuk watched all this, talking to me so softly and angrily at times that I couldn't understand him above the roar of fire and the spitting of burning wood. There were moments when I felt the poor woman who had lost her husband would be incinerated herself, but the sons brushed all cinders and flaring shards away, and I could see by the pyre's light that each was crying.

At last Kylhuk went to the widow and knelt on one knee on the flattened ground before her, his head bowed. Ellys put a circlet of white flowers on his head and he passed her a ring, which she accepted. The two youths, surly in their expression, hugged the big man when he stood and he spoke to them for a few moments, one boy listening, the younger looking angry. This boy rode away soon after, and I saw that his mother was distressed and being comforted by her elder son.

Kylhuk led me back to the table where Gwyr sat among Kylhuk's closest retinue, all but one of whom was drunk, all of them wearing short, colorful cloaks, bright torques around their necks and arms, and the white streaks of grieving on their cheeks and breasts. Two of the ten were women, including the hard-faced Raven, who sat apart from the others, adrift in her own thoughts, seemingly unbothered by the chatter and wild laughter that was again rising around her now that the courtesy to Manandoun's family had been completed.

"Where's Guiwenneth?" I asked Gwyr. "I'm worried about her."

"Issabeau is with her," the Interpreter replied. "Not far from here, by a shallow stream. Someone son of Somebody is close to them, keeping watch. The strange oyster eater, too." He meant the jagar.

"Does she know that Manandoun's pyre is burning?"

"Of course. While you were elsewhere, she carried the body here herself. She spent time with him, and brought the head to Ellys for the last kiss. Her own father, a man of high rank, was killed a long time ago and Manandoun adopted her. But because of a *geisa* that Manandoun won when he was a younger man, she cannot be here while he passes to his Island. That is why Issabeau is with her."

"I should be with her, too," I said, and I meant it. Nothing that had happened so far had moved me to tears, but the thought of Guiwenneth being banned from the funeral of a man she had loved made me angry because I could imagine her sadness and I wanted to be by her side, even with Someone and Issabeau, and help her through her grief.

"She will want you later," Kylhuk said through a mouthful of fruit. I hadn't realized he'd been listening.

"She'll be glad of you on her cloak of grass. Have you been there already?"

For a moment I didn't understand the words. Then the meaning came to me.

"I am more than fond of Guiwenneth," I said to him, standing from the bench. I was incensed at his comment, and my head had started to whirl with drink and rage. "And it is none of your business how she feels for me. None of your business at all! All I know is, she is distressed and I feel for her. Your cheap jokes, your callous tongue, your . . . your *fat* tongue and your *fat* wits, you should be ashamed! Gwyr, take me to Guiwenneth. I want to be with her!"

Every warrior in Kylhuk's retinue was standing, staring at me, none making a move to draw their weapons, every one of them waiting like a hound at the start of the course.

Kylhuk spat out the plum he had been eating, stood and faced me. How hard he now looked, how narrow his gaze, how grim his scarred lips. His breath was slow and even. He towered over me, his gold-and-bronze funeral decoration rattling on the hair and the ears that held it. He looked very powerful, and he was very angry, and I flinched as he drew his dagger and held it by the blade, handle toward me. But his words were very soft when he spoke them.

"What was said was wrong. I will have none of what was said. A tongue spoke, but the heart did not mean the words. If you sit back at my table, I will be the richer man for your kindness. As this good man Gwyr will tell you, Guiwenneth asked to be alone with Issabeau, but she will be glad of your company later. And I will be proud to ride behind the two of you when you share one saddle."

I noticed that his retinue were relieved by this gentle declaration. When I sat, they sat, and when they had sat, Kylhuk sat, and when he was seated, he poured me a cup of sweet-sour honeyed liquor. Gwyr waggled his eyebrows at me, then pretended to be engaged in eating.

I found out soon after that one of Kylhuk's *geisas* was that he should always apologize for the first angry words, whether his own or someone else's, spoken after the death of a friend.

And when Guiwenneth told me this, I wondered what might have happened if that particular *geisa* had already been "called in"?

The offer to ride behind the two of us when we shared one saddle was his self-invitation to be (in whatever terms the society of six hundred years B.C. thought of it) my "best man." On this subject, I had my reservations.

And when he had said, "A tongue spoke, but the heart did not mean the words . . ." whose tongue was he talking about? Mine or his? Had that been necessary apology or infuriating forgiveness? I decided on "courtesy" and kept the thought to myself.

Legion was at rest, and the wildwood it occupied was alive with fires and the conversations and laughter of many different times, protected by the subtle, concealing magic of twenty thousand years. As Manandoun left us, and Ellys and her companions danced within a ring of thorns to the thunderous beat of bone on skin drums and the wailing and howling of bronze trumpets, so Kylhuk broke his short-lived fast, and with the first intake of meat and the first swallow of beer he, too, passed on from this funeral, remembering that he had a special guest to whom he had made promises; and in the way of a storyteller, he told me a little of his life,

and I'm sure you will not mind if I present it in the formal
way that Kylhuk expressed it.

But it was only later that I realized how he had used the
story to answer my question "What is a *slathan*? Why have
you marked me?"

CHAPTER 13

The story of Kylhuk and Olwen (as told by Kylhuk himself):

When the child of a great man is born, and Kylhuk's father was a king in his land, there is usually a portent: A star falls from the sky, perhaps; or a great storm washes away a fortress on a high cliff; a cow gives birth to a lamb; or a poem cannot be made to rhyme.

There were no portents when Kylhuk fought his way to life, though a storm that had been building in the west suddenly vanished, and if this seems remarkable, bear in mind that Kylhuk, even when in the womb, could affect the world around him.

Kylhuk was born with the portents *inside* him; he had swallowed them by using his mother's mouth, and they would be useful later.

As the unnamed child lay in its applewood crib, one of the sons of the giant boar Twrch Trwyth burst through the palisade wall and attacked the dogs in the stronghold, killing six on its tusks. Badly wounded by a spear thrust from the child's father himself, the boar rampaged into the roundhouse and shook the child from its crib, screeching angrily as it did so, trying to impale the infant, but succeeding only in wedging the tiny boy between its tusks.

The boy clung to the tusks as the boar ran from the stronghold and into the forest, pursued by hunters and hounds. The chase lasted for a hour, and though the boar tried to shake the child from its tusks to see where it was going, the boy held on. Eventually the boar ran blindly into an oak and stuck there fast, to be quickly caught and slaughtered.

Seven days later it was roasted, and Eisyllt Cleverthreads, the king's favorite daughter, cut the hide so skillfully that she made four cloaks and two masks from the skin of the pig.

The valiant child was named Kylhuk, which means "running with the pig," a very great name, greater than CuCullain, which means "running with the hound"; though these two heroes would meet one day and become great friends.

When Kylhuk's beard had begun to itch but not to sprout, his father married another woman, his first wife having died.

At the games to celebrate the marriage, Kei Longthrow challenged Kylhuk to a spear-throwing contest. Kei cast the first spear and after several hours it was seen to strike the side of a distant mountain, seven days' ride to the east. Then Kylhuk threw and after several hours his spear was seen to glance off the summit of that same mountain. But Kei cast again and the spear sailed over the summit. It killed an ox that was peacefully grazing on the other side, though this wasn't known until the complaint arrived, some time later.

"You will not do better than that," said Kei in triumph.

"I will," said Kylhuk, "though you think otherwise."

And Kylhuk circled four times where he stood, summoned the storm he had swallowed as a child, and cast his spear. The spear disappeared into the distance, flying over the summit of the hill.

"It is a tie," said Kei Longthrow, "since we have no way of seeing which spear has gone the farthest over those hills."

"Be patient," Kylhuk said, "the throw is not finished."

The sun set, and the host slept, and in the morning Kylhuk and Kei were still in their places.

"You are a bad loser if you do not accept the draw," said Kei.

"Be patient. The throw is not finished."

At dusk, Kylhuk turned his back to the hills. In front of him a flight of geese was suddenly disturbed as a javelin came flying out of the setting sun. He snatched it from the air and tossed it to his challenger.

"There. I win. Keep the spear, Kei. It is my gift to you. It will come in useful."

"I am impressed by that throw!"

But the contest had consequences.

Kylhuk's stepmother was also impressed by the throw. She was still a young woman herself and fell quickly in love with her stepson. Kylhuk, being the man he was, rejected her interest, but out of kindness to his father kept the betrayal to himself.

Angrily, that night his stepmother cursed him.

"By my head, you will wed no one until you have first won Olwen, the daughter of Uspathadyn, and you will not win her because Uspathadyn is a champion in his country, and a giant besides, and twenty-three severed heads, all brothers, all of them still singing of Olwen's charms, make up his table decoration! When Olwen is won, Uspathadyn must kill her lover, or be killed, as part of a *geisa* that he carries, but he is keen to live and has no intention of letting his daughter go. So there. That's that."

"I will win her," said Kylhuk coldly, "though you think otherwise."

Kylhuk had accepted his first challenge, but to Kei he confided, "I could have wished for a better start to my life of adventure. Olwen's father is a giant of a man, and will be hard to kill, though I can do it, I'm in no doubt about that.

But Olwen herself is half again as tall as me, and though she is certainly shapely, I have heard that her thighs are like Greek columns and can easily crush an ox; when her teeth chatter it might be rocks falling from a mountain. And she makes oak logs into kindling by *twisting them into knots*! Kei—as a man, and with a man's passions, I fear those hands more than I fear her father."

"By my head, Kylhuk, I'm glad it's you and not me that must sleep with this woman."

"What shall I do?"

"If it were me, I would chain her hands to the bed posts!"

"I mean, what shall I do *now*?"

Kei scratched his chin. "Go to Pwyll. His fort is only ten days' ride away. Ask for help there. That is my advice."

"I shall take that advice, though I'm sure I am wrong to do so."

So Kylhuk went to Pwyll's fort, but hesitated at the gates, again reflecting that to ask for help in his first task was a cowardly thing, and might have consequences. But he was too young to think it through clearly, and too eager to win and then dispense with Olwen, so that he could continue his life of adventure.

He begged his way through the gates, then rode to Pwyll's hall. He was so nervous that he forgot his manners and rode straight into the hall where the meal was being taken.

When he had stepped down and been seated and fed, and had told Pwyll of his quest, the king stood.

"Kylhuk, you are the son of Kylid, who once took a blow that was intended for me, but this is neither here nor there. There are a hundred men in this fort, and a hundred women, and every one of them is a great man or a great woman."

And he proceeded to name them all, which took some time.

Then he said, "Kylhuk, you are welcome to take one or

all of them to help you in your task, since I am bound to
grant the wish of any beardless man who rides his horse into
this hall without his weapon drawn, which you have done.
But if you take more than two I shall know that you are
younger in heart than you are in body, and that will not be
good for you."

"I will take two men only," Kylhuk said, but in his heart
he knew this was also a grave mistake. He should have taken
no men at all, accepting only the good advice he would have
been offered and Pwyll's hospitality.

He picked one of the older men, and one of the younger,
Manandoun and Bedivyr, and some days later Manandoun
used his wiles to gain them entrance to the fort on the white
hill where Olwen was the favored daughter of Uspathadyn.

Uspathadyn gave them hospitality and a chance to abandon the quest and keep their heads. When he spoke, the
whole of the hall shook from floor to rafter. Olwen looked
longingly at Kylhuk, and Kylhuk looked nervously at her
hands. But he smiled at her and she smiled back, blushing
and lowering her gaze.

Manandoun and Bedivyr teased Kylhuk until he silenced
them. On the table, twenty-three oiled heads, their beards
trimmed, sang mournfully of their love for Olwen.

Olwen's father stared at Kylhuk for a long time along the
length of the table. Then he said, "Of all the men who have
come here to ask for my favorite daughter, you have the
fairest face and the best manners. Why, you have not even
drawn your sword, which is quite unusual for visitors to this
household."

"Give your consent to my marriage to Olwen and my
sword will never reflect the flames of your fire, that great
fire over there, where the ox is roasting."

"Well said indeed," said Olwen's father, slapping a hand
on the table so that all the heads jumped and lost the rhythm
of their song. "The more you say to me, the more I like you.

It is a shame, then, that I must ask you for three wedding gifts. And since you will fail to get them, it is a greater disappointment that I must kill you and put your head here, on this table. But I will place you at the top of the table, where I can talk to you like a father to his battle-slaughtered son. Yes! That is how much I have come to admire you."

"I will get your wedding gifts, whatever they are, and at the wedding it will be your own head that is at the top of the table and singing, and *I* will talk to *you*—as a son to his battle-slaughtered father."

Uspathadyn roared with laughter. "By Olwen's Hands! The more you speak, the greater is my admiration for you, Kylhuk son of Kylid. I have never had so nice a man here. Your manners are impeccable. Your spirit is everything a proud father could wish for. And so it grieves me even more that you will never get the wedding presents that I insist upon, but there we are, that is that, your head will still be a comfort and joy to me and to Olwen."

"I will get the gifts, though you think otherwise, just as soon as you tell me what they are."

Olwen's father sighed. He was enjoying this company, but now business had to be done, and necks made ready. "The first gift is that you will plough and sow the great field that lies to the west of this stronghold. It is bordered by four tall stones, and there are other stones inside it. And a few mounds of earth, as well as trees in groves, and pits with swords and shields and pots—a few bones, some trinkets, other bits and pieces—nothing to concern you. The wheat that you will then grow there will make the bread for Olwen's wedding, since as her father I must supply the bread for the feast."

"Ploughing a field is a task for lesser men than me," Kylhuk said. "I will find it no hardship at all."

Olwen's father stared at his nails, each the size of a dagger. "To be done by morning. I forgot to tell you that it must be ploughed and sown by morning."

"It will be easy to do that," said Kylhuk.

"I don't think you will find it easy," said the other man.

"What else do you want me to fetch? Quickly, I must get on with the ploughing."

Olwen's father thought hard for a moment, then said, "If this marriage is to take place, there will be so many guests that I could not possibly afford to feed them all without Cerithon's hamper."

"Cerithon's hamper?"

"Yes. A small thing, made of briar and willow. Four men can carry it easily and once opened, it can feed everyone with their particular delights."

"I have never heard of it. But I will get it for you easily."

"I don't think so."

"Oh, but *I* do . . ."

"And the horn-and-silver cup of Votadinos, which will supply strong, sweet drink endlessly, and therefore save me a great deal of money. Yes, you must get that, too. Neither man will part with his treasure, though."

"They will be easy to get."

"Don't be so sure. Others have tried it."

"It will be easy to get them," Kylhuk declared. "But you must tell me where they are."

"That's a good question. They are hard to find. You must ask the houndsman, Mabonos son of Modron, who was stolen from his mother when a boy."

"And where is he?"

"I'm not sure. You should ask his cousin, Yssvyl, who lives with the Oldest Animals."

"And where are they?"

"I'm not sure, but if you can find the boar called White Tusk, you will find the hunter Othgar in close pursuit, and he will help."

"And where shall I find him?"

"I'm not sure, but the houndsman Gordub son of Eyra, will certainly know."

"And where is he?"

"Again, I'm not sure, but if you can find the Long Person, she may answer your question."

"Enough!" said Kylhuk. "We could stand here all night only to grow older by ten years. I must get to the field and plough and sow it."

"I forgot to tell you. You'll need the spotted oxen of Amathaon son of Don for that."

"I'll get them easily. Where are they to be found?"

"I'm not sure, though Caratacos the Wanderer will know."

"And where is *he*?"

"I'm not sure, but if you find—"

"Enough!" shouted Kylhuk.

"Remember your manners," Olwen's father said angrily, and Kylhuk apologized. He glanced at Olwen, who rose to her feet, her cheeks blushing, her eyes filled with love. Kylhuk stared up at her and felt the muscles in his neck straining. He tried to think of an endearment, something romantic to say to the Tall Woman, a love token.

"I'll be back," he said in his strongest voice.

"Hurry," said Olwen. "And be careful of tricks."

"Tricks? What tricks?"

"I'm not sure," she replied. "But the brother of Dillus the Bearded will know——"

"Good-*bye*!" said Kylhuk in exasperation, and with Manandoun and Bedivyr he hastened from the hall and set about his task.

He had ploughed one strip of the field when Manandoun rode up to him from the west, his face whitened with chalk, a white pennant tied to the blade of his spear. "Kylhuk! This is not a field, this is a burial ground."

"I know," said Kylhuk as he hauled on Amathaon's spotted oxen, keeping the second furrow straight.

"Those are not piles of earth, they are mounds covering the tombs of kings."

"I know," said Kylhuk. "And they are harder to flatten than I'd thought."

Now Bedivyr charged at him from the east, wheeling round nervously, white pennants of protection on shoulders, elbows, knees, ankles, and around his neck and waist.

"Kylhuk, these are not pots and bones and bits and pieces. You are disturbing the dead!"

"I know. I can hear them shouting as the iron shares cut through them and turn them over."

"Those are not rocks at the edge of the field, they are carved stones, older than time."

"I know, Bedivyr. I have seen them. I will haul them down later." He turned the oxen to begin the third furrow.

"You must leave this place alone. As you plough the field, the dead are being called back from their islands!"

"I know! Do you think I can't hear them riding toward me?"

"You are bringing terrible consequences upon yourself!" shouted Manandoun as his horse reared with sudden fright.

"I will confront those consequences later. First, I must plough this field."

"Olwen's father has tricked you!" pleaded Bedivyr.

"I *know*! And when I have finished ploughing the field, I will think what to do about it!"

They left him alone and he got on with the job. When he returned to the gates of the fort on the white hill, Kylhuk found them closed. Manandoun and Bedivyr were there. Inside, there was music, a great feast, and the sound of Olwen's grief and her father's triumphant laughter.

"You were tricked," said Manandoun.

"I know. But knowing *that* I was tricked is less of a burden than knowing *how* I was tricked."

"You should not have ploughed over the tombs in the field."

"There's more to this trick than just that," said Kylhuk, trying to think through everything that had been said in the hall earlier.

"Nevertheless, you should have stopped the ploughing."

"When I start something, I have to finish it."

Bedivyr slapped him on the shoulder. "Well spoken! Such a quality in a man is both a good thing and a bad thing!"

"Thank you," said Kylhuk.

"And on this occasion it was a bad thing," Manandoun muttered pointedly as they rode away, the angry dead in slow pursuit.

Unable to find hospitality that night, they camped in the forest.

"I have learned one thing at least from this difficult encounter," Kylhuk said as he drank from his cup.

"That you are a fool and easily deceived?" Manandoun suggested.

Kylhuk finished the cup, then wiped his lips.

"I have learned two things at least from this difficult encounter," he amended. "Manandoun has referred to one of them, and I have learned that lesson and no one will deceive me again."

"Ho-ho," said Manandoun.

"Indeed. Ho-ho. But we'll see about that. The other thing is that something has been passed on to me, some burden, and Uspathadyn is celebrating because he is a free man. He has tricked me into calling down the anger of the dead. But he has also set me the task of finding this hamper and the silver horn."

Bedivyr muttered darkly, "There is more to those gifts than meets the eye."

"There is more to the *pursuit* of those gifts than meets the eye," Kylhuk said.

And Manandoun added, "By the head on my shoulders, you are right to say that. The danger is in the pursuit of the beast, not in the beast itself! I am game for this, Kylhuk. I was born for this hunt. And may my arm fail me if I ever call you a fool again."

The two of them embraced, while Bedivyr shuffled uneasily by the fire, saying, "I have come this far and God knows, it is not a long way back to the place where I started—"

"Which god are you referring to?" asked Manandoun dryly.

"Whichever one follows me noting my deeds in combat."

"I'd noticed a certain absence of gods," Manandoun said, looking round at the night as he stoked the fire.

"I will ignore that discourtesy. My point is, I will not return to Pwyll until this man Kylhuk is free of the burden."

"Thank you!" Kylhuk said. "Manandoun . . . Bedivyr . . . My good friends! This is just the *beginning* of something!"

"Indeed!" said Manandoun.

"I have no idea what that something is," Kylhuk went on. "Except that it involves a hamper of food and a silver horn filled with drink. When it is ended, we will all three of us look back and celebrate its ending. We will *rejoice* in its ending. Whatever it might be that has ended. I cannot say fairer than that. Shall we stay together?"

"I will not leave your company by my own will," said Manandoun.

"Neither oxen nor the wain-ropes they pull will drag me away from this small band," agreed Bedivyr, "terrible though this situation is."

"Well spoken," Kylhuk said. "And my head on this: I will

not abandon either of you until Olwen's father's own head is on the end of my spear."

"That's that, then," said Manandoun. "We are all agreed. And you will certainly need a big spear for the head you propose to sever. But now we must think about what to do next. I would suggest that the three of us are not enough to take on everything that is behind us, and everything that is ahead of us."

Manandoun's counsel was wise. And besides, on the hill behind them a line of men had risen and stood watching their fire, but try how he might, Kylhuk could see no features on them, only shadow, and he knew that they were ghost-born.

He, Manandoun, and Bedivyr fell to thinking.

CHAPTER 14

A fight had started at one of the tables, a disgraceful insult to the memory of Manandoun, and Kylhuk had been increasingly aware that he should intervene on behalf of his friend.

When he reached the point in his story which signaled an end to the beginning and an anticipation of the ending, where the three of them were "falling to thinking," he stopped the narrative.

"Gwyr may feel inclined to explain what happened next," he said to me, and rose and crossed the forest glade, where the two men, naked but for kilts and metal torques on their arms, were hacking at each other with great determination, shouting insults and laughing in each other's faces. Blood had not been drawn, and would not be drawn, since among the clans that these people represented such an act would bring instant execution. But the duel was rowdy, and the watching crowd was becoming excited. Outside the taunting ring of Celts, puzzled legionaries, dour Saracens, ice-eyed Vikings, and dismayed Courteous Men kept a watchful gaze on the proceedings, but did not interfere.

Kylhuk entered the fray and the fighting stopped.

I had thought that would be that, his authority stamped on the squabble, but he was not in a good mood and he snatched the sword from one man and beat him unconscious with it (without drawing blood).

The other man backed away, then walked stiffly through the gates in the temporary palisade. I never saw him again, and suspect that an act of contrition had occurred that had left him for the forest to reclaim.

Gwyr said, "You have heard the first part of the story and now have the general idea. Sometimes, when Kylhuk recounts his tale, I wonder about Olwen, that poor Tall Woman who was so attracted to the feisty youth. Is she still waiting? Does she know how fat her beloved has become?" He grinned, then went on. "Truthfully, Kylhuk was so afraid of her he would never have completed the tasks, those simple tasks as he thought of them. He would have found some way to delay the ending of the adventure. But as you have heard, Kylhuk's quest is a harder task than anyone would have thought. We seek the hamper, we seek the horn, but those were just Uspathadyn's way of tricking Kylhuk into adopting something very dangerous, which Uspathadyn had sworn to do and was unable to do, despite the consequence of his failure."

"What consequence?" I asked, disliking the word.

"A rather final one," said Gwyr pointedly, "and with no prospect of an Island at the end of it." He meant death without the Otherworld. Then more brightly, "But Kylhuk will achieve the task, now that he has you."

"So I'm to be tricked, too. . . ."

"In one way, you have been tricked already, but Kylhuk is a different man to Uspathadyn, and if you choose to abandon him, he will let you go. But without you, the great task he is sworn to accomplish will never be accomplished."

"Because I am marked as *slathan*," I said, realizing that Kylhuk had still not told me its meaning.

"Yes. Whatever it is, that term he uses and will not explain."

"Gwyr, I fear that word more than I fear Kylhuk himself, or this quest that he has drawn me into."

"Well said; bravely admitted," Gwyr said with great affection. "And as long as there is a head on my shoulders and a foot on the end of each of my legs, I will stay close to you and make sure there is no further trickery. But my feeling is, it is some magic, or a certain knowledge or memory that you possess that Kylhuk needs."

"What is the task, Gwyr? Has he told you, now that Manandoun is dead?"

"Yes. But only a handful of us must know. We will accompany Kylhuk himself. We have been chosen for our various skills."

"And what exactly are we to do?"

"We are to undertake a rescue. We are to attempt to rescue Mabon, who is imprisoned at the very gates of the Underworld, in a place that is savagely defended. Mabon! Son of Modron! I heard about him as a child and just to say his name makes my hair stand on end and my skin crawl. This is a *terrible* task. But that said, you must believe me, Christian, this rescue—which many have attempted, but none with success—will have a wonderful consequence for each man and woman who takes part in it. Kylhuk is undertaking a great task, perhaps the greatest of them all. No one is born who doesn't soon hear about and grieve for the cruel way Mabon was entombed alive."

"Entombed alive?" I repeated emptily. Why did that sound so familiar? Echoes of Merlin from my childhood's reading!

"What happened after Kylhuk and his two companions had ploughed the field and unleashed the dead?" I asked.

"A good question, Christian, well asked—"

"Get on with it, Gwyr," I snapped impatiently.

He was taken aback. "Your first discourtesy. I'm surprised by that. However, to continue:

"Manandoun advised that before they did anything at all they should try to understand precisely what had happened, and the first task was to work out precisely what tasks had been set them by Uspathadyn. Although the field had been ploughed, the whole journey to fetch Cerithon's hamper and the drink horn of Votadinos involved a total of thirty-six individual deeds, and buried among them was the Great Deed, the rescue of Mabon from his terrible prison.

"Most of the tasks were simple. *Tall Men* had to be killed for their *whiskers* for use as *leashes* for great *hounds* to run with great *horses* to be ridden in great *hunts* on enchanted *saddles* that only *dead men* could fashion. . . ."

He paused for breath and I took a chance and said, "The whiskers of giants? It sounds ludicrous."

"I agree," he said, shaking his head. "You are not the first to comment on it. But nothing will work without them."

He went on. "Kylhuk and the others worked steadily through the list, finding some of the tasks hard and others easy. But everything no matter how simple, had a *consequence.*"

"Consequences," I said bitterly. "Yes. This is certainly turning into a game of consequences."

Gwyr stared at me, thinking about my words, perhaps, and their modern allusion. Then he nodded abruptly. "Indeed. When Kylhuk caught the hound, he released the hounds of *hell,* which now follow behind us! And wherever the hounds run, they summon the ghost-born of their kind so that it is not one pack of hounds that pursues us, but hundreds, a legion of them, and all slavering, all with great eyes—"

"Yes, yes," I said. "I get the picture. Get on with it, Gwyr."

He raised his eyebrows. "Your *second* discourtesy. You are not quite the man I thought you were. However, to continue:

"When the hamper of Cerithon is finally taken and opened— Yes, I see you are surprised by the thought of this quest. But the hamper is said to be of endless capacity, so it seems quite reasonable for Kylhuk and the rest of us to eat our fill before transporting it to Uspathadyn—when the hamper is finally opened, the ghost of every man and every woman and every child and every dog that has fed from that hamper will rise from the earth and come in pursuit. This has already happened with the silver horn of Votadinos, which Kylhuk found last summer. It was a worse experience than could be imagined, because the ghosts were drunk, and a drunken ghost is less reasonable even than a drunken man— they are argumentative and confused—and I feel that you are experiencing this feeling even now, even as I talk to you, answering the question that you put to me—"

"Get on with it, Gwyr!"

"Three! Three discourtesies!" He looked me steadily in the eye. "I feel a fight is coming on."

"I will not fight with you."

"Will you not? We'll see. But to continue," he said warily:

"One of the tasks within the task was to hunt the great boar that had sired the boar that gave Kylhuk his name . . ."

"Twrch Trwyth," I said.

"Indeed. And to hunt Twrch Trwyth, a huntsman was needed, and this was Kuwyn son of Nodons. Kuwyn was a young man in whom were imprisoned the thousand ghosts who had first ventured into the Underworld. These ghosts had ruled the shadows and the islands of the Underworld from the beginning of time. But one day their time was up and they were routed and cast out, to be passed from one man to another among the living, any man who had the strength to contain them—there are many stories to do with this, I can assure you—"

"I have no doubt about it. Even a maggot in this Legion has its story it seems."

"Four! Four discourtesies!" Gwyr looked delighted. "My sword hand is twitching! Your white throat looks so exposed! But to continue:

"When Kylhuk found Kuwyn, the demons were released from him. Kylhuk was not a fit man to accept them, however, so there they are, behind us, with the dogs, the risen dead, the sons of Kyrdu, and all the rest, a great army of shadows and evil that presses close to us and is kept at bay only by the forces that Kylhuk, Manandoun, and Bedivyr sensibly began to muster around them as they rode through the wilderness of woodland, river, and rocky crag, shortly after that moment when they had fallen to thinking, that moment Kylhuk told you about."

"And how did they muster those forces?"

"A very good question, very well asked . . ."

Gwyr waited for my response, but I kept a prudent silence.

He frowned and went on. "He could not go back to Lord Pwyll, though Pwyll, being the man he was, would not have hesitated to help. But the consequence to Kylhuk would have been too great in terms of the repayment of the favor. This has all to do with courtesy and honor, as I believe you are beginning to understand in your simple way. . . ."

Gwyr waited for my response, but I kept a prudent silence.

He frowned and went on. "There was only one other stronghold with sufficient brawn to supply Kylhuk's needs— an army of swordsmen and spearmen, charioteers and horsemen, runners and jumpers, madmen and brutes, strategists and the far-sighted, those who are sound in hearing and vision, smellers, sniffers, and frighteners of the shadows that occupy this great wilderness, these old trees, these timeless woodlands, and that stronghold was held by . . ."

I leaned toward him questioningly, as courteous as I could possibly be.

He leaned toward me and concluded: "Uther."

"Uther?"

"Uther!"

"Arthur's father?"

"The father of all the Arthurs. Uther himself."

"Arthur's father, Uther. No other?"

"No other. Only Uther."

"Uther and his little Arthurs."

"Yes. Are you mocking me?"

"I'm joking with you. It's not the same thing."

But unfortunately, to Gwyr it was.

As he stood, he struck. When I had regained consciousness, it was to the awareness that my lower incisors were loose and my mouth was full of blood. Gwyr stood over me, looking anxious. Kylhuk was by me, holding out a hand, which I accepted. I was hauled to my feet.

Looking around, I realized that the whole of the host, that feasting host, those who had come to say good-bye to Manandoun, were gathered around in a ring. I took silent comfort from Gwyr's earlier information that at the funeral of a friend, blood should never be drawn in any personal combat. I resolved not to let Kylhuk see that blood was flowing from my battered gums. It might be the worse for Gwyr.

"Are you ready for the fight?" asked Kylhuk, and I mumbled: "What fight is that?"

"Gwyr has counted it against himself that he struck you in anger, and therefore you may have the first blow."

I mumbled through my swelling jaw something further to the effect that I was sorry, very, *very* sorry for any insult that might have been perpetrated on a man whom I needed in my life like air itself, and that I was simply under the influence of strong drink and not in control of the lively horse called "impatience" that was currently bucking below me.

Kylhuk laughed.

"Well said, Christian! Well said indeed . . . Whatever it was you said," he added as an afterthought. "But I have decided that Manandoun would want to see this fight, and would want to see a head taken, since the two men who have decided to fight during his long ride to the Island he has chosen are such fascinating men, and each with different skills and different *tricks*"—he looked at me as he said this. A very pointed comment!—"tricks which can be tested one against the other."

"Please don't ask me to fight," I said, bitterly regretting my earlier conversation with Gwyr, or had it been Manandoun, about my combat skills.

Kylhuk ignored me. "I am relaxing all rules of courtesy and hospitality in order for you to have this fight which I know is important to you both, though I have changed my mind and will not allow a head to be taken, nor more blood to be drawn."

"Thank you."

"But I expect this matter to be resolved, and at the end of it, I will expect to have two friends who are still friends with each other, even though their bones may be broken and parts of their bodies twisted into strange shapes."

"By Olwen's hands, I hope that does not happen," I said, and Kylhuk went white, giving me a look that combined alarm with unwelcome memory. He stepped up close to me.

"That is a good thing you say," he said softly. "I had forgotten about Olwen's hands in the excitement of seeing the two of you about to fight."

"So the fight is off?" I asked hopefully.

Gwyr was waiting impatiently, stripped naked, all weaponry out of reach. "Hurry," he said to Kylhuk. "I want to get at him."

"That is a discourtesy you do to me, asking me to hurry!"

Gwyr fell silent.

Kylhuk scratched at his beard as he stared at me, then said, even as he was thinking, "Why are you still wearing your weapons? Take them off."

I unbuckled the belt which held my sword. But the further look he gave me made me realize that I was expected to strip naked, and I performed this task with as much indifference as I could muster, which was not very much at all, since Guiwenneth and Issabeau were watching from the outer circle.

Guiwenneth smiled at me. Issabeau whispered in her ear. Guiwenneth giggled. I felt humiliated and let my stomach relax. Guiwenneth watched me with affection.

"There," said Kylhuk. "We are ready for the fight. But I still have to decide on the rules."

I spoke quickly. "Knowing Manandoun for the short time that I did, I would nevertheless say that he would want us to fight only with our feet."

Kylhuk stared at me in bemusement. Gwyr frowned.

Kylhuk asked, "Why would he want to see that?"

I thought very fast. Very fast indeed. "Because of Cryfcad his mare, his great horse, that great beast that is now in my charge and which has taken to me gladly though with sadness, but will allow me to ride her. She is a feisty creature, and her kick can disable four men, one behind the other. I'm sure Manandoun would want us to use only our feet. It would amuse him."

"I am impressed with this explanation," Kylhuk said, and it was Gwyr's turn to look shocked.

"Go to it," said the overlord, and slapped his hands together.

Gwyr approached me. I summoned all my strength, remembered the training in unarmed combat I had been given in '42, and kicked out to disable him when he was least expecting it. He went down, stunned, conscious, and in pain.

"I have never seen that done before," Kylhuk said thoughtfully as he stared down at Gwyr's groaning figure.

"It is not often that I have done it," I said in triumph.

I should more truthfully have said, "I've never seen it done before either. And I've certainly never done it, except to a straw-filled dummy."

So that was that, and Gwyr and I became friends again, and everything went on as if nothing had happened, except that afterward he nicknamed me "Quick Foot."

I would never come to a full understanding of the way nicknames were used in Legion, those at least among Kylhuk's Celtic gathering. For example:

"Carried a King," "Fought in the River," and "Survived Gae Bolga" had all done these things.

"Leapt over Trees," "Savaged the Boar," and "Makes Women Sing" were named so because the opposite of these events had happened.

"Face of Stone" was a woman who never looked at the man who had let her down. "Face of Shadow" was the man who had slighted her. "Face of Moon" was a woman who aspired to greater things. "Face of Horn" was a woman who had passed her prime, but would not accept the fact. "Spear of Horn" was a man with the same reluctance to accept his age, the reference to horn being to "the truth that is there for all to see."

(Horn for truth, ivory for the lie. If I noted these things at the time, I let them pass!)

Everyone had many nicknames and by those nicknames you could summarize an individual. If you were a man, you were named by your children, by your wife, by your parents, and your wife's parents. Also, by your closest friends, by the chief, by the chief's first wife, and by the druid and any tale-teller who might be passing.

Respect for an individual was often reflected in the balance of courteous nicknames ("Reliable Spear") to discourteous ones ("Stabs His Own Foot"). If the balance was unfavorable, a combat could be arranged to win back an unfavorable nickname and convert it to a favorable one. No nickname ever stuck for long and new ones were adopted constantly. Everyone seemed to be attuned to these changes. Indeed, to refer to someone with a nickname that was out of date was an insult.

After death, one nickname would linger and would come to reflect the person, and around this particular name the "bright story" would be told, which is to say, the story of that person's life. "Wise Counsel" for Manandoun, for example. ("Thinner than the Willow" for Kylhuk? I wondered idly.)

But in short, it was best to think of people as they had been named at birth, although this might cause problems, since if a nickname was used in a conversation about a third party, and you failed to recognize that party, the man or woman who was doing the talking could accuse you of discourtesy.

In short, the less said about anything the better. . . .

A few minutes after our brief combat, however, Gwyr had relaxed again, taken a drink, and concluded his summary of the formation of Kylhuk's Legion.

During the years following that first encounter with Uspathadyn, Kylhuk completed all but a few of the tasks set him by Olwen's father, but had turned Legion into an industry, accumulating and accomplishing the quests set to others, and exacting a very heavy fee, though always inheriting the consequences. Bedivyr had died because of one such screeching Nemesis. Legion itself had become dedicated to one thing: finding the Long Person; opening the gate to the rescue.

Early on, he had negotiated with Uther, and Uther had supplied horsemen, charioteers, and runners, all well trained and eager for adventure, and they had been a great help in the beginning. But none of Uther's knights could resist undertaking their own quests whenever the opportunity arose, and more often than not the tragic or sinister consequences of their actions came to burden Kylhuk.

Uther's sons—the Three Arthurs, all of them identical—were particularly difficult to handle. They had been born fighting, Gwyr told me, little fists in faces, tiny feet in mouths, and it had taken nearly a week for the midwife to separate them and stop the squabble.

Because Uther had prepared only one name for his son, only one child ever spoke at any one time. They passed a small sword between them to indicate whose turn it was to voice his opinions on this or that, usually a criticism of their father, or an expression of love for their father's sorceress, whom he had housed in a cave below the hill.

As they grew up, the Three Arthurs rode together to the far North and South of the land and gained a reputation for great actions, great battles, and great conquests. They joined Kylhuk's legion for a few years, then one day had a fierce argument with each other and rode off in different directions. But because they were identical, their exploits far and wide became known as the exploits of one man only, and Arthur's name became associated with magical appearances and the ability to ride the length and breadth of Albion in a single night.

Kylhuk had been glad to see the back of them. I was fascinated, but Gwyr was unforthcoming on any further details of this unlikely legend.

By this time, Legion was already like a great whale, nosing through the ocean of the forest, sensing for danger ahead, trailing behind it a great wake of angry ghosts, the armored dead, and vengeful sanctuary spirits. Riding among these, using the powers and insights of this spectral army, came Eletherion and his brothers, Kyrdu's sons, seeking the entrance to the Underworld, to begin a course of plunder and outrage in the caverns of the earth that, according to legend, would change the earth itself!

Kylhuk tried to shake them off, but the Sons of Kyrdu were jackals that had found the scent of prey. They stalked around the marching garrison, attacking at the front, sometimes at the flanks, sometimes from the rear, killing and taunting, holding on to Kylhuk with teeth of bronze, because they had seen that Kylhuk's quest contained the answer to their own!

The *Underworld*.

Gwyr used the word deliberately where usually he expressed the idea as "Otherworld." He seemed unhappy at the thought of a place so dark and dismal. Being Celtic, his own afterlife would be an Island of his choice, endless hunting, endless pleasure, occasional returns to the world of his birth to check on the behavior of his family. The gloomy, ghastly caverns of Hades were not at all to his liking, and he was confident that only Greeks, Romans, and the Sons of Mil would go there.

I intuited that Gwyr had little time for Greeks, Romans, and the Sons of Mil.

But his mention of the Underworld brought back thoughts of my mother, and the strange thing Elidyr had said to me. *Her death was not as you think.* I imagined her there, in the dark caverns, walking with the other shades.

And if the rescue of Mabon could unlock the gate to that Underworld . . . what chance, I wondered, of bringing her out of the Valley of the Crow, back into the light?

Was that what Gwyr had meant by "the rescue of Mabon will have wonderful consequences for each man and woman who participates"?

Despite everything I had come to know, I chose to believe so.

CHAPTER 15

I had paid my visit to Kylhuk, and my respects to Manan-doun. I had fought with a man whom I regarded as a friend, and agreed to a fast that I had no intention of keeping. I had become almost anxious at the realization that my father was abroad in this wilderness, and melancholy at memories of my mother, dizzy with the thought that she might be "rescued." I might then understand what she had said that day, when she had dangled from the tree.

At the moment, however, I wanted to be with Guiwenneth. I needed her. I imagined she needed me as well.

I found her by the narrow river, half a mile from the center of the camp where the bank was clear. Her feet were in the water and she was leaning back on her elbows, staring at the night sky. Issabeau sat beside her, idly flicking at the stream with her carved staff.

As I approached, Someone rose from where he had been keeping watch and greeted me softly, clearly glad to see me.

"How is she?"

"Doleful," he replied. "But the tears have dried. And she will be pleased to see you."

"And how are you?"

"Hungry. But not for Kylhuk's plums and water."

"There's meat as well."

"I'm glad to hear it. But I'm not interested in eating, now."

He stood before me, an imposing figure, gently stroking the luxurious mustaches that framed his mouth. He was a man scarcely a year older than myself, and yet he carried weight and authority, from the steady gaze to the careful thinking, to the immaculate state of his garb—a simple kilt of green cloth, an open deerskin shirt, skin boots tied around his calves with twisted gut . . . and his sword, slung from a shoulder belt, its ivory pommel carved to suggest a bull.

He said, "You have paid a great respect to a man you didn't know."

"Manandoun? I did as I was told to do."

"Nevertheless, you showed a great respect."

"I feel as if I know him without ever having known him. I have a picture of him. It would have been nice to have known him better."

Someone touched his right hand to his breast, a gesture of affirmation. But he said, "Manandoun's death is terrible for us all. He was close to Kylhuk. He kept Kylhuk in hand. Without Manandoun, Legion is in a greater peril than even Issabeau suspects."

He had pronounced "peril" in the way of the French-woman. And it was clear that Manandoun had been a con-trolling influence on Kylhuk, and that Someone—perhaps *everyone*—now feared Kylhuk's behavior.

"Shall we send for Elidyr? The guide?"

"Elidyr has gone," the Celt said bluntly.

"Do I have a role in this?"

"We all have a role in this."

Someone looked away, frowning. "If I could just find my name—if I could just understand the taunting words of the hawk. It sits on my chest while I sleep, pecking at me, and its demands are strange and frightening. Until I understand them . . ."

Again, that bright, hard stare at me. "Until then, Christ-ian—you must stay close to Gwyr, and think hard after everything you say or do with Kylhuk."

"He is a fat man—" I began to say, but the Celt cut across me.

"He is no such thing. Neither fat, nor a man, in my opinion. He has played a fine game with you. Don't always believe what your eyes tell you. And if I could explain more, then I would, but like you, I am a stranger in this Legion. But enough of that for the moment. Come and be with Guiwenneth. She's been waiting for you."

We walked to the river. Issabeau looked up at me, then at the Celt. She reached out a hand and Someone took it, helping her stand. Issabeau looked at him and smiled, then said to me, "*Bonzoire,*" before she and Someone walked away.

I sat down on the damp grass by Guiwenneth and put my arm around her. She nestled into me and sighed.

"So that is that," she said, presumably meaning the departure of Manandoun.

"So that is that," I agreed.

"I know he will be happy. But I shall miss him so much."

"I know you will. But as you once held on to him, please now hold on to me. I am not wise, and I am not old, and my beard itches rather than grows, and his horse tolerates me, but only just. But I love you; I know it. It's a true feeling, Guiwenneth. Whatever happens to you, I want to be a part of it."

She turned to me, put a hand on my cheek, and urged me closer. Her lips on mine were sweet and soft. The kiss deepened. She sighed suddenly and lay back, her grip becoming firmer on my hair.

I sighed, too. For all my inexperience, my hands found her, and my mouth found her, and nothing happened that needed to be thought about; everything that happened by that river happened as if we had known it all our lives.

A splash, a laugh, and the sound of "Hoosh!" made us sit up suddenly, drawing Guiwenneth's cloak around our naked bodies to block the chill of the night air.

"What was that?" I asked.

She looked at me delightedly. There was mischief in that glance.

"Quickly," she said, and pulled on her clothes, shaking the grass from her long, auburn hair. Silencing my chatter with a finger to my lips, she led the way along the river, to where the stream widened and formed a pool.

From the cover of the underbrush we watched Issabeau and Someone son of Somebody swim lazily together, he on his back, she across his belly and between his legs, arms outstretched to propel them forward. They circled the pool slowly, whispering together, their pale bodies almost translucent above and below the water.

Guiwenneth tossed a small stone into the middle of the pool. Issabeau and Someone glanced toward us, then returned to their leisurely swim, eyes only for each other, laughing together.

"Come away," I said, suddenly embarrassed. "This is none of our business."

"I knew it would happen," Guiwenneth said as we walked hand in hand through the wood, back toward the Keep. "There is something that connects them. I could tell that from the moment they were recruited to the Forlorn Hope. Anyone could tell it who had half an eye for love."

"I thought she was with the Saracen," I said. "They were together when I first met them."

"No. They shared a similar magic. They were powerful together. But Abandagora had no heart for love."

Her voice was strange and I looked at Guiwenneth as we walked.

"*Had* no heart for love?"

"Has no heart at all, now," she said quickly. "Eletherion took it in that same skirmish when he took the life of Manandoun."

CHAPTER 16

And so I began my long march with Legion, a journey of many weeks, many months. I find it hard to be more precise than that. The column, as it progressed, shifted so often through time, and into so many different seasons, that even day and night became meaningless. And Kylhuk worked me hard at the various stations throughout the marching garrison, sending me on many night watches and occasionally on wild rides outside the forest wall.

He kept me close to Guiwenneth, however, and I was grateful for that. Her company was a comfort and a delight, and the mischievous sense of humor a great relief among this army of mostly dour and silent adventurers.

Only on two occasions did I come close to disaster. The first was one summer's day, when we finally discovered Cerithon's hamper!

Kylhuk had abandoned that particular task the moment he realized it was just part of Uspathadyn's trick to make him search for Mabon. But there had always been a grumble of opinion that the hamper should still be sought since it promised such a feast, and very often the food in Legion was worse than "dog's paw and baked fur," as Issabeau so delicately put it. (She liked fine food, it was clear, and it was always very difficult sitting near her at mealtimes since she spent the time sighing with despair and sulking heavily as she contemplated whatever was on offer.)

So when the Forlorn Hope brought back the fattest child I have ever seen, a boy so rotund that he could have been rolled into camp like a beer barrel, his skin covered with rashes, stings, and spots, a child who stank of honey and whose mouth and fingers were so sticky with the same that no matter how hard we tried, we could not remove the dead leaves and grass from his hands, there was a sudden air of excitement among Legion's uncouth hordes. The word had gone round that this boy had been "feeding at the hamper."

"There is a slight problem," said the Carthaginian woman, Dido, who had been given charge of the boy.

"And what problem is that?" Kylhuk asked irritably.

"The hamper is protected by a force of nature."

"Then it will find itself assaulted by a force of *Kylhuk*!" said the grizzled man with a grin at me.

"The force consists of flying stingers."

"So does mine!"

Without further discussion, our small band rode through the forest wall for a first look, the sound of appetites being whetted ringing in our ears. But as we left Legion, a new sound struck us: the hum of bees, a buzz that rose in volume along with the black cloud that we could see flowing toward us as we entered the true wood.

The swarm was on us in a moment, wasps, bees, and giant hornets smashing into our faces, crawling through our hair, pouring through the gaps in our clothing to sting and die, or sting and sting again.

"Get the bee-boy!" Kylhuk shrieked in pain, using his cloak to sweep the air around him. "Find him! Bring him! The *bee-boy*!"

Guiwenneth returned quickly to safety, her flowing hair seething with these flying stingers. The rest of us flung ourselves to the ground, covered our heads and bodies and rolled as best we could to squash the invading insects. How long this agony lasted I can't remember. It seemed forever.

Then, suddenly, the swarm detached from us and the horses became calmer. The air was still electric with the buzzing of a billion wings.

The bee-boy had come, I realized, a tiny lad from prehistoric Crete, a country which had been famous for its honey from a time long before even the jarag had stalked his Mesolithic shores. In his kilt and loose shirt, the bee-boy was running in a zigzagging, circling dance, imitating the bees that he sought to control. Soon, the black swarm rose into a funnel, a whirlpool of wind and motion, widening around the dancing boy. We flung ourselves close to him, finding merciful shelter in the stillness at the eye of this storm, and the boy led us to the distant mound of seething black and yellow.

As we approached this restless hill, we stepped among seated groups of children, all of them as bloated as the boy who been brought to the camp, all of them encased in glistening honey, all of them red raw with stings. As the bee-boy danced up to the mound, the crawling mass of insects rose in a single movement to join the swirling vortex around us. Beneath the thick and sluggish flow of honey, the vague shape of a wicker hamper could be seen. As the honey rose and spread like lava, so it carried flat, round loaves of bread, which lay encrusted all around, a landscape of crystalline, stone wheels.

"Well, well," said Kylhuk irritably. "And not a haunch of meat in sight."

Gwyr talked to one of the children and came back to us, chuckling and shaking his head.

"Uspathadyn tried to play a second fine trick on you."

"Did he, indeed."

"Indeed, he did. It seems that Cerithon was not a king at all, but a royal child."

"I can hardly bear to listen further."

"One day this child distracted two bears from their attack on an old man, who turned out to be Merlin."

"I might have known it."

"Merlin granted Cerithon a wish and the boy, being a greedy lad, asked for an ever-filling picnic hamper. And Merlin asked what he would like in the hamper. And Cerithon said, Nothing more than bread and honey! Which is what he got."

"Children!" Kylhuk muttered, severely disgruntled. I expect he was thinking of his reception when he returned to Legion.

"Cerithon himself lies in the center of the hamper," Gwyr went on. "Long dead, and preserved in the honey he so coveted."

"Good," said Kylhuk. "It's where he deserves to be."

"These children are visiting from their dreams, from many lands, since the story of the hamper is one of their great delights."

Kylhuk looked around him thoughtfully. Then he reflected out loud that because these dream visitors looked so much like pigs themselves, and were already fattened, perhaps we might pacify the hungry mouths of Legion by—?

He stopped in this reflection when he realized we were all looking at him in horror.

A few weeks after I had joined the column, Kylhuk attached me to a knight called Escrivaune, armored as his *squire*, carrying his shield (a black gryphon), battle spears, and axe. Sir Escrivaune had assumed the appearance of a questing knight called Mordalac and was returning to a castle called Brezonfleche where Mordalac's fair lady waited for him. Escrivaune, on Mordalac's behalf, had killed the son of a giant who was terrorizing the castle, and now carried the giant's gold-embroidered sword belt, an item of clothing so heavy it needed two packhorses to transport it.

The belt itself was of no use to Kylhuk, but the terms agreed on with the cowardly knight included a fourth of Mordalac's dowry, and a hundred head of cattle, which Mordalac had promised from his own estates.

Unfortunately for Sir Mordalac, he had become drunk after Escrivaune's triumph in his place and indiscreetly revealed that he had no estates of his own and was simply a "chancer," living by the lie, the worst sort of trickster, since their guile was usually so successful.

Furious at the deceit, Kylhuk had challenged the knight and the challenge had been haughtily accepted. I counseled against such a combat—full metal jacket against a torque around the neck?—and Kylhuk squeezed my nose between thumb and forefinger, shaking his head.

"What do *you* know about it? Stay out of my business!"

He then stripped naked but for his blue battle kirtle and the bronze necklet, selected a narrow, leaf-shaped bronze sword only twenty-four inches long, and stood in the middle of a clearing, arms crossed, sword resting lightly on his left shoulder.

Mordalac, mailed and helmeted, had ridden down on Kylhuk with a pennanted lance, but at the last moment, Kylhuk glanced at the horse, which shied with fright and threw its rider.

Kylhuk helped Mordalac to his feet and gave him time to draw his sword, a four-foot-long, half-foot-wide, double-edged steel weapon of tremendous weight.

Nevertheless, Mordalac swung it with such speed that Kylhuk yelped with shock and had to dance quickly to one side. He had to leap four feet vertically as the sword sliced horizontally in a continuation of the first movement, then duck almost double as the blade flashed back in a blur.

"You're better than I thought," Kylhuk said, as again the broadsword swept through the air like a samurai's blade, skinning him, shaving his beard, pricking the end of his nose. "By the hands of that woman! You've been trained well!"

The silent knight came grimly forward, cutting swiftly. Kylhuk somersaulted over the blade and howled like a hound when a return blow bit deeply into his right buttock. Hand up his kilt to hold the wound closed, he danced backward, the bronze sword held limply before him.

"Even your horse is well trained!" he shouted in astonishment. "Here he comes!"

The knight drew back, glanced round (his horse was standing silently at the edge of the clearing), then looked back, staggering slightly before leaning heavily on his sword.

Kylhuk stood quietly before him, arms folded, the blood-stained leaf blade resting on his shoulder again.

"In case you're not aware of it," he said, "I've just cut your throat."

Sir Mordalac swayed twice, then fell forward with a rattling of chain mail and a throaty gurgling of blood.

Kylhuk knelt on one knee beside him. "Though I called you coward, you were a finer fighter than I'd realized, and the next few painful days in the saddle will keep me constantly reminded of the fact. Perhaps there were unspoken reasons why you asked Escrivaune to double for you. It's my loss, I realize, to have killed you, Mordalac. The truth is, I could never have trusted you."

Then, clutching his bloody backside, he left the arena, returning the sword to its owner, who made an immediate gift of it to Kylhuk.

Kylhuk accepted gratefully.

But a certain deal had been struck with Mordalac to do with the Lady of Castle Brezonfleche, and Kylhuk, being the man he was, felt obliged to honor that Cherished Lady's request. Mordalac had been a chancer, but she would survive a broken heart better if she felt her suitor had died nobly, for a noble cause, rather than ignominiously because he was a cheat.

It was a weakness in Kylhuk that he cared for this sort of chivalry, the sort that existed to diminish the hurt in people, rather than to celebrate the honor expressed to them. Which is why he had formed the Marrying Men, a band of stalwarts combined into knight and shapechanger, brute force and magic, to which I had just been assigned.

I had wanted Issabeau as our shapechanger, but Kylhuk had sent her to another part of Legion, to learn more about Mabon. The jarag would have done just as well for that, but Kylhuk had other plans for him, too. So Sir Escrivaune and myself rode through time and the forest to the Castle Brezonfleche in the protective company of that same ethereal woman who had greeted me on my first encounter with Legion, a silent figure, timeless, exquisite, somehow more elemental than human. She went ahead of us with instructions to leave a strip of rag, tied to a tree, on the path that led to the gorge where the castle had been built.

White cloth for safe progress; green for danger.

The castle seemed almost to be growing out of the depths of the gorge, tall, thin towers reaching from the dense forest below, rising high against the craggy, tree-strewn cliffs, their gray, weathered walls pierced by tiny windows. Flocks of crows circled the gray-slate, conical turrets. Mist hung halfway down, clouds too tired to rise higher. From far below came the sound of wind and the creaking of wooden gates and stretched ropes. Occasionally, as we listened hard, we could hear the sounds of dogs and horses.

"It looks safe enough to me," said Escrivaune unconvincingly. "It's a steep path down, though."

We dismounted and led the horses. Halfway down, winding around the chasm toward the distant bridge across the river, we encountered a green rag tied to a tree, its edge cut by a knife in a significant pattern.

Escrivaune sniffed hard. "Have you noticed?"

"Have I noticed what?"

"No wood smoke. No fires. No welcome."

I looked at the green rag, at the discreet cuts that had been made in it. I struggled to remember my lessons in cypher from Kylhuk's sorcerers, and realized that I had become bewildered rather than enlightened during those long, concentrated sessions. But I was fairly confident as I articulated aloud each of the shapes of the jagged divides in the simple cloth, and summarized finally what the cuts implied: "All not as seems."

"All is not as it seems," Escrivaune repeated, then looked at me quizzically. "Meaning what, exactly?"

"Things are different to the way we look at them," I hazarded. Adding, "Don't trust your eyes. I'll not trust mine. Trickery is afoot. Beware!"

He scratched his jaw, tugged on the bridle of his charger, stared into the space between us and the magnificent and imposing stone turrets. "Trickery?"

"Trickery!"

"Eyes untrustworthy."

"Don't trust your eyes."

"Beware, you say."

"Be *very* aware. Trickery. Danger. It's all here." I waved the green cloth.

"Seems safe enough to me," said Escrivaune.

"They'd want you to think that."

He glanced at me blankly. "*Who* would want me to think that?"

"The people doing the tricking. The inhabitants of the castle." I waved the cut, green cloth again, but Escrivaune simply frowned as he surveyed the castle.

"But I can see nothing wrong. Only the absence of wood smoke from the fires you might expect to be burning in this season. They must be a hardy lot. . . . I hope they have a fire for *us*."

"Where's our guide?" I asked nervously, and as if in answer to a prayer, she appeared suddenly, startlingly, misty and wan of face, stepping between trees.

Sir Escrivaune took the green rag from my hand and waved it. "How dangerous is it?"

She said, "I can't tell. But I can tell you this. That half the castle is overgrown with red and yellow briar-rose. The other half is rotting below black ivy. It is a desperate place. Its corridors are alive with snakes. Dogs are howling from the ivy towers. I can see dead women's faces in the towers of rose. There is the stink of corpses, the stench of moon's blood, the sweat of fear, the bristling tension of treachery."

"It might be wise to be on our guard, then," Escrivaune said thoughtfully.

I looked at the castle and saw only the stone, the wood, the windows, the drifting mist and circling carrion birds . . . and felt such a sense of ruination and desertion that I was inclined to think this was an abandoned place, all human life long since departed, only wist-hounds, scald-crows, and rats left to scour and haunt its passages and chambers.

"Which part is in the rose?" Sir Escrivaune asked.

"The main hall. And by the entrance gate, by the bridge over the river."

He looked at me. "We'll make the transaction there. Don't be tempted into the inner court."

"I'll be sure not to," I said, but since I could see nothing of the flower and ivy that was enveloping the castle, it was hard to know where safety ended and danger began.

Escrivaune was in control, a proud knight, proudly displaying. His beard was cut like Mordalac's and dyed black (Sir Escrivaune was an older man, quite grizzled, but still lean and lithe and full of passion, with all the charm and power that goes with age and experience, though sadly lacking in common sense) and had been treated with simple cosmetics to give him the look of the knight for whom he would substitute.

Magic—the "altering of looks"—was all very well, but it was an extravagant use of resources when dyes and dress and imitation could accomplish the same end! And anyway, Sir Escrivaune would not be expected to sleep with the Cherished Lady for more than a week, and in his own words, "She'll not have time to take breath in that week! As long as my back holds out! So I don't expect to be tested on my nature or my honor!"

"You don't think she'll want to wait for a wedding, then . . . ?"

His quick glance in my direction suggested that he was not happy with my observation. But he said nothing.

"And her father?" I persevered.

"What about her father?" he grumbled as we slipped and slid down the steep, wet track, descending the valley walls.

"I imagine he'll want to entertain you. To talk to you. To learn your intentions. Is he going to be happy with your immediate and no doubt vigorous—*congress*—with his daughter?"

"Congress?"

"Intercourse!"

"Conversation?"

"*Lovemaking!*"

"Sweet words? I only have a week!"

"You know what I mean, Sir Escrivaune! You know very well what I mean! Carnal lust!"

"Mind your manners! Is my shield polished?"

His comment confused me. He repeated it. "Is my *shield* polished?"

"It is."

"Then polish it again."

"I will. But the question won't go away."

"I don't feel inclined to answer your question. Polish my shield!"

"I'm leading the horses. I can't lead and polish at the same time."

"Then just lead the horses. Stop talking about her father."

"I will. But the question won't go away. And think as well of her *mother*! What about her mother?"

He turned on me furiously.

"My task is a simple one, Christian! Do you understand me? Simple! I enter the castle. I become that *slit-necked* chancer whose quest I accomplished, that Beloved Knight, that *Mordalac* for seven days and seven nights. My armor shines! I drink, I eat, I laugh, I *service*!"

"Not in your armor . . ."

"Of course not in my armor! And at the end of the seven days and seven nights, my squire brings me news of a challenge! Don't forget *that* part of the plan! *Squire!* I leave full of bravado, and I do not return! I have been defeated in fair combat. The *slit-neck's* helmet and sword are returned to the grieving Gracious Lady. In due time, when the grieving is over, she finds comfort and consolation on her back with someone else! In his armor or out of it! In that same time, I am getting on with my own life! *Don't condemn me,* slathan *of Kylhuk!*"

"Sorry. I'll shut up, now."

"Polish my shield."

"I'm leading the horses."

"Then lead them better!"

"What about the rose and ivy? The castle is in disguise."

"So am I. Two masks will surely be a block to the truth for as long as I need it!"

"Will they?" I asked nervously. "Are you sure about that? Is that a Truth or a Guess?"

"It's a Hope," said Escrivaune. "And in case you're not aware of it, Christian, Hope is a two-edged sword every bit as dangerous as that sword of Mordalac's, that steel blade which Kylhuk danced around and still got stung by. Hope is both challenge and despair. We weave our lives around hope, and succeed or die according to the pattern of that weave. Enough now, *slathan*. What little wit I have I'll need if I'm to secure the dowry. If you smell rotting ivy, retreat. More importantly: keep the horses on half-rations so that they'll run fast when we leave. But water them well; keep them gently bridled but not saddled, lightly tethered and facing the gate."

"And your shield polished to perfection?"

"The shield is more than just a shield. Your *forlorn friend* is in the gryphon. The better polished, the safer our escape."

"I'm glad you told me," I said, wondering what friend he could have meant, and assuming he meant Issabeau, who among my "forlorn friends" was the only one I was confident could assume the shape of an animal.

But a *gryphon*?

Our ethereal guide had seen a castle in two halves, covered with rambling rose and ivy; we had seen a castle that exuded an air of desertion. But as we came through the woods to the drawbridge, we might have been stepping toward Camelot. The walls were painted white, the towers streaming with colored pennants. The courtyard into which we were led was alive with the activity of animals, wagons, and the inhabitants of the stronghold. Yes, the place stank of the farmyard, but the smell of fires was also a warm and welcoming odor; and the aroma of cooking, and of the honeyed ale that I had come to associate with this medieval period, soon overwhelmed our senses.

We were greeted by the baron, the Lord of Brezonfleche, and Escrivaune, in his guise as Mordalac, was received with grace and charm by the astonishingly beautiful Lady Brezconzel.

"God's Truth," he murmured to me through the laughter as we stood in the mud by the main steps, "I think I'll stay forever."

"I suspect that's exactly what they have in mind for you," I retorted and Escrivaune glanced at me sharply.

"Meaning what?"

"Meaning this castle changes its look as you approach it. Please summon that little wit you referred to earlier."

"S'Truth! You're right."

I slipped away, leading the horses, and found the animals grain and stabling as close to the gate as possible. I did as Escrivaune had instructed, but noticed that I was watched by eyes expressing puzzlement, the castle's ostlers confused as to why I left the steeds half ready.

"It's the way we do things in my country," I said, but without Gwyr to interpret, my words might well have been in the language of the Devil.

That night we feasted in style, seated at a long table, facing a roaring fire at the side of the hall. Eight immense hounds, fur the color of bracken, lean bodied, muzzles like the dead-eyed features of a python, prowled the hall, eating bones and fighting among themselves. Thin, insubstantial music was played from a gallery and Escrivaune and his Lady danced a sedate routine alone before circling the hall and drawing all the other knights and their ladies, the squires and the daughters into the spiral dance.

I was on my guard all the time, but when I finally succumbed to sleep that night—on a bench a few yards from the glowing logs, among others of my status—I dreamed well, and woke at dawn to find everything in its place, and all quite normal.

And except for the feasting, it was like this for five days.

I began to feel relaxed. Castle life was cold, busy, noisy, and dull, but since my tasks consisted only of looking after our horses, supervising Escrivaune's bodily needs—water to wash in, if a quick splash of face and chest could be called washing, and a sharp blade for his cheeks since his Lady's own skin was looking noticeably raw from his intimacy—I managed to find time to myself.

But on the sixth night, as Escrivaune made his bedtime preparations, he whispered to me, "Polish the shield."

The gryphon shield was hanging on the wall among the shields of other guests and knights under the baron's protection. I took it down and cleaned the soot and grime from its face, then laid it on the floor below my bench as I slept.

In the dark hours, with the fire now a dull glow in the deep hearth, I woke to find the gryphon standing over me, eyes bright, breath foul, jaws open to reveal gleaming teeth. Its tail flexed angrily, its claws flashed as they extended from the pads.

"Follow!" it whispered.

"Issabeau? I thought Kylhuk had sent you elsewhere."

"Follow!"

Was this Issabeau in animal disguise?

The voice had not been hers. I crept after the shadow. It rushed through corridors, down spiral stairs, then out into the yard, a shape almost invisible against the night, so swift, so silent that sleeping dogs stayed still, and tethered horses hardly shifted from their stations.

The gryphon led me deeper into the castle.

Suddenly I could smell decay. Suddenly the air was full of desolation. We entered a tower and ran lightly up its winding staircase . . . entered a room where dark, still shapes hung from the rafters, turning slightly with the breeze of our arrival. Discarded armor lay everywhere, catching faint rays of light.

Above us, the wooden ceiling creaked and whined in erotic rhythm, and I could hear a man's voice howling in pain, a woman's laughing.

"Get the skin!" hissed the gryphon.

I looked into the darkness, but the shadow had fled, though it stopped in the entrance to the tower and repeated, "Get the skin!"

Suddenly the ceiling opened and light spilled down. A shape tumbled toward me, screaming, attached to a rope around its neck which sprang taut and stopped the fall. In that moment of spilled light, before the ceiling closed, I had seen the skinned men hanging around me, the snakes around them, intimately entwined, bulging eyes turned to me in anger at the interruption of their congress. Escrivaune's partly flayed and bloody carcass swayed among them now, his scaled Lady wrapped around him like a python, her jaws holding a glistening, sickly sack.

His skin!

I could hardly think what to do. The tower was alive with hissing. The hanging men were crying feebly, all save Escrivaune, who was screaming with all his lungs.

The fall had not killed him then.

I had only my sword and my strength. I ran to the Lady and tugged at her tail, pulled her from the knight and cut the hissing head from her body. The sack of skin seemed to wrap itself around me, hugging my arm like a terrified and grateful pet. I jumped and jumped again, slashing at the rope that held my friend, and eventually he fell down, screeching with pain as his raw flesh contacted my touch and the floor.

We ran through the night. The gryphon danced ahead of us, sending the bloodhounds scattering, and by effort of illusion, shape-shifting and pure determination, we found the horses. I had still kept them half-bridled, and they reacted violently to the smell of my friend's half-skinned torso, but this only served to make them livelier. As the gryphon ran like a cat up to the ropes that held the bridge, loosening the blocks that held the pulleys and letting the wooden road fall across the river, so Escrivaune clung like grim death to his charger, galloping through the gate, his squire in frantic pursuit, dogs in pursuit of the squire, but dogs only, as if no human life existed that could be roused and riled to follow.

*   *   *

And that was that. A half-flayed man, who should have died of his wounds, was made well again when his skin was retrieved from the sack. His shield gleamed in starlight; the gryphon was gone; Issabeau, escaping her duties with Kylhuk to hide in the shield, Issabeau was gone.

Our guide appeared, a dreamy, flowing shape, narrow faced and beautiful, beckoning to us, encouraging us back along the path to Legion.

By morning, Escrivaune's skin had reassembled. Naked and humiliated, but alive and experienced, the man rode slightly higher on the bare-backed stallion as we finally encountered the forest wall, and the protective attentions of the Forlorn Hope. His awkward posture in the saddle had nothing to do with his pride.

"You did very well," Guiwenneth whispered to me as she lay across me later that night, still warm and wet from our lovemaking. She had tugged the cloak over our heads and we lay, cheek to cheek, in moist and pungent darkness. "But I was worried about you."

"Is that why you asked Issabeau to hide in the shield?"

"I asked her to follow you. I didn't know how she'd do it, but she agreed."

"She was wonderful. A gryphon!"

"A what?"

"A mythical beast. A shadow. Without her, Escrivaune and I would both be alive and in pain forever, and forever the source of food and satisfaction for those succubi."

"Succubi?"

"Reptiles. Demons. *Lamia*. I don't know how to describe them."

"Don't try," the woman said and brushed her lips over mine. "Don't try and remember. Just be a source of satisfaction to me."

"A prospect that fills me with joy, since I love you so much."

"I'm glad you think that way. And we still have so much time."

"We have all the time we want in this strange, strange world."

"We have the time we have," she said quickly. "Let's not waste it."

But before I could think about her words, her teeth had closed briefly on my breast, nipping me to attention, and she had wriggled down, reaching below her belly to find me, gently easing me into a second "conversation."

For a while, as my time with Legion continued, I was too busy and too confused to think clearly. I saw very little of Kylhuk himself after the funeral respects for Manandoun had been paid, and had no chance to push him on my strange role as *slathan*. Most contact with Kylhuk was fleeting, usually on horseback as he brought me new instructions, or a new guide to my circuit of the garrison. He always brought me a gift, anything from honey or meat to a small knife, or a cloak pin that he had thought would appeal to me. And once: a bow of strong ash, half the length of my body, and a leather quiver of arrow shafts ready to be tipped.

"You should give him a gift in return," Guiwenneth hinted one day, and in the absence of anything better, I begged a slice of thin, polished birchwood from a carpenter, red and black pigments from my "forlorn" friend Jarag, a strip of leather from the young Cleverthread I knew as Annie, and to the best of my ability painted a snarling boar on the face of the wood, staring straight out of the amulet. In charcoal around this image, as if inscribing a coin, I wrote: From dream you came; to dream you will go.

"For me?" Kylhuk demanded when I gave it to him. The look in his eye was of surprise and suppressed delight. His companion, the silent Fenlander, was uneasy behind his bronze-featured face plate.

"What do these runes say?"

Kylhuk meant the inscription. I was ready for his question.

"That you will one day return to the place from which you came."

"One day I will return to the place from which I came?"

"I couldn't have put it better."

"Nothing too profound, then."

"Hardly. I'm too young for profundity."

He gave me a quick, sharp look, almost quizzical. "But not a curse . . . ?"

"Certainly not!"

He seemed relieved. "I like this old tusker!" he said (he was referring to the boar) and kissed the red-and-black image on the birchwood slice. He tied it round his neck and grinned at me. "I'll hunt him one day. This big, bad pig. I'll bring you his crest! All those sharp spines in one crest!"

"I do believe you will."

"I know I will."

Then with the same ceremony, he gave me the cut and battered leather glove from his right hand, which left his sword hand exposed, and I could see that Guiwenneth was astonished . . . and perhaps alarmed?

"I *like* gifts," Kylhuk said loudly. "I like gifts of food and I like gifts of love. But the best gift is that gift which can only be given once. So guard that glove!"

"I will. And thank you. I'll wear it with pride as I undertake my tasks for Legion."

"You will! I'm sure of it. But you won't like this next task, *slathan*."

"This doesn't surprise me."

"You must do it anyway."

"To the best of my ability."

That was when he assigned me to Escrivaune, the adventure I have just recounted.

*   *   *

Two evenings after my return from Castle Brezonfleche, I asked Guiwenneth about Mabon son of Modron, whose rescue lay at the end of Kylhuk's quest. I had tried to raise the subject before, not just with Guiwenneth, but encountered only shrugs, impatience, confusion, or avoidance. Tonight, however, with some ten of us sitting round a good fire, succulent and spicy food and warmed sweet ale for company, Guiwenneth stood up, brushed down her tunic, shook out her long, auburn hair and raised her hands as if to say, "Silence."

She was drunk.

"Mabon's story," she said, "is tragic. There are few people who have even heard of him, and few facts are known about him, though for some of us his fate is entwined in our lives like a braid of dried grass in our hair. When I was a child, my mother told me the story of his miraculous conversation just after birth. It went like this. . . ."

And she began to act with her body and with different voices, to the amusement and applause of several of our dinner companions.

"So!" she said, looking at me with a grin. "So! The babe is in his purple swaddling, still shocked from what his mother, the Queen, has just proposed! And what has she proposed? His answer will make it clear."

"It is not right that a young dog should lie with an old bitch, even if she is his mother!"

(Howls of horror from around the fire.)

"It is perfectly right," shouts Mother angrily. "No *whelp* will result from the union. What will result is only that special knowledge that the Young Dog who is Divinely Born, as you are my son, Mabon, needs to have about his *mother*. How else will you inherit the knowledge of the land? More than *whelping* is achieved when Divine Son lies with Divine Mother."

So! Struggling in his swaddling, Mabon's face distorts into a furious mask, the hair sprouting on chin and cheek as the man he will become rages from the skin, fire dancing in his eyes for a moment before he is the peaceful babe again. "This whelp is too small and too young," he shouts. "It would suckle gladly, since it is hungry, and its eyes are on those swollen paps! Milk! Milk! It is all I have on my mind, Mother. Is there nothing to be learned from suckling?"

Mother pulls her cloak across her fat breasts to deny milk to the infant. "Suckling is for the ordinary dog," she snaps.

"Then I am ordinary. Put me to your breast, or there will never be hair on my chin!"

"You are not ordinary and I will make you aware of it!"

"You may try, Mother, but you won't succeed."

Furiously, she reaches for the babe to chastise him, but Mabon is too quick for her.

Confined in his purple swaddling, only his head exposed, he wriggles away from her and squirms like a maggot around the hall. Mother races in close pursuit. Round and round they go, the worm wriggling faster, little rump rising and falling, until he slithers up a roof pole and sits on a rafter, out of reach, staring down at the disheveled woman and her weeping breasts.

And Mother cries out, "The ordinary dog has always howled when it loses the scent. But a Royal Hound should listen to that howling and should always know the scent that is trailed through time and the forest. You are a *royal* hound!"

"I am content to howl with the other dogs. I will be an ordinary man!"

"You are not ordinary," roars the harridan. "And I will make you aware of it."

"You are welcome to try," shouts the infant, "but you will not succeed."

"I *will* succeed," says Mother, soft and grim. Then in a raised voice: "In the forest, the strongest tree grows alone in the clearing where a great tree has fallen. Our family is that sunlit glade, Mabon! Hallowed, a place of worship. You are the sapling that will grow during the Mother Moon and outstrip the rest of the wildwood. Ordinary men will hang their trophies from your branches."

"First hounds, now forests," sneers the child with a coarse laugh. Oak leaves sprout from his ears and a hound's muzzle from his mouth. "This world into which I have come through your gate confuses me."

"Hounds or forests, there is always One who can run farther and faster than the rest, or reach higher and wider."

His face that of a babe again, Mabon says, "Mother, listen to me. I am content to run in circles with the pack and grow in tangles with the thicket."

"You are *not* content with that and I will make you aware of it."

"You are welcome to try, Mother, but you will not succeed."

"I *will* succeed, because I have already dreamed of what will happen to you!"

The babe laughs. "That dream is for tomorrow and the days after, Mother. *I have time to turn your dream to dust!*"

"You are welcome to try, Mabon. But by the power of the gate that passed you into this world, you will *not* succeed."

Guiwenneth was stroking my face, looking at me earnestly. "What is it, Chris? You've gone as pale as the dead."

"Something you said—nothing more than that . . ."

"Something I said? In the story?"

"Brought back a bad memory."

She seemed to understand, fussing at me, but I assured her that I was well, just a little shaken.

I have already dreamed of what will happen to you!

When Guiwenneth had used those words as she had sketched out the story of Mabon, I had shivered with the awful recollection of my own mother, holding herself alive against the branch, watching me with eyes that expressed nothing but contempt.

What did that old woman say to you? I had wailed, thinking of the unkempt old woman I now thought of as the "dolorous voice."

Nothing I hadn't dreamed of already. Nothing that wasn't already pain.

My mother's words; the admission that had left me desperate.

What have I done?

Nothing . . . yet, she had said.

Please don't die, I had implored her.

And she had whispered, *My son is gone. . . .*

And dropped.

And snapped.

And left me alone.

Mabon's tale was strange and frustratingly incomplete, like everything, all stories in this realm, from Someone with his unfinished name and Kylhuk with his unfinished tasks, to Issabeau with her unfinished passion, and Gwyr in his own form of Limbo, a man in a waiting place, both dead and alive.

"When did this happen to Mabon?" I asked Guiwenneth and she replied, "When he was an infant."

I'd realized that!

"I meant, how long ago?"

"That I can't answer. Not recently, I think. My grandmother knew the story, so it must be very old."

It seemed that shortly after his bitter row with his mother, Mabon had disappeared.

Talking among the travelers with Legion, I heard various accounts of what might have happened:

That he had been sent for fostering for seven years to a neighboring clan (a common practice among the early Celtic aristocracy); that his father had hired hunters to take him away from the stifling and sinister attentions of his mother; that he had crawled to the animal huts and suckled on a cow, but the bull that guarded its herd had hooked the child by its woolen wrap and carried it into the forest, passing it to one of the Oldest Animals for protection.

Mabon now became a hunter. He flew like a bird of prey, pounced as a cat, stalked as a wolf, lurked in the deepest of lakes as a pike, swam fiercely like a salmon, and watched the world cannily and dangerously as an owl. The spirit and features of all these creatures he wore as a mask for his face and a cloak for his body.

There was a ludicrous element to the fragment Guiwenneth had enacted, which suggested that by her own time in history the story was *already* old and being recounted with typical Celtic exaggeration. Others in the circle that evening—even though they had laughed at Guiwenneth's eccentric performance—were adamant that the furious exchange with his mother had occurred when Mabon was many years older. Two accounts made it clear that it was not just his mother, but his sister as well with whom Mabon was expected (because of his rank) to "lie with." In one version, Mabon had two sisters, both older than him, and he was expected to sleep with each of them once a year for seven years before going with them into the forest maze, at whose heart lay the Divine Gate.

The reference seemed clear: The sisters were both lovers to him and his chosen executioners, and Mabon was having none of it! He had fled the scene—he felt himself to be an ordinary man!—denying his royal status.

A cheerful, charismatic red-haired warrior called Conal had a tale from the cycle that was a little more ambitious. Perhaps it contained a grain of truth? I think it unlikely:

"It's a true fact that when Mabon was fourteen years of age, no more than that, he heard that his mother's hunters were only two valleys away from where he was hiding, their dogs like mountains, their horses each with eight legs—I've *seen* such beasts, so I have!—carrying spears that could fly round corners! These are the facts, now, so pay attention!

"Mabon was hiding in the woodland when this news reached him. He began to eat stones and rocks, the trunks of trees, and to swallow clay from the river. And that's a big appetite in a man, in case you're not aware of it. As fast as Mabon ate these stones and trees, so he grew. The rocks built up around his belly, the trees formed into sturdy gates, the clay shapes into massive ramparts. He kept eating. Stone towers rose on the walls and an inner stronghold grew up. Do you now see what's happened? He had formed his body into a stone fortress!

"When the hunters came near, what did he do? He spat splinters of wood the size of javelins at them! The riders failed to recognize him, but the spears were cutting them to pieces, so they passed on by. Now Christian, listen to me! That's a wonderful achievement by any account, and a story that's as true as the fact that I'm sitting here telling it, though I may have got some of the details wrong, I can't be sure of that. It's a long time since my own dear mother nursed me. But it certainly saved Mabon's life on that particular day. That's the story I heard as a child, so I did, and it's a true tale."

There was a period of silence, all eyes on Conal, then a sort of collective sigh.

Guiwenneth glanced at me. "The Irish," she whispered in exasperation.

I soon realized that knowledge of Mabon was very fragmentary and confusingly contradictory. The fate and ill-fortune of a young "dream-hunter," as he was often referred to, was known from Ireland in the west to the mountainous land of the Kurgan in the east, and by the disheveled heroes and heroines of many ages, in particular the Bronze Age Minoans, though the jarag from ten thousand years in my past did not recognize Mabon in any shape or form.

Mabon's story, at its heart, seemed to be that of a princeling born into a matriarchal society—perhaps on one of the Mediterranean islands such as Corsica or Crete—who had refused to conform to the rituals of that society: marriage to his mother, immolation at the hands of his sister, and had escaped sacrifice as a youth, fled, survived by his wits and muscle in the wild, but had finally been tricked out of hiding and either buried alive or imprisoned—but certainly confined alive in a grim place.

He was "divine"—half human, half god.

And by *all* accounts he had been born out of "an animal's dream" on a mountainside, in the heart of a land surrounded by ocean.

In prehistoric times!

"How is it that Uspathadyn was searching for him?" I asked Guiwenneth, in bemusement. "The man lived in the Welsh mountains, thousands of years later."

"He'd inherited the task, of course. The task has been passed on since that terrible time in lost memory."

"And Kylhuk inherited the task from him."

"Tricked into doing so."

"And now Kylhuk is waiting to trick me in turn."

"You've asked this of Gwyr already," Guiwenneth said slyly. "And Gwyr still doesn't think so. You are not man enough for the task. You are too much an outsider. But your presence has persuaded Kylhuk that the rescue can be achieved. The result will be amazing."

"Yes. And it still amazes me that until recently, I had never even *heard* of Mabon!"

PART FOUR

THE END OF
WANDERING

Though I am old with wandering
Through hollow lands and hilly lands,
I will find out where she has gone,
And kiss her lips and take her hands;
And walk among long dappled grass,
And pluck till time and times are done
The silver apples of the moon,
The golden apples of the sun.

—W. B. Yeats,
from *The Song of Wandering Aengus*

CHAPTER 17

A tall, black-maned cat came running at me from the bushes on its hindlegs, startling me as it flung itself onto my body, the feline features melting to reveal Issabeau in her wildcat furs. I fell to the ground, caught in her embrace. She straddled me, her dark hair flowing over my face, her breath sweet. "If you value your life," she whispered, "don't fight against this kiss."

And she pressed her wet mouth against my own, pushing my head to the ground. Her fingers squeezed my shoulders, keeping me still.

Eyes open as the kiss continued, I could see that she was listening. When I tried to move, she urged me down again, her own gaze flickering left to right, her mouth eating at mine. It should have been intimate, but Issabeau was elsewhere and very frightened.

And an image flashed into my eyes: a raging sea, a rain-swept shore, a girl running from horses!

A few seconds later, in the real world as I knew it, the woodland stirred. Something gigantic walked past on this lazy, summer's afternoon. I heard its growl. A second creature followed it, and to the other side of us was a third, stalking through the forest. Turning my head slightly, I glimpsed a figure like an upright wolf, but its massive head was like the skull of a dog, covered with thin, gray skin. The skulled face turned to look down at me, came closer, a foul sight. It sniffed, snarled, licked at its bony chops, then turned away. It grumbled several words. Growls were answered. This awful troop moved on and Issabeau, after a circumspect few moments, disengaged from me, wiping a hand across her lips.

"They didn't see us. Kissing can be useful."

"Thank you for the kiss."

"Thank you for not moving. If they had sensed you, they would have sensed me, and we would both be dead. I could only protect us with that kiss."

"What were they?"

"Good news and bad news," she said, helping me to my feet. She was amused by something now, looking me up and down.

"What were they?" I repeated.

"Scaraz," she said. "Winter creatures. Like wolves, but like the *bones* of wolves. They eat flesh. In summer, they are green and often friendly. Then they are known as *dauroz*. I think it means 'green man.'"

"But this *is* summer," I said, and she smiled.

"That's the good news. It means we are close to the Long Person. The Scaraz have come down here, that much is obvious. That's why they are displaced and not in their time or in their season or on their guard. Didn't you smell them?"

"No."

"They smelled of *time*. The Long Person! We are almost there."

"If that's true, we should tell Kylhuk—"

But Issabeau said, "Wait a moment."

She stepped up to me and put her nose against my neck. "You smell of the ocean . . . the salt sea! What did you see when I protected you with the kiss?"

"A girl running. A wild sea by a rocky coast. Just a glimpse. Was it you?"

Issabeau had gone quite pale, a look of alarm on her face.

"Well, well," she said after a moment. "I let you in. I let you see. I didn't mean to do that."

"*Was* it you?"

"Yes," she said. She was close to me, staring at my eyes. "You are a strange man, and I don't understand who you are. But I trust you, which is saying a lot. Christian. . . . We are almost there, almost to the Long Person, and when we have reached her, nothing will be the same again. There is something that puzzles me, something that haunts me. I don't know why, but I think you may have an answer for me. Will you try?"

"Yes. Gladly."

"Will you take another kiss to see the kiss that saved my life?"

"What can I possibly say? I had no idea that magic was so stimulating."

Issabeau smiled wryly. "I thought you loved Guiwenneth."

"I do!"

"Then put a little *winter* where it counts," she said, wriggling on my hips pointedly as she lay down and embraced me again.

The sea again, surging against the girl's legs as she lay in the surf, aware of rain falling and a sky lowering and darkening. Her mother had crawled from the water, dragging her infant son. The crates with the animals in them were spread along the beach, among the spars and flotsam from the wreck. Too tired to lift her head, too dazed by concussion from the rocks, the girl could only stare across the billowing waves at the ship's stem, still high above the heaving ocean,

"My animals . . ." she whispered, but there was no sound from the broken cages, though she was half aware of the drowned shapes curled within them.

After a while, the cages were dragged away. She could

hear them being moved across the shingle. The rain grew more drenching before it receded. Slowly the girl's senses returned. Distantly, she could hear the dull canter of horses coming toward her.

She forced herself to her feet and stared along the shore. Seven or eight riders, still far away, one of them a woman with billowing black hair, one an old man. They moved almost eerily through the misting air, but they were riding hard.

She ran up the beach, into the shadow of the cliff, then scampered from sea cave to sea cave, looking for a hiding place.

In one, its passage reaching deeply into the hill, she saw her crates, her creatures, and she flung herself among them.

"Owl! Cat! Oh no! Roebuck! Eagle! Oh, no, no!"

Each corpse she stroked or held, but there was no way of bringing life back to them. "Who dragged you here?" she cried. "Who tried to save you?"

A woman's voice shouted angrily. She crept to the mouth of the cave and saw her mother, terrified, disheveled, running from the hunters. The corpse of her infant son lay naked in the tidal zone, limbs shifted by the waves. The hunters rode after the poor woman, passing the sea cave without a glance.

"I have to hide. I have to hide. . . ."

Her thoughts selfish, now; all about survival.

She drew her skinning knife and slipped the feathered pelts from the owl and eagle, the hides from the deer and the cat, sticking the skins to her face and her arms and across her clothes. The skins moved into her, swallowed her. Her eyes sharpened with the owl, the eagle put murder in her mind, her senses heightened like a cat's, her limbs grew sinewy and strong.

Dressed as this strange, many-coated beast, she crouched in the sea cave and watched as her mother was ridden into the ocean, pushed back into the swell by a mailed knight and by the sorceress with the wild, black hair, who screeched abuse at her until the poor woman stumbled and slipped into the turning tide, dragged suddenly away, and down into the deep, and out of the world.

"I will kill you for that murder, Vivyane," the girl-beast whispered, but it was a foolish thing to have done, since the old man with his tight growth of gray beard, who had sat back from the troop of armored men, suddenly glanced her way, as if her words had reached him. The girl felt her heart squeeze as the dark eyes spotted her and the mouth formed into a silent, triumphant word.

His glance was noticed by Vivyane, who screamed angrily at her steed and galloped the animal up the shore.

The sea-cave girl in her skins cowered back. The cat snarled and the owl watched. The deer made ready to bolt. The eagle chattered, anxious to kill.

Vivyane appeared in the cave entrance, breathless from the ride, damp with rain. She looked into the darkness, eyes bright like a wilder cat than her prey.

"Where are you hiding?"

She looked to where the girl was concealed behind her creatures; she frowned, then took a step forward. . . .

A youth moved suddenly out of the shadows of the sea cave. He was tall, wiry, dressed in brown leather and linen stained black with the ocean and hanging with weed. What little facial hair he possessed was white with salt.

"Leave my pet alone!" he shouted defiantly.

Vivyane stood uneasily in the cave mouth, staring at the sea-crusted man who had risen from the darkness.

"I have never seen a creature such as this," Vivyane said, pointing to the girl in her skins.

"You've seen it many times," defied the youth. "You should open your eyes. This creature is my pet and I will not see it harmed."

"What's your name?" Vivyane asked. She was holding a

short, pointed staff, wickedly sharp, its haft carved with the signs of her strengths.

"What's your *name*?" she asked again as the youth stood defiantly silent.

"If you can see it," he said, "then by the Good Christ, you can have it, and my pet as well. And me, too, for that matter. Because as God Knows, if you can see my name, nothing will matter *but* the name. That is my challenge to you."

His words provoked Vivyane to a fit of fury. Her figure filled the mouth of the cave. But she didn't step inside, kept at bay by the challenge and by confusion. Instead, she screeched abuse at the cowering, pelt-covered girl and flung her staff at the crouching creature. The hard wood turned in the air like a knife and its point pierced the buck's skin covering on the girl. A moment later, Vivyane was gone, riding furiously back toward the fort, the sharp-stubbled old man and his knights galloping behind her.

The youth ran out of the cave and threw stones after them, mocking them as he did so, then went back to kneel by the girl, pulling away the ragged clothing of skins and feathers, shocked by the wound he saw. Outside, the sea was still raging, the wind howling, but inside this place there was only calm, and the dying girl.

"Has she gone?" the girl asked.

"Yes," said the unnamed youth. "And I don't think the Good Christ is in her heart, but only the dark lady of the crossroads."

"Hecate. Didn't you recognize her? That was Vivyane. And Hecate flavors her bile."

He could hardly take his gaze from the blood on her breast. "I would think so. There was an old man with her, but when I looked at him, I had a strange thought: that he is either a young man pretending to be old, or an old man who would be young, because as God is my witness, he seemed ageless and frightening."

"Merlin," the girl whispered. "He is training a new protegée. Vivyane. But he doesn't trust her and would prefer to be instructing me, having met me at my father's court before it was destroyed. The protegée will not hear of it. She wants me dead. Merlin watches. Vivyane and I are pitted against each other in this cold-hearted, young-old man's scheme. And do not mention God in the same breath as his name, because it is Hecate's Master that guides him, and all the Hounds of Hell."

She looked at the youth gently, her eyes still alive with light, though she was slipping into darkness.

"My name is Issabeau," she said.

"Well, well. Are you half boy, then?"

"I am *not!*" she chastised him as loudly as she could. "I was christened *Yzabel.* But I was called Issabeau by my parents, and now that they are both dead, I wish to remain as they thought of me, in that fond way, that softer name. And there is *nothing* of the boy in it!"

"Issabeau it is."

"I'm dying of that young hag's magic."

The youth glanced furiously at the sea beyond the cave. "She is dying of her own magic, though she doesn't know it."

"You're very confident to condemn a sorceress so easily."

"Trust me."

"I don't," said Issabeau, gently amused, "since it's only bravado that makes you say what you say. But thank you for trying. And I hope you're right. She didn't manage to guess your name."

The youth sat back on his haunches, gazing through the mouth of the cave to the violent sea. "By the Virgin's Prayers, she tried. She certainly tried. I felt her magic in my head. I felt stripped and beaten. I felt exposed and naked, with crows pecking at my eyes and ears and heart. The Cruel Saracen could not have inflicted more pain on me than did that hag as she sought my name."

Issabeau was impressed. "Then how did you hide it?"

The youth stared at the girl for a long time, a twinkle in his eye. "There was nothing to hide, Issabeau. I was never named."

"*Everyone* is named."

"*Someone* was not! That someone was me. My father died before the name could be given."

"How did he die?"

"The truth of that is lost with my name."

"If he knew your name, then the name is still there, but in the heart of a dead man."

"The Good Christ Knows, Issabeau, I have clung to that hope. But there is a good reason to never find it. Five reasons, in fact."

"Amd they are?"

"*Because* I was not named, I was given five gifts."

"That's generous giving."

"I agree. One gift for each limb: one each for my arms, one each for my legs"—he stared at the girl, a mischievous look on his face—"and one for the smaller limb that is speaking to me even as I look at you."

Issabeau smiled knowingly and tossed a pebble at her companion. "Put winter in that limb! I'm still too young."

He grinned. "I'll do my best. My very best. But as to the other gifts, the four that I can show you are as follows: that I can give back a life to one who has died. But this will cost me the strength of my right arm, which will be my sword arm, so it will be a gift given carefully."

"A wise comment."

"Secondly, I can give a kiss that will bring freedom. That's my left arm gone, though I can live with that. Thirdly: I can hold the Holy Grail of Christ as long as I fast from all things physical while I carry it. My left leg is the price for this privilege, when it's done."

"When it's found!"

"Indeed. But the Grail has to be somewhere in the heart of the land."

"But which land?"

"Indeed. A wasteland, apparently."

"Among the many that we hear of."

"Some knight will find it. Someday."

"Much good may it do him."

"I agree. The knights I meet often wonder what will be done with the Grail once its hiding place has been revealed."

"Tales will tell, no doubt," said Issabeau. "And the fourth gift?"

"I can confuse sorcerers as long as my True Name is lost."

"Amply demonstrated," said the girl. "Vivyane's head will ache tonight!"

"Indeed. But if I find my name, I lose a leg. So I think I'll continue to *confuse*. And as regards courtesy, you can call me whatever comes to mind."

Issabeau sighed. "Since I'm dying, none of your gifts are of use to me except the first, the bringing back of life, and you should save that gift for a greater friend than me."

The youth smiled at her. "I *will* save that gift, though I have no greater friend than you at this moment. But the kiss will suffice, I think, and I'll give it gladly."

He leaned down to Issabeau, pulled aside the tunic over her small breast to expose the bleeding wound from Vivyane's staff. The blood was still flowing. He lapped at it, licked the wound, then put his lips against the torn edges, kissing fiercely.

Issabeau watched him, then reached a finger to touch his glistening lips. "I feel stronger for that kiss."

"And I feel a chill in my left shoulder."

The left side of his body froze, became gleaming stone. They both marveled at the transformation. Fingers flexed, wrist flexed, arm bent at elbow, but this was a stone arm, now, white marble shot through with streaks of green and red; and yet he could feel with it, and was strong with it.

"God's Truth, by kissing you I've made myself invulnerable to attack from the left."

"That's because the kiss was given gladly."

"It was a True Kiss."

"And stopped the wound to a True Heart."

The youth leaned toward Issabeau, his brow creasing with love and desire, his crimson, rosebud mouth soft with need. "Issabeau, I feel so much older then I am. . . ."

"And soon you will be," she whispered, brushing her lips on his. "And that will be good for us both."

Then she pushed him back firmly, shaking her head, half smiling. "But for now, I think I'll stay intact."

"Must you?"

"Yes! I must! I wish I knew your name, though."

"It will find me soon enough, no matter how fast I run."

"Yes. I suppose it will." She sounded forlorn. "And then you'll be prey to sorcerers."

"But the Good Christ is in my Heart, Issabeau. His Enduring Cross will be my strength! And no one can kill me from the left."

"Bravely said, stone-knight," murmured Issabeau. "And I think you must be of noble birth, with gifts such as yours; and also by your clothes and your confident look."

Suddenly she was fighting back tears. The boy put his arms around her and hugged her. "What is it?"

"Hell has just drowned my mother and is on our tails. I will miss her dreadfully. She had such wisdom. This will be a desperate time."

"A desperate time, indeed," said the youth. "But if Hell has taken her, Hell can give her back. I will do what I can for you to make her live again, and protect you from Hell in the process!"

*　　*　　*

The seascape faded and I emerged from the dream, dizzy with the images and heady with the scent of sea air. There was a weight on my belly and I realized that Issabeau was straddling me, her hands resting on my chest. My mouth ached from the prolonged contact that had induced the memory.

She sat there, dark against the bright sky above, staring down at me.

"Did you see?"

"Yes. What happened next? Between you and the youth?"

She sighed. "We had different paths to follow. But we agreed to meet at the sea cave in a year's time."

"And did you?"

"I was there. He was not. And I never found him again."

But in a way she had, I thought to myself.

"*Haven't* you found him?"

She shook her head. "I'm confused because—"

"Because of Someone son of Somebody? That proud Celt with his drooping mustache and golden hair?"

"The barbarian," she said wistfully, repeating, "barbarian!"

"But you think you recognize him. He's a good few years older. . . ."

"He is not the same boy grown into a man!" she insisted. "He is nothing like him. When I met him in Legion for the first time, I was frightened of him. Something about him was familiar. All I could think of was that it was Merlin, disguised to trap me. Or Vivyane, tricking me into complacency. . . ."

Her sudden look at me was innocent and lost.

"But I am in love with him, and I feel I am betraying the boy, that sea-cave boy, I have promised to find. Do you have an answer for me, Christian? Tell me what is happening to me!"

"I have an answer," I whispered. "I'm sure of it."

Issabeau's body was tight against my loins and I was

aroused and embarrassed. She wriggled on me, her fingers clawing at my breast, her eyes wide with anticipation.

"But I think I should talk to Someone first," I went on. "I need time to think. And if Guiwenneth finds us like this . . ."

"It will be bad for us both, I know. This isn't love, Christian. It's comfort. And very comfortable, too. You make a good chair," she added with a mischievous laugh before rolling off me, standing, and brushing at her clothing.

I needed time to think.

I hadn't lied to her. How could I explain to her what was obvious to me: That she and Someone were part of the same story, but a story in two versions, hers from medieval France, his from a Celtic land hundreds of years before the Romans had conquered northern Europe, from before *Christ,* as she would have understood it. A story had been told generation after generation, and it had been adapted by the telling over fifteen hundred years.

What would happen next? I had no way of knowing. But perhaps it could help the love between these two people if I could find out Someone's version of events.

Were these to be "star-crossed" lovers? Or would they live happily ever after? I was amused and alarmed by the thought. If the story they represented ended badly, it would be too bad for them. But if one version of the story was agreeable, they would need to direct themselves in that direction, as long as they stayed inside this forest.

Distantly, a horn was sounding, but it came from the direction of the Long Person and not Legion. Issabeau shuddered noticeably.

"We *are* close," she said. "You find Guiwenneth and the jarag. I'll find Kylhuk."

CHAPTER 18

I had found out quickly enough that the Long Person was a river, her "parted legs" the place where twin streams joined, each flowing from the heart of the wildwood, but bringing very different boats and travelers!

In the months that I had journeyed with Kylhuk's Legion, we had crossed many rivers. The Long Person was something different, however, and Issabeau, like all the enchanters, could "smell" that difference since the river flowed not out of the hills of the world, but from the forgotten past of the world. And though Issabeau could not describe to me the smell of "time," it was clearly something pungent and exotic to her, and that smell had clung to the Scaraz, as it would soon cling to Legion.

Issabeau, small staff in her mouth, transformed into a fast runner and went back to the garrison, urging me to be cautious as I probed onward toward the river itself. She whistled for Someone, who answered from a distance. Guiwenneth was scouting elsewhere with the jarag and I tried to call for them.

In the six months I had marched with Kylhuk, I had taken a turn at the Silent Towers, behind the column, watching that terrible darkness follow us, seeing men die by sword and spear and by unseen hands, or claws that snatched them into the black sky, shredding them like paper. There were always fires burning in that darkness, and to pass beyond the Silent Towers was to enter a realm of eerie sound, calls and cries, screams and howls, and sounds that are beyond description, but which suggested primitive, angry language. And above all, the steady gallop of horses, an endless ride toward Legion, neither encroaching, nor receding, but someone keeping pace, the steady drumming of hooves, riders biding their time.

I had spent time as well in the center of the train, dispatched on several small quests.

But in the end, something drew me back to the Forlorn Hope, and my companions from that first encounter. Kylhuk was certainly aware of the bond between us, and though Gwyr was often called away to help with interpreting the language of captives, or acquisitions to the garrison, the six of us worked well together, Issabeau and Jarag using magic as a defense against danger, Someone and myself using brute force. I had taught Someone simple martial arts; he had taught me to use the leaf-blade sword, the shield, the chariot, and the javelin. He didn't believe in bow and arrow, a dishonorable weapon. Gwyr, of course, used his wits, his newly acquired trumpet, its mouth like a grinning bronze boar (which, though it sounded a piercing and terrifying bellow when used as warning, could also be played with delicacy, a sort of vertical horn with a range of seven or eight notes); and his speed—in retreat!

No fool, Gwyr, but a shadowed man, often to be found alone, silent and melancholy, his cheeks glistening until a sleeve wiped the sheen away and a quick smile broke through his beard at the approach of a friend.

It was Gwyr, now, who rode up behind me as I trotted along a rough track that had appeared within the greenwood, still calling for my companions. A river flowed ahead of me, out of sight, but not out of smell, though its odor was a familiar one to me from my boating trips along the Avon and the Thames.

I heard his horse thunder toward me and turned defensively, relaxing as the Interpreter jumped from the bare back of his mount, hauling on the reins to stop it grazing as he led the animal across to me, his gaze over my shoulder.

"Kylhuk is following," he announced. "Issabeau says this is the place."

"I can smell a river ahead of us. Issabeau told me she can smell *time itself*."

Gwyr was elated. "We've found her," he said in a delighted whisper. "The Long Person. Now it begins, Chris. Now it begins. . . ."

And with a quick glance at me, he added, "And for some . . . it ends. . . ."

We ran on, Gwyr's horse trotting behind us, glad to be unburdened.

The woodland opened out; the way ahead became dazzling with reflected light.

We came to the tree-fringed, gravel bank of the Long Person and gazed at the broad ribbon of water and the crowded forest on the far side.

Gwyr looked to the left, toward the setting sun, to the source of the river where the forest was in gleaming, ruddy twilight. "That's the direction we are headed. It will be hard rowing!"

At that moment, the forest shifted, the land heaved, Gwyr's steed reared in alarm. Legion's outer wall had arrived and as we turned, the wildwood opened and Kylhuk himself galloped through. He jumped from his horse's back, letting the beast walk free, reins dangling. He strode past me, prodding me painfully in the stomach.

"You should have kept me company!" he barked.

Kylhuk had not broken his fast, except to eat an occasional fish, game bird, and loaf of bread, since his diet of plums had soon given him diarrhea. But he was lean and hard now, wearing nothing but a dull green war kilt, and a short cloak pinned over his heart. His sword was slung from its belt across the other shoulder, and his sandals were Roman, taken from a corpse.

He dropped to a knee on the gravel by the river's edge, put his hand out and tentatively touched the flow, trailing his fingers for a while and looking thoughtfully upstream.

Then he called to me.

"Touch the water," he said as I crouched beside him. I obeyed and felt a strange flow of life from the fluid to my skin and up my arm, not a tingle, not a charge, but a breath of presence.

Kylhuk extended his hand and I took it, and the river mingled in that grip, and there was a look in his dark eyes that I couldn't fathom. "You have come a long way," he said to me.

"Yes."

"I have come a long way, too. Of all the tasks I was set, finding the Long Person was going to be the longest journey. Sailing her will be the most strenuous. What we achieve at her source will be the hardest. I had only the omens of my seers and Cleverthreads to get here: Issabeau could smell her; Ear son of Hearer could bury himself in the ground and *hear* her—he can hear an ant walk on a leaf when he is quiet like that—and Falcon died at the claws of the Scald Crow, ascending to let his Far Look gaze across this wilderness. All of them were right. And here we are."

"Here we are," I agreed. "What happens now?"

He stood, slapped me painfully on the shoulder, and barked, "We build a boat, of course. By Olwen's Hands, you're getting fat, *slathan*! You're no good to me carrying such weight on your shoulders."

"If I knew the full meaning of the word, perhaps I'd agree with you."

He didn't respond. He had told me only that a *slathan* was the "sharer of his burden." He returned to his horse, reached into a pouch and tossed me an apple, grinning before he rode furiously back into Legion.

I had seen no boats in the garrison. I had assumed that a period of tree felling, carpentry, nailing, and rigging would now occur, but I was wrong. I had forgotten the carts and wagons. And indeed, as these vehicles were dismembered like wooden puzzles, and rearranged to form a wide-hulled, low-masted ship, even the wicker chariots were pressed into use, to form row locks, hatches, and storehouses.

For several days the camp along the river's edge was a hive of activity as this bizarre transformation took place, and on the gravel shore, above the waterline, the lean, low-prowed longship was constructed, its shallow keel sharp so that it could cut the water as it was rowed upstream, sail slung low to catch any favorable wind, deck wide so that men could easily stand and handle the oars that would drive us up against the current.

There was no fussy design on the ship yet, no figurehead, no iconography to challenge the world of myth and superstition into which we soon would sail. Just wood and metal, wheels, rope, and cloth.

The vessel would carry a crew of twenty-seven (that number again!). I was certain to sail on it, with my friends from the Forlorn Hope and with Kylhuk and his personal entourage. Meanwhile, a long and difficult process of selection was occurring behind the forest wall for the men and women who would make up the number. This involved games, tests, combat, trials of wit, and the casting of lots. Guiwenneth watched it all with deep fascination and brought me lurid accounts of the activities and the often fatal consequences of the contests, some of which turned my stomach. I will not recount them here. At the end of it, the ship was crewed, and a feast was held to celebrate the finishing of the task.

But as for the rest of Legion, when the celebrations were over, it would have to follow along the edge of the river itself, a slow and dangerous journey and without a leader.

As I waited for Kylhuk, I glimpsed for the first time the extraordinary flow of life that was erupting at the river's source; and of the death that it was drawing back, against the stream, as if the impulse to life was the easiest, that to death the hardest, all notion of entropy ignored.

A broken tree floated down the center of the river, turning in the flow, its roots high above the water, a man and a woman, exhausted and afraid, clinging to its trunk. They saw me and called, but the Long Person swept them on.

Later, dogs swam past, six or seven of the creatures, leashes trailing, baying in desperation, their owner drowned perhaps. And a glittering barge, light shimmering from metal on its hull, white sails catching the breeze and tipping it slightly as the helmsman struggled, and four cowled figures stared into the distance, unmoving and unmoved by the voyeur on the bank.

Then upstream, rowing hard against the current as soon we would be, too, came a ship that looked so grim I drew back, half into the cover of the forest. A low, mournful horn sounded at regular intervals as it stroked its way against the river. Its blackened hull might have been tarred or charred. Faces peered at the shore from jagged holes hewn in the sides. The rails around the deck were lined with men who watched the forest. I could hear the complaints of animals and the stamping of hooves from belowdecks. A single mast trailed a shredded sail, so holed and rotten that the opposing breeze hardly ruffled it as it hung, half furled.

The horn moaned as it passed me, and suddenly a man's voice shouted. There was immediate activity on the deck and a hail of arrows flew toward me, one grazing my cheek, another striking the tree next to me and spinning round to crack against my skull. A spear thudded into the ground, trailing red ribbons and black feathers. A second hail of arrows whispered past me, and stones struck and clattered among the rocks.

This terrible ship of the dead pulled away and I cautiously stepped out of cover to watch it go. A last arrow wobbled toward me in the air, a curved, crude shaft that was suddenly snatched from its flight as Someone stepped in front of me. He looked at the weapon, then scratched his jaw with the chipped stone point as he stared into the distance.

"We go that way, too," he said after a moment. "But I'll be glad to let that ship get ahead of us."

"How many more ships like that on the Long Person?" I asked and Someone nodded soberly as he glanced at me.

"Very many, I imagine. The challenge of the twin gates is too seductive."

Although I had talked to Someone about his life of adventure, I had never thought to ask him about his childhood after the events of his father's death by combat. The opportunity arose that night, as we camped by the open water, a few miles downriver from the main camp. Kylhuk had taken a band of forty men and ten specialists to guard the bank, since omens had suggested that Eletherion was there.

A torch-lit barque drifted past us, lighting up the river. A woman's voice sang sweetly, though the woman was not revealed. A black hound watched us, paws crossed on the rails.

"What is your earliest memory of love?" I asked the Celt, and he glanced at me with a frown, tugging at his mustache.

"Why?"

"I'm interested to know. You've told me of adventure, and the search for your name; you've told me of the haunting presence of the tasks you feel obliged to perform. But you've never mentioned passion. Has it been a lonely life until you met Issabeau?"

He prodded the fire with his knife. "Truthfully, it has, though not by my choice. When I was very young I met a girl in the dark forests that filled the valleys to the north of my father's fortress. I have never mentioned this before, and I don't know why I should tell you now, but I will. Perhaps you can answer a question for me that has been bothering me for some time . . . !"

"I'll do my best," I said, and he drew breath, stared into the distance and began.

You will remember, from what I told you when we first met, that my father was summoned to a combat a few hours before my birth and before he could name me, challenged in a dispute about the stealing of a famous white bull and five cows that were being taken to honor Taranis. They were to be sacrificed, a sacrifice of great importance, and my father in his envy of the bull intercepted it with his warrior band and made the offering himself.

My father, you will remember, was killed outright by Grumloch's first throw across the river, a truly lucky strike.

Because I hadn't been named, Grumloch spared me. I was taken out onto a forest lake in a small boat. My father's finest knights were murdered there, and dropped into the pool. I was left in a coracle with a wet nurse, forbidden ever to return to the fort, though of course being only a babe in arms, I knew nothing of what was occurring.

When I was weaned, the woman left me in one of the deep forest glades, one dedicated to Sucellus. She placed me in a hollow between the feet of the great wooden idol, where it was warm and protected from rain and wind. At night, the great gods roared at each other across the forest, and Sucellus strode around the glade, beating at branches. But he, like all of them, was tied to this place.

Every so often, masked people came and sacrificed or left offerings at the feet of the idol. I ate whatever was left and Sucellus never complained. Only later did it occur to me that because I had no name, the god could not see me.

Then one day—I had lived in the shadow of this monstrous, shouting tree for ten years or more—animals began to visit the place. I remember a small, black bird that watched me for ages before flying off. And an owl settled on the wooden head, high above me every night for a week. Then a gray-furred cat came slinking around the glade. And a small deer that I tried to snare, but it butted me and escaped each time.

These creatures all came through the forest from one direction at the edge of the glade, close to where I had dug out my stink pit. I found a hidden track there and one morning, after the statue had returned to rest, I began to follow the trail. And after a while I found a glade where two great wooden idols, one of a man, the other a woman, stood locked in an angry embrace. They were wrestling, their legs stretched out for balance, their arms around each other's head, their mouths gaping in pain, the wood of their muscles swollen with tension. During the night, they were clearly fighting. During the day, the trees had grown together. They cast a vast and sinister shadow in the sun. I soon recognized them as Cernunnos, Lord of Animals, and Nemetona, Goddess of Glades.

There was a stink pit here, too, and the trees were hung with knots of grass, the stems of flowers, with strips of hide, and dolls made out of feathers. Another prisoner, then. But who was she—I felt sure it was a girl—and where was she hiding?

I stayed at the edge of the clearing until nightfall. As the moon rose and the last of twilight was swallowed to the west, the statues began to detach from each other. The forest began to echo with the screaming of the wooden gods in their sanctuaries and these two began to wrestle and scream until I was deafened. They staggered about the glade, tearing at the bark on their faces, clubbing at each other so that splinters and strips of wood flew like spears around me. At midnight they released each other and prowled the glade, pulling back the trees, prodding at the bushes, calling in their strange tongue. I cowered back as Cernunnos leaned toward me, gape-mouthed and slack-eyed, but the monstrous horned head moved away. It hadn't seen me.

They were looking for something, and I imagined it was the human occupant of this place.

Cernunnos stalked off through the forest. Nemetona hunkered down, growling, then turned her head to stare at the bright moon.

And at that moment a voice whispered, *Don't give me away. This one will tear me apart if she finds me. . . .*

I tried to speak to the girl, but she pressed a sap-scented finger against my mouth. *Wait until morning. It's not safe until then.*

And then she pulled me to her body, holding me against her against the cool of the glade. I felt a soft fuzz of hair on her face. Her breath was sweet with wild herbs. She was as thin as a carcass, bones prominent below the flesh. She stayed awake all night, I think, because when I came out of my own forest dream, in the dead, dark hours, the first thing I saw was her starlit gaze on me.

At dawn, the wooden idol rose and bowed its head, hardening into the tree from which it had been so crudely hacked.

"We're safe, now," said my newfound friend. She ran to the stink pit and squatted over it, then kicked leaves from a pile into the hole. I followed her example, fascinated by the way she had painted her body. She sat down against the heels of the idol, legs stretched out in front of her and face upturned, quite relaxed now that the night had passed.

What a sight she was! Not an inch of her skin was not painted with the tiniest of animals. What seemed like lines or circles on her face and arms were in fact a hundred creatures drawn so close together that each ran into its neighbor. I saw every creature I knew and a hundred that I didn't. They ran across her features like deer on a bare knoll, like a flock of birds, wheeling at dusk.

"What's your name?" I asked her.

"Mauvaine," she replied. "What's yours?"

"Only my father knows, and he's dead, killed by a spear on the day of my birth."

"I shall call you Jack of the Glades. Who killed him? Your father."

"Grumloch, his brother-in-law."

"Why was he killed?"

"Over the matter of a bull and five cows, which had come his way."

"You mean he stole them in a raid."

"Yes."

"The Oldest Bull was called Tormabonos," Mauvaine said. "I have him painted here." She indicated a spot on her left side, close to where her small breast scarcely stretched her clothing. "All of the Oldest Animals are painted on me."

"Who painted them on you?"

She sat quite still, hands on the ground, feet splayed as she stared at me. "Taranis. When I was an infant. I think he knew what he was doing."

"They're magic animals, then."

"Yes. They're the Oldest Animals! Unfortunately, I can't raise all of them, only a few. I was trapped here when I was too young. Nemetona keeps me here, and she will kill me, given half a chance. Cernunnos tries to take me away for his own ends, but their struggle is an endless one. She is not as powerful as he, but she has a secret which drains him of full strength."

"What secret is that?"

She looked at me with amused disbelief. "If *I* knew the answer, it wouldn't be a *secret,*" she said.

"Indeed."

"She steals his knowledge and his power when they fight at night. But the animals that rise in the wood from my painted skin stalk her and bring some of that power back to him."

Because of their struggle, Mauvaine was caught in this wilderness, a piece in a game that was beyond her control. When I suggested this to her, she snarled at me.

"Yes. But only if I fail to escape. And I intend to escape!"

"I feel the same. But whenever I try to leave the glade, I end up back where I started. Something drives me in circles. At least you can disguise yourself as an Old Animal and run."

"Easy to say. Not easy to do."

And she explained that Cernunnos had more control over her when she was in animal form than he could exercise when she was in her human guise. The animals ran, and her animal senses were heightened, but they were obedient to the call: a whistle for the hound, a song for the cat, a breath for the owl, a clacking of tongue for the ouzel, a bark for the buck. They could run and fly widely through the blackwood, but always came home at dusk.

"We must burn the idols during the day. Set fire to them!"

"I've tried it. As Nemetona burns, so I burn." And Mauvaine showed me her right leg, where the skin inside the ankle was red and scarred by scalding.

"I am trapped here," she added forlornly.

"I had had the same thought. Then a cat enticed me away from my own prison."

"That was me."

"I know it was. Mauvaine, all we need is the way to break the charm that holds you here."

"I am charm itself," the girl said with a wry smile, lying back and stroking her body through her clothing. "My skin crawls with magic, but not my dreams."

"My own skin crawls with lice. So I'll look to my own dreams for a way to save you."

I remember the way she laughed at that, but that night I crept into her arms, sheltering her from the raging giants, shielding her from the splinters of wood that flew from the angry gods.

And when the moon was high, and the idols were off somewhere, stalking the night forest, I dreamed such a strange dream: perhaps a memory of my time as an infant, after my father's death.

A face was hovering above me, old and wise, half toothed, deeply scarred; a man who said, "I am your grand-father. I cannot tell you your name, since my son is dead, but he would have told you that you must always welcome any scarred-faced man to your hall if he pays you courtesy during the rising of the moon, and pay heed to his words. If his hair is black, you must pay him tribute. If he has lost a hand, you must allow him to depart in his own time."

Then a woman came full of gall and spirit, gray hair like the glow of the moon around her shrunken face.

"I cannot tell you your name, but your father would have told you this: That at the beginning of each season you must offer advice to every child you meet in your fortress, even if they don't ask for it. Nothing you say to them will ever be forgotten, even if it makes no sense."

A druid crowded in on me in my dream, black bearded, hungry eyed, foul breathed, a gold lanula round his neck dangling and glittering above me. "I cannot tell you your name, but you must give back a life before your death, or your death will be an ending and not a beginning. Give back a life! Don't forget that. And because of your rosebud mouth"—he touched my lips with his stinking finger—"a kiss from this mouth will put new life in a dying heart, but only once. Once only."

I woke from the dream to find Mauvaine deeply curled into my chest, her face and mouth close to my own as she slept, her breath so sweet in the night that I could think only that with a kiss I could take her away from the torment of this glade: I could put life into a heart that was dying.

And so I kissed her. And as I kissed her, her mouth opened and the kiss deepened. And her hands ran over me as she slept, and her fingers were in my hair, and she had rolled back to pull my body on top of hers, lifting her simple dress to expose her belly and pulling me onto her, trying to pull me into her. . . .

In her sleep.

But I woke suddenly to find myself in a coracle on a cold lake, surrounded by freezing mist through which the forest could be seen as a black, brooding fringe of winter limbs.

The kiss had not released Mauvaine, it had released me!

I spent years exploring that forest, searching for the glade where the painted child was imprisoned, but I found nothing but pain, loneliness, solitary adventurers . . . and finally Legion.

I have never forgotten that girl, and though the pain has gone, the betrayal remains.

I said, "You had dreamed of the taboos that would be placed upon you by your clan. These were your *geisas*. They have haunted you since your infancy. You cannot be blamed for using one of them inappropriately when you were still so young—"

I managed no more of the thought. The Celt rose angrily, glaring at me, and stalked away into the forest. I ran through my own words again, and realized that nothing could have been more inappropriate than my empty-headed advice to the man, and no doubt I would have to make amends.

But I had him!

I knew him, now. Though not his name!

The ship was finished. All of us who would sail in her stood in a circle around the sleek vessel on the shore, holding torches. Kylhuk stood before the prow, swathed in a cloak of feathers. The frightening woman, the dolorous voice, whispered to the wooden barque, moving slowly around the hull, her hands spread on the planking. The Fenlander and the grim-faced Raven cut notches on the wood with their blades and Kylhuk made his own mark between their signs. Each of us then carved a symbol on the right side of the hull and nailed a crudely fashioned shield above the mark. The shields were made from bark, or cloth, or shards of wood tied together and were gaudily and variously decorated. Everyone seemed to know what to carve and what to paint on the shields, but when the blade was passed to me, Kylhuk gripped my hand in his, directed the point to his own crudely scratched symbol—a tusked boar inside an oak leaf—and made me carve a *C*.

"You don't need a shield," he said with a smile. "Because you are protected by my own. I hope you can row," he added quietly, as I gave him back the knife.

"I expect I'll learn soon enough. Are you going to name the ship?"

"What do you think we've just been doing?"

"That's a complicated name we've given her. Twenty-seven in all . . ."

"It will help to confuse the enemy."

As supplies were put aboard the vessel, and a slipway to the river constructed out of logs, Guiwenneth found me and tugged me away from the river. She led me at a run through the tangled forest, saying only, "What have you done to Someone?"

"What do you mean?"

"I'll show you. . . ."

The Celt had hacked down small trees to make a glade.
He had piled the trimmed trunks into a wigwam shape, with
a gap so that he could enter. He sat inside, carving a statuette
by the light of a single torch rammed into the soft earth.

"Do you have an answer for me, Chris?" he asked without looking up.

"I have an answer for you. But it will be hard for you to
understand."

I glanced at Guiwenneth. "Find Issabeau . . ."

But Someone said, "Issabeau is here. She is in the forest.
When I have finished the cat"—he turned his carving
slightly and I saw that its features were feline—"she will
come back to me."

And he was quite right. A while later the undergrowth
was stirred by stealthy movement and the torchlight picked
out two quick, green eyes. A moment later, Issabeau stepped
into the clearing, her stick-of-shapes held firmly in her right
hand.

"Do you have an answer for me?" she asked. Someone
stepped out of his dream lodge.

I made them hold hands, then reached out to take that
loving grip in my own. Guiwenneth stood behind me, her
arm around my waist.

"I am an Outsider in this forest. Everything is new to me.
But of one thing I am certain: And that is that you are the
same children who met in the sea cave—Issabeau—and in
the idol glades—Someone. You do not recognize each other
because Someone is far older in time, because time has
passed, and in a way which will confuse things if I start to
explain it. But as Guiwenneth is my witness, and by the
power of hindsight that I carry with me, I now pronounce
you *versions of the same myth*. You have already had the
honeymoon. Now you must start to find a common path.
What the future holds for you I can't say. You have told me

the early part of your story, but the end of your story is not yet resolved. Only Kylhuk can glimpse such events."

They were looking at me blankly, then turned to gaze at each other, as if seeing each other for the first time, despite the fact that their relationship had been intimate for months. But somehow the difference in detail of that Celtic and medieval story had fallen away. They were not Issabeau and the Sea Cave Boy, nor Mauvaine and Jack of the Glades, but Issabeau and Someone son of Somebody.

Guiwenneth and I left them to their embrace.

Besides, away by the river Gwyr was sounding his horn and there was something urgent about that doleful howl. We returned at once to find out what was happening.

Kylhuk had had a trance-dream, it seemed; omens had supported his vision; he had even drowned a dog with its rider and watched the way the fleas had jumped. He was in no doubt that the time was right.

The ship would be launched immediately, despite the darkness, to begin its journey toward the heart of the forest, where Mabon was imprisoned.

CHAPTER 19

The simple ship had already been pushed out into the river, only the keel below its prow biting the mud of the bank; its aft was tethered to trees, which bent and creaked with the strain of holding the vessel still against the flow. A shaky ramp had been extended from the prow to the shore, and supplies were being carried aboard by torchlight. The oarsmen were at their stands below the deck, practicing their stroke to the steady rhythm of a drum.

Kylhuk was standing impatiently at the water's edge, the Fenlander beside him. Gwyr was already aboard; he stood in the stern, occasionally raising the carnyx and sounding the note that would summon all of the far-flung and the Forlorn Hopes who were attached to Legion.

"Where have you been, *slathan*? I told you to be at hand at all times!"

Kylhuk's fingers pinched my arm with irritation as he spoke, but he forced a smile as he waited for my answer.

"I've been learning about two of your best and most trusted scouts," I replied evenly. "And I've been helping the course of love."

This took him by surprise. "Love is a hard sort of thing," he said bitterly, the frown on his face deepening as he thought, no doubt, of Olwen. "You should not be wasting your time with it."

Someone and Issabeau had gathered their belongings and with quick and furtive glances toward me were making their careful way up the ramp.

As if he had seen the edge of my vision, Kylhuk glanced their way, then looked back at me with a wry smile.

"The course of love?"

"The course of love!"

"Well, well. I hadn't realized. Are they in the Delightful Realm?"

"Indeed. They might have been made for each other."

"Then for the moment," Kylhuk said agreeably, pinching my arm again as he stared at the romantic pair, "I'm all for love. Let's hope it lasts. I am very fond of that husky-voiced trickster. Now—Christian!—fetch your weapons, your blankets, find Guiwenneth, get aboard. I want to get moving on the river while it's still dark."

"Because Eletherion is on our tail?"

Kylhuk exchanged a brief, amused glance with the Fenlander before saying, "No, *slathan*. Because Eletherion has gone ahead of us. He has a quicker mind than I'd thought, and my Forlorn Hope—too busy journeying in their own Delightful Realm from what you tell me—have brought Legion to the river too far away from our final destination."

To the sound of horns, high-pitched ululation, and the somber chanting of the knights left behind, the boat of shields heaved against the river, the water flashing as the oars struck and lifted, soon finding their rhythm, a silent, steady stroke that was at first unsettling and then became smooth, so that we seemed to drift between the overcrowding forest.

Kylhuk took us to the middle of the stream. Two men with torches leaned out on each side of the prow, watching ahead for trees or other boats. On the raised stern, two people marshaled the spirits of the night to guard our rear: One was an elderly man wrapped in a voluminous cloak of bearskin, the skull rising above his long gray hair. Around him the night boiled with movement, elementals summoned by him and kept under his control, sent darting to the forest to scent and sense for danger. The other was Issabeau, her face in its cat form, her eyes reflecting green in the torchlight as she sniffed and listened to the animal world. Someone sat close by, keeping a watchful and protective eye on her.

For the rest of us there was nothing to do but sit, or sleep, or love, and I found a place behind several crates where there was a degree of seclusion and wrapped myself inside Guiwenneth's cloak, huddling snugly against the weary woman.

I woke at dawn. There was no sound except the gentle splash of water as the oars dipped. The slight forward surge of motion with every stroke was hardly noticeable. The mist-shrouded forest seemed to glide past us. A flight of cranes swooped over us as we lay, staring at the brightening sky, shivering with the damp.

We were on a river journey to the heart of the world, and already I felt as if we were in the deepest wilderness imaginable. At night, the forest echoed with cries and growls, sudden movement and the violent shaking of great trees. By day, only silence, each bend in the river bringing us farther toward the source, but showing us nothing but the wall of wildwood. There were no rapids, no broken water, no sand banks . . . only fallen trunks and statues, sprawled and broken where they had toppled from their sanctuaries on the shore. And an occasional boat, drifting downstream, its occupants invariably wearing the blank expression of the newly born, their gaze fixed ahead, their awareness not yet wide enough to encompass the boat of shields that stroked so lazily past them.

We drifted through space and we drifted through time.

Winter came and passed away in a matter of hours; thunderclouds blackened the horizon, a drenching rain shattered the river, drummed off the deck; and then a hazy sun warmed us. The forest shed its leaves, then went into green budding life, then was rich with the colors of late summer. Days had passed, perhaps weeks. Guiwenneth's cycle suggested more than two months, but again, how could I be sure? She was as much a part of this wilderness as the geese and cranes that flew above us, as the giant, ridge-backed salmon that occasionally broke the surface, swimming ahead of us, out of reach of the lines and hooks that Someone and the Fenlander cast in desperation for such a catch.

Every so often we passed a sanctuary, the forest cleared to make space for an idol, or a temple, sometimes rude constructions out of wood, sometimes shining marble, sometimes no more than a giant boulder, deeply carved with a symbol or rune that the sorcerers on the boat of shields anxiously tried to identify, their arguments becoming heated.

We put into the bank only once, at a shrine to Freyja, one of the northern goddesses, whose weeping, falcon-faced statue in rough stone dominated the shore. A spring of clear, fresh water bubbled from the cliff behind the ring of stones and the weathered statues of wolves and wild pigs, and we drank greedily. Someone had heard that this goddess wept tears of gold, but we found only mossy rock and rotting wood. Issabeau took on the shape of monkey and scaled the cliff, then stood guard against the wilderness beyond as all of the twenty-seven came ashore in groups to drink and wash, to touch the earth.

But after a while the spring turned suddenly sour and the sky darkened. The ground around the stones started to shake rhythmically, as if at a gigantic approach. Issabeau found her eagle's wings, came down to the shrine, alarmed and unashamedly in retreat. "A falcon flies this way!" she said.

We flung ourselves back along the ramp of our boat of shields and cast off.

Though we stared at the shrine for several minutes, we could not tell what or who had arrived there, and had soon left the place behind.

I took my turn at the oars and my back strengthened, my arms thickened, my mind deadened. Increasingly, we sailed through deep, cloying banks of mist, emerging to new locations, a river subtly changed. Reeds and rushes crowded the banks, then crumbling cliffs, their fractured ledges home to desperate thorns. But always we came back to the forest, meandering through the silent walls of summer green.

One dusk, Gwyr's cry of alarm roused me from lassitude and I joined the others at the starboard rail, staring at the indistinct shape of a giant walking parallel to our course, away in the woods. We could make out its head and shoulders above us, a cape of patterned furs. It carried a staff. A deep, resonant booming was its voice, the words indistinct as it called to a second walker on the other side of the river. This one was female, long hair flowing like golden water around a pale, pudgy face as she loomed hugely toward our boat, peering down at us, before turning deeper into the forest, her grumbling words like thunder. This stalking pair dogged our passage for a few hours through the night. Then, shortly before dawn, the male stepped across the river ahead of us, the wind from his swirling cloak of skins rocking us in the water, and the two of them disappeared into the wilderness.

We all became slightly mad.

Gwyr played his bronze horn in a rhythmic but melancholy way. Issabeau and Guiwenneth sang in a shrill, harmonizing duet, in a private, nonsense language that they had invented, laughing hysterically at some of the ululating trills they accomplished as Someone and I sat bemused and idle during our resting period. A grizzle-bearded hero from Finland, Vainomoi by name, constructed a six-note reed pipe and became quite accomplished on it. A crinkle-faced, weather-tanned, wolf-skinned shaman whittled a kazoo out of a long bone which he had tugged from a gigantic skeleton half submerged in the river.

And under the direction of Kylhuk, the rest of us made drums.

This combined voice, wind and percussion then commenced, under my guidance, to create a version of Beethoven's Fifth Symphony that would have had the composer jittering in his grave. We became crazy. The sounds filled the space of the river, sent whole flocks of crows circling into the night sky. The stroke of the oars changed to reflect the dancing around the many blazing torches that illuminated the upper deck.

At dawn we were still playing, entranced, tranced out, lost in time, lost in space, the beat of the drum filling our heads, our legs moving effortlessly as we circled and twirled, arms outstretched, moving slowly through the fires, chanting and stepping out to the monotonous, all-consuming, four-note rhythm.

A shadow had appeared ahead of us, but none of us had seen it at that time.

The shadow grew, and if we began to see it, we could not accommodate it in the dream vision.

The boat of shields pulled onward, up the river. The shadow reared, grew tall, grew more distinct.

We were dancing in a circle, like the Greeks, my arms around the delightful Guiwenneth and the pungently animal Jarag, who had taken to this ritual formation with exuberant delight, grinning, singing, and breathing on me at every possible moment.

"Good dance! Good dance! We dance this way on river shore before collect fish and shell. Good dance!"

I had never known the prehistoric hunter so vociferous.

Opposite me, the impeccably trimmed and dressed Gwyr was squashed between Kylhuk, who was half naked and very drunk, and Issabeau, who was in a dreamy state, her face a fluid film of animal features, all vying for control over the darkly beautiful human.

When the circle juddered to an awkward stop, I looked up. Gwyr had ceased dancing and was staring beyond me, his face a depiction of pure astonishment. Slowly the music faded away. The oars struck relentlessly as the boat surged forward, but on the upper deck there was only silence as we turned to stare at the massive tree that had at last loomed large in our awareness.

"Olwen's Hands!" Kylhuk breathed in amazement. "So that's where he is. I had no idea . . . no idea how vast!"

"It's drawing us toward it," the jarag said, leaning over the bow and staring at the water. The river flowed past us, away from the tree, but we were caught in a deeper current drawing us forward and the oars were struck, the effort of rowing being wasted.

Still the tree rose ahead of us, its dark trunk a writhing mass of faces, shapes, and glowing fires, its girth blocking the horizon, its height and widespread branches smothering the dawn sky.

"Divine Son of the Mother! The bitch didn't mean her bastard to escape from this!"

The words were again the astonished words of Kylhuk, a strong man again, eyes wide, sobering fast.

Then Issabeau shouted out, "By the Good God! What is that?"

But we had all seen the swirl of water, the great whirling maelstrom that was sucking us toward its deadly mouth.

Kylhuk shouted, "Back oar! Can you hear me below? Back oar now! Or the pool will suck us in! Get the rhythm! *Back oar!*"

With a clatter of wood and the uncertain beat of the

stroke-drum, the oarsmen tried to find a reverse stroke. Several oars splintered, the boat lurched, the water thrashed as blades struck in confusion, the ship of shields beginning to twist and turn as it was sucked toward the pool.

"Drag it back!" Kylhuk screamed angrily, dropping from upper to lower deck. The drum had stopped. The oars trailed deeply in the water. We clung to the rails, the mast, even the flimsy hutches for support as our progress toward the swirling water below the bulging roots of this towering growth was slowed.

Again the boat of shields lurched, throwing several men over the side. The shields clattered against the hull, some detaching and falling away, taking their protection with them. The defenses were weakened. Then the prow dipped, the hull reeled drunkenly, slewing to the starboard. The ever-determined Jarag and two others leaped into the white water, holding ropes, and tried to swim to the bone-strewn bank to find stones or trees around which to tie the tethers. They were sucked out of sight, whipped down into the deep like leaves in a storm drain.

The end came so suddenly I have little clear recollection: The ship broke in two, splintering across the hull and pitching everyone else on the upper deck into the swirling river. I remember seeing Kylhuk flying backward, his face contorted with pain; I remember Guiwenneth grabbing for me, her saturated hair wound around her face, her eyes full of despair in the instant before she was flung from me and lost into the river. Someone grunted loudly, somersaulted as a spar struck him and vanished in a plume of blood. I went under the water. The current had taken my feet and I was dragged down so fast that within seconds I was in the silent realm of the dead, my lungs bursting as I held my breath, my arms flailing as I sought feebly for anything on which to gain a hold.

Then my vision darkened. A corpse swirled past me, gape

mouthed, fish white, dull eyed. Issabeau's black hair floated
in my vision, the woman turning almost peacefully, her arms
across her chest, her eyes closed. She had resigned herself to
death.

I reached for her, but she was caught in the spiraling flow
and spun away from me, and at that moment I, too, began to
resign myself to the cold and to breathing out for a final
time, my mind suddenly clear and calm—

When a force like a vise pressed into my head. A finger
the size of a baby's arm blocked the vision from one eye.
Something huge had risen up below me and grasped me in
its hand!

I felt myself pulled up, then freed from the water, letting
go of the stale breath and sucking in air gratefully, and with
a sobbing cry of relief. A second powerful hand was on my
arm. A mass of dripping weeds *blinked* at me, eyes in the
river wrack, a grinning mouth—

Elidyr!

Then he grunted with effort, heaved and flung me onto
the bank, literally that: lifted me and threw me. A branch
broke my flight and bruised my arm. I fell to the turf, next
to the groaning bodies of Guiwenneth and Issabeau. A moment later the ground shook as Someone thumped down, his
face twisted with pain, his soaking hair red with his own
blood. Guiwenneth crawled toward me and slumped over
me, her mouth on my cheek, her fingers digging into my
flesh. She was still only half-conscious. As I sat up, cradling
the woman carefully, I saw Kylhuk some yards away. He
was on all fours, retching up water and shaking his head.
The jarag was beside him, slowly getting to his feet and staring at the weed-draped giant who had just hurled him to the
shoreline.

Elidyr, the green-haired monster, stood in the maelstrom
and stared back at us, the weed writhing like snakes. I

shouted out, "Where is Gwyr? We need him, Elidyr! We need our Interpreter!"

After a terrible moment of silence, the boatman grumbled words that were incoherent against the noise of the swirling pool.

Then he shouted," Gwyr!" and raised his arms. The lank shape of the Interpreter of Tongues was drawn from the water, draped across Elidyr's palm like a rag doll. A moment later, Elidyr stepped through the wild water—he could not have been touching the bottom of the whirlpool!—and emerged onto the bank, the weeds drawing back into his body just as once the flowers and fruits of the forest had drawn back into his supernatural skin.

Elidyr turned the Interpreter upside down, holding him by his legs. Soon, Gwyr vomited water and twitched with consciousness. And soon he, like the rest of us, was sitting huddled round a glowing fire, Elidyr back in the shadows of the wood watching us, his favorite place, it seemed.

When I was warm and dry, I went over to the boatman, who frowned uncomfortably as I approached. He was crouching, but still looking down at me through the deep ridges of his eyebrows, his jaw working beneath the heavy beard.

"I thought I was a dead man at that moment. Thank you for my life."

He nodded quickly, then looked away.

"Have you been with us all the time, Elidyr? Are you following us? Why not stay with us?"

"Go away," he grunted, then reached out and prodded me away from him as easily and indifferently as I might shift a cat that was snuggling too closely against me on a sofa.

Thank God for Gwyr! As the rest of us had succumbed to whatever spell had been cast about us, the Interpreter of Tongues had managed to stay in touch with the hidden sounds and sights of the world around him. Even from his own dreamtime, his function—to see the hidden meaning in words and sounds—had enabled him to surface suddenly and see the danger. Without that moment of vision, the maelstrom would have taken us suddenly and devastatingly. I suspected that not even Elidyr could have saved us.

Kylhuk agreed with me. But for Gwyr, he said darkly, we would have been swept below the arching, giant roots of the tree, and would have been lost. Others before us had managed to break the spell—there was evidence around us to testify to that fact—but it was clear that even those had often fallen foul of the defenses of this massive prison.

Stunned, disorientated, shivering in the shadow of the towering oak, we looked around at the desperate place on which Elidyr had "beached" us. Ten or so others of the Legion had survived the drowning and dragged themselves to where they could smell the fire.

We were camped, now, among the sad and rotting hulls of ships, some extending above the water, some broken on the banks or among the trees of the forest's edge. There were bones of men as well, and of animals, some of them grotesque, many of gigantic size. This whole place was a graveyard and the roots of the tree had reached to encompass the remnants.

And it was not just ships and creatures that had fallen foul of Mabon's prison. A city had once stood here. As the light grew brighter, Kylhuk pointed to its gates, its turrets, its once-proud walls, all of them now absorbed into the gnarled, black bark of the tree, sucked upward as the tree had grown, broken into its components, but still recognizable.

We had come ashore in the corrupted remains of its harbor. The bridge to the land was still visible, impressed within the high-arching roots that spanned the double flow of the river.

At the tree, the Long Person divided; or rather, her two branches, flowing below the roots, joined, forming the whirlpool, to continue through the land to a long forgotten ocean.

"Are those the Gates?" I asked Kylhuk in a whisper, glancing back as he stood behind me. His hand was a gentle pressure on my shoulder, his breath sharp and stale after the dream dance.

"The Gates? Ivory and Horn? No. That isn't how the Cleverthreads weaved them for me. But the two branches of the river have flowed through them."

"Bringing the truth and the lie," I repeated, remembering our earlier conversation. I could see no difference between the two branches of the river, and no sign on the huge arches of wood and stone that might distinguish their origins. "Which comes from which?"

Kylhuk's hand gripped my flesh painfully and when I looked round at him again, he was grinning at me, his eyes twinkling.

"Why *Christian*! That's for *you* to find out!"

"Because I'm *slathan* . . . I should have known it."

"By the rough love in Olwen's Hands, I'm sure you will succeed! I have that much confidence in you. Besides, you are hardly alone. I selected your companions carefully. And I notice that we are all here, all but Abandagora, and you can replace him adequately."

"The Forlorn Hope?"

"Tried and tested in the fire, like Annanawn, my father's sword. I despaired only once, when I truly thought they— and you—had been destroyed by Kyrdu's bastards. But my *slathan* surfaced in the wilderness, as my dream had told me he would, and brought them back. And here you all are. Not Forlorn. Not dead. But alive! Determined!"

I looked quickly around me, at the activity, the shelters being built, the boats of past adventurers being looted for

fuel, crude shields being hacked and shaped, idols and pro-
pitiatory structures being erected. I could see Guiwenneth
among them, and Someone son of his father scraping the
whiskers from his cheeks with a small bronze dagger as he
stared up at the tree and its glowing, running figures.

Kylhuk broke through my distraction. "What's on your
mind, Christian?"

"Only that I have no idea what you expect of me, or what
I'm to do."

"Your task is to find your mother. Isn't it? Isn't that why
you came here?"

I couldn't read him. His voice was gentle, his icy gaze almost soft. The smile through his beard was neither triumphant, nor sarcastic. It might almost have been encouraging.

But I didn't trust him!

"I saw her dead and dancing by the neck," I murmured,
and Kylhuk reached out to squeeze my arm.

"You saw what you were told to see, Christian. You were
just a boy at the time. Now you're a man. What you saw is
in the past. This is the present. And tomorrow is the future."

I would have laughed at the simplicity, but his eyes were
alive with energy and triumph. He went on. "In the future,
dreams remain undreamt! Don't you see, Christian? If the
dreams are *waiting* to be dreamed, we can choose to *shape*
that dream. There were men and women on the Boat of
Shields, and in my Legion, who do such things all the time,
only they don't know how to use their skills to the best effect—which is why," he added quietly, "they're all so
scrawny, scruffy, and obsessed with wild, familiar spirits!"

I saw what I was told to see?

"What did you mean by that?" I asked Kylhuk, whose attention was beginning to wander as the need for raising defenses became more urgent. "What did you mean that I saw

what I was told to see? *Who* told me? *What* did I see? Are you saying my mother didn't die?"

"Mabon will show you." Then he laughed out loud, adding, "Just as soon as we can tease him out of the tree! Relax, *slathan*. Something wonderful is about to happen to you."

And he walked away, as cryptic as ever—he had never explained the full meaning of *slathan* to me—as dismissive as ever, a man drawn to the task, this final task, the rescue of Mabon from his tree.

Odd, though, the way he had said, "tease him out."

As if, despite our best efforts, Mabon himself might be reluctant to come. . . .

CHAPTER 20

Where was Eletherion in all of this; and his brothers, the other Sons of Kyrdu? The question was asked repeatedly of Kylhuk, who simply answered, "I imagine they are close by."

It was oddly circumspect behavior for a man who had recently seemed so confident, so aware of things in the future. And I guessed, before Guiwenneth suggested the same thing to me, that his true talent for far-sight and that uncanny sense of all-knowing had come from the Dolorous Voice and the Cleverthreads, none of whom were with us now.

Perhaps Kylhuk was on his own for the first time in a long time, although he had his Forlorn Hope at his side, the small band that he had nurtured and guarded with his warriors' lives. He had sent all other survivors from the boat back down the river to set up camp and wait for his call.

But Eletherion was on our minds, and despite Kylhuk's almost violent objection, now that we were down to seven, Someone and myself scouted into the forest for a mile or so, while Guiwenneth went back along the river with Issabeau. Jarag, his body daubed with moss and lichen from the damp rocks, crept as far toward the first rise of the towering tree as he dared, sniffing the air and tasting great handfuls of river mud, riverwater, and the earth from the higher bank.

Strange things were happening, I realized later, but for the moment I only noted the oddities in behavior. I had passed through several forest glades, taking the *sinister* side (as Issabeau called it) while Someone took the other, and was waiting for my companion in a shaft of welcome sunlight when a towering, upright *boar* ran at me from the edge of the glade, and through the edge of my vision.

I swung round to protect myself against the jutting tusks and gaping muzzle of the charging beast, and found the proud Celt standing there, breathless and hot as he quickly dropped to his haunches, recovering from his run.

He looked up at me and smiled, then frowned as he saw my shocked expression.

"Is something wrong?"

"I don't know. You took me by surprise. . . . Is something hunting you?"

"This forest is alive with ghosts. They are from the prison, I'm sure of it. Kylhuk warned me that we might encounter them." He looked round nervously. "I feel strange," he went on. "My skin itches. I want to scratch against the bark of a good old tree. I can smell things below the ground, and they're making me hungry! I suspect that Mabon has sent his own defenses into the wilderness. Can you feel them around you, too?"

I couldn't, but didn't say so. Instead I closed my eyes, breathed deeply, turned where I stood, trying to experience the presences that had alarmed my friend, wondering again whether Mabon was trapped or hiding, or both. When I opened my eyes, I was startled by the brightness of the sun through the summer foliage. And as I turned away from the glaring light, the boar was rising beside me, leaning toward me!

Again I stepped back, looked directly at the beast and saw only Someone, son of the Defeated King, reaching toward me anxiously.

"You seem disturbed," he whispered.

"I keep seeing the image of a wild boar. On its hindlegs. Very big, very menacing. But when I look at it, the boar vanishes. . . ."

I decided to say no more than that, to leave Someone temporarily in the dark about the apparitions associated with his own welcome features.

The Celt tugged at his beard, pale eyes glowing with agreement. "Yes! I sense it, too. Mabon is certainly aware of us—legend has it that he hunts boar in the form of that same creature!—he is probably watching us. Come on . . . we must go back. If Eletherion *is* here, he's biding his time!"

The sky was darkening toward night and the massive trunk burned with the faces and shapes of the lost. Guiwenneth and Issabeau stood with their arms around each other, staring up at the *melange* of movement, occasionally crying out as they recognized some beast or a figure from their own legend, sometimes startled as a face formed and leered at them, a boyish physiognomy, with flaring fire as its hair and a mouth that grinned, then went hard; this apparition was fleeting and very rare.

Standing naked between two torches, close to the first swell of root, his hair caked in mud, his body still plastered with moss, Jarag was silently staring at the same blaze of masks. He had been like this for several hours now, and Kylhuk sat close by, watching him, wrapped in a heavy cloak, sword across his lap, as motionless as the prehistoric man.

This was the second strangeness, but Someone by now was very disturbed and very remote from me, standing by the edge of the river, staring back at the treeline, a deep furrow between his deep eyes.

I picked a little food from the spit over the dying fire and huddled down between the spread roots of a thicket, only to move quickly away as the roots kicked at me. It was Elidyr, disguised and silent, and he glowered at me from the foliage.

"Go away."

"Sorry. Didn't see you there."

I crawled to a less intrusive haven. But even here I was suddenly prodded in the back, startling me so that I choked on my first mouthful of supper. Turning, I realized that Gwyr was sitting behind me, swathed in a horse blanket he had rescued from the river. He grinned at me through his trimmed beard.

"What are you doing here?" I asked him.

"Keeping out of the way. Elidyr is lurking in the woods and I don't like the way he looks at me."

"Elidyr is ten feet away," I whispered, cocking my head to the left. Gwyr glanced nervously into the gloom, then scowled and turned back to contemplate Someone, by the river.

"What's he doing?" I asked. "Do you have any idea?"

Someone was standing with his back to the river, ankle deep in the wiry grass that grew from the muddy edge. He was in trousers, bronze cuirass strapped to his breast, a gleaming torque around his neck, arms folded. His eyes were open. Issabeau, in her catskin cloak, her hair tied in a flowing ponytail, stood near to him, watching him carefully, but not moving.

"We have always looked after each other," Gwyr said. "Now more than ever we must be aware of what is happening in our group. Issabeau is guarding Someone. Kylhuk guards Jarag. You must pay attention to Guiwenneth."

"Who guards *you*?"

He laughed forlornly. "My task is almost done, if not done completely."

"Interpreting."

"Certainly. And keeping my eyes open. Once the Oldest Animals have been summoned, if the jarag can speak to them, then all I'll be good for is to fight against the Sons of Kyrdu, if they've survived the maelstrom, if they're still around."

The way Gwyr spoke confirmed that everything was happening according to a plan of Kylhuk's devising. His own role was almost finished. Someone and Jarag seemed to be coming into their own. Issabeau and Guiwenneth were still behaving in an ordinary way, as was I.

"But what does Kylhuk intend for me?" I breathed rhetorically, watching the huddled man as he gazed steadily at the naked shaman.

I hadn't expected Gwyr to hear my words, but he whispered, "Be on your guard. From everything I see and hear, you are the key to Mabon, though I don't know how."

The same words, more or less, that he had spoken to me many months ago, when we had first ridden through the wildwood together.

"Look. He's here!"

Gwyr's words directed me to Someone. A dark shadow flickered around the tall Celt. The man's face dissolved into an evil muzzle, torchlight on jutting tusks and a raised spine of quill-like gray hairs on his head. The face of the boar was fleeting. The man wailed and writhed where he stood, eyes bulging. Again the boar inhabited him, its pizzle curling from the poor man's groin, lashing like a coiled whip. Then gone again.

Issabeau was clapping her hands delightedly. Kylhuk was standing, tensed and ready for something. The jarag was racing back and forth along the river's edge, stooping, grabbing, touching, and reaching his face to the heavens to howl or bark.

"What the *hell* is going on?"

Gwyr said, "Kylhuk said this would happen. Mabon has been nosing for us, sniffing us out, testing us. But for some reason he can't fathom Someone. The Celt has upset him. Kylhuk knew this in advance, but I have no idea why it should be."

I did, though.

And I told Gwyr, "It's part of his *geisa* . . . or one of his *geisas*. I'd never heard of *geisas* until I met your forlorn band."

"A *geisa*?"

"Yes. He can confuse sorcerers until his true name is known."

That particular talent, though, was not from Someone's own story, but from the medieval romance of Issabeau and the Sea Cave Boy.

"Having been unnamed before his royal father was killed," I hazarded, "when he is close to a sorcerer he must make himself available for their inspection, though he will confuse them in the process."

Gwyr nodded as if everything was now clear. "That sounds right. It's very much the sort of imposition that would be placed around the neck of a king under the circumstances you mention, being unnamed at the time of his father's death. It had never occurred to me before now that Someone, with his wild hair, is invisible to sorcerers. How useful . . . how very useful."

So Kylhuk had used the Celt to draw Mabon, son of the Mother, to the edge of his prison stronghold, where he had reached out to probe and peruse the Forlorn Hope and found a man he couldn't recognize or fathom, inhabiting the Celt in his boar-shape as he tried to break the man's identity, failing in the task but revealing himself.

Mabon was both prisoner and ruler of his domain.

From everything that was happening by the river, both Gwyr and I agreed that Mabon's stronghold was weakened and vulnerable, and that we would soon be passing from the wildwood into the smouldering Tree of Faces, closer to the enigmatic hunter who was the object of our quest.

I *needed* to know what would be expected of me!

But before I could articulate this sudden, angry thought to

Gwyr, Kylhuk had shouted, "*Slathan!* Show yourself. Now! They are rising all around us!"

"The Oldest Animals!" Gwyr gasped beside me, his face a mask of astonishment and admiration. "By the Cauldron's Depths, the man has done it!"

"*Slathan!* Gwyr! Show now!"

Kylhuk was storming toward the forest's edge, great cloak flowing. He stopped when he saw us emerge from cover, waved us to him angrily. Someone and Issabeau were in an embrace, mutually enveloped in the faint phosphorescence that outlined the uneasy giant boar, Mabon's ghostly presence at the events now unfolding.

The jarag was walking backward in a circle, eyes wide, mouth gaping, his beard and breast wet with the saliva that seemed to pour from his mouth. Suddenly he wiped his chin, stopped the retrograde movement, and grabbed for a torch, holding it above his head and peering at the river.

Beyond him, the vast, overleaning tree glowed more brightly, and the movement and action of creatures seemed to be drawn toward us, as if we were the focus of that great stampede.

Kylhuk smacked me around the back of the head, impelled me before him, dragging Gwyr by the arm until we were within scenting distance of the overripe shaman.

"They are rising around us," Kylhuk said. "The Oldest Animals. Jarag has performed his task better than I could have hoped. When they turn and run—the creatures—we must follow them. They will take us into the land beyond these roots, and Mabon won't have time to flee."

His grip on my shoulder tightened suddenly. "There!" he whispered, pointing to where the surface of the whirlpool was bulging as a silvery shape rose through the water, a man-fish, a leering salmon!

"Clinclaw!" Gwyr muttered, then urged, "And there!"

The turf close to the forest had swollen into the shape of a giant manlike figure, resting on his back.

In the greenwood itself, the trees were arching and twisting, as if being pushed apart by an unseen force. Feathers began to swirl and rise on the breeze. An owl's face watched us from the darkness.

"Cawloyd . . ." Gwyr whispered. "That's how the owl is known in my country, but it will have an older name which Jarag has used. . . ."

The swelling turf opened and the man stood, as tall as Elidyr, if not taller. His face was a hound's muzzle below the broken, jagged stubs of antlers. His body was clothed in the limp forms of pine martins, rats, weasels, and stoats, all the vermin of the forest, attached to his body by their teeth, clothing him in corpses.

This one was called Rhedinfayre, oldest stag, according to Gwyr.

From the river, the fish-headed man stepped to the shore, pike and perch and carp and eels thrashing from his skin, where they hung by their tiny, bony teeth.

And the owl, too, was clothed in the fluttering bodies of birds: ravens, robins, scintillant kingfishers, and the single, massive shape of an eagle, its beak hooked through the ligaments of the man's neck, hanging across his belly, wings stretched like a living golden breastplate.

I was so enthralled by these monstrous visions that I failed to see what was happening to the Mesolithic hunter-shaman, the naked jarag whose forgotten talents had summoned these ancient echoes. He was crouched on the ground between his three remaining torches, incontinent, terrified, shuddering with a fever of fear.

Kylhuk leaned over him quickly and ran a powerful hand down his back, then touched his neck and lank hair. Jarag looked up. I was shocked to see the skull leering from his face. Corpselike, emptied, he lay quietly down on his side and

Kylhuk spread his cloak across him, covering the ghoulish features.

"That is that, then," said Gwyr.

"*Slathan!* Stay close!" Kylhuk bellowed. Good God, was that a sob in his voice? For all that the jarag had kept his own, strange counsel, was this inheritor of quests distressed at the dying of the primitive man?

"*Slathan*, he stay close," I muttered archly. The Tree of Faces flared, the flow of movement represented by the glowing shapes in the bark quickening slightly, and the sudden light made the Oldest Animals seemed starker as they stood in wood, on earth, by water.

Then the boar stalked past me, glaring at me, and when I met its gaze, I saw my friend Someone. He stared at me inquisitively, head cocked, mouth working strangely. I turned away from him and the black pig was there around him, Mabon surveying the events from his attachment to the unfathomable Celt.

Someone stared at me, but his eyes were not his own. And those eyes were curious about me.

He asked, "What do you seek?"

Gwyr nudged me meaningfully and I answered, "My mother. I seek my mother."

"How did she die?" Mabon asked through the lips of my companion.

"She took her own life. On a tree."

"What is served by finding her?"

What was served by finding her? What did *that* mean? I stood and stared blankly.

Gwyr nudged me again and I pushed him away angrily. I didn't answer. I didn't know *how* to answer.

Someone stalked away.

But then a vague memory of a story came back to me, of Arthur and his knights and their Grail quest. I remembered my mother leaning down toward me, as I snuggled below the blankets, my mind alive with those castles and gleaming knights.

"The *truth,*" I called to him. "The *truth* is served by finding her."

That was when the cat leaped from the river!

Sleek, lean, a blur of movement, the gray-furred feline snatched at one of the fish hanging from the body of Clinclaw, then crossed the bank to tear and snarl at the dangling form of an otter on Rhedinfayre's chest. But it was the eagle that was her target. As the owl-faced Cawloyd raised its arms defensively, the cat was on the eagle, chewing at the great bird's feathered neck.

The eagle released the owl, and bird and beast rolled in a blur of feathers and angry movement, their harsh, hoarse cries and wails deafening as they struggled for supremacy.

Then the eagle took flight, a slow beat of massive wings, a slow rise, the cat held in its claws, still screeching and twisting. The eagle seemed to have doubled in size, the cat to have shrunk. It flew across the root of the tree, across the river and to the farther shore. The salmon-faced man had returned to the river and his silver form could be seen swimming the edge of the whirlpool. The owl and the dog-stag were running away from us, following the eagle.

"Come on!" Kylhuk cried. In his kilt and breastplate, with little else to cover him, he was in close pursuit of these oddities from the past. Gwyr was running, Someone, too, and I could see Guiwenneth, spears in hand, head low, red hair streaming behind her as she raced toward the tree, having established with a quick glance that I was behind her.

Where was Issabeau?

I passed the covered body of the jarag in his half circle of torches. I looked back along the river. And then I realized that she was the cat who had attacked the eagle.

Curiouser and curiouser, this use of animals to breach the fortress-prison.

We were running along the root of a tree that loomed immense and alive with fire above us, its branches reaching out to cover the sky. The trunk leaned away into the heavens, but the roots were formed from the broken stones of a city, and soon, as the river dropped farther below us, I realized we were passing through a place of broken, petrified wood, and crumbling wood-cracked stone. Twisted iron gates, crushed wooden doors, echoing shafts and tunnels besieged the senses as Kylhuk led us in the heated pursuit of the eagle and the flowing, ghostly animal forms of the fish, the dog, the stag, and the owl. Like specters, their shapes shifting between the myriad forms of the creatures they comprised, they flowed ahead of us, returning to the security of the stronghold.

Kylhuk was a barking, baying hound at their heels, his laughter and his anger sounding in equal measure, and time and again I heard him demand that his *slathan* keep close to him.

In all of this, I would never have known which passage into the tree to take. The entrance was disguised not by subtlety but by quantity. We had crossed the river. Our world was the world of gray stone, fractured pillar, and twisted wood, a labyrinth of alleys, paths, and shafts that boomed with sound as we traversed them.

The eagle dropped the cat!

The cat snarled, arched up into human form, Issabeau naked and slick with sweat, padding quickly in pursuit of the giant bird of prey, then standing and pointing to the arch of marble, ivory, and horn through which the bird had flown and into which the writhing shapes of the Owl of Cawloyd and the Stag of Rhedinfayre were passing.

The salmon, Clinclaw, was in the river, finding its own way home, no doubt through the maelstrom.

"Quickly! Quickly!" Guiwenneth called to me as she followed Kylhuk and the wary Someone through the entrance. I exchanged a nervous glance with Gwyr.

"You don't have to come," I suggested.

"He hasn't told me to go back. And with Jarag dead . . . if these Oldest Animals need to be understood . . . who else is there but me?"

"You are too noble, Gwyr."

"No, Christian," he retorted with a grin, "I am long lost!"

"Look after yourself."

His sudden look at me was full of pain. "I tried. But you should have found me sooner."

"SLATHAN!"

Kylhuk was framed in the arch, bronze-bladed sword in hand and thrusting toward me, then using it to wave to me, to summon me to him, and as if ropes were attached to the point of that sword and to my legs, I ran to where he waited. I entered the gate, Gwyr on my heels, Guiwenneth a sudden presence in my arms, her face radiant with the glow of this inner realm, a light that emanated from the ten towering statues that stood in a semicircle about us, watching us with strange, stone faces.

"I have heard of these ten," Kylhuk whispered in my ear. His blade was bright as he weaved a pattern between the watching figures. "You can see the fish, the hound, the bird of prey . . . their names come back to me: Silvering! Cunhaval! Falkenna! That is the child in the land, *Sinisalo*. That one is the shadow of forgotten forests. *Skogen*. Beware of it! And that's the shape of memory, the storyteller: *Gaberlungi*. And that one's old mother, and young mother . . . I can't remember what they're called. And the face of death, *Morndun*. And of grief . . . look at them. . . . Look at them, Christian!"

I looked without understanding at these crude stone carvings, blank-faced masks hacked out of the hard gray stone.

I listened without understanding as Gwyr whispered the strange names himself, the names of these stone guardians:

"Skogen, Gaberlungi, Sinisalo, Morndun . . ."

"What are they, Gwyr?"

"The Oldest Animals. The oldest memories . . . I've heard of them all my life. They mark the way to the realm of *Lavondyss,* the unknown land, the beginning of the Labyrinth. It's a place of mystery. The unknowable, forgotten past. These are one way inward. They have often been sought. Never found!"

He was almost breathless with awe.

But we were here, we had followed them to where Mabon was imprisoned, and we *had* found them. Some reckless impulse in me made me smile and think aloud that they could not hurt us now.

"We'll find out soon enough," was Gwyr's wise and whispered counsel.

Kylhuk turned to me. "Look more closely. What do you see?"

Between the stone pillars he had called *Cunhaval,* the hound, and *Morndun,* death, and between *Gaberlungi* and *Sinisalo,* memory and the child in the land, I could see a cornfield, summer trees on the ridge, blue sky. I suddenly realized I was looking at the field behind Oak Lodge, the place of my mother's death!

"It's my home," I whispered.

"*One* of them only," Kylhuk said thoughtfully. "One is the true dream of that place, one a false dream. Look carefully, *slathan.* Everything now depends on your making the right choice. *These* are those gates, those Ivory and Horn gates that test and torment us all. Which one seems to speak most honestly to you?"

I was looking at the place of my mother's passing. Morndun? But I was looking too at a *memory* of that passing. Gaberlungi? I couldn't decide. I opted for memory and pointed through the gate between memory and the child in the land.

Kylhuk grunted, then turned to Gwyr, prodding him in the chest.

"Go back if you wish. You've done enough."

"I'll stay, if it's all the same to you," replied the Interpreter nervously.

"Don't move from this place, then. I'll make you my marker. You'll mark the way out when this business is done!"

"Take my cloak," said Gwyr. "You look cold."

He removed his short woolen cloak and passed it to Kylhuk, whose flesh was pale with the chill in the air. Kylhuk accepted gladly and covered his shoulders and arms with the garment.

"When you pass this ring of totems, through the gate which we hope is Truth," he said to Guiwenneth, "you must remember that childhood ride you made out of the wood, when you reached the end of the world, with the *slathan,* here. When he was a boy. Mabon will remember, too. That's how we draw him out."

"I remember the ride," Guiwenneth said. "Manandoun was my guardian at the time."

"Indeed. He was an angry man that day. You rode too far. You did more than you were told."

Guiwenneth glanced at me awkwardly. Without taking her eyes from me, she said, "But I *did* the deed I was told to do. I obeyed your instructions. And I fell in love with the boy."

"I'd noticed," Kylhuk said. "A little love will help. Everything now depends on Mabon himself. Remember that childhood ride. He will *catch onto it*. That's how we will draw him out, though that's all I can tell you. It was the last third of the tapestry. . . ." He opened his hand to reveal a crushed piece of embroidered cloth. It fell away to dust as he held it. "My life has been informed by a weave of silk," he said with a wry smile. "But nothing lasts. Not even a promise. Go and find Mabon! Go!"

CHAPTER 21

It was that same summer's day, the fields of barley flowing in the warm breeze, the edge of the wood a dark,
brooding wall. I had run here, on my way back from Shadoxhurst. I had used a stick to strike at thistles. I had jumped
the brook, then heard something in the wood. For a while I
had stood and stared at the trees and just as I had turned for
home, the girl had come, cantering suddenly toward me.

I was here again, a man in a boy's body, and I turned
where I stood and stared at the sky with its drifting, summer
cloud. My hands felt small, my face smooth, my ribs prominent. I laughed and explored this memory of my early youth.
The scents of summer were strong.

Distantly, the clock on the church tower was chiming
three.

Where was she? Where was the girl? From the wood
again . . .

A flurry of wings drew my attention back to Ryhope. An
owl was looping in the bright air, then a hawk, then a black-
bird. A tall, red-brown flank moved through the underbrush,
a stag edging too close to the open space. I heard a growl
and a grunt, then the soft complaint of a horse being kicked
forward, and a moment later she rode out of the wood, just
as I remembered her.

She cantered toward me, white hair flowing, white mask

solemn. The crop she held was trailing by her left leg. Her short tunic seemed simply draped on her, this girl child, coming toward me.

There was that same hint of boyishness, that same tension in limb and posture.

Suddenly she kicked the horse into a gallop, charged down on me, struck me gently with the feathered crop, laughed—a deeper laugh than I remembered—turned and came back, haughty in the saddle, peering down through the uncracked layer of white paint.

"Is this how it was?" a boy's voice asked. "Do you remember her like this?"

"Who are you?"

"Who do you think I am?"

"Mabon?"

"Of course Mabon! Some people take on the shapes of animals. I take on the shapes of people! Through their memories," he added. "Climb up behind me, I want to remember the girl rider."

He reached down, grabbed my arm and hauled me onto the broad back of the gray. He yelled out loud, kicked the animal, and we rode like the wind into the barley field, but it was no thin, soft girl that I held on to now, but a hard-muscled man-boy. His breath was not sweet like Guiwenneth's, but sour and stale. Aged! His back, below the silly tunic, was covered with graying hair. He was so much older than his white mask made him seem. He laughed boyishly, though, as the gray stumbled and struggled through the tall corn.

"Was it here?" he shouted suddenly.

I didn't know what he meant, but he suddenly reined in, threw the horse to the side, sent me tumbling, went sprawling himself.

He stood and turned in the barley, striking the ripening

heads with his hands. "Yes, it was here that she fell. I can feel it. Where is the tree? Come on! I want to see the tree."

Again he mounted the tired horse. Again he hauled me up behind him. He galloped to Strong Against the Storm, staring up at the dark branches, the rich green foliage.

"What a tree!" he whispered. "Yes! A good place to die. A very good place to die."

Then with a shout, "But she isn't dead yet! Her death is still days away! Where is she?"

"My mother?"

"Of course your mother! Where is she? I want to see her."

"In the house, I expect."

"Show me!"

I pointed to Oak Lodge and he thrashed the flank of the gray and we galloped round the wood and over the fence, to ride right up to the windows of my father's study.

I had thought Mabon would stop there and dismount, but he kicked the animal viciously and the horse smashed through the windows. Mabon rode us twice around the empty room, hitting the cabinets with his crop.

"What's this?"

"His specimens. My father's specimens."

"Is this where he worked?"

"Yes."

He rode into the hall, then through the parlor and into the kitchen, striking the metal pans hanging on the wall, sweeping the storage jars from their shelves.

"What's this?"

"The kitchen."

"Did she work here?"

"My mother? Yes. She did the cooking for the family."

"Why isn't she here?"

"I don't know. Perhaps she's gone to one of the villages."

"She should be here." He beat his crop against the pans,

drumming on them and delighting in the various tinny sounds.

Then back through the parlor and stumbling up the stairs. The horse bucked and whinnied, but Mabon thrashed it. On the landing he paused, leaned forward over the gray's nape, looked at the doors, then made the animal kick into Steven's bedroom.

My brother lay fast asleep and Mabon rode round the bed, peering down at him, flicking the feathered crop at the face in repose.

"Who's this?"

"My brother. Steven."

Mabon peered at him closely. "His sleep is charmed."

Yes, I thought. It is! But this was Steven several years after the time when young Guiwenneth had come from the wood, years after our mother's death. This was an image from later in our lives. I was confused, hanging on with one hand to the restless man-boy, nervous in anticipation of the next wild move or gallop. It would not have surprised me if Mabon had leaped the gray out of the window, a long drop to the garden below.

Had I chosen the gate correctly? Had I sent Guiwenneth—had I followed Guiwenneth—through the *Ivory Gate* into the land of lies? Confusion tormented me, and yet . . . And yet this seemed *right*. From the moment I had smelled the field of barley, and the summer air, I had felt that this was the same place that I had once inhabited.

Mabon said, "Stop talking."

"I'm not talking."

"You are! You are talking incessantly. *Is it true, is it real, is it a lie?*" His voice mocked me. "My head is hurting with your doubts. All that matters is that we see the truth of her death."

"My mother's death?"

"If you know of another death, I'd like to see that, too. But, yes. Of course! Your mother's death. Where *is* she?"

I tried to remember what had happened that day of Gui-wenneth's wild ride. Had Jennifer Huxley stayed away overnight? Where had George Huxley been? My brother, Steven, had been away at school. This strangely isolated image from my past had so much that was true and so much that was false.

At last I remembered that Jennifer had spent the evening staring at the fire, the unnecessary fire that she had laid and maintained during the warm summer's night. But though the wood in the fireplace was newly set, there was no sign of my mother at all.

We had come through the wrong gate.

"Not at all," Mabon whispered as he rode the horse back through the kitchen and out into the late afternoon, blinking against the light, staring at the silent wood.

There was no food in the house. In the evening, Mabon walked outside, whistled into the dusk sky, and a while later his eagle flew in with a chicken clutched in its claws. Mabon took the dead creature, stripped some feathers, sniffed the flesh disapprovingly—"Smells young. No blood!"—then went into the kitchen, clattering among the pots and pans, running cold water from the tap, laughing and complaining, delighting in the long, sulphur-tipped matches, which he called "fire sticks," finally boiling the stripped and gutted fowl, which we ate with our fingers after dark.

My mother did not return.

While the chicken was still boiling, however, the man-boy walked with me to the woodland's edge.

"I'm glad you brought me here," he said. "I like your house. I like the warmth in the rooms. I like the fire sticks, I like the iron pans, I like the way it is clean and orderly. I like this dry garden, that gentle field of yellow grass. I like the strong trees, the way they stand alone in the fields, like watching giants. This is a strange yet lovely place in which you live."

"I never thought so myself. It always seemed very empty."

"But what made it seem empty? Did you ever ask yourself that?"

"No."

"Was it the land? Or was it the father? It certainly wasn't the mother."

"No. It wasn't my mother. It felt very lonely in the house at times."

"Because a father was missing!"

"Yes. Because a father was missing."

"In the forest."

"You know a lot about me, Mabon. . . ."

He grinned through his white mask, which was beginning to crack, revealing the older face below. Every hour, the youthful and female look of his disguise was degrading into a harsher, aging masculinity. "I know nothing about you at all, Christian. That's why I'm here. Feeding from your dreams! I want to see for myself. I don't need to know you to know that your father was as distant as that cloud up there. I don't need to know you to know that you loved your mother to the point of fury with your father. I don't need to know you to know that you love Guiwenneth, whose shape I took, though I've shed it now. I prefer my own body to a woman's and especially to a girl's. I know you for the man you are, though you look like a boy. But I know that you did something in your boyhood that you cannot face. I did something in *my* boyhood that I cannot face."

"What was that? What did you do?"

He laughed. "If I knew that, there would be no point in all of this!"

I couldn't help smiling at this admonition, since it reflected Issabeau's words, from her own account of her story with the Sea Cave Boy, the lad who had asked her the secret that kept her in the glade: *If I knew that, it wouldn't be a secret.* . . .

This place was neither real nor false; it had echoes of many memories, and from what I had seen, the memories were accurate. I felt as if I had come home, but this was not my home at all, and Mabon was a visitor creating the familiar landscape around us in order to explore my own childhood.

And yet, knowing that the place was both real and unreal did not discomfort me. Perhaps if I had passed through the Ivory Gate, there would have been terrors and nightmares gnawing at my consciousness as I surveyed this Dreaming Land. Here, though, there was familiarity, peace, and an impending sense of discovery.

Full of fowl, our thirsts quenched with strong tea, which Mabon enjoyed, I lit the fire and waited for my mother, staring at the flames as they consumed the wood, feeling the sweat run from my skin in the stifling room. Mabon watched me from the corner, curious, quiet.

"Your father is here," he whispered suddenly, and when I looked up, he was holding out a hand to me. He smiled, then put a finger to his lips. He looked so odd, in his short tunic, his hair lank and white with lime, his face like a cracked, Japanese mask.

I followed him to the study. Huxley was hunched over the desk, writing furiously in his journal. He looked up as we entered, frowned, changed his spectacles from the horn-rimmed reading pair to the slightly larger, horn-rimmed lenses that he used to see into the distance, stared at me and stared right *through* me, then rose and walked to the shattered windows, his hands behind his back. He peered at Ryhope Wood for a long minute, then came back to his desk;

changed glasses again; picked up his pen and continued to write.

I couldn't get over how young he looked. His hair was full and dark, shaved smartly above his ears, parted precisely on the left side of his crown, hair cream reflecting the light from his desk lamp. There were no lines, no shadows on his skin. His mouth was pink and youthful. He was enveloped in a cocoon of inspiration and enthusiasm. This was my father as he must have been when he first realized that he had discovered something wonderful, literally in his own back garden.

I tried to think how old he might have been—not much older than Steven upstairs, perhaps. Or perhaps just as old as he was—and he had seemed monstrous to me, and wretched with age, only because I had seen him with the eyes of youth.

I saw him now through Mabon's eyes. Mabon and I were two ghosts haunting the scientist as he recorded his latest insights, his most recent observations.

What date, I wondered, what day, what year was this? I peered more closely at the tight, neat writing.

. . . from the wood again.

I must keep calm. I must maintain control over the physical and mental environment. I have seen these creatures in the flesh, the forms of the Green Jack, of the Hoods and Arthur, Hereward, Finn, Tam Lyn, Tom Rhymer—all the brutal, stinking forms that have come down to us as heroes. I can smell the woman. She is around me always. She is watching me. Why? I cannot answer the question, but I know this: These myth images are watching me, and are curious about me, with the same intensity that I watch them and am curious for my own part. Here we are, at the edge of two worlds. My careful curiosity drives me to question their past. Their own curiosity drives them to question their present. And I must fight against the arrogant assumption that I am superior. . . .

They haunt me every second of the day. They are here, watching me. I can glimpse them from the edge of vision, and because my mind is frail in its way, I think I see my son Christian; and the girl, of course. The girl from the wood.

Like laughing clowns, they crowd down on me and peer at my scrawl.

GET AWAY!

But why should I write that? I *welcome* these hauntings. My life depends upon them! I have not yet found the way into Ryhope Wood, the way deep. Perhaps these ghastly reflections at the edge of vision will harshen, harden into the true ghosts they are, and take me by the hand, and guide me gently into a place I wish to know so well, and which I do not know at all—I am an Outsider in my own life. I long to be inside the world of *mythago wood*!

I whispered to him, "My son Christian is a sensible boy. He will 'guard the fort. . . .'"

My father wrote the line.

Mabon whispered, "There is a beast that is at the heart of the world."

There is a beast . . . at heart of the world. . . . Huxley wrote, and I caught my breath.

"Shall we call it Urscumug? Call it Urscumug!" mocked the white-faced Mabon.

I call it Urscumug. Manlike, but with the tusked features of a boar. It is the first hero. . . .

"Oh this is good, this is good," said Mabon with a laugh, clapping his hands together across the hunched form of the young man, my father, that young-old man.

"What are you doing?" I asked. "This isn't real. My father's discoveries were his own. We weren't here then, all those years ago, haunting him."

"We are here now, haunting him," Mabon whispered through Guiwenneth's crack-faced features.

"But we are not in the past. This is just a play on the past!"

"Really? Are you sure? Breathe on his neck. Go on. Breathe on his neck. He will feel that breath!"

"I know he will. Look at his writing!"

Huxley had written:

> . . . they are near me. I feel their breath on my neck. They are watching. This is wonderful! I have no rational way of explaining it. It is as if inspiration is falling from a bright, yet unseen sky. I document not my own experience, but the whispered fears and fantasies of men and women long dead, heroes, heroines, the forgotten folk of time who have been waiting to express their hearts and their stories to someone, anyone who would listen. This wood, this wonderful, ancient forest, has waited in time for a moment when someone . . . someone like me . . . some man, some woman, some entity would sit quietly at its edge and hear its whispered tales of terror, of beauty, and of great deeds performed in great times when there was no man, no woman to remember that moment.
>
> George Huxley is here, though. I am here! Whisper all you want, I will deny you nothing. Just tell me the names. Tell me the names of those ancient heroes. . . . Urscumug? What in God's name is that? But I will write it down. I will remember it.

"Just a piece of invention," mocked Mabon over the frantic, possessed figure of my father. "Do you hear me? Just a piece of fancy. A piece of unreality. A little tale from the Ivory Gate."

The ghostly whisper was confusing my father.

I raged at Mabon: "You said we had come through the Horn Gate. The 'true' gate."

"We have. I'm teasing this fool! I know those gates well, in all their forms, and I have learned how to draw a little sustenance from each of them!"

"Was my father's work a lie, then? Were you here, years ago? Have you made his obsession into something that is false?"

"If only I had that power!" Mabon said. "Alas! Only in our lives can we turn something true into something that is a lie. It's a human failing; and it is also a human strength. If Huxley did that to himself . . . if he created his own lies, his own visions in this place . . . then there was a reason for it. And that reason has nothing to do with my own interference, now *or* in the past."

"Unless you are lying about it," I whispered, and Mabon grinned boyishly from his ancient mask.

"We create stories to illuminate truth. We create lies to hide pain. Don't we?"

"Stories to illuminate truth? I would think so. Yes. Fables. Yes."

"And don't we create lies to hide pain? The truth is *masquerade*?"

"As Kylhuk might say, that's getting a bit too profound for me. Go away for a while, Mabon. I want to be alone with this dream."

Like Puck making his exit from the glade, Mabon's light winked out.

I stared down at my young father and after a while he looked up at me, his focus not quite on my eyes.

"I've found her," I said. "And I've found love. I don't *care* from whose mind she came. We love each other. I'll never let her go! I know you loved her, too. And I know you are looking for her still. But if you can hear me . . . if you can hear these words . . . stop looking for Guiwenneth. You can never find her, not as *I* have found her. She will never love you, because you can't create the love you need!"

Huxley smiled at me, or seemed to; and a moment later bent to his journal, writing in an impassioned scrawl.

I half dozed, half dreamed in front of the roaring log fire, the sweat running from my body, hot on my chest, cooling on my back. The flames seemed to lick out of the wood, curling like mocking tongues about me. I shivered in that heat. There was movement around me, the murmuring drone of voices, the dull clatter of crockery. Touches on my shoulder . . .

Whispers in my ear.

But I half dozed, half dreamed, and I dreamed of Jennifer Huxley. Is this how she had felt, those last nights of agony before she had walked to the solitary oak and calmly, calculatedly hanged herself?

There was a crashing of glass, and a sonorous, moaning sound that might have been music on a gramaphone slowing to a stop. I looked up at the clock, but the glass face was steamed up, time invisible behind the condensation. I rose and walked unsteadily to the study, stood in the doorway for a moment, staring out at the night, and at the shapes that moved around the room.

I was beckoned to the desk and stood with my legs against the mahogany edge. The smells of the night mingled with the smell of the leather covering to the desk, where Huxley had written away his life and mind. I dreamed I was my mother for a moment. . . .

An old woman in garish clothes, layer upon layer of skirts, a shawl above a shawl, the glitter of metal on her ears and nose, gray hair hanging in ringlets, walked up to me and whispered something in my ear.

The words were incomprehensible, but my blood turned cold, my heart began to race, my head filled with terror!

And a voice whispered, "Is this how it was? Is this how it happened? Or should I say—is this how it *will* happen?"

Daylight flooded the room. I stepped into the garden, walked around the house to the yard, with its chicken huts and sheds. The wood was ablaze. Steven stood there, with Guiwenneth! And another man, staring at the fire, the forest fire, frozen in their movements as if statues, though their hair moved and the woman's dress flowed slowly with the heat.

I stood behind them, dreaming a dream that made no sense, seeing events that were meaningless to me, though the way my body reacted, surged with fear, brought them horribly alive.

Golden shapes tumbled from the fire, hawk-faces on running bodies.

Horses came through, and tall, dark men.

An arrow struck the stranger who was my brother's companion, sent him tumbling toward me, clutching at the shaft that had entered his chest. His face was marked, as if burned; he was in agony as he died.

Rough men struck Guiwenneth, bundled her over the back of a horse, led her away. An ageing, scarred man flung a rope around my brother's neck, pushed him against the shed, kissed his lips, then walked away. And a man I recognized—the Fenlander!—pulled the rope tight over the roof of the shed so that Steven hung there, limp and strangled. The fire consumed the figures again, but the ageing man looked back for an instant, blew a kiss, and through the beard that covered his face I recognized someone I knew.

I had seen myself!

I had seen myself through my mother's eyes.

I had seen her eldest son kill her youngest son. Myself killing my brother, Steven!

And Mabon whispered again, "Is this how it will be? Is this what must happen?"

*   *   *

She was running through the tall barley. I followed as fast as I could, calling for my mother, but she ran so fast, in her best suit, with the blood from her eyes splattering on the ripening ears and broken stalks. I called to her, but she seemed not to hear. She ran to the solitary oak and wept for a few seconds, then saw me coming, tried to fling the rope across the bough, but her throw wasn't strong enough, even though the branch was within jumping distance of her outstretched hands.

By the time I had reached her, though, she had secured the noose loosely around her neck and stood there watching me, tearful and bloodstained, sobbing as she swayed on her feet.

"What are you doing?" I screamed at her, but she shouted back at me.

"Go away, Chris. You can't help me—only yourself!"

She looked up and again flung the rope across the branch, and this time it curled over the bark and draped back down. I stood in terror, staring at the half-hunched shape of my mother wracked with pain and tears, blood on her shoes, her breast red with blood, her pearl earrings catching the light as she held the free end of the rope, as if still reluctant to complete the act she had planned.

"I don't understand what you're doing!" I wailed at her.

"Nor do I," she said through her tears, her head shaking, her arms around her body as if she was cold. "But I am in such pain now. I must end the pain. I must start a new life, somewhere away from all of you, *all* of you!"

She was still not on the tree.

"I love you!" I shouted at her, and she cried and wailed more loudly, staring at me through a face that was crushed with grief and fear and tears.

"I love you, too, Chris," she managed to say, her voice

small with despair. "My little boy . . . oh, my lovely little boy . . . how could you become such a thing—such a terrible thing. . . . How could you kill him. . . ?"

I ran to her, put my arms around her, but she pushed me back as if frightened of me.

"What are you doing?" I shouted, terrified at the rejection. "What have I done?"

"Nothing . . . you've done nothing. . . . Not yet, not yet! You're too young. But it will turn out so badly for you. I have seen it. I have seen what you'll become. I can't bear it—I can't bear the pain—"

It hasn't happened, I wanted to scream at her! *That fat, scarred man killing Steven wasn't me! I'm just a boy. The old woman lied to you. And if it wasn't a lie, it was nothing more than a prediction! She was giving you a prediction only—you can act to stop the dream from coming true!*

What I said was, "Don't believe what that old woman said to you. What did she say to you? Don't believe it!"

"You are your father's son. I had dreamed what she said already. It was already pain in my life."

"I've done nothing! Nothing you think I've done ever needs to be done! Don't die, Mummy!"

"My sons are gone. My poor boys. My poor little boys."

"I'm here! I love you!"

"Both of them . . . gone. I've seen their going. I've raised a *devil* and a *hanged man.* Gone, now . . . gone forever."

It hadn't happened like this. These were "almost" words. They were "not quite right" words. I didn't remember it like this at all. This day was no longer mine!

And behind me Mabon whispered, "It *was* like this. And this day *is* yours, though you remember it with a different voice. You've come this far, now see it through. We always remember *part* of the truth. We always *forget* a part in equal measure. This is how it was, Chris. See what happens next!

Face the truth. And *then*—" He laughed in my ear. "And then I might let you have her back from the dead."

"My mother? You can do that?"

"No. *You* can do it. But to bring her back, first she has to die!"

I turned to look at Mabon and cried out with shock.

It was my father who stood there, but he was so disheveled, so ragged, so filthy, his face painted black and white with the features of a tusked pig, that for a second I didn't recognize him.

Naked, his belly sagging, his beard scrawny, the muddy mask falling away from his features, all I could see was how he stared at Jennifer, his mouth twisted into a grimace of hate.

"Why don't you do it?" he roared at her. I closed my ears with my hands, ducking away from this terrifying, stinking apparition that had moved upon me so silently through the field of barley, coming from the wood.

His voice, and my mother's voice shrieking back, were just the drones of bees and engines, and I pressed my fingers hard into my head to stop the words of hate forming.

Listen, Mabon whispered. *Listen.*

My mother was screaming, "Go back to her. Go back to that girl from the wood. . . ."

"Don't you think I would? I can't find her. If I could find her, do you think I'd stay in this love-forsaken place?"

"Look at you! Look at what you've become! Nothing but a beast. Leaves, mud, filth, the marks of the savage on your face and body . . . you are filth, George! You are savage! Go back to the wood. Go back to your filth. Go back to that girl!"

"Let me go!" my father roared. "I beg you, woman. Let me go! Each time I get close to her, you call me back. Each time I find the scent of her in my nostrils, your stink, the stink of my house, the stink of my sons calls me back. Let me go for once and for all!"

"I will be glad to do that. And may God have mercy on your sons while they are boys, because as men they are doomed to a terrible death!"

"Then I will be free of them, too. Dance for me, Jennifer! Dance and let me go! Come on! I'll help you!"

Like the wild animal he had become, this boar, this man, this *Huxley* leaped to the bough, pulled hard on the rope and wound it round the branch, knotting it. My mother screeched, then gasped, reached up to hold the tree, hauling with all her strength to take her weight. Her eyes, half closed with strangulation, half opened now to stare at me, and I rose from my crouch, stepped toward her, aware that she was imploring me silently to help her.

My father, legs splayed, urinated on the woman below him, leaping like a wild man on the bough, making it bend and buckle, making the woman dance below him.

I couldn't speak. I was horrified and appalled. My mother's lips moved and perhaps she would have reached for me, but she was gripping the branch until her knuckles were white while her husband rocked her, rocked her, the pale yellow piss streaming from the fat, slack stub of his ash-gray member and drenching her hair, running from her shoes.

All I could see was her face, bloated and bilious, puffing and pathetic, the eyes bulging, the nostrils beginning to seep blood.

And she dropped, and the rope stopped her fall, making her gasp horribly, making her instinctively scrabble at the hemp around her neck.

Still the beast danced upon the tree, my father inhabiting the primal form of Urscumug.

They take from us. They reflect us, and they take from us.

And this is what my father thought I had seen as a child! This is why he had been so "frightened" of me.

I had to save her! I had to throw my father from his perch. I ran toward her, leaped to reach for him, tried to grab the branch, tried to get a grip upon his feet, to throw him down, to stop this killing.

But my jump fell short. I had jumped with the expectations of a man, and achieved only the success of a child. As I failed to touch the bark, my arms clutched for comfort around my mother's waist and my weight dragged down, tugging her down suddenly before I could release her, and in that quick, sharp movement I heard the wet and sickening snap of the twig that was her life.

I fell down, wailing, my head being drenched in warm and stinking water. The bough above me did not break but creaked, and the shadow of the woman swung across the tough grass below the old oak, a limp thing, drifting left to right, left to right.

"That's that, then," said the naked man in the tree in a low voice, as if talking to himself. "The boy has done the deed quicker than I could have done it myself. She's dead. No bringing her back. But he saw what I *did*. He knows what I've *done*. He was here, a witness . . . what to do? What to do? He knows what I've done. Though by the look of him . . ."

Blows were struck at me as I lay in agony and I curled into my body. A boar's savage teeth gnawed at my neck, while fingers squeezed my throat.

"What to do? What *shall* I do?"

And the voice of this primitive creature, this "Urscumug" as my father had called it, this half-man, half-animal, whispered:

"I do believe you've been charmed. Charmed into blindness. Charmed to forget. Well that's good. Thank God for that. Better get dressed. Better wash and change my clothes.

Can't be seen like this. Paperwork. There'll be paperwork to do."

And I heard my father run through the corn like a young dog released from its leash, keen to use its newfound freedom.

"Dear God . . . *was* it like that?" I whispered in horror to Mabon. I was suddenly sick, retching and wretched with the vision of Jennifer's death that had been revealed to me. "*Was* it like that? Like *that*? No wonder the day is no longer mine! Did the two of us conspire in my mother's death? I don't want to believe it, Mabon. But I *do* believe it! Mabon! Mabon . . . ?"

But my answer was only the wind and the sibilant rustling of the tall corn. As I turned over on my back, staring at the sky through the spreading branches of the oak, I realized that no woman's body hung there now. And no girlish man, face cracked with white paint, stood grinning at me.

I sat up and called for the wild rider, the strange man who had been the presence of my conscience in this imaginary place . . . my guardian to the truthful vision. But Mabon was nowhere to be seen. And when I stood and looked around, I realized that I was not in the cornfield at all, but in a field of wild grass and thistles. Strong Against the Storm was only one among many great oaks that surrounded me, an open clearing, a bright glade with many bright paths leading away from it. The air was hot and heavy, fragrant and still, not the air of England but of the dry and aromatic islands of the Aegean.

I began to walk toward Oak Lodge, to where it should have been, and after a few minutes I saw stone ruins in this wildwood. I had crossed a stream to get there, but the "sticklebrook," as Steve and I had called it, was wider and deeper and flowing in two channels, each flowing hard into the forest.

I approached the ruins through the undergrowth and began to smell honey and spices. Where Oak Lodge had once stood, now I could see a white-stone house, fronted by marble pillars painted in exotic blues and reds. The roof was made from rounded, terracotta tiles, gently sloping. Small windows, their shutters opened, seemed to watch me darkly. This was how I imagined ancient Greece might have been, the air so hot and dry, perfumed with rosemary and thyme and lavender, so still and silent that time itself might have been suspended for the moment of my passing through.

I stepped to where the door to the kitchen had once been, ducking below a stone lintel into a square, white-walled room, where a fire burned in the corner hearth, and a stocky, muscular man in a black tunic and leather sandals, his dark hair shining and tied back with coils of copper wire, his beard a thin line around the angle of his jaw, stirred the contents of a wide, copper pan slung above the flames.

He looked up as I entered, then beckoned me over, scooping some of the stew into his spoon and holding it out to me.

"Careful! It's hot. I think I've used too much honey. I could die for honey. But too much can spoil good meat. Taste it, Chris. Tell me what you think."

This was Mabon, I realized from his voice, but without the mask, without the chalk-streaked hair, and without the clothing that he had copied from Guiwenneth. His legs were dappled with tiny red-and-yellow animal symbols, I noticed, like freckles, and I thought of Issabeau's tattoos of the Oldest Animals. Thinking of Issabeau, I noticed Someone son of Somebody's rough cloak in the corner. The proud Celt had been here, too, then.

"It's fish," Mabon said, still holding the spoon toward me. "Pike, to be precise. A great lake-water hunter. I caught it from a pond while you were sleeping after seeing the truth of your mother's death. Go on, Chris. Taste it."

His statement confused me. Had I *slept* after the vision of Jennifer's murder? It hardly seemed likely! And I certainly couldn't remember doing so. But I couldn't find the words to raise the question as Mabon stared at me, his offering held out toward me. I accepted the spoon and ate the morsel of pike. It was good, very succulent, a little sweet and aromatic for my taste, though again I didn't see the need to comment. I could see the fish's head on a platter, gawping at me grotesquely, all jaws, teeth, and evil, still eerily alive despite its being severed from the body.

"It *is* sweet, but it's good," I said after a moment.

"This is a dish we cook when an old friend comes home," Mabon said, again stirring the pot. "Or when a new friend arrives: a birth, perhaps; a union of families; or the return from war of a man who knew a dead son and has brought his armor and his sword hand back to his village. The head of the fish, with its teeth and savage jaws, is cut away. That means no more pain, you see? Only the sweetness and succulence of the flesh remains, which symbolizes the comfort of friends. The honey is important. The dead stay fresh for a long time if placed in honey. We preserve a lot of things in honey, from mothers and sisters to ideas and hopes. So friendship and life can stay fresh, too, if preserved in the *idea* of honey."

What in God's name was he talking about?

"I don't understand what is happening," I said sorrowfully. Then the tears I had been fighting back suddenly surfaced. "I killed my mother! I thought I was trying to hold her up, hold her own weight against the pull of the earth around her neck! But I hung on to her like a child at her breast, and I heard her neck go! I heard the snap! I killed her . . . and my father, dressed in skins, danced on the tree, danced and sang on the tree!"

I think I cried out loud. I screamed at this black-clothed man for thinking about nothing but fish and honey and the preserving of the dead. He seemed a callous presence in a dream that was filled with pain and fear, and terrible grief.

I could still feel the boy's weight of my body, slung on my mother's waist. I had done to her—without intending it—what the families of hanged men in centuries past had been allowed to do to quicken the death by execution of a loved one.

And I had only been trying to save her from the rope and from the brute who had ceased to love her, the man who had become obsessed with becoming free from his wife's demands upon his time, his mind, and his heart!

After a while I realized that gentle hands were on my face. Fingers smeared the tears across my cheeks. Honeyed breath scented the air as Mabon crouched beside me and whispered to me.

"You must understand—before you could have her back, you had to know the way she died. There are no quick paths through the forest, Chris. No shortcuts. You were 'charmed' that day, that terrible day, charmed into forgetting the truth. That is why you called to me. That is why I am here to help you. Mabon. My name means Remembering Shadows. I am *Memory* brought back through the broken dream. You were charmed into forgetting truth. Someone cast a spell on you."

"Someone? The Celt?"

"Not him."

"Who, then? Who made me forget the truth? Who charmed me? My father, of course," I added with anger. "I don't know why I bother to ask. . . . If he could hide himself on the branch of the tree, if he had been there, he certainly could have blinded me."

But Mabon said quietly, "It was not your father."

"Well it was certainly not my brother. Not Steven!"

But as I said the words, I felt a moment's shock, remembering the state of the man when I had left him, deep in a charmed sleep that had been cast on him by . . .

"Guiwenneth! Oh, God—Guiwenneth herself . . ."

My heart suddenly ached, and my chest tightened. She had certainly charmed Steven. She had been present in my life as a brutal, feral savage; and then again as the woman I loved. A trickster! A charmer! Had she charmed me, too?

"Not Guiwenneth!" Mabon said with a frown. "Not directly."

"You, then. You seem to know all about me. Of course! You. But how? You weren't there—"

"*Not* me, though you have done me a service. I knew nothing about you until you came here. Once you arrived, you were as transparent as the waters of the streams outside. . . ."

"Then as I have always suspected . . . *Kylhuk*. It was *Kylhuk* all along. Tricky, canny *Kylhuk,* a man consumed by the trickery of others, tricking me. . . ."

"Not Kylhuk," Mabon said, again adding, "not directly."

"Then who? For God's sake *who*? My mother? Mabon! I'm running out of possibilities."

"Yes," Mabon said coldly, his fingers on my cheeks, turning my tearful face to look at his own hard, bronzed features. "Yes. It *was* your mother who charmed you. Just as my own mother charmed me."

My last guess had been a flippant one. I was astonished by his calm answer.

"My mother didn't know the time of *day* most of the time," I raged back at him. "She was in a dream! She was in despair! She bottled tomatoes in her Sunday clothes, Mabon, her *best clothes*. She lit fires on hot summer days. She was lost in a world that my bloody father had created, and she could no more have tricked me, or charmed me, than she could have taken wing and flown south for the winter!"

"She took wing in her own way, though—and summoned

help. Help *from* that world your father had created, used to get her *out* of it, I suspect."

I stared back at the man as he sniffed at the copper vessel, stirring the thick lumps of fish and fussing with the height of the pan above the glowing wood. He seemed so confident in his comments to me. He knew so much about me, or appeared to. *My name . . . Memory brought back through the broken dream. . . .*

A mythago! *My* mythago. Brought alive by my own need, from my own unconscious.

I watched him, and again heard his words: *She took wing—summoned help. . . .*

I said angrily:

"Then tell me this: *Whose* help did my mother summon?"

Mabon poured himself wine from a clay flagon and sipped it, watching me, half amused.

"*Your* help. Why else are you here?"

"*My* help? I'm helpless!"

"Hardly helpless," Mabon said with a laugh. "But as to mothers—mothers, you may have noticed, have a way of making things happen. My own mother, when she couldn't get her way with me, when she couldn't catch me in the chase after I had fled her stronghold, when she saw that I would not submit to the demands of her Sanctuary and spend my life a captive to her Goddess, and my death as bleached bones built into her altar—my own mother contrived by pure genius to imprison me at the entrance to the Underworld itself! Which is where you are now, by the way, in case you weren't aware of it. Christian!"

No, I had not been aware of it. And as I looked around the kitchen of this ancient house, Mabon laughed and shook his head, rose to his full height and kicked some cold embers onto the fire to damp down the heat. Then he walked to the door, standing there for a moment before he said, "It's this way."

"The Gate of Horn?"

"The open mouth that will lead you to your Grail. You passed the Gate of Horn earlier. You saw that truth lay between Memory and the Child in the Land—two things which people often think are false, but which hold the seeds of our lives!"

I followed him back toward the twin streams, then through the woods, through sanctuary clearings, ruins, and between tall, mossy rocks.

Suddenly a face loomed ahead of us, carved from stone, a broad, narrow-eyed monstrosity of leaf and flower, a greenman's face looming hugely, its nostrils flaring, its mouth gaping darkly. A hollow wind blew from the cavern. The twin streams were running like tears from its eyes, the beginning of the river along which I had recently rowed.

Mabon placed a hand on my shoulder.

"When my mother trapped me here, she made it so that I could never enter the Underworld, only *guard* it, in whatever way I wished. I am old and tired, Christian, and I have longed to make the journey into that silent and peaceful realm. I could only do it when a man came and shared the truth of his mother's death. That was the spell she put on me for denying her my love. Love as *she* saw it. You have broken that spell for me and I am grateful. I will gladly lead you into this Beautiful Realm. Once you find your mother among the Shades, lead her out. But when you do so, don't speak to her, no matter what she says to you, nor look back at her. . . ."

"I know the rules," I said. "I've read the story! Have you encountered Orpheus?"

Mabon seemed surprised and delighted. "Yes! A long, long time ago. But he was impetuous and lost the woman he loved. He looked back. . . ."

"I *know* he looked back. I'll be sure to take more care."

"Come on then."

But I stood my ground, nervous and edgy. "Not yet. I must go back to the others first. I need to see Guiwenneth before I enter. . . . Will I be able to go in—to Hell—on my own?"

Mabon smiled. "Of course. One trip inward. One life returned. My gift to you. And my thanks for releasing me, Christian," he added as he turned to walk toward the mouth of the green and monstrous, sighing head.

The air hissed sharply and an arrow struck him in the shoulder, throwing him forward, screaming. Behind me, horses thundered through the tall rocks. Two more arrows streaked past me, one clattering against the rock face, the other catching Mabon son of Modron in the arm as he staggered to his feet.

A man yelled triumphantly, riding down on me, a lance held low, its shaft tied with colored streamers. I flung myself to one side as Eletherion stabbed at me, and I felt the crack of the wood as he missed with the point and struck with the shaft.

I was defenseless, and Mabon was badly wounded. The five horsemen rode over him and dismounted at the mouth of the Underworld, peering into the windy gloom. Eletherion took off his hawk-faced helmet and flung it into the void. Then he laughed with triumph, made a fist and banged it against the stone lip above his head.

Raggedly dressed, save for their gleaming helmets, the Sons of Kyrdu turned to look at me. Eletherion's eyes were bright with bloodlust, his teeth gleaming white through the heavy, russet beard.

Then he hefted his javelin above his shoulder, drew back his arm, aimed—

Reeled back as a slingstone caught him above the eye!

He turned where he stood and sent the javelin into the

rocks, but it came back at him and struck one of his brothers. Kylhuk and Someone stepped quickly into the space before the gorge, armored and smiling, Kylhuk in battle kilt and torques, daggers strapped to each thigh and each forearm; Someone in a purple cloak, his hair meticulously shaped above his crown, his whole bearing prouder and more magnificent than I had ever seen.

"I will take your head and heart for the life of my friend Manandoun," Kylhuk roared, and leaped at Eletherion.

The man's brothers barred his way and he struck furiously with his long, iron sword. Someone entered the fray, using sword and axe, sending a spray of blood each time he struck at one of Kyrdu's sons. But these warriors were harder than they looked, and they spun and danced, weaving between the two Celts, drawing blood on the enemy themselves, screeching in their ancient language from behind the bronze masks of their conical helmets.

"*Slathan!*" Kylhuk shouted at me, and a dagger was flung to the ground at my feet. Eletherion was standing in the very entrance of the cave. Mabon was still breathing, I noticed, but his body was crushed by hooves and split by arrows.

I picked up the dagger and hefted it. Eletherion glimpsed the movement and as the blade streaked toward him—a good shot, I was quite surprised—he raised an armored forearm and caught the weapon, picking it up and grinning.

Kylhuk could make no headway through the four brothers and his roar became frustration.

"Fight! Fight me for the honor of the man you slaughtered!"

But Eletherion could not understand the words, though he certainly understood the anger.

Suddenly he barked an order. His brothers began to fall back, stepping nimbly, their bright blades deflecting the heavier, stronger iron of their opponents. With a quick laugh, Eletherion turned and entered the Underworld, the others following so fast that Kylhuk, unbalanced, could not reach far enough to strike at their backs. He raced to the mouth of the cave, screeched furiously into the darkness, but could not pass, of course. There might as well have been a stone wall there.

Someone son of Somebody was licking the wounds on his arms, looking curiously at the void that marked the way to Hell. Kylhuk threw his sword to the ground, then leaned back against the stone, holding out his arms as if crucified, his eyes closed with frustration; the water from the left eye of his face washed the blood from his left arm.

Then I noticed Someone grinning at me. He looked back at Kylhuk and said, "Are you refreshed?"

"Why?" asked the man.

"Because if you are refreshed, I shall call Eletherion back to you."

Kylhuk stood up straight, then carefully reached down for his sword. He stared at the unnamed Celt quizzically.

"How can you do that?"

Someone scratched his newly trimmed beard. "I'm not certain I can . . . but I can certainly try. This poor, dying man here, this Mabon, has released my name to me. I know my name now! I know who my father was, who my mother was, and I know who I am, and I am astonished to discover the truth of my name, since my identity could hardly be more noble, more legendary, more famous in the world in which I have sought it. I am my own hero! I have sat with men and talked about the lost hero, and the lost hero was me! But of this triumph, more later. For the moment, all that is important is that I know who I am and what I can do. I have seven *geisas* on my life, *seven*! Only one man ever was issued with seven, and all my life seven has been a special number to me. I have always known myself without knowing the truth of myself. What a fool! How blind a man can be when he is lost in the wilderness. But seven *geisas* are mine to use, and I have only used one of them. A second is that I can summon to account for himself any man who sets his brother to fight against me in his place! When you are ready, Kylhuk, I shall call Eletherion back to account for himself, since he raised no weapon against me in this skirmish, but only set his brothers to do the task."

"Do it!" yelled Kylhuk, standing ready, strong and tensed in front of the cave mouth. "Do it, and my life is yours for the taking!"

"Thank you for the offer. If your life remains for the taking at the end of the fight, I'll make a gift of it to you."

"I accept," said Kylhuk impatiently. "Now bring that bastard out of Hell!"

The proud Celt stepped to the cave. In a voice that boomed like thunder he shouted words in his own language, and over and over again the name "Eletherion" was embedded in that abusive, angry, *furious* exhortation, that exercising of his *geisa* against the eldest Son of Kyrdu.

After a minute of this shouting, Someone fell silent, stepped back from the entrance to the Underworld and crossed his arms. Kylhuk stood there, a hound straining at the leash, the muscles of the arm that held his sword standing out so strongly that I thought they might explode.

How long he waited I can't say; it seemed forever, and then suddenly a figure rose in the darkness, the helmeted and masked shape of Eletherion, walking hesitantly into the day. Even though his face was covered, it was clear that the warrior was confused by what was happening to him. He had stolen the secret of entering Hell—part of his legend—and now he was being dragged back to the world he had left.

Frustrated in his ambition to loot the Underworld, he now found himself confronting the looting of his life by a man whose friend he had callously and tauntingly murdered.

"This for Manandoun," Kylhuk breathed and struck the helmet from Eletherion's head, revealing startled, bloody features.

"And this!"

He struck again, cutting deeply into the man's shoulder.

Now Eletherion came alive, spinning round on the spot, his bronze blade flashing in the bright air, catching Kylhuk off guard and sending him sprawling. Someone stood impassively, motioning me back as I involuntarily stepped toward Kylhuk as Eletherion charged down at him.

But Kylhuk turned, used his feet to trip his opponent, stood quickly, and backed away. As Eletherion, too, found his feet, they rushed at each other. There was a quick, sharp ring of metal on metal. Then Eletherion's face went loose, his body went down on its knees, his arms dropped, and a moment later Kylhuk was sawing furiously at the sinews of the head he was claiming in triumph.

When it was off, he spat in its face, then tucked it into the belt of his kilt by the long, russet hair.

"Don't worry, Christian," he said to me. "I shan't ask you to prepare *this* one for the pyre!"

Then he faltered in his step, and Someone and myself went to his aid. I realized suddenly that Mabon was nowhere to be seen. In the fury of the last few moments, he had vanished completely, though a thick trail of blood led to the mouth of the stone head. I felt aggrieved and ashamed that in his dying moments, Mabon had had to haul himself to the place he had so longed for, and which for so long had been denied him by the sorcery of his mother.

I cleaned and bound the wounds on Kylhuk's body. He watched me all the while, a half-smile on his face, then reached out to squeeze my shoulder.

"I'd had plans for you," he said. "But things have turned out better than I'd expected."

"What does that mean?" I asked.

He closed his eyes. "Good-bye, Christian. And the best of fortune. It won't be long until we meet again."

And then he drifted into a recovering sleep.

I went in search of Someone son of Somebody, and found him staring into the distance, away from the Underworld. He was restless, that much was obvious, and I guessed that he was as keen to get back to Issabeau as was I to Guiwenneth.

"How is Kylhuk?"

"He'll live. He has more blood in him than most of us, and I saw a lot of it in his face today, as he avenged Manandoun."

"He fought like a boar cornered by hounds. He fought well. This is a good ending for him."

"And he called me Christian," I added with a smile. "Christian. Not *slathan*. Though I don't suppose the courtesy will last."

To my surprise, Someone laughed out loud. "He's released you. He had told me he would. You are no longer the *slathan*. He will keep Legion for himself. For the moment, at least."

What did the man mean? Kylhuk would keep Legion for himself? Had he intended to make a present of it to me?

"Yes," the Celt said simply, "exactly that. Well . . . not so much a present. He was going to pass it on to you. To trick you into taking it. To rid himself of the burden—Legion, and the quest for Mabon, and all the consequences of his questing, have been a burden on the man for years, exactly as they were for Uspathadyn before him. Uspathadyn tricked Kylhuk into taking on the quest for Mabon; Kylhuk was *slathan* to the giant, you see? In his quest for his own *slathan*, however, he found a boy—Christian Huxley—who could become the key to the rescue of Mabon himself, a boy whose mother could shape the boy's life by a lie she was led to believe in, and who could have the truth revealed to him only after he had come of age. Kylhuk planted the lie in your mother, then harvested you later, to help end the quest.

"I'm quite sure," Someone went on, "that he would have left you the responsibility of Legion, and therefore the anguish of fighting and fleeing from everything that is crowding and looming on its tail. But he can't do it. His honor prevents him. As his *slathan* you were both his guide and his heir; the word means simply *disguise*. He had disguised your true nature from you. That was part of the trick. Now, though, you are free to go, free of him, free to enjoy the lusty Guiwenneth—" he clapped his hands together spiritedly—"as I will enjoy that husky enchantress, that Issabeau, that divine, raven-haired creature to whom you have married me, Christian Huxley, and my thanks, my arm, and my life for your life on that!"

"Don't forget," I said to him quickly, "that now you know your real name you can no longer confuse enchantresses!"

"So she has told me. But that particular change in my talent isn't in *my geisas,* not as I now know them. I will *always* confuse and confound enchantresses. One, at least!"

"And your name? This great name? I can't keep calling you Someone . . . ."

He turned to me proudly, then made a small bow of respect. The sun shone sharply on his waxed hair. "My name is that great name, the name I have always known, a name that will be as familiar to you as the sound of the lark on a hot summer's day."

I waited almost breathlessly, my mind running through all the great heroes, all the giants of myth and legend that I had read or heard about in my scant years on the earth.

"My name is Anambioros son of Oisingeteros!"

He paused for a moment, to let this information sink in. "Yes, Christian. I am that man. And despite what I must now do to fulfill the immense ambition attached to that name, I am always . . . *always* at your service."

"Say the name again?" I asked nervously.

"Anambioros son of Oisingeteros," he said quickly, with a frown.

"Anambioros! By Olwen's Hands, I thought you'd be older!" I said with a laugh.

He seemed relieved. "I'm still young. There is a great deal of adventure ahead in my life to put the years on me. I'm delighted you recognize me. I had thought—being the strange man you are—that you would not have heard of me."

I didn't disabuse him. "Pleased to meet you at last, Anambioros! And what *geisas* do you have left?"

He drew himself up to his full height. "Just these: That I must give a word of advice to every stranger I meet, even if they don't request it. I must address the first child I meet after the night of Beltane as if they are royalty. I must shave and trim the hair from the head of a proud enemy taken in battle, and have the head to my right at the first feast, and address it in conversation without mockery. I can give back one life before my own death. I must not enter the house or stronghold of a stranger unless a red-haired woman enters first."

I didn't have a response that seemed appropriate. All I could think of was how strangely mundane they seemed, these *geisas,* compared to the elaborate and supernatural versions that had been devised fifteen hundred years later.

"We should let Kylhuk rest, now," Anambioros said. "He's quite safe. And it's a long walk back to the stones, and to the others."

He paced off, walking with a new swagger in his step, cloak flowing behind him.

"Anambioros son of Oisingeteros," I murmured as I followed. "I'll do my best to write your name into the storybooks when I get home. But if you had been called 'Arthur' or 'Mordred' it would have been a lot easier."

CHAPTER 22

From the confident way he strode off, away from the house where Kylhuk lay asleep, I thought Anambioros knew exactly where he was going, and jogged along behind him through the forest. He was fitter than me, despite his wounds, and his pace was furious, a combination of swift walking and steady running that soon had me falling out of sight of him, though he kept calling to me.

I caught up with him by a river. He was standing, confused and uncertain, looking to left and right.

"You've got us lost," I said. "And no *geisa* to help us find the right track."

"Not lost . . ." he said. Around us the wildwood stirred with wind. There was the scent of flowers on the air, and above us birds circled silently, as if preparing to roost for the night.

"Do you know where we are?"

"I thought I heard Elidyr call. I was following the sound of Elidyr's voice. He told me to listen for him . . . as soon as I'd found you. But I can't see him. Why would he hide from us?"

We spent a minute or so calling for the boatman, but to no avail. Anambioros then suggested we go separately along the river for a few minutes, meeting back at this starting point. Knowing the realm as well as I did, with its shifts and uncertainties in time, I thought this was a very bad idea; but the Celt was insistent and we parted company.

After a while I came to a part of the river where flowers in full bloom and swollen fungi grew from riverbank and tree trunk, hanging in great loops, plates, and fronds from the branches, even rising in full, red-and-yellow petaled splendor above the flowing water of the river. Insects buzzed and fed on nectar, dragonflies swooped and hovered, birds chattered and took wing, and Elidyr came toward me through the water, huge and menacing, his gaze hard as he watched me. He was dragging three small boats behind him. My heart began to race as I realized, shocked and horrified, who lay in them.

"I have to take them now," Elidyr growled at me as he passed. "They have had long enough."

"NO!" I cried, and stumbled into the water. I could see Gwyr's ashen face in the nearest boat, and the tumble of Guiwenneth's auburn hair in the middle one. I waded toward Elidyr, blinded by the tears in my eyes. "Oh, God, please no! Don't take her!"

"Time to go," the boatman snarled again. "One kiss. Quick!"

One kiss?

He had stopped in the stream. The boats swayed in the current. I wiped a hand across my eyes and peered quickly down at the Interpreter, his face peaceful now, no sign of the charring that had destroyed him, his hands resting over his waist.

"Gwyr . . ." I whispered quickly. "Thank you for friendship. . . ."

"Hurry," Elidyr growled again.

I spent a moment staring at Issabeau. Her eyes were half open and seemed to shine, but she was quite dead, the blossom of blood on her breast from the wound that had killed her covering her heart.

I held the sides of Guiwenneth's boat and leaned down to kiss her cold lips. I reached out to touch her icy hands, folded on her breast. I didn't understand. How had they died? I didn't understand. . . .

"All died before," Elidyr said. "Now I must take them."

Before? In the skirmish? "I thought only Gwyr had died," I protested. "The others seemed so alive in the boats."

"*All* died," Elidyr murmured. "Kyrdu's sons killed all. I gave them back for you. For pity. But only for a while. I told you!"

Yes. Yes, Elidyr. You told me. You showed me the flower garden and the dead knight with his mourning lady. But I had thought you were warning me about Gwyr. Only Gwyr. I hadn't known the skirmish had eliminated the whole Forlorn Hope.

Guiwenneth! Dear God, I couldn't lose her now. I hugged her cold body and wept for her, but Elidyr reached over and pushed me firmly away, back into the water.

"All over," he said harshly. "Now go away."

Anambioros appeared on the bank, a sudden, screaming figure, leaping into the water, his face filled with despair and fury.

"Issabeau!" he howled.

Elidyr transformed. His giant's body thickened even more, his face became that of a snarling hound, his pelt became wolf-gray. He lashed out at the Celt, who drew his sword and struck back, only to have the weapon snatched from his hand, snapped quickly, and tossed away. Then Elidyr had swiped a hand across the proud man's face, knocking him backward, below the river.

Baying and howling, angry and frustrated, crying out, "I *have* to do this!" Elidyr tugged at the ropes that held his burden and continued his journey toward the Underworld, to enter the place through the route of the dead, along the river that flowed below the gaping mouth of the green-man cliff.

I swam to Anambioros and dragged his unconscious body to the shore. After a few minutes his eyes opened to stare at the sky, then his face twisted into grief and rage, his hands clenched into fists as he lay there.

When he was more composed, he went back to the water's edge and crouched down, crying softly, mourning the death of his beloved Issabeau. I stood behind him, numb and confused, my head reeling with memories of Guiwenneth, and with the events of the last few hours. I felt suddenly alone and totally helpless, aware that I was far from home and without the woman who had become such a part of my life that I had not noticed how much my fear of this wilderness had been soothed by her reassuring presence.

I didn't know what to do now. I didn't know what to do next.

"I took it for myself," Anambioros was saying softly, angrily. "I took it for myself. I could have given it to her. I *should* have given it to her. . . . The boatman didn't give me the choice."

What was he talking about? I crouched down beside him, my arm round his shoulder. "What are you saying, Anambioros?"

"I had the right to give back a life. It was one of my privileges. I died with the others, that awful day in the forest, when Eletherion attacked us. Elidyr has let me live because of my own *geisa*. But I would have willingly given it to Issabeau."

And then she would have been alive and alone instead, I thought, but I didn't voice the words. Anambioros was almost inconsolable, and by helping him through his grief, I was able to delay the onset of my own deep sadness.

Or perhaps my strength at this moment was not because of the weeping king beside me, but because I was increasingly aware that Guiwenneth, now, was in the same Underworld realm as my mother, a terrible place opened to me by

Mabon for a single journey only, for a single rescue only, his thanks for releasing him from the prison that he had guarded and which had guarded him in turn.

I felt almost faint as I stood and stared back toward the stone house, the narrow passage through the rocks and the grotesque face carved around the entrance to the deep.

My mother was there. Guiwenneth was there.

And I could go into that Dark and see them. I could sit and talk to them.

But eventually . . . I would have to choose between them.

Chapter 23

I was not greeted by Cerberus as I entered Hell; no five-headed hound snarled and snapped at me. But Mabon was there, old and gray, robed in black and smiling through his beard.

"You took your time," he said.

"It was about time I did something for myself," I replied. "I wanted to think. I wanted to be with Guiwenneth. From the moment I entered this wilderness of time, trees, and gateways, I have been led, pushed, shuffled, tricked, deceived, manipulated—"

"Loved?"

"Oh, yes. Certainly that."

"But love itself is also something that *happens* to you," Mabon agreed. "Not something you can make happen. Yes. I think I understand how you feel."

"Love is wonderful. And I'm glad it happened. But now . . ."

He stood quietly as I struggled with my fears and feelings, staring beyond him to the bright land, a world of woods and fields, not at all the gloomy, grim incarceration that was the construct of Hell of his own, original time.

This was the Otherworld of the Mabon of my own legend, the Celtic Lordly One; I looked beyond him at the wonderful ideal of death of the wild and optimistic clans of Iron Age

Europe, and not at all the gray and dismal shroud of ancient Aegean philosophy.

"Well, well. At least I can agonize in summer."

"Which is more than can Eletherion," my Shade-guide said, and I followed his gaze to the skeletal figure that was strapped by chains to a jagged rock in the gloom. Eletherion's wounds bled copiously, his eyes blazed furiously, but his mouth, though it worked angrily, emitted no sound, no sound at all.

"His brothers are finding their own deaths, deeper in the ground," Mabon added. "But that is another story for another time. Look for it in your books, Christian, when you get home."

"I will."

"Home is where the heart is. How many times have you thought that, recently, I wonder?"

"Very many. Very many indeed."

"Keep walking, keep following this path. Home and all your heartbeats are there, and if you remember the one simple truth: That you must not question your decision! If you remember that, then you can bring her out alive."

"And how do we then get home? To my true home!"

"Elidyr will take you. He's the boatman, remember? He doesn't just transport the dead. You can trust Elidyr to take you home. Off you go, now. Time is passing faster than you think."

I had run across the field from the wood and now stood breathless at the gate to the garden of Oak Lodge. Smoke curled from the chimney. Hens clucked and pecked, watching me nervously. Somewhere in the house music was playing, and I thought I recognized one of my mother's favorite symphonies, by Vaughan Williams. It was peaceful and beautiful, but I had never taken much interest in classical music and I could do no more than recognize the gentle, pastoral theme.

My heart lifted, my spirits lifted. This was a wholly different return to my childhood than the encounter with Mabon. I might almost have been home, properly home, on a hot, still summer day. . . .

But there was smoke from the chimney. . . .

I opened the gate and walked up to the house, then changed my mind about entering and continued to walk around the garden, peering in through the French windows at the study. Everything was intact, nothing broken, the desk polished and gleaming, my father's journal on one side, two books on the other. No Huxley sat there, however. The place was just a shrine, a memory of intellect.

And so I entered my home and found my mother by the fire, sweat on her face, her gaze focused on the flames, her shirt stained red with the juice of the fruits she had been preserving.

I sat down beside her, clasped my hands together, and stared at the flames. We spent a long time in silence. I couldn't find the words to express my feelings. I looked around: at the clock on the mantelpiece, the pictures on the walls, the table with its thick green cloth, the shelves, dark stained and ornate, with their wretched rows of plates and mugs. The room was stifling, and not just because of the fire blazing on this hot, still day.

After a while, my mother said, "She's in the study. She's waiting for you."

"Who is?"

"Guiwenneth. Go and see her."

"I've come here to see you," I said, tears flooding my eyes as I stared at my mother's sad, bowed head. She was more forlorn than I could remember. She licked her lips, wiped her hand across her nose, clasped her hands in her lap, each tense, restless motion reflecting a thought or a memory that was haunting her and hurting her, and yet which she would not speak.

"Go and see her," she repeated softly.

"I've come to take you home, Mum. I've come to find you. To take you home."

She was suddenly crying, but her voice stayed strong. "No. That's not true. It was true once, but it's not true now. And I wouldn't want it differently. Go to her, Chris. You only have one chance. I'll be all right. It's only while you're here that I feel the pain. Once you're gone, once you are finally gone, my life will go on. . . . Go to her. She needs you. . . . And you need her. If you take her home with you, then the terrible things I've seen might not come true at all."

"I know what you've seen. It's not going to happen. I will not become like that man you saw!"

"I saw Grief make a monster of you."

"I am not a monster."

"I know. That's why you must trust me. You must take Guiwenneth. I love you too much, and I'm too frightened of what you might become, to let you take me in her place."

"Everything you saw, all that horror, that vision of me as an old man killing my brother. . . . just a dream! Just a lie! I will not kill Steven. I promise you, Mum! I will not kill Steven. . . ."

"Not if you take the girl from the wood. Take her home, Chris. Do what you have said and make the dream a lie! Perhaps when the time comes, and the dream breaks and dissolves into dust, perhaps I'll know it. Besides"—she turned to me, put her hands on my cheeks and after a moment, a restless, moist-eyed and searching moment, kissed my mouth—"Besides . . . you long for her more than you long for me. You have found love, then lost it cruelly. Now you can retrieve it. I long for your life to be long and loving. Go to her, Chris. Go to her. . . ."

*   *   *

ROBERT HOLDSTOCK

There was someone in the study. I could hear the murmured words, the rustle of the pages of the journal being turned. I opened the door slowly and saw the spill of light from the garden through the opened windows. Issabeau sat weeping at the desk, her tears staining the scrawled writing of the journal as she read. She looked up at me, sorrowful and forlorn, her face as pale as snow, a small, sad oval in the tumble of graying hair.

"She's been waiting for you," the enchantress whispered. "She will be so glad you came."

"Where is she?"

"In the garden. She's been waiting a long time for you."

I walked past the desk. Issabeau drew breath, fighting back her own sadness. "How is he?" she asked in a small voice. "Will he remember me?"

"Oh, yes. He will remember you. Grief will not make a monster of him, he's too proud of that. But he will not be the same man again."

"I loved him so much," she said. "I hope he knew that."

"He knew it, Issabeau. And God willing, I will make sure he never forgets it."

"Look after him."

"As much as I'm able, I swear I will. Issabeau. . . ."

She looked up at me, a lovely face crushed by pain. "Go to her. . . ."

Her fingers shook as she ran her nails down the lines of my father's writing, raking through his thoughts and observations, and I left her there, lost in her own considerations, her own world, her own magic.

I finally found Guiwenneth by the sticklebrook, sitting on the dried mud of the bank, her bare feet in the thin water. This was the very place where, as a child on a gray horse, she had trotted round me and struck me with her feathered coupstick. She seemed to be remembering that moment pleasantly, her head tilted up, hair still luxurious and full, face almost serene with delight, eyes closed.

"Hello," I said, and she opened her eyes and looked up at me.

"Do you remember this place?"

"Of course. You whacked me with a riding crop. Then we rode together, into that field there, and fell from the horse."

"And Manandoun came to rescue me and was furious with me. I thought he was going to kill you, but I think he just wanted to make sure I understood how dangerous it was to come to the edge of the world and to go galloping off after stray, strange boys, small boys, gullible, and gorgeous boys."

"Is that how you thought of me? Gullible and gorgeous?"

"But you are, aren't you? Sit down beside me."

I sat down. She reached out a hand to stroke my face, then tugged my hair and pulled me back, so that we lay on the earth, our faces to the heavens.

"Once upon a time," Guiwenneth said quietly, her fingers entwining with mine, "once upon a time there was a young man, fair faced and full of life, who loved a girl. But the girl died. The young man rode the length and the breadth of his land, seeking in every forest and every valley and on every mountain for the way into the land of the dead. He sacrificed everything he could lay his hands on. He kissed every stone and undertook every quest that was asked of him. He slaughtered the beasts that inhabited the edge of the wood and the edge of the lake, even if he wasn't asked to do so. He fasted, then feasted, then fasted again, then turned himself inside out and upside down, walking backward for a whole season, and speaking his words in reverse. And at last he had done enough to enter the world of the dead, and there he found the girl he had loved.

" 'I've come to fetch you,' he said, and she looked at him in horror.

" 'Who are you?' she asked.

"'I am the young man you loved,' he replied.

"'Well, if you are,' she said, 'you left him behind a long time ago. Things have changed. And you have certainly changed.'

"'You are as beautiful as the day you left me,' said the sad old man.

"'Alas, I cannot say the same to you. Go away. What we once had was wonderful. What has happened since cannot justify your waste of life. Go away.'

"'I have spent my life trying to find you.'

"'I was dead and in a wonderful place. You were alive and behaving like a dead man. You have wasted your life. There were better things for you to do. You have one life only, and there are always other lovers.'"

She turned to me, smiling mischievously. "Did you like my story?"

"Not very much. What are you trying to tell me?"

"You have one mother and you can take her back; you can start again; you can use her dream, her terrifying vision, to make sure that the dream remains unreal. As for me . . ." Her face changed from happiness to sorrow, though she tried to hide it. "As for me," she repeated, "you can find me again. I am always in the wood. There are more of me than you can imagine; all I ask, my dearest love . . . all I ask . . . just dream me well. Dream me beautiful. And dream me happy, and with a heart that can fulfill all your own needs and love. . . ."

These last words had been spoken through tears and she crushed me to her, sobbing quietly, her fingers digging into my back and neck. "Just dream me well, Chris. . . ."

"I don't need to dream you at all. I have you here, in my arms. I can take you out of here, I can take you home. I have won that right, and I will claim that right. . . . "

"You came for Jennifer. You came for your mother. Don't imagine I don't know that. She is alone, Chris. She needs you, she needs this life more than I do. Chris . . . you can find me again so easily! Just dream me well," she repeated firmly. "We can *always* find each other again. You *must* take your mother out of here!"

"I can't leave you, Guiwenneth."

"You can't leave her!"

"She wants me to take you. . . . You want me to take her. . . . What am I to do? I want you both. I want you both so much!"

"Good memory is a great comfort," she whispered. "Eventually, that is all we can ever hope for. I have loved my time with you. If you are sensible, we can find that time again. The same cannot be said for Jennifer. So go home, Chris. Go back to the beginning. *Take your mother home!"*

I had come to Oak Lodge across the field from Strong Against the Storm. As I walked back to the entrance to the Otherworld, I realized that I was following the same path through the tall corn that my mother had carved, years ago, when I had followed her to her death. This was not quite the same field; nor the same sky, nor indeed the same tree; though to my right, the edge of Ryhope Wood watched me with its hidden eyes as it had watched my family for tens of years.

Somewhere here, I remembered, the trail through the corn had divided, a part of my mother's spirit taking off to flee into the safety of the wilderness beyond the forest.

Or perhaps . . . the mark of a spirit joining her?

Eventually, walking stiffly and carefully, repeating to myself that I must not look round, I must not speak, I must not even hear the murmuring and breathing of the woman behind me, I came to the rise of land from which ordinarily I would have seen the spire of the church at Shadoxhurst, away in the distance.

This ridge of land, this focus of my memory, close to the

hanging tree, was where the bright realm ended and the grim, gloomy passage to the surface of the world commenced.

I stepped forward into this stygian night, and behind me footsteps shuffled on the bare rock.

Ahead of me, the new day was a glowing circle, the inside of the mouth of the green-man's painted, stony face.

The walk took hours, or so it seemed.

No Mabon greeted me to say good-bye; no Eletherion screamed silently from his rock. The presence of the shrouded dead was visible literally as shadow, the movement of shape and memory on the walls on either side of me, and I dared not look too hard in case, inadvertently, I glimpsed my passenger with the edge of vision, and dispatched her back to eternity.

Silently and steadily I led her from the world of the dead.

Anambioros was waiting for me as he had promised he would, spear at the ready, his sword exposed and resting on its sheath in case any of Eletherion's brothers should make a bid for their own freedom, like birds flying in the wake of a ship.

He stood up as I emerged, grinning broadly. And then his face dropped in astonishment as he saw who was following me out of Hell.

"What's happening?" he asked blearily. "What's going on."

"Is she free of the cave's mouth? Has she emerged from the shadows?"

"Yes," said Anambioros, and I took the chance and turned to look at Issabeau, who stood there, blinking against the light, as young, as husky, as raven haired as when I had first met her.

"Go and kiss him," I whispered. "I think he needs it."

"By the Good Christ, I thought I was dreaming," she said, and I laughed, though my heart was breaking. I had wanted to amend her thanks to: By the Good Christian!

It was enough to see the two of them in each other's arms, reunited in love and purpose.

Later, Anambioros found me in the stone house. Kylhuk had long gone, returning to his Legion, pursuing his own fortunes. I had made a fire, polished the tarnished cooking equipment that Mabon had left, who knew how long ago, and made a broth of vegetables and wild pig, speared at great effort with the Celt's own weapons, while he and Issabeau were lost in their Delightful Realm.

"My father was a king among men," he said, "and so am I. But I am a man with a true king for a friend, and I will never ask you why you saved the life of Issabeau and not one of the two people who mattered to you most. Christian, I will not die until I have saved your own life once! This is my promise to you. It is a *geisa* that I am willing upon myself, and the price is all the others, which I hereby abandon, send back, deny, and part with. If I am ever asked to explain my actions, I will claim the friendship of a man of courage—and offer my own life as forfeit."

"Thank you," I said quietly. "How many lives do you have, Anambioros? You seem to conjure them out of the air."

"I do, don't I?" he replied. "I seem to have the lives of a cat. And I have a cat in my life! Thank you again for that. My heart goes out to you in your loss; may good memory be a great comfort to you."

"Gentle words, my Guiwenneth's words, too, and I will cling to them gladly."

He leaned down and kissed my cheek and chin.

"By the way, Elidyr has come for you. He says he can wait until you're ready, but not to leave it too long. He's by the river. I shall miss you, Christian. But I will make your name famous!"

And with that he left me, returning to his own world, leaving me to mine.

CODA

If I have been in the Path of Stone and the Wood of
    Thorns,
For somebody hid hatred and hope and desire and fear
Under my feet that they follow you night and day.

—W. B. Yeats, *He mourns for the Change . . .*

We must all eventually awake from the dream, unless we have been stolen from our passage through the wood of thorns, from the path of stones. While I dreamed in my boat, Kylhuk passed by, together with his Legion, many on horseback, most on foot, some in chariots, some in wagons. They overtook my slow boat on the winding river, moving by on each side, each face peering down at me, smiling, bidding me farewell, blowing me kisses.

The last to pass were the woman, Raven, and the Fenlander.

Raven said wryly, "You might have made more of me, but your mind was elsewhere."

I didn't understand her words. She had already cantered on ahead.

The Fenlander said, "Our time has not yet begun, Christian. I look forward to it!"

I remembered the vision through my mother's eyes, of myself as a fat, scarred warrior-chief, cruelly killing my brother, Steven. The Fenlander had been there, my right-arm man, my friend. . . .

"I don't," I whispered. "I don't look forward to it. Not at all . . ."

He grinned, held his masked helmet high, then rode on.

And so they had gone, and slowly the earth ceased to shake with the passage of that army. The boat drifted on.

Did my father pass me as I dreamed? I heard the growling of a boar and a dark shape leaned low one dusk, a white, animal face painted below lank, black hair.

"It is not finished yet. . . ." the apparition breathed. "When you come back, I shall be waiting for you."

"I looked for you this time. I followed in your footsteps. I came into Ryhope along the Hogback Ridge, but I couldn't find you."

"I hid from you," my father said.

"Why?"

"You had other things on your mind."

"I had Guiwenneth on my mind. And now I've let her go."

The man leaned down toward me, but behind the savage, snarling mask of chalk, the eyes were sad and gentle. Almost like Elidyr's, I thought. . . .

"Yes. You did. And now, like me, you will pursue a dream. And we pursue the same dream, Chris. That dream has become your life. You don't know it yet. And that is why I will be waiting for you. *When* you return."

He drew away, growling and grumbling, towering over my supine form, following the boat for a while almost protectively, until quite suddenly he turned away from me and was gone from my vision.

The boat rocked. If Elidyr pulled it, he was invisible. I saw only the moving of branches against the clouds and the changing colors of the heavens.

The journey seemed endless, a journey without hunger or sleep, without pain or pleasure, a journey through winter and summer, a gentle passage along a narrow stream, through an age of forests.

Eventually I succumbed to sleep, made drowsy by some hidden charm, but delighting in the anticipation of oblivion.

And this morning, when I opened my eyes and saw the spring sky above me as I lay in that shallow boat, I realized that my long journey from the heart of the forest was over.

I had come home again.

If only for a while. . . .